By Sophie Snow

TOUCH AND GO SERIES

The Rule of Three

SPICY IN SEATTLE SERIES

Legally Binding

Legally Binding

SOPHIE SNOW

First published in 2024 by Sophie Snow
This paperback edition first published in 2024

First Edition

ISBN: 978-1-7394450-2-7 (paperback)
ISBN: 978-1-7394450-3-4 (eBook)

SOPHIE SNOW

For everyone who grew up believing love was conditional —and the therapists, friends, lovers, and romance novels that taught us it shouldn't be.

Content Warnings

Legally Binding is an adult novel that features explicit content and some topics that may be triggering for some readers. The following is a list of topics featured in Legally Binding:

Age gap relationship, alcohol, blood/injury, boss/employee relationship, body modification (nipple piercings), controlling relationship (former), drug use (mentioned), explicit language, explicit sexual content (biting, bondage, daddy kink, fingering, masturbation, oral sex, orgasm denial, rough sex, spanking, vaginal sex, voyeurism), misogyny, parental neglect, pregnancy (past) and discussions of remaining child free, smoking, work-place sexual harassment.

You can read about these content warnings in more detail at www.sophiesnowbooks.com.

Author's Note

Legally Binding is a work of fiction and is not intended to be used as an educational tool.

As much as we all love reading spicy romance, the sexual acts described in Legally Binding are not intended to be used as a guide. Please always do plenty of research and have clear discussions of consent before trying anything new.

CHAPTER ONE

Maggie

"Michaelson and Hicks, Maggie speaking. How may I direct your call?" Maggie fought a yawn as the words spilled out on autopilot, her face resting on her hand.

The line was quiet before the disembodied Irish voice of her boss replied, "Is today boring you, Miss Burlington?"

Maggie rolled her eyes and leaned back in her chair, balancing precariously on the back legs. "No more than usual, Mr. Michaelson."

A low chuckle sounded. "You spent about twenty minutes yawning before drifting off for a second there."

Shit. That was the result of having too much on her plate, though knowing that did nothing to change it.

"I didn't sleep well," she admitted, twirling the

fraying phone cord and fighting another yawn at the mere mention.

"Trouble settling in?"

"No, the house is great," she replied quickly. Buying a house was a distant dream for most twenty-seven-year-olds, and if she'd bitten off a little more than she could chew, she wasn't going to complain about it. Sure, the house was a little bigger than she was used to, a little more quiet and drafty, but it was *hers*.

Maggie turned to face the camera that covered the office and raised a brow. "Why are you watching the camera feed, anyway?"

"I accidentally clicked something on my computer and now I can't get it to go away."

Maggie snorted. Cal Michaelson: the most successful business lawyer in the Pacific Northwest and absolutely awful with technology.

"I'll come up and fix it," she offered. "Were you just calling to shout at me for dozing off, or did you need something?"

"When have I ever shouted at you?" her boss spluttered, and Maggie hid her smile in the roll of her turtleneck. "I can't find the agenda for the ten thirty with Okcho. Could you run a copy up?"

"On it," Maggie replied, squinting at the clock. How was it only ten a.m.?

"Thanks. And Maggie?"

"Hmm?"

"Quit leaning on your chair like that. I'm not buying you another one."

"You can afford it. And quit watching me. It's creepy." She stuck her tongue out at the camera and put the phone down on her boss's insufferable chuckle.

She made quick work printing another two copies of the agenda for the Okcho case. Though Cal never read anything in advance, she liked to have everything prepared as early as possible. He was one of those annoying people that just showed up and aced whatever he was trying to do with zero preparation; Maggie checked the menu a week before she was due to go out.

She gathered the papers up and stood with a groan, her calves burning. She'd been up past midnight, on her hands and knees, removing tiles. Renovating the house was grueling, more exhausting than working out. But much more fun.

Maggie stepped into the elevator and leaned against the cool glass with a sigh. The elevator shot up to Cal's office, past the main offices, the consultancy rooms and senior offices, and Mr. Hicks' floor. Michaelson and Hicks' downtown office building wasn't big, but it was tall. Cal had fallen in love with the view from the top floor when they'd toured the building two years ago, then won the top floor from Mr. Hicks in a single round of poker.

It wasn't unusual for Maggie to hide out in Cal's office, avoiding the din of the first floor. Home to the paralegals and associates, the first floor housed three dozen of Seattle's brightest up and coming legal experts —and they were so loud.

Maggie stepped out of the elevator onto the fourth

floor, her heels sinking into the soft carpet that covered the floor of the cozy lobby outside Cal's office. She fluffed and straightened the throw pillows on the plush couch before knocking on Cal's door and opening it without waiting for a response.

Cal Michaelson looked up from behind his desk, his green eyes twinkling. "Thanks, love," he said as she handed over the agendas. Even after six years working for Cal, her stomach still fluttered at the term of endearment. "I know you gave me them at the start of the week, but…" He trailed off and Maggie followed his gaze to the tray full to the brim with unorganized paperwork. She grimaced and swiped the tray from the desk. "You don't have to," Cal protested as she took a seat opposite him and began sorting through it.

"I really do." If she didn't, she might as well give up on trying to relax over the weekend. "I don't mind. Are you all set for the call?"

"Yeah, I'm good to go. Are you staying?"

She nodded, setting aside a stack of outdated files for the shredder. "I'm going to tidy up in here a bit. I'll be quiet."

"Thanks, love." She returned his smile before turning back to the pile of paperwork.

Cal, for all his disorganized ways, *was* a great boss. She'd been his assistant for five years, and an intern for a year before that. It had taken her a while to get used to working for someone so easygoing, not to mention how long it had taken her to adjust to his strong Irish accent and the way he called her *love*. It was an Irish thing, apparently; his parents also used the pet name when they called, and oh boy, did they call. Cal's parents like to speak to him at least three times a week and, since their calls went through Maggie, they liked to chat to her three times a week too.

Cal's kind nature was clearly genetic; Maggie didn't have a bad word to say about him. He paid her well, trusted her to get shit done, and, perhaps most rarely in the legal world, he was a genuinely nice guy. Since her internship, Maggie had met thousands of lawyers, and very few of them didn't make her skin crawl. Cal was an exception to a sad rule. His co-owner, Ben Hicks, was so creepy that she avoided the third floor like the plague.

She crossed the room to Cal's filing cabinets and unlocked them with the master key she wore around her neck to file the documents not destined for the shredder.

"Any plans this weekend?"

She jumped and looked over at him. Though he had the agenda clutched in his hand, his eyes were on her.

"Um, no, not really. I'll probably just be working around the house," she said, turning back to the cabinets. It was the same answer every Friday. Though, for once, she *did* have plans. They just weren't the kind she could share with her boss, no matter how chill he was. "Are you up to anything nice?" She knew his schedule was clear, but she didn't always schedule his weekend plans.

"Nothing much," he replied, his eyes scanning the agenda. He set it down. "I might see if Liam is around and wants to grab dinner or something."

"Liam's in Banff this weekend for a bachelor party.

He left this morning," she said, and Cal let out a noise of protest.

"How do you know what my son is doing this weekend and I don't?"

She shrugged, fighting a laugh. "He used your air miles. I booked the ticket for him."

Cal frowned, tapping a pen on the desk. "He asked you to do that? You know you don't have to do that kind of stuff."

"He didn't ask me to do it, he just asked about your miles. I offered. I don't mind, really." Maggie picked up the shredding pile as the calendar alert that signaled Cal's meeting was about to begin sounded. She sighed and clutched the papers to her chest.

"I'm going to take these downstairs to shred. I'll be back up in a few. Coffee?" she asked, on her way to the door and Cal nodded, that smile back in place and turning her insides liquid.

"Thanks, love."

She nodded and stepped out of the office, holding her breath until she was safely in the elevator.

Perhaps she did have a bad word to say about him after all; between the twinkling green eyes, the dimples, the smile, the Irish accent... God, the accent... Cal Michaelson was lethal.

CHAPTER TWO

Maggie

Maggie wasn't sure how, but she was somehow both overdressed and underdressed. Admittedly, her google search of *what to wear to a sex club* hadn't been particularly helpful. There was surprisingly little information, and her best friend, Jasmine, the reason she was here in the first place, hadn't answered a single one of her calls while she'd been getting ready.

Maggie's wardrobe was mostly office-appropriate skirts and sweaters, and paint splattered shorts and t-shirts, and a lot of cozy loungewear. She'd had to dig through her closet for this number—and hold her breath while trying to squeeze into the bandage dress she hadn't worn since college.

Jazz leaned in to say, "I'll grab a booth if you want to grab drinks."

Maggie nodded, splitting in the opposite direction

towards the bar, stepping through the throngs of people. It was busier than she expected, though she hadn't really known what to expect. Jazz had been given the tickets by the guy she'd been hooking up with for the past three months before he ghosted her, and she'd begged Maggie to accompany her.

"It's a live show, but like… a sexy one?" Jazz had done her best to explain. "We can leave before it devolves into… more."

Maggie hadn't bothered to ask what she meant by *more*. Her imagination filled in the gaps. Jazz had always been the more adventurous of their little duo, and though Maggie dreaded the outings she planned before she got there, she usually ended up having a good time. Besides, it had been a while since she'd gone home with anyone, and where better to find a casual hook up than a sex club?

She finally landed against the bar, teetering on her heels, and smiled at the bartender. "Vodka soda and a large glass of red—merlot if you have it, please."

She leaned on the wood, peering down the long bar. Despite the hundred or so people crowding the room, there was a calm hush, as if everyone was whispering. It was easy to spot the veteran attendees, laughing and smiling, perfectly at ease, amongst the newbies like her, wide eyed and huddled together, wondering where to look.

There were already people in various states of undress, and several of the booths were occupied by groups getting started before the curtain had opened. She looked away. *What had Jazz gotten them into this time?*

"Scotch—neat, please."

Maggie's heart fell into her stomach at the familiar voice coming from right beside her. *No. Surely not, it can't be...*

"You got it, Cal." *Fuck.*

She turned her head slowly, taking in the side profile of her boss, horror spreading through her. As if feeling her gaze, Cal turned to glance at her, his eyes widening.

They stared at each other, open-mouthed, until the bartender cleared his throat and slid their drinks across the polished mahogany. "Vodka soda, large glass of merlot, scotch, neat."

"Thanks," Maggie said quietly, opening her clutch and pulling out her card. She didn't get the chance to hand it over before Cal slid his card across the bar.

"Can you put them on my tab, Raph?"

The bartender, *Raph*, looked between Cal and Maggie, an amused look on his face. "Sure. Enjoy."

His raised eyebrow and surprised smile told Maggie two things: not only was Cal clearly a regular here, but he didn't usually buy drinks for anyone. She had no idea what to make of that.

Raph moved on, leaving them leaning against the bar, staring at each other.

"Thank you. I didn't schedule this for you, did I?" she blurted out and Cal blinked, a bark of surprised laughter bursting from him.

"I think that would be inappropriate."

"Maybe," she agreed, though it wasn't as inappropriate as running into your boss at a fucking sex club. If she could command the ground to open up and swallow her whole, she would. "My friend Jasmine dragged me here," she added quickly, as if she could justify her presence with the fact that it hadn't been her idea to come.

She nodded across the room, to where Jazz had commandeered an empty booth, and was watching the two of them over the back of the leather seat. She gave Maggie a thumbs up and appreciative nod. Maggie groaned. "Oh my God, please ignore her."

Cal just laughed, shaking his head. "Is this the same Jasmine that took you axe throwing and smashed your phone last year?"

"The very same," she confirmed, as they started towards her best friend. "She's always roping me into stuff I wouldn't usually do."

"Not your scene?" Cal asked, and there was nothing but curiosity written on his face when Maggie looked up at him.

Maggie shrugged, clearing her throat as if she could clear away the awkwardness she was feeling. "I'm not sure yet. It's my first time. Not your first time, I take it?"

"Not my first time," he said, which confirmed it *was* his scene, and that was more than Maggie ever expected to know about her boss. Sure, she might have imagined... but thinking about that was dangerous.

They stopped beside the booth, and Jazz popped up, grinning at them. "Hey, I'm Jazz."

Maggie pressed the vodka soda into Jazz's hand and gave her a warning look. "This is Cal," she said, and Jazz's head swiveled between them.

"As in... your *boss*, Cal?"

"That's me," Cal said, rubbing the back of his neck, and Maggie was glad she wasn't the only one feeling awkward. "It's nice to meet you. Maggie talks about you all the time."

"Yeah, likewise," Jazz said, then added, at Maggie's horrified expression, "I mean, she talks about work all the time, not you, of course. I mean, like constantly. She's such a workaholic, really. Can't take her anywhere without her checking her emails. I'm going to shut up now," she finished wisely, and Maggie took a long sip of her wine. She should've ordered liquor.

"You know, I can go. This is your domain, and I don't want to…" She trailed off with no idea how to finish her sentence. She was utterly out of her depth.

For a moment, they just stared at each other, Maggie urging her eyes *not* to travel down to the slice of his chest exposed by the shirt he'd left unbuttoned at the top.

"Stay," he said, finally. "We're all adults. It's fine."

"Okay," Maggie replied, still considering making a break for it.

"You want to sit with us?"

They both turned towards Jazz, whose cheeks colored as she realized the implications of her offer.

"I'm good, thanks," Cal replied, not unkindly. "Enjoy the show," he added, slowly, as if unsure of what else to say, before turning and walking to the other side of the room.

Maggie blew out a breath and slid into the booth beside Jazz.

"Well, fuck," Jazz said, shaking her head in disbelief.

"Tell me about it."

Jazz peered over her head, presumably looking to wherever Cal ended up before slumping back in the booth. "You know I'm not religious, but if there was ever proof that God exists, that man would be it."

Maggie rubbed the spot between her brows. "Jazz."

"Yeah?"

"I love you. But please shut up."

Jazz snorted, but zipped her lips and threw away the imaginary key just as the lights dimmed and the curtains parted.

S *mack.*
    Maggie leaned forward, so engrossed in the woman currently strapped up on stage being spanked, that she jumped when the seat shifted beside her. She turned, coming face to face with a leering blond.

"I'm Dax," the man said, leaning too close to her for comfort.

Maggie leaned into Jazz. "Hi?" She didn't mean for it to sound like a question. It wasn't like she didn't know *why* Dax had planted himself beside her; she was sure most people went to sex clubs with one goal in mind.

"What's your name?" he asked, oblivious to her disinterest, resolutely ignoring the fact that she was leaning away from him.

"Maggie."

A smile split his face. He was around her age, dressed

head to toe in black satin, the watch on his wrist worth more than the deposit on her house. "Ah, Italian!" he said, and Maggie frowned.

"What?"

"Maggie—it's an Italian name," he replied, slowly, as if she was stupid.

"I don't think that's true." She knew it wasn't. *Everyone* knew it wasn't, except Dax, apparently.

"No, it is." He waved a dismissive hand. He leaned in close enough that she could smell the liquor on his breath. "So what are you—"

"Move."

Dax frowned, turning his head. He took one look at Cal's thunderous expression and sprang to his feet. "Sorry man, didn't realize she was yours," he rushed out before scampering off.

Maggie watched him go before turning her attention back to Cal. "Thank you. He was… Thank you."

"Anytime, love." Cal looked around for a moment before taking Dax's vacated seat with a sigh. He left a decent gap between them, setting his glass on the table, but the implication was clear to anyone considering bothering her: don't.

It might have annoyed her—she had planned to go home with someone, after all—but she wasn't sure she could bring herself to leave with anyone with Cal watching. She exchanged a second-long look with Jazz, who was watching them with an entirely too excited expression.

"So, what are your thoughts so far?"

Maggie turned to him. "Huh?" Cal nodded to the stage, and Maggie looked back at the couple *performing*. They'd moved on from spanking to tickling, the woman enjoying it far more than Maggie would have—she was far too ticklish for that. "It's a little tame, to be honest," she replied, after clearing her throat. "I expected... more, I guess."

A shadow loomed over the table, but the man approaching turned away when he spotted Cal's face. He blew out a breath and slipped an arm around her shoulders, resting it on the back of the bench. *Holy shit.* Jazz was practically vibrating beside her.

This was bad. Dangerous, even. They should have left as soon as Maggie spotted Cal. Over the past six years, she'd become a pro at blocking out the part of her brain that lit up like a Christmas tree when she looked at her boss. When she started her internship, she could hardly speak to the man without drooling. She'd even slipped up once or twice in the beginning and almost called his name out in bed; she'd only managed not to piss off her ex by turning *Cal* into a forced gasp.

Maggie looked at Jazz out of the corner of her eye. Her best friend was fighting for her life, trying not to laugh at how awkward she must look.

"Give it time," Cal said, drawing her attention back to the stage. "The audience usually joins in around the third act. That's when it gets more exciting."

They were the audience. But surely they weren't going to join in? Obviously not. She had to get herself under control.

Maggie leaned forward, drained her glass of wine, took a deep breath, and settled back into Cal's arm. "Good to know," she said, before quickly changing the subject. "It's weird that we've never run into each other outside of work, huh?"

Seattle wasn't a small city, but most things were pretty centralized. Then again, Maggie more or less had Cal's schedule memorized, and, though she didn't go out of her way not to cross his path, she would hesitate to go somewhere she knew he would be.

"Yeah, it is," Cal agreed, his gaze roaming over her with his dimples on full display. "So this is what you look like when you're not at the office."

Was that a note of appreciation she detected?

"Not often," she corrected, her cheeks warming. "I don't usually go around dressed like I'm going to a sex club."

"Oh yeah, me either."

Maggie let herself look him over. His gray hair sat perfectly, just one strand falling across his forehead, and his beard was razor sharp, and she knew from his calendar that he'd had an appointment that morning to get it tidied. He really was devastating. The charcoal suit and white shirt he was wearing were familiar to her, the sleeves pushed up just enough to show off the watch that he actually used to check the time, because he could never find his phone. A longtime client had gifted the Rolex to him after he retired and closed his business, and Maggie wasn't sure she'd ever seen his wrist bare of it.

"Didn't you wear that suit on Tuesday?" she asked, dragging her eyes back to his face.

"I did, but no tie. See?" He gestured to the sliver of skin peeking through his shirt, with a laugh, and Maggie most definitely *did* see. She was just too busy trying to keep her tongue in her mouth to reply.

"It's a g*rea*t look," Jazz cut in, saving her from having to respond, and Maggie closed her eyes for just a second, because if she didn't take a break from looking at the man beside her, as the sounds coming from the woman on stage grew, she was going to implode.

Cal chuckled, the sound sending shivers down her spine. "Thanks. So, is this a girl's night thing? Is that why your boyfriend isn't here?"

Maggie opened her eyes and frowned, confused. "What?"

"Your boyfriend—Nathan, right?" Cal asked, squinting uncertainly.

"Oh. Right." His name alone was enough to douse her in cold water. "Um, he's not my boyfriend anymore, actually."

Cal's face fell, but he didn't get the chance to respond before Jazz added: "Yeah, he proposed."

Cal's look of sympathy morphed into surprise. "Oh, congratulations, love. When did that happen?"

Maggie scowled at Jazz. Why the fuck would she phrase it like that? "On my birthday a couple of months ago," she said slowly, looking back at Cal. "But I said no. We broke up."

Cal was quiet for a moment, and Maggie wished she

had wine left to occupy her hands. "Shit," he said finally. "That was a rollercoaster. I'm sorry. On your birthday?" She nodded. "Christ."

"He planned this huge surprise party and proposed in front of like everyone they knew," Jazz leaned in to add, and the shock on Cal's face morphed into horror.

It hadn't been everyone they knew; it had been everyone Nathan knew. The party had been full of Nathan's family, friends, and co-workers. Aside from her parents, siblings, and Jazz, he'd invited none of Maggie's friends or co-workers. Which was, perhaps, for the best given the outcome. Sure, she'd thought some of Nathan's friends had been her friends too, but they'd all cut contact with her the second she'd turned him down.

"It was brutal," Jazz continued, shaking her head and sipping her drink. "They opened all the champagne in advance, and Nathan was live streaming the whole thing to his Facebook page. Everyone took his side after the breakup. Even Maggie's parents said…" she trailed off, her attention caught by something over Cal's shoulder. Maggie followed her gaze to see a woman with waist-length braids crooking her finger at Jazz. Her best friend turned to her, her eyes pleading. "Are you guys good? Because I want that."

Maggie couldn't help but laugh as Cal opened and closed his mouth, apparently speechless at the chaos that was Jazz. "Have at it. Be safe," she called after her, as her best friend sped from the booth. "She's a lot, but she's pretty great," Maggie told Cal.

"I like her. She's exactly how I imagined her," he replied. "I'm sorry about Nathan, love."

Maggie waved him away. "It's fine, really. I'm much better off without him."

"I can't believe I didn't know," Cal answered, shaking his head. "I guess we don't actually know that much about each other outside of work. Although, even I would never think you'd want a surprise party, let alone a public proposal."

"Thank you," she said, throwing her hands up. No one who'd ever spent five minutes with her could possibly think she would have wanted that. "I feel like I know you significantly more outside of work now than I did this morning. Possibly more than I should," she added with a wry smile.

"True," Cal answered with a laugh. "Still a little tame for you?" he asked, gesturing to the room.

Maggie tore her eyes from him to look around the room. He hadn't been kidding when he'd said it would get more exciting. There was a group on stage now, and Maggie could hardly tell where one person ended and another began. The audience had become part of the show, and bodies writhed in booths, smacks and gasps echoing through the room. To their right, two women were tying a man up in the most intricate knots she'd ever seen. But somehow, she'd still expected... more.

"A little," she confessed, looking back at Cal. She didn't recognize the dark look in his eyes, but her skin warmed beneath his gaze, goosebumps spreading every-where it touched.

"Interesting," he mused. "I guess I know you a little more now than I did this morning too."

"I guess so." He trailed his eyes over her arms, her chest, and finally met her eyes. *Was she still breathing?*

"Mr. Michaelson?"

Cal blinked himself back in control, taking a shaky breath as he turned towards the woman who stopped beside the booth. "Yeah?"

She held out an ornate dish full of jewel toned foil packets. "Condom?" she offered and Cal's eyes cut briefly towards Maggie before he shook his head.

"No, thank you."

The silence between them was taut as the woman left with a smile, their eyes glued to the show before them. How could Maggie be so unaffected by the dozens of naked bodies in her line of sight, yet fall to pieces at the sight of one of Cal's dimples?

He cleared his throat and gestured to a server. "Another glass of wine?" he asked, and Maggie shook her head.

"No, thank you. I'm driving."

"Sensible."

Maggie bit her lip. "That's me. Sensible." Her hands fussed with her skirt, smoothing non-existent wrinkles as she closed her eyes and took a steadying breath.

For a split second, in the heat of Cal's gaze, she'd considered not being sensible at all.

CHAPTER THREE

Maggie

Maggie collapsed onto her bed, panting. When she'd struggled into the bandage dress earlier, she'd hoped to have someone to help her unzip it by the end of the night, but, unlike Jazz, she'd left the club alone, with enough pent-up sexual energy that she thought she might burst into flames.

Maggie had lived with Nathan for five years, and she'd expected the worst part of living alone to be coming home to an empty house, with no one to ask about her day or give her a hug when she wanted to cry. She'd been dead wrong. It was the little things: the top shelf of the cabinet she couldn't reach without pulling out a step stool, the spiders that she'd just had to learn to live alongside because there was no fucking way she was touching them, and she was too softhearted to vacuum them up, the constant leftovers because she still hadn't learned how to cook for one, and the zippers that required honest-to-God acrobatics to do alone.

She sat up with a groan and kicked her heels out of the way as she dragged her feet to the bathroom. For all the house's flaws, the clawfoot tub wasn't one of them. She turned on the faucet, sprinkled winter-spiced Epsom salt onto the surface of the water, and sank into the depths with a satisfied sigh.

The salt eased her aching muscles, and Maggie stretched her body out like a cat in the sun. With everything else she had going on, spending an hour in the tub was a luxury she couldn't afford as often as she liked, so she closed her eyes and let the water soothe her soul alongside her muscles.

Her phone rang from the thrifted side table beside the bath and she frowned at it, drying her hands on the towel hanging over the edge before picking it up. Her stomach did a somersault as she took in Cal's name. He hated texting; he always called when he needed anything, but never this late at night.

She cleared her throat before answering. "Hey."

"Hey. Oh good, I didn't wake you."

"Nope. What's up?" She shifted, cringing as the sound of the water rushing down her body echoed through the bathroom.

Cal was silent for a moment before asking, "Where are you?"

Maggie wracked her brain for any explanation that didn't involve her lying naked in the tub, but came up short. "I, uh, I'm in the bath." A soft bang sounded through the phone, and she frowned, sitting up straight in the splashing water. "What was that? Are you okay?"

"I'm fine, yeah. I just banged my knee on the table," Cal replied, his voice strained.

"Oh, okay. So, um, what's up?"

"Right. I just… I know tonight was a little weird, and unexpected, so I just wanted to make sure we were okay," Cal said, stumbling on the words.

"Oh, yeah. We're fine," Maggie said quickly. The less they spoke about it, the better.

"Good." He sounded relieved. She could see him in her head, sitting with a lowball glass on the table, running a hand through his gray hair and blowing out a breath. "I wouldn't want to make you feel uncomfortable."

"You didn't at all, I promise. I didn't make you uncomfortable, did I?"

"Not at all," he assured her quickly.

"Cool."

"Cool." They were quiet for a moment, their breaths and the soft ripple of the water the only sounds. "Did you have a nice time tonight?" Cal asked, his voice hushed, like he knew he shouldn't be asking.

Maggie bit her lip, her stomach fluttering. "I did, thanks. Did you?"

"I did," he agreed, with a long breath.

"Good, I'm glad."

"Yeah, same," he agreed, and she knew him well enough that she could tell he was smiling by his voice. "I should let you enjoy your bath. I'll see you on Monday?"

"Of course. I'll see you Monday." she answered, pulling her knees up to her chest.

Cal paused at the sound of the water coursing. "Sweet dreams, love."

"Thanks. Sweet dreams, Cal."

She heard the start of a sigh before the call disconnected, and she held the phone to her chest. *Sweet dreams, love.*

She dropped her phone on the table and sank further into the water, her heart racing. *Sweet dreams, love.* When she'd first met him, and he'd introduced himself with that flawless Irish accent that hadn't wavered in the four decades he'd been living stateside, she'd had dreams about it. She wished she could blame it on the accent alone, but the longer she spent with him, the more detailed her dreams became. And now, six years on, when she closed her eyes, she imagined his lips skating over her skin, whispering in that accent with so much detail, it might have been a memory.

I wish, she thought, her fingers absentmindedly following the trail his lips left behind in her mind. Her skin tingled as she dragged her nails across her collarbone, down her ribs, before settling on her thighs.

There was a line, and she knew imagining her boss touching her while she got herself off in the bath was crossing it, but that didn't stop her from spreading her legs and groaning as she grazed her clit.

At least she'd known she wouldn't miss sex when she left Nathan. The man seemed to forget how to touch her the moment they handed him his diploma; she'd faked it for five years after they graduated, but she'd learned how to take care of herself over the years.

Maggie knew that would never be a problem with Cal. He did everything with intention. Every word was weighted, every look had a purpose, and every touch... She could only imagine. And imagine she did.

It was Cal's fingers she felt teasing her with small circles, his beard tickling her thighs as he replaced his fingers with his mouth. It was him she imagined sinking a finger inside her, his teeth brushing her clit.

And when the spring coiling within her snapped and she tumbled off the edge, sparks crackling over every inch of her, a single word slipped from her tongue like it was made to be there: "*Cal*."

"*Maggie*."

Cal slammed a hand against the cool tiles as he came, the shower beating down on his back. He released his cock and let his body fall forward, his forehead pressing against the tiles.

He'd been so good. For six years, he'd held it together. Sure, he'd noticed that Maggie was beautiful when she joined the firm, but he'd never been the kind of man to lust after women half his age, and she was so young.

Besides, she'd been seeing someone, and she'd

always seemed a little uncertain around the office. Until the leaves had turned a couple of months ago, and Maggie had changed alongside them. He'd noticed when she'd shown up with a new air of determination, though he hadn't thought much of it. Now, when he did the math, he realized it had been right after her birthday—right after she'd broken up with her ex.

Cal understood that. Both he and his ex-wife, Eliza, had changed for the better after their divorce. It had taken *them* more than a couple of days to bounce back, though.

He finished up in the shower, trying to scrub the shame away and wash it down the drain, but he still couldn't look at himself in the mirror when he stepped out of the water. He'd crossed so many lines tonight. The moment he'd spotted her in the club, he should have left. When he'd seen that asshole leering at her, he should have asked security to step in, not growled at him and then taken his seat. And he definitely shouldn't have asked her how she was enjoying the fucking show. All of it was an HR nightmare.

Any of the lines he hadn't crossed, he'd fucking obliterated picturing her while he fucked his hand in the shower. He might have been able to control himself if he hadn't been stupid enough to call her.

I'm in the bath. He'd almost upended his coffee table at the speed he sat up. Every single sound of splashing water that made it down the line had made the picture in his mind clearer; Maggie, on his lap, in his jacuzzi tub, her dark brown hair curling at the ends from the steam. He could picture her perfectly, her smooth, warm skin, her dazzling blue eyes, more gorgeous than they had a right to be.

He didn't know exactly how old she was, but he had to be twice her age. Not to mention her boss. Maggie was the best assistant he'd ever had, and he'd had a lot over the years. She never batted an eye at the demands of his clients, and, though she'd had no actual legal training, she'd learned so much, so quickly, that she could answer their queries without even asking him. Some days, he sat in his office twiddling his thumbs because she'd streamlined everything so much and he had nothing to do.

He couldn't afford to fuck this up. Maggie had been through enough with her ex without him making her uncomfortable. She'd assured him he hadn't, but would she have been honest with him if he had? She was a newly single home owner; she was probably scared to risk her job.

Not that her job would ever be at risk. Cal didn't know what he'd do without her, not to mention how much he just liked being around her. She met his sarcastic sense of humor two-fold and made the office brighter just by being there. In another world, they might have been friends.

Cal sank onto his bed and rubbed his face, groaning. *Friends.* Perhaps that was the answer, a way to get closer to her without being an inappropriate asshole. There would have to be rules, even if he just kept them to himself.

No mutual sex club visits; that felt like an obvious one. No masturbating to the thought of her in the shower.

Or in his bed, or anywhere at all. No calling her late at night when she was naked in the bath. No picturing what she would look like with his hands all over her... He wasn't sure that was possible. Maybe *friends* wasn't in the cards.

Cal lay down and tugged the comforter over himself. He just had to stay professional. He could do that. Maybe.

He groaned as he leaned over to drop his glasses on his nightstand, before burrowing his head in a pillow and closing his eyes.

Immediately, her face appeared behind his eyelids, blue eyes wide and smiling.

Sweet dreams, Cal.

He was so fucked.

CHAPTER FOUR

Maggie

S he wasn't *actively* dodging Cal. If she had his
schedule memorized and avoided being in the same
room as him for the first half of the day, that was just a
coincidence. And if she had held onto the paperwork in
her hand for two hours longer than she usually would
have, waiting for a time she knew he wouldn't be in his
office to drop it off... Well, okay, she couldn't explain
that away as easily.

She still knocked when she stepped out of the elevator, stopping outside his office door, and pretending that
she wasn't relieved when there was silence in response.
According to his calendar, Cal was in a consultation with
one of the junior attorneys on the second floor.

Maggie usually gave herself more time to set up his
virtual consultations, but there was the whole matter of
avoiding him...

She made quick work of setting the paperwork out on his desk, leafing through it to make sure it was ordered how Cal preferred. The paralegal who'd handed it over that morning had all but shoved the papers into her hand before rushing off to work on something else.

Once the paperwork was organized, Maggie filled Cal's glass decanter with water from the dispenser in the lobby, and searched around his desk for his favorite pen in vain. The desk wasn't messy, but Cal had an aversion to putting things back where they were supposed to go. She'd seen his apartment briefly when dropping stuff off, so she knew his disorganized nature was exclusive to his desk. That, or he had a housekeeper she didn't know about and that seemed unlikely considering she handled all of his appointments.

Maggie found the pen hidden inside a legal pad and set it on top of the paperwork. The clock on Cal's computer confirmed she had ten minutes until his meeting was due to finish. That was plenty of time to tidy his desk up, at least a little.

She set all the loose pens and pencils in the bamboo holder, flicked through the papers in his *to do* tray, removing those he no longer needed, and stacked up the legal pads and half-finished notebooks. She unlocked his desk drawer to put them inside, but stilled as she pulled it open.

She wasn't snooping, but… why was her staff file in his desk drawer? They kept staff files in his filing cabinet; Maggie was usually the one to file them. She'd only ever seen them on his desk when something was wrong.

Shit. She should have left the club. That *had* to be what this was about. How was she going to pay her fucking mortgage if she lost this job? Sure, she could bounce back and find something else, but she wouldn't find a job she loved nearly as much. Or a boss that treated her so well.

But she didn't know for certain that's what was happening. There was no point in catastrophizing. She would just ask him if there was a problem, and, if there was, she would fix it. A little groveling went a long way, and she wasn't above begging to keep her job.

Her hands shook as she put the notebooks in the drawer and locked it, gathering the paperwork she had to file in her arms and taking a deep breath as she walked towards the filing cabinet.

Cal appeared in the doorway just as she was finishing up, the filing cabinet closing with a soft thud.

There was a split-second delay before he spoke, his cheeks rosy. "Hey."

She turned to him, forcing a neutral smile onto her face. "Hi. How was your meeting?"

Cal's eyes narrowed. Perhaps she wasn't doing as good a job with her expression as she'd hoped. "It was good. Are you okay?"

"Of course." Her voice was too chipper. "Everything is ready for the Corsovick call," she added, nodding towards his desk.

Cal crossed the room and sank into his chair. "That's great. Thanks, love. Can you stay? They always ask a million questions, and it'd be helpful to have a list of them."

"Sure." Maggie locked the cabinet and dropped the key back around her neck.

"Are you sure you're okay?" Cal asked, his eyes roaming over her face as she turned around.

"Yeah." She nodded emphatically, but Cal raised an expectant brow. Maggie groaned and dragged a chair around his desk to sit beside him. "I... Am I in some kind of trouble?"

Cal frowned and rubbed a hand across his jaw, smoothing his beard down. "Why would you be in trouble?"

She took a deep breath and chewed on her bottom lip. "It's just when I was tidying your desk, I found my staff file in your drawer."

Cal's eyes widened a fraction, realization dawning on his face. "Ah. You're not in trouble. I promise."

What a relief. It wasn't an explanation for the file, but as she opened her mouth to ask for one, the calendar alert on Cal's computer sounded. The meeting. So, instead, she just nodded. "Okay, good." She grabbed her own notebook and pen and sat back. Cal's gaze stayed on her until the Corsovick team appeared on screen and he turned towards them.

Corsovick, a Tacoma based accountancy firm, was a longtime client of Cal's, but she'd forgotten what a mess their team was. Thirty minutes into the meeting, and they'd already devolved into several arguments that neither Maggie nor Cal needed to be present for. But they were paying by the hour, so if they wanted to waste their money on arguments, Cal wouldn't stop them.

Maggie fought to keep a straight face as the people on screen argued over the word choice on the contract they were supposed to be asking Cal about. Cal leaned forward and cleared his throat, stealing their attention. "Why don't we give you a few minutes to talk it over? Just let us know when you're ready."

The team uttered their thanks, and Cal muted his microphone before turning them down and sitting back in his seat.

"I pulled your staff file to check how old you are."

Maggie turned to look at him while she processed his words; he was staring straight ahead, his face a blank mask, but his cheeks were pink.

Why would he care how old she was? She could only think of one reason, and surely not...

She had no idea what to say, and when she opened her mouth, all that came out was, "Oh."

"You're twenty-seven," he added, still not looking at her. He gripped the edge of the desk, white-knuckled.

"Yes, I did know that."

Cal flexed his hand and rubbed the spot between his brows. "I'm old enough to be your dad." *Oh.* "You're *younger* than my kid," he added, shaking his head as if he couldn't quite believe it.

So she hadn't been imagining the way his eyes had darkened at the club, lingering on her mouth. Somehow, her boss, *Cal*, wanted her.

Maggie tried to fight the smile tempting her lips, but

she wasn't entirely successful. "You're actually older than my dad," she said, and Cal blew out a long breath before finally turning to look at her with a pained expression.

"You know how old I am?"

She nodded, fidgeting with the pen in her hand. "Fifty-five. But I took the millennial route—I googled you."

Cal snorted, a little light flashing back into his eyes. "I didn't think of that."

She neglected to mention *when* she'd googled him (three days into her internship.) Nathan had caught her and grilled her until she'd made up a story about checking his zodiac sign so she could adjust her assisting style accordingly.

He was still staring at her, like he couldn't look away, and she felt raw under his intense gaze. "You're a Cancer," she blurted, and he blinked, an amused smile finally falling onto his face.

"I am, but I have no idea what that means."

"Um, Cancer is known as the nurturing sign. Protective, tenacious, loving," she checked them off on her fingers. "Possessive, devious."

He considered that, but nodded, agreeing with the traits. "Huh. What are you?"

"I'm a Virgo. Independent, hardworking, control freak." She wrinkled her nose and Cal laughed.

"That doesn't sound like you at all," he lied, fighting a laugh. "You're really into the whole astrology thing, huh?"

She shrugged, her cheeks coloring. "Not really. Jazz is, though. She's really into astrology, tarot, yoga, dancing naked in the woods..." she trailed off, snapping her mouth closed, while Cal's popped open. *What was wrong with her*? "You know what I mean," she finished lamely.

The Corsovick group called them back to attention, saving Cal from having to think of a response, and Maggie turned back to her notes.

The rest of the meeting passed without incident, though the team had, as expected, a million questions. Maggie wrote them all down and handed the list over to Cal when they'd finally said goodbye.

He scanned the list before handing it back to her. "That's great, love. Can you make copies of this and ask Hamza to look over it? Is there anyone we have spare that can help him? They ask too many questions." She could already see Hamza's face falling when she handed him the list.

"Addison is at a dead end with the McKinnish case. I'm sure she could help," Maggie offered.

"What's going on with the McKinnish case?"

Maggie gave Cal a quick rundown of the case while she walked over to the copier and slid the list in. A surprising amount of her job was waiting; waiting for clients to send over files, sign shit, actually pick up the phone and call her back. She spent hours every week chasing people and, though the Michaelson team never rushed her, she didn't like to keep anyone waiting.

"Thanks for keeping on top of it," Cal said from right

behind her as she finished updating him. Maggie jumped, squeaking. How did he move so quietly? Cal chuckled, stepping closer and leaning over her slightly to unlock the filing cabinet. "Sorry, love."

He reached into the cabinet and she followed his hand as he placed her staff file back. He locked the cabinet, and when Maggie looked up, his eyes were on her. The copier beeped, spitting out the copies of her list.

Cal leaned back against the cabinet. "You know I don't know what I'd do without you, right?" he said softly, his voice making her blood rush.

Maggie snagged the lists from the copier and held them close to her, warm in her hands. "Then it's a good thing I'm not in trouble."

"Did you really think you were?"

Maggie shrugged, her cheeks burning. "I've only ever seen you pull a staff file when you were letting someone go."

It felt like his eyes were staring straight into her soul as he replied, "There's no chance of me letting you go, Maggie."

She sucked in a breath that stuck in her chest, the room suddenly too quiet. Maggie swallowed, and, though she struggled, she tore her eyes from Cal. They landed on the carpet. "Noted," she said, her voice breathier than it had a right to be in the workplace. She cleared her throat and held up the lists. "I should get these downstairs."

Maggie fled Cal's office before she said or did something she couldn't take back.

M aggie all but collapsed onto her desk when she made it to the office on Friday. *Was it possible for a week to last an entire year?* Between the exhaustion of trying to renovate her kitchen, constant calls from her parents, a to-do list longer than the West Coast, and the ever-growing tension between her and Cal, it certainly felt like it had.

She'd whittled her to-do list down on Thursday, and had spent an hour before bed trying to clear her inbox, but she turned on her computer and groaned at the two dozen new emails waiting for her. The sleeves of her sweater were damp as she rolled them up, thanks to the torrential downpour terrorizing Seattle, and opened the oldest email.

A half dozen emails later, the shrill ring of the phone stole her attention, and she took a long draw of coffee before answering. "Michaelson and Hicks, Maggie speaking. How may I direct your call?"

"Ah, Maggie. Wonderful, just who I was hoping to speak to. It's Ben Hicks." Maggie fought a groan. Who else would he be speaking to? He'd called her direct line.

"Morning, Mr. Hicks. What can I do for you?"

"Well, you can start by calling me Ben, you naughty thing. Mr. Hicks makes me feel old." The man was in his sixties, only a decade older than Cal, and yet… Maggie's mouth twisted in disgust. *Naughty thing.* Gross. "Now, onto business. You know my new assistant, Karolyn?"

Maggie's face fell into her hands. "Do you mean Kristen?"

"Yes, yes," he replied dismissively. "She called this morning and quit without notice, if you can believe it." Maggie could absolutely believe it.

"Oh no, I'm sorry to hear that." Good for Kristen. Maggie picked up her coffee. There wasn't enough caffeine in the world for this conversation.

"Yes, it's quite unprofessional. Anyway, I see from Cal's calendar that he has a quiet day today, so I was hoping I might borrow you."

Maggie almost choked on her coffee.

She wracked her brain, trying to think of something, anything, that she might have forgotten to put onto the calendar, but Maggie never forgot anything, and she couldn't think of anything she could add last minute. "Well..." She looked around her desk for inspiration, but came up short and closed her eyes. "I can't think of any reason why not."

"Excellent." She could practically see him rubbing his creepy hands together. "Bring me up a coffee, won't you? And hurry along—I have a lot for you to do." For the first time in her life, Maggie considered faking sick.

But she'd already agreed, so she gathered her shit together, poured half a cup of coffee and filled the rest with straight heavy cream for Mr. Hicks, just how he liked it, and headed towards the elevator, dragging her heels.

"You alright, Maggie?" Josie, one of the veteran paralegals, asked.

Maggie paused at her desk. "Yeah, everything's fine. Hey, if Cal's looking for me, can you let him know that yet *another* of Hicks' assistants has quit without notice and he's asked to *borrow me* for the day?"

Josie grimaced. "Borrow you to do what?"

"God only knows," Maggie groaned. "Wish me luck."

CHAPTER FIVE

C al drummed his fingers on the desk and glanced between the clock and the door. He'd fucked up. There was no other explanation for the fact he hadn't heard a peep out of Maggie all day.

Though his schedule was empty, she usually planned his Fridays that way so they could spend a couple hours in the morning gearing up for the following week. And even on the days she had nothing to go over with him, she always checked in. Her car had been in the parking garage when he'd arrived, so she *was* in the office, but Cal had checked the camera in the first floor office throughout the morning and hadn't spotted her.

The tension between them had been… palpable since their conversation on Monday. He could have made something up, rather than admit to looking up her age in her staff file, but he hadn't. And then she'd admitted to doing the same. Where that left them, he wasn't sure.

It couldn't leave them anywhere anyway. She was his assistant; she was *twenty-seven*... Younger than Liam. *Christ*. He had to fix whatever he'd broken. Cal couldn't bear the thought of another week of her flitting around, clearly uncomfortable.

He groaned and headed out of his office, down the elevator, and stepped into the first floor office. It was always too loud and busy. Three dozen paralegals, legal assistants, and junior attorneys discussing cases filled the room, mountains of paperwork covering almost every desk. Cal didn't blame Maggie for hiding in his office so often. He'd offered to move her desk up to his floor permanently, but she liked to be accessible to everyone. Though she was technically *his* assistant alone, he wasn't sure she'd ever said no to anything she'd been asked to do.

He kept his head down as he wandered through the fray to her desk; the last thing he wanted was to be peppered with questions when he was so focused on Maggie. Her desk was, unlike his own, organized to a tee, empty of loose paperwork, errant pens, and unwound paperclips. It was also suspiciously empty of Maggie; the ridiculous oversized metal water tumbler she carried with her, the tablet that was semi-permanently glued to her hand... missing.

Cal turned to leave, knocking her mouse as he did so. The screen flashed to life, bringing up Maggie's LinkedIn page. He loathed social media, but it was necessary for hiring and keeping an eye on their competition these days. Their PR person handled the company's page, but he knew Maggie had a profile and monitored it. He wasn't *trying* to read her messages, but the screen had opened to a message from a familiar name and profile picture: the CEO of another law firm in the city.

Hi Maggie,
How are you?
Just checking in to let you know that, if you're looking to make a move, my offer from six months ago (and every six months before that!) still stands. We would love to have you on board at Raban-Willis, and we're willing to discuss whatever it takes to get you here.
Let me know what you think and we can set up a dinner.
Regards,
Christopher Raban

Cal sucked in a breath, his blood pounding in his ears. Why the fuck was Chris fucking Raban trying to poach Maggie?

And every six months before that. How long had this been going on for? Neither of them had mentioned it, and he bumped into Chris every couple of months at court. Hell, they'd gone for drinks three times in the past six months.

Apparently Maggie hadn't been tempted six months ago, but would things be different now they were so…

strained between them? He couldn't let it happen; Chris might be willing to do *whatever it took*, but that had nothing on what Cal would do to make her want to stay.

Cal turned to the adjacent desk. "Hey Grant, have you seen Maggie?"

Grant peered up at him through his glasses, his cheeks coloring. "Um, she hasn't been around much today. Last I saw her, she was talking to Josie this morning," he stammered. Grant was new and, according to Maggie, *hopelessly in love with Cal*. He offered him a smile and a thank you and, as Cal walked away, Grant dropped his head to the desk.

Cal fought a smile as he made his way across the office to Josie's desk. She looked up at him as he approached, a pencil tucked in her black, curly bun.

"Hey, Cal. What brings you down here?"

"Hey. Have you seen Maggie today?" he asked her, and she winced. "What?"

"Mr. Hicks' new assistant quit without notice—"

"Again?" Cal interrupted in disbelief, and Josie pursed her lips as she nodded. Though he'd never been friends with his co-owner, Cal had never had a problem working with him. They'd both been attorneys at a business law firm that had gone under twenty years ago, and, though it had been Cal's idea to set up his own firm, Ben had been instrumental to the early days of the firm.

Cal's side of the firm handled a range of businesses, assisting with contracts, to employment law, to taxes, while Ben's side of the firm handled their corporate clients. But Ben rarely took his own clients these days, choosing instead to hire more attorneys under his name than Cal did. Cal was a quality over quantity kind of boss; Ben was just coasting until his wife forced him to retire.

"Again," Josie confirmed. "He called Maggie this morning and asked to *borrow* her." Derision dripped from Josie's tone and the two paralegals flanking her desk looked up, their faces mirroring the disgust on Josie's.

"Poor Maggie," Twyla said, while Demi groaned.

"What am I missing here?" Cal asked, staring at the three of them. While he wasn't thrilled that Ben was piling extra work on Maggie when she already did so much, he wasn't sure it warranted so much disgust.

He and Ben had always worked with their own staff, though the two teams would occasionally collaborate on cases. But Maggie... Maggie was his. The thought brought him up short. *Possessive*, she'd said when discussing his Zodiac sign. Asshole might have been more fitting.

The women before him raised their brows and pursed their lips at each other in silent conversation. They turned back to him and Demi leaned forward on her desk. "Mr. Hicks is a creep. You wouldn't catch me in that office alone with him."

"Me either," Josie agreed. "Especially if I were Maggie. Have you seen the way he stares at her?"

Twyla voiced her agreement. "She always looks stressed out when she's been to the third floor, poor thing."

Red tinged the edges of Cal's vision. At least Maggie

wasn't avoiding him because he'd made her uncomfortable, but he hated the thought of her stuck with someone who treated her like Ben apparently did.

"Why would no one tell me this? I don't want any of you to feel uncomfortable." Especially not Maggie, but he couldn't say that.

"Well, we just assumed you two were friends," Twyla said with a matter-of-fact shrug.

"We're not friends," he replied firmly. "I'll go upstairs and get Maggie. And make it clear that he—"

Cal was cut off as the door to the office opened and an aggravated Maggie appeared, her blue eyes full to the brim with icy fire. She paused in the doorway, closing her eyes and sighing deeply, then schooled her face into a neutral smile and stepped into the room. Her eyes roamed over the chaos, settling on him, and the smile on her lips softened into something more genuine.

Cal ignored the sheer fucking audacity of his heart to race at the sight.

"Hey," she said as she approached, and God, why did it feel like it had been days since he'd heard her voice?

"Hi, love."

They stared at each other until Demi said, "This is weird," and Maggie turned to face her, narrowing her eyes.

"It's not weird." She turned back to Cal and nodded towards her desk. He followed her through the office. "I'm sorry I haven't been up to go over next week's schedule with you. It's been a busy morning. I can try to squeeze—"

"Let's get lunch." The interruption surprised Cal as much as it seemed to surprise Maggie, even though it had come from his mouth. They stopped beside her desk and Maggie's brow knit together as she shouldered her purse.

"Lunch, like... not here?" It was out there now, so Cal nodded. Maggie swallowed. "We don't do that."

Though she regularly picked up lunch for the two of them and they holed up in his office, working through their lunch hour during peak times, they'd never gone out. He hadn't intended to ask her to lunch; it had just... slipped out. He needed to get them back on steady ground; maybe lunch would do the trick.

"We *can* do it, though."

Maggie sighed. "I only came down here because Hicks wants me to pick up lunch for him. He specifically told me to *hurry back*."

Cal fought the growl building in his throat and leaned closer to Maggie to slide her phone across the desk. His mouth watered in such proximity to her; she smelled like sweet lilacs. Cal punched in Ben's direct line with more force than was necessary and held the receiver to his ear. It rang for entirely too long before Ben's nasally voice sounded down the line.

"Ben speaking."

"Ben, it's Cal," he ground out, pleasantries be damned.

"Ah, Cal. What can I do for you?"

"I'm afraid I need Maggie for the rest of the day."

Ben tutted. "What a shame. I was enjoying having her around."

Cal took a deep breath before responding. "I can imagine. Hey, if you want to *borrow* any of my team, can you give me a heads up next time? I don't always keep my calendar updated."

"Yeah, yeah, of course I can," Ben replied dismissively. "I don't suppose you have anyone who would make a good assistant? I just can't seem to find anyone who wants to work."

"Afraid not," Cal replied, weighing up the pros and cons of hanging up on the asshole.

Ben chuckled. "It's a shame we can't share Maggie, huh?"

And that was his limit. He gritted his teeth. "I've got to go, Ben. Talk soon."

He placed the handset down and pushed the phone as far away as he could without it falling off the desk, as if it was tainted by Ben's mere fucking existence.

"That fixes that. So, lunch?"

Maggie chewed her lip, looking uncertain. Cal rolled his eyes, faking the picture of nonchalance, as he held out a hand for her purse. "Come on. I don't bite."

Maggie narrowed her eyes, but, finally, dropped the bag into his waiting hand. "I don't believe that for a second," she muttered, shaking her head. "Lead the way."

Less than a sixty-second walk from their front door, Ethel's Diner was a staple in the day-to-day of every Michaelson and Hicks employee. Cal shuddered to think how much he'd eaten here since they'd moved to this spot two years ago. The benefit was that they knew the menu like the back of their hands, and he and Maggie placed their orders the second they sat down.

Maggie shed her coat and folded it neatly on the seat beside her, then tapped her nails on the table in front of her as Ethel filled their cups with coffee. They offered their thanks to Ethel, dissolving into silence as she walked back towards the kitchen.

"This is weird," Maggie declared, though she seemed more uncertain than uncomfortable.

Cal snorted and pulled his coffee cup closer. "We were drinking together in a sex club last weekend, but *this* is weird?"

"That was weird too," she pointed out, but some of the tension fell from her shoulders and a small smile appeared on her mouth. Cal had to drag his eyes away from the perfect blush pink of her lips, but not before Maggie spied his gaze and her cheeks turned rosy to match.

He took a long, too hot drag of coffee. "Tell me about your house."

Maggie blinked in surprise. "My house?"

"You're renovating it, right? How's it going?"

"Oh, yeah. It's going… fine," she offered, her nose wrinkling. "It's good. I just finished tiling the kitchen last night, actually. This weekend I just need to figure out the plumbing situation and I'll finally have running water again. Hopefully."

"You don't have running water? How long have you

been without it?" Cal asked, an unwelcome worry winding its way around his bones.

"It's fine." She waved away his concern. "It's only been a few days, and I shower at the gym before work. I do miss my bath," she allowed, and Cal swallowed as memories from the previous weekend flashed in his mind. "It took me longer to learn to tile than I hoped. And I had a lot to do. The kitchen is huge."

The scent of fresh basil and tomato interrupted them as their lunch arrived, and Cal's stomach rumbled as he inhaled.

"I can't believe you're doing it all yourself. You must be exhausted," he said as he unwound the napkin from his silverware.

Maggie shrugged, laying her own napkin on her lap. "I'm managing. I mean, I had no idea what I was getting into when I bought the house, but I really love learning so much and seeing it all come together."

"Why'd you do it?"

He understood wanting to own your own home—and how much easier it had been when *he* was in his twenties —but buying a fixer-upper with zero experience was a lot for anyone, let alone someone doing it all alone.

Maggie dragged her spoon through her soup in a spiral. "After Nathan and I broke up, I moved in with Jazz for a couple of weeks, but then I saw the house in a real estate ad online and it just... excited me. It was messy and falling apart, and it felt like a fresh start. Not to mention it was dirt cheap. I bought it on a whim, to be honest. Which, if it isn't obvious, is really unlike me."

Cal fought a laugh. "Oh, really? You strike me as the kind of person who thrives on mess and chaos, love."

"It's been a bit of a trial by fire," she admitted, scrunching her nose. "But I'm holding it together."

Because Maggie held everything together. He'd done the math after looking in her staff file; her birthday weekend, when she'd broken up with her ex, had fallen just days before the office had lost power three times, a week before they were due to take one of their biggest cases of the year to court. And Maggie hadn't once wavered. If she'd exhausted herself running back and forth to Ethel's for coffee, to the library to print and copy files, and on constant calls with their electric company, no one would have known. Just days after uprooting her life, she'd been taking care of everyone else. He'd never considered that she might be doing it to her detriment.

Cal set down his silverware and sat back in his seat. "Why didn't you tell me about Ben?"

Maggie's hand stilled, her spoon halfway to her mouth, concern flooding her blue eyes. "What? Oh shit, this morning. I'm sorry. He totally rushed me upstairs, and I figured I'd get the chance to call you or drop in but—"

"No, that's not... About how he treats you, I mean," Cal clarified.

"Oh, that." Realization dawned on Maggie's face, and she laughed, shaking her head. "It's fine. Don't even worry about it. I'm a woman in America, and you're the exception, not the rule. I'm used to it."

Cal was no stranger to misogyny. He was a business

lawyer, for Christ's sake—he'd handled enough sexual harassment cases to breathe a sigh of relief that he had a son, and pray to God that they'd done enough to drill into him how not to be an asshole. But it wasn't going to fly in his office. "Just because you're used to it doesn't make it okay, Maggie," he said gently, and she sighed.

"I'm not saying it's okay, it's just… if it's not Hicks, it's the clients. If I'm not at work, it's the guys at the grocery store or my neighbor's creepy dog walker. And really, I'm lucky. There's a reason Hicks has to hire a new assistant once a month and I still love working for you after six years."

As reassuring as that was… "My job is to make sure you're safe and comfortable at work," he said, ignoring the roaring in his chest that he should *also* make sure she was safe and comfortable at the grocery store and with her neighbor's creepy dog walker. "I can't do that if I don't know what's going on."

"I suppose that's true," she relented.

"No more Hicks *borrowing* you," he told her, his mouth twisting in disgust at the term. What an asshole. "And if any of our clients are anything but polite and respectful, tell me. I'll deal with it."

She was quiet for a moment, and he couldn't read the emotions flashing through her eyes. But finally, she nodded. "Okay. Thank you."

Cal picked up his spoon but paused. "When I didn't see you this morning, I thought… I thought *I* made you uncomfortable, and you didn't want to be around me."

Maggie's eyes widened, and she shook her head.

"What? No, not at all. I know things have been a little awkward lately." She winced. "But I promise, I always feel totally comfortable and safe with you."

Relief filled Cal, a weight lifting from his chest. "And you're not… considering other firms?"

Maggie frowned in confusion. "Why would I be considering other firms?"

Cal sighed, rubbing his face. "When I was looking for you this morning, I accidentally woke up your computer and there was a message from Chris Raban offering you a job."

Realization lit Maggie's eyes, and she waved a dismissive hand. "Oh, that. Yeah, I get calls and emails every couple of weeks from firms across the city. I've always made it clear I'm not interested."

Surprise rippled through Cal. *Why had no one mentioned this to him?* "How long has this been happening?"

"Since the Hemminger West case a few years ago," she explained, and Cal understood immediately. They'd represented another law firm in the city when the two brothers who owned it had parted ways, after one accused the other of embezzlement. It had been messy, and every person connected with the legal world in Seattle had watched the case eagle eyed. The courtroom had been packed, and no one—him included—was sure who was actually in the wrong or which way the case would go.

Maggie rarely went to court with him, but he'd been so stressed about how many eyes had been on the firm for that case, that he'd had her by his side every day in court.

She'd been a godsend, keeping him organized and making sure he had everything before he even knew he needed it. They worked perfectly in sync, Maggie anticipating his every move. Clearly, it hadn't gone unnoticed.

He couldn't say he was surprised; the pressure had gotten to everyone during the two weeks in the courtroom, and the opposition stumbled at the final hurdle. The only reason Cal hadn't struggled was because he didn't have to think about what he was doing. She'd done it for him.

"So you're not—"

"I'm not going anywhere," she said firmly, with a smile that made his stomach flip. "And, for the record, I don't like Chris Raban. He cheats on his wife."

Cal raised a brow at that. Chris had married the daughter of a senator, and their wedding had been plastered all over the local news. If that ever got out, he could kiss goodbye to his firm. "How do you know?"

"Because he's propositioned me every time I've seen him over the past few years, and when I've said no, he's moved on to someone else." She shrugged. "Something tells me he's not just looking for an assistant."

Cal's jaw tensed, and he busied his hands with his coffee cup. Something told *him* he wouldn't be having drinks with Chris fucking Raban again.

And that something was in dangerous territory.

CHAPTER SIX

Maggie

W hat the fuck had possessed her to buy a fixer upper? Maggie groaned at her tablet, the video on screen giving the world's least helpful instructions on how to connect the water to her sink. She hadn't even considered the dishwasher yet—God help her.

All she wanted was a bath—an hour or two to soak in dessert-scented bubbles while listening to music and trying not to think about work or her parents or the house or her boss. Especially not her boss.

Despite hours of searching the previous weekend, Maggie hadn't found a way to turn the water off for just the kitchen, so she'd been without running water for six whole days. She was sure it was possible, she just didn't have the skills to make it happen.

Maybe she should have called a plumber, but that

defeated the purpose of proving she could do it herself. And she *could* do it herself... probably.

The doorbell chimed, and she narrowly avoided knocking her head on the underside of the cabinet as she withdrew, frowning towards the hallway. She stood up, brushing dust from her bare thighs and watching it gather on her knee-high wool socks instead. She wasn't expecting anyone, and she definitely wasn't dressed for visitors.

Maggie considered grabbing a sweater to throw over her tank, but she was so dusty. "Fuck it," she declared, before stalking down the hall towards the front door. The rusty iron lock had warped long before Maggie had gotten her hands on the house, but she forced it until she heard the telltale click and wrenched the door open.

She really should have grabbed the sweater.

Cal stood on her moss-covered steps, a bag slung over his shoulder and... jeans? How had she never seen him in jeans?

"Hi," she said, confusion clear in her voice. Cal was at her house. Cal, whose eyes were making their way up her body from her wooly socks. And Maggie wasn't wearing a bra. Had she even brushed her hair this morning? His gaze was heated as it traversed her, and Maggie swallowed as Cal's eyes landed on her face, the sun painting flecks of gold in emerald green.

"Hey. I couldn't in good conscience let you live without running water, so I came to help."

"You didn't have to do that," she said automatically. "But also, thank God you did. It's not going well. Thank you." She stepped aside, and he chuckled as he crossed the threshold into her house. *Cal was in her house.* This didn't bode well for her trying not to think about him if she finally got that bath later.

She led him down the hall and he whistled appreciatively at her tiles when they got to the kitchen. "Maggie, this is amazing. You seriously did all of this yourself? And it was your first time?"

The blush and gold tiles had been a labor of love, but mostly labor. Still, she couldn't deny how fucking proud of herself she was. She nodded, and Cal smiled at her. "You did amazing, love."

Maggie's stomach fluttered at the praise; she was surprised how much she liked it. "Thanks. Coffee?"

"Always." Cal set his bag on the island with a clink while Maggie grabbed a cup for him. She gave the bag a questioning look. "I wasn't sure what we'd need in terms of tools, or what you'd have, so I brought a little of everything."

Maggie set his cup in the coffeemaker and popped a pod in before pressing *start*. "You don't really strike me as a DIY kind of person," she admitted, leaning back against the counter. "I figured you probably just hired people for this kind of stuff."

"I do, usually. But I knew if I tried to do that for you, you'd probably shut the door in my face," he said.

"And you said you didn't know much about me."

He laughed as she handed the cup over, wrapping his hands around it and closing his eyes for a second as he breathed it in. It was how he responded to every cup of coffee, taking just a second to truly appreciate the aroma before downing it.

"My dad owned a couple of contracting companies over the years before he retired," he explained. "Most of my siblings still work for the one he set up when they moved back to Ireland. We all worked with him when we were kids, so I learned a lot over the years."

A soft smile lit up his face as he spoke about his family, and Maggie felt her own lips lifting in response. "What?" he asked.

"You just look really happy talking about your family."

He shrugged, his cheeks turning pink. "I don't get to see them often. I miss them." He hesitated for a moment before asking, "What's your family like?"

That was a rabbit hole she didn't want to lead him down, so she simply said, "My parents own a cafe in Marysville. I see them a lot."

"Do you have siblings?"

"Three," she answered. "Cassie, Danny, and Hallie. Yeah, my parents did the matching name thing." She wrinkled her nose.

Cal grimaced. "I'm guessing you're the oldest?"

"What makes you think that? My crippling perfectionism?"

"You said it, not me," Cal protested, laughing. As expected, he drained his coffee in seconds, then set the cup on the island. "Let's get your water running, shall we?"

C al Michaelson was an excellent teacher, but Maggie already knew that. In the six years she'd worked for him, she'd learned more about business law than she needed to know, just because he explained things so well. In her first year, she'd taken a couple of online legal workshops, but had quickly given them up when she realized she learned more by just being around Cal.

He crouched on the floor and stuck his head under the sink without flinching and, once Maggie got over the sight of him in casual clothes, she took a seat beside him.

Cal explained what did what and had her jump up and down to test the water. In no time at all, Maggie not only had running water again, but a fully functioning dishwasher. *Finally*.

"You're amazing. Thank you," she gushed as she set lunch out on the table between them. She'd ordered in, insisting on feeding him as thanks for his help. "Just out of interest, are you bad at anything?" It was ridiculous, really, that he spent Monday to Friday running the top business law firm in the Pacific Northwest with relative ease, then fixed her plumbing on the weekend. *Some people*.

"Anything to do with technology," he answered, and she had to sound her agreement. The man could barely send an email.

"True, but you have me for that." She didn't offer to teach him; she'd tried once, but teaching had never been her strong suit. Huffing and puffing until she inevitably said, "*Just give it here and I'll do it,*" was more her style.

"Thank God I do," he said, his dimples peeking out and making Maggie's stomach flutter.

Maggie loaded their plates into her shiny new dishwasher once they'd finished eating.

"Is there anything else I can help you with while I'm here?" Cal asked, gathering the takeout bags and tossing them in the trash.

Maggie opened her mouth to decline automatically, but paused and bit her lip. "How do you feel about spiders?" she asked, her cheeks burning.

Cal laughed. "Lead the way, love."

Maggie led Cal up the stairs, pointing out her renovation plans as they went. They paused by the bathroom and she showed him the clawfoot tub that had sold her the property. "It's the best tub I've ever used," she gushed. "You've made my whole weekend by fixing the water, you know."

Cal swallowed, his green eyes focused on the tub, and she wondered if he was thinking about their phone call the week before. Maggie blew out a breath. "The spider's in my room."

She led him down the hall into her room—*holy shit, Cal was in her room*—and pointed out her unwanted eight-legged roommate on the wall.

Cal gaped at it. "Fucking hell, that's massive."

"Mhmm," Maggie agreed, keeping distance. "I named her Margaret."

Cal turned slowly to stare at her. "That's your name."

"I figured if we had something in common, she might be more likely to respect my boundaries and stay out of my personal space."

"And how's that going?" Cal asked, fighting a laugh as they looked at the spider sitting a foot above her headboard.

"Wonderful, thanks for asking."

He shook his head, smiling, as he considered the situation. "I think I'm going to have to get on the bed," he said, finally.

Maggie gulped. "Have at it."

He kicked his shoes off and kneeled on the bed with more grace that she would have managed. Cal was on her bed. She had to sleep there.

"This is also huge—the bed, I mean," Cal said, approaching Margaret slowly.

"It was the first piece of furniture I bought when Nathan and I broke up," she explained, patting the comforter fondly. "I had *big* plans for this bed. Unfortunately, I'm also a workaholic who bought a fixer upper so there hasn't been much time for said plans." Maggie closed her eyes and shook her head. *Why the fuck did she say that?* Thank God he couldn't see her.

"You don't go out?" Cal asked, and she could hear the smile in his voice.

"Not often. And the one time I did, I didn't meet anyone because I ran into my boss." Cal snorted. "You're technically the first man in this bed." The words slipped out before she could stop them, and Cal faltered, his hand slipping down the wall as the spider scuttled away.

"Shit." He reached out with lightning reflexes and closed his hands over the spider. "Got it."

Maggie hurried to the window, wrenching it open with a concerning creak. Cal didn't hide his grimace at the sound as he deposited Margaret outside the window. She ran down the wall like her life depended on it.

"Good riddance," Maggie said, pulling the window closed and breathing a sigh. She led Cal back downstairs and made him another cup of coffee, rummaging in the cabinet for the fancy shortbread cookies he'd gotten her hooked on during her first year at Michaelson and Hicks. She arranged them on a plate Jazz had painted for her at one of those paint and sip places and, though he blinked at it, Cal didn't question the abstract portrait of Maggie and Jazz.

"Thank you for today," she said, sitting across from him. "I owe you, big time."

"Helping you fix your water and moving a spider doesn't come close to covering everything you do for me."

"You pay me for that," Maggie pointed out.

He raised a brow. "I pay you from nine to five, love. As much as I struggle to send an email, I can read the timestamps on the ones you send."

"I don't sleep well." It wasn't exactly a lie. She didn't sleep well when she knew she had shit to do, so she just did it. Then she would inevitably remember something else she had to do and… It was a vicious cycle.

"How long were you and Nathan together?" Cal asked, the question catching her by surprise.

"Six years, officially, but we hooked up on and off before that." What a waste of her twenties he'd been.

"God, I didn't realize it had been so long. You know you could've taken time off after," he said gently, but Maggie laughed.

"Honestly? I didn't even cry. I felt more myself the second I walked out of our apartment than I had in years. Which, I realize makes me sound like an asshole, but it is what it is."

"You don't sound like an asshole," he confirmed. "Eliza and I were both the same when we got divorced. We were just relieved."

"That was exactly it. Relief."

"Had things been rough for a while?"

Maggie considered, toying with the pompoms hanging from her socks. "It wasn't rough, per se, it was just... dull. He got down on one knee and I wasn't excited. I couldn't remember the last time I had been excited, actually. I tried, over the last couple of years, to do more exciting shit, trying to be happier, you know? But Nathan didn't like it."

"He didn't like you trying to be happier?" Cal asked, his voice laced with disgust for her ex.

Maggie shook her head with a sigh. "At first, I went out with Jazz a lot more, but he didn't like that. He doesn't like Jazz, period." Nathan hadn't liked any of her friends, and Jazz had been the only one to stick around when he threw fits over Maggie going out without him. "Then I bought a bunch of new clothes, but I had nowhere to wear them since I wasn't going anywhere.

Nathan didn't like them, anyway, so I ended up just donating them. I even got my nipples pierced."

Cal choked on his coffee. "Christ, Maggie, you've got to warn someone before you drop that."

She tried and failed to hide her laugh in her cup. "Sorry."

"Tell me he at least enjoyed that," Cal asked, his voice pained, as he adamantly avoided looking at her chest.

She scoffed. "Nathan... Okay, it's noon on a Saturday and you're my boss, so I *definitely* shouldn't be talking about this, but we did watch a live sex show together last Saturday." She shrugged. He'd spoken to her while she was naked in the tub. He knew she had her nipples pierced. He'd been on her bed. The lines between them were already blurry. "Anyway. Nathan liked to have sex in front of the mirror, but not in a kinky way. He just liked to stare at himself."

Cal winced. "You're kidding me."

"I wish I was. You could have replaced me with any nameless, faceless woman, and it would have made no difference to him. He was entirely focused on himself for exactly six minutes every time."

"Six minutes? That's it? But that's not even enough time to—"

"Yeah, no, trust me—I know," she interrupted, holding up a hand. "And before you ask: no, I don't know why I stuck around for so long." She was lying, but admitting she'd stuck it out because Nathan and her family had convinced her she couldn't manage on her own was fucking embarrassing.

"You've seemed happier—more excited—lately," Cal told her.

"I am," she replied, the smile on her face a little forced.

Cal saw right through her. "But?"

"No buts," she lied.

Sure, it hadn't been entirely what she'd expected, not that she'd really known what to expect, but she was managing. And she was managing on her own. If it took staying up until the wee hours of the morning and still spending every day exhausted just to get everything done, she was still managing. And the loneliness was… manageable. Maybe her big plans for her big bed had yet to pan out, but she was managing. Alone, with her fancy new tub and forbidden thoughts of the man before her.

Cal pursed his lips in a way that made it clear he didn't believe her. "You know, I think I might know you better than I thought I did."

"How so?"

"Well, I know you're bullshitting me, for one," he pointed out, but there was no heat behind the words and his smile softened them.

"No comment," Maggie replied with a laugh.

"Maggie?" Cal said, and she fought the shiver that yearned to run down her spine at the sound of her name from his lips.

"Yeah?"

"Whatever it takes to get rid of those *buts*? You should do it." Cal hesitated for a moment before adding, "Unless whatever it takes is quitting on me. Please don't do that."

"What do I have to do to convince you I'm not going anywhere?"

"I don't know what it is," Cal said. "Every time you walk into my office, I'm convinced you've figured out you're too good to be my assistant and you're going to leave me." He laughed it off, but Maggie recognized the genuine worry in his green eyes, in the set of his jaw.

"Hey. I love being your assistant, Cal." She put as much conviction as she could into the words and watched some of the tension fall away from his face. "We're a good team."

"Yeah, we are," Cal agreed, his voice a little softer and his eyes a lot brighter.

Maggie's face warmed; how had they gone from talking about her nipple piercings to how boring her life had become? She cleared her throat. "Well, since we've talked about my nipple piercings and my ex-boyfriend's sexual preferences, I think I can probably ask about the club."

Cal snorted, his cheeks turning slightly pink. "I think that's fair. What do you want to know?"

Everything, Maggie thought, though she knew better than to ask for the dirty details. They might have sat together at the club, and he might be in her kitchen, but Cal was still her boss.

"Are you like... a regular?" she asked, and Cal shrugged.

"Not super regular. I go maybe once a month. It's a good place to meet people with minimal effort."

"I can see that," Maggie agreed. Though she hadn't gone home with anyone, thanks to Cal's presence, Jazz had hit the jackpot, and all she'd had to do was wait for someone to beckon her over.

"Do you think you'll go back?"

Maggie wrinkled her nose at Cal's question. "I think running into my boss at a sex club once is probably more than enough."

"We could compare schedules to make sure it doesn't happen again," Cal pointed out.

"Or just put it on your calendar—I pretty much have it memorized."

Cal and Maggie stared at each other for a moment before dissolving into laughter at the idea of adding *Visit Sex Club* to his calendar.

"Maybe not," Cal said, as he stood, shouldering his tool bag, his shoulders still shaking.

Maggie walked him down the hall to the door and ignored his frown as she warred with the lock. She would get to it; her neighborhood was safe... ish.

"Thank you for today. Seriously, I would still be stuck under the sink if you hadn't shown up, and I think Margaret was getting ready to climb into bed with me."

"Anytime," Cal offered, squinting at the winter sun as he stepped out onto the top step. "I'll see you on Monday, yeah?"

"Definitely. I'm not going anywhere—remember?"

Cal laughed, turning to leave but pausing. "Maggie?"

"Yeah?"

"I meant it. Do whatever it takes to find the thing that excites you. And if it's something I can help with, you know where I am." The words themselves weren't suggestive, but the edge in Cal's green eyes had Maggie wondering if the same ideas that were swimming around in her head were in his.

It would be so easy to reach out a hand and invite him back in; so easy to lead him upstairs and break in her new bed. But it would be absolutely unbearable come Monday morning, when they had to walk into work and figure out how to work together after blowing any sense of boundaries out of the water. It was a terrible idea, regardless of how pretty it looked in her head.

She shook herself. "I will. Thank you. And thank you, again, for today. I'll see you on Monday."

Cal lifted a hand in goodbye and walked down the path. She watched him climb into his Tesla and drive off with another wave, before closing her front door and leaning back against it with a sigh.

CHAPTER SEVEN

Maggie

Maggie groaned as she pushed against the glass door in vain. The weather report had been calling for a storm for days, but, although she'd spent every one of her twenty-seven years in Washington, the awful weather still pissed her off.

How the fuck was she going to drive in this? That was a problem for future Maggie—future Maggie, who somehow figured out how to lock up the office so she could leave.

She winced under the weight of the door, the wind a howling racket, until two strong hands landed above hers, relieving the pressure. Maggie could have moaned in relief, but that definitely wouldn't help the thick tension that lived between her and Cal these days.

"I'll hold it closed if you lock it," he said, close

enough that his breath tickled her neck. Butterflies swarmed in her belly.

Maggie nodded, afraid that if she spoke, her voice would betray the heat spreading through her despite the cold air. She released the door and sank to her knees to grab the keys from the spot on the floor where she'd dropped them during her first locking attempt. When she glanced up, the veins were visible on Cal's bare arms as he strained to hold the door closed. Maggie swallowed and shoved the key in the lock, breathing a sigh of relief when she felt it click into place.

She looked back up at Cal, who was looking down at her with an expression that did dangerous things to her insides, and nodded. "It's locked. Do you think it'll hold?"

"Only one way to find out." Cal slowly released the door and stepped back. They watched the rain beat against the glass, but the lock held strong. "Lets hope it lasts the weekend," Cal added, offering her a hand. Maggie hesitated for a moment before taking it; it was strong, uncalloused, and... how had she never noticed how big his hands were? She let him pull her to her feet and shook herself.

This had gone on long enough. She'd gone too long without sex. Even longer without *good* sex. But tonight, she finally had plans to change that. She'd listened to Cal's advice and, good idea or not, she was going to find a little excitement tonight.

All it had taken was one perfectly timed, slightly suggestive, bath time selfie, posted to her Instagram story and ten minutes scrolling through the replies until she found an old college hook-up, Rebekah, asking what she was doing these days.

It had been almost too easy. She'd made her intentions clear, and Rebekah was only in town for a couple of days anyway. It was the perfect solution to getting Cal out of her system. Come Monday morning, she'd be able to walk in here and look Cal in the eye without wanting to jump on him. She just needed one night of really good sex and—

"I don't think we're getting out of here tonight."

No. She had to get out of here tonight. Maggie closed her eyes and pinched the bridge of her nose. "You know, I think I could..." she trailed off as the wind howled loud enough to make Cal wince. "I could probably still walk."

He looked at her like she'd grown another head. "You want to walk all the way to Ravenna in gale force winds?"

"Oh no, I have plans nearby. It would only be a fifteen-minute walk." As she said it, they watched a woman being dragged along the sidewalk outside the office by the wind. Maggie sighed, her plans blowing away at fifty miles per hour. "I guess I'm canceling." She pulled out her phone and sent a message letting Rebekah know. "Getting stuck here overnight has to be a new level of workaholic-ness."

Cal laughed. "It's not my first time getting stuck at the office. The weather here is unhinged. I sprung for the comfier couch in my office after the second time."

"Sensible."

"I'm going to head down to the parking garage and grab my gym bag so I can change. You want me to grab anything from your car?"

"I'll come," she said. "I have my gym bag too."

They took the stairs, forgoing the elevator in case the power cut out. Maggie's phone chimed, and she checked it to find a sad face and *I'll hit you up next time I'm in town* from Rebekah. She frowned at the phone.

"Where were you supposed to be going tonight?" Cal asked as she tucked her phone back in her pocket.

"The Paramount on Pine Street."

"The hotel?"

"Yeah."

They stepped into the parking garage, the wind echoing around them. "Is something wrong with the house?" Cal asked as they stopped by her car and she wrenched the trunk open.

Maggie paused. Why did their conversations always end up on unsteady ground these days? She rummaged around in the depths of the trunk for her gym bag, dodging the paint cans, bags of loose screws, and wall-paper paste. "No, the house is fine. I was supposed to be meeting someone."

"Like a date?"

"I wouldn't call it a date, no. Just a one night trying to find the thing that excites me kind of deal." Her hand closed around the strap of the bag and she pulled it out, turning around just in time to see Cal schooling his face into something slightly less stormy than the Seattle night.

The wind chose that moment to pipe down, leaving

the silence between them taut until Maggie closed her trunk with a soft thud and it cut the tension. Cal held out a hand for her bag. "Oh, I'm okay." He didn't drop the hand, just raised an eyebrow until she rolled her eyes and handed it over. He shouldered it with ease. "Thanks."

"I'm sorry the weather messed up your plans," Cal said, finally as they made their way to his car.

Maggie shrugged and cleared her throat. "It's fine. I'll try again next weekend." Perhaps next time, she'd post a picture of the knee-high socks he hadn't been able to take his eyes off last weekend.

Cal grabbed his own bag, and they headed back into the warmth of the office.

"Did you meet someone online?" Cal asked as they finally reached the fourth floor. He set their bags down gently by the couch.

"Huh?"

"The person you were meeting tonight."

"Oh," Maggie said, dropping onto the couch and rubbing her eyes. "No, it was someone I hooked up with back in college before Nathan and I got together. I haven't seen her since we graduated, but she's only in town for a few days. I've never really tried the online thing."

"I tried it a couple of times," Cal said, taking a seat beside her.

"Shut up. You never even text."

"Kind of feels like you just called me old, love. Liam set it up for me when he was about to graduate high school. He was worried I was lonely. It was a lot of effort with little payoff. I do better meeting people in person."

"It's the accent," Maggie confirmed, and Cal just rolled his eyes. "No, I'm serious. Dating apps have voice prompts now and you'd kill it. Jazz scrolls through them for fun."

"I do well enough without them," Cal said with what, on another man, might have looked like a self-deprecating shrug. On him, it looked matter of fact.

"I bet," Maggie replied without thinking, and his green eyes twinkled as they landed on hers. His gaze was heavy, and Maggie swallowed under the weight of it. "Should we head down to the kitchen and try to pull some dinner together?"

"I could eat," Cal said, and the words were almost obscene when he was looking at her like that.

Maggie shook her head. "Holy shit," she muttered under her breath as she stood and followed him towards the door.

"What was that?"

"Nothing."

Running outside for a cold shower in the Seattle downpour was looking better and better.

Maggie kept the office kitchen well stocked, and though their dinner of ramen, cookies, and seltzer water was hardly a luxury affair, it hit the spot.

By the time they made it back up to the fourth floor,

night had fallen over the city with the rain, and the wind had settled into a steady howl.

"Do you want to change in here and I'll go into the office?" Cal asked and Maggie agreed, pulling her gym stuff out of the neatly packed bag. It wasn't much; cycling shorts and a cropped shirt, but it would be comfier than sleeping in tights and a pencil skirt. She changed quickly, eyeing her reflection in the rain flecked window. It *really* wasn't much. The shorts weren't booty shorts, but they were close, and the cropped shirt left a wide strip of her torso exposed. She hadn't packed a sweatshirt, since she usually just threw her work sweater or cardigan on top to drive home.

Maggie picked up her itchy wool cardigan and sighed. There was no chance of her sleeping in it.

"Can I come back in?"

Maggie shoved the cardigan into her bag. "Yeah, I'm decent." *Barely.*

She didn't immediately look up as Cal walked back into the lobby, but when she did, she almost toppled over. Her mouth watered as she took him in. He was devastating.

"What are those?" She tried to force her voice to sound level and calm, but it just sounded hollow.

Cal frowned, looking down at himself before realization dawned on him. "What? Oh, you mean my glasses?"

Yes, she meant his glasses. Black framed and sleek, sitting perfectly on his stupid, perfect face. "How did I not know you wore glasses?" Was she whining? It felt like she was whining.

Cal chuckled, setting his bag down by the couch. "I usually wear contacts. I just don't like to sleep in them."

"But I've never even booked an appointment for you."

"Eliza's an optometrist. She just texts me and tells me when to show up."

It made sense. It didn't, however, stop the heat pooling between her legs. "Oh."

Cal gave her a confused, yet somehow amused, look. "What?"

"Nothing," she bit out too quickly, her brow furrowed. Cal just stared at her, an eyebrow raised in a clear *bullshit* position. "Ugh," Maggie groaned. "How am I supposed to sleep here knowing you look like *that* in glasses?" She regretted it the moment she let the words slip out. Cal's mouth dropped a little, but his face lit up with mischief. "Shut up."

Cal held his hands up, eyes dancing. "I didn't say anything."

"Your face said it all," she grumbled, and he bit his lip, clearly trying not to laugh.

"It's a pullout couch. Shall we?" he asked, taking pity on her and changing the subject.

"Lets." Maggie packed the rest of her work clothes away in her gym back with vigor before dropping it beside Cal's. Metal groaned as they pulled the three seater out into a bed. Someone, presumably Cal, had tucked blankets and a comforter inside the queen mattress. Maggie looked from the soft fabrics to Cal and back. He tossed the throw pillows to the top of the bed and seemed to realize at the same moment she did, his hand stilling in mid air.

She was an assistant lusting over her millionaire, much older boss, and stuck overnight in the office with him because of a storm... with only one bed. What a fucking cliché.

"You take the bed, love. I'll sleep in the armchair." Cal leaned down to fluff the pillow—her pillows—and seemed unfazed at the thought of sleeping in the adjacent chair.

Maggie took a deep breath. She should keep her mouth closed. She should accept graciously and— "We're both adults who've had a long week. We can share a bed for the night without making it weird, right?"

She wasn't supposed to say that.

Cal paused on his way to the chair and turned slowly to face her. "I don't want to make you uncomfortable."

She took a seat on the edge of the bed and almost moaned at the dreamy soft mattress. Of course, when Cal said he'd sprung for the comfier couch, it had probably cost more than her car. "You don't make me uncomfortable. I promise. Can you just trust me that I'll tell you if you do?"

Cal sat opposite her, his white t-shirt riding up a little and revealing the tiniest sliver of skin. Maggie snapped her eyes away. "You are, without a doubt, the biggest people pleaser I've ever met. So, no, I can't really trust you to tell me."

She considered protesting, but it was a fair assessment. "Okay, so we'll pinky swear." She held up a pinky, and Cal loosed a surprise bark of laughter.

"Pinky swear?"

"Come on, you have to know what a pinky swear is. They're legally binding, Cal," she told him, deadpan.

He shook his head, but he was smiling when he leaned forward and curled his pinky around hers. "We called them pinky promises in Ireland."

"Well then, I pinky promise to tell you if you make me uncomfortable," she said, the heat of his little finger branding her.

"I feel like I need to promise something in return to make it binding," Cal said, making no move to drop her pinky.

"You *could* promise to stop messing up my spreadsheets by leaving gaps and writing the date in the wrong format," she suggested, and he scoffed.

"Something achievable, love. Okay, I promise to be perfectly respectful and professional, despite the fact that we're sharing a bed tonight and it's kind of awkward."

"It's a deal." She tugged lightly on his pinky, as if shaking his hand. Maggie immediately felt the absence of him as she pulled back, and couldn't help dragging a finger from the other hand over her lonely pinky.

Cal stood and crossed the room to turn out the big light, leaving them in the glow of the table lamps and the moon outside. He squinted at the windows. "I really should have hung blinds."

"I like seeing the rain," Maggie admitted, climbing under the blankets with as much grace as she could manage. She couldn't help the gasp that slipped out as her bare legs grazed the silky sheets. Cal's eyes snapped to hers, widening. Maggie felt the blood rush to her cheeks. "You come across like a pretty normal guy, for the most part, but God, rich people have the best bedding."

"Bedding and towels," Cal agreed. "They're the first things I splurged on when I realized I could."

"A worthy investment," she said, leaning back and stretching like a cat with her eyes closed. When she opened them, Cal was holding his side of the blankets and watching her with a soft smile. She held his gaze as he climbed into the bed beside her and lay down.

It had been months since she'd shared a bed with anyone, Margaret the spider notwithstanding. She'd forgotten how it felt to have the steady heat of someone lying beside her.

"What?" Cal asked, and she jolted, realizing she was just staring at him.

"Glasses," she said, clearing her throat and looking away. "They are lethal."

She stared resolutely at the ceiling as the silence stretched between them.

"The socks," Cal said, his voice gravelly.

She turned her head to look at him, her brow pinched. "What?"

Cal's eyes flicked down the bed and back up before he answered. "The socks you were wearing when I came over last weekend. *Those* were lethal."

"Huh." Cal's eyes followed her throat as she swallowed. "Is it a foot thing, or…?" she asked, successfully piercing the tension as Cal chuckled.

"Definitely not a foot thing." He wrinkled his nose. "It's, uh, a thigh thing." He loosed a shaky, pained breath.

A thigh guy. Interesting. The devil on her shoulder was suddenly grateful for her tiny gym shorts. "Good to know," she said. "They're my favorite—" There was a short crackling sound, and the lamps went out, plunging them into darkness. "—socks."

Maggie's eyes adjusted to the glow emanating from the window, bathing them in silver and gold from the moon and the streetlights. She blinked, Cal's eyes dancing with speckles of light and tickling her skin. Every inch of him demanded she pull closer.

"They're definitely my favorite too," Cal said, an attempt at humor that fizzled out among the electric sparks that had only grown stronger with the power cut.

Maggie bit, though, trying to claw them back from the precipice. "I have like ten pairs. They're so cozy—you can borrow a pair sometime."

The corner of Cal's mouth lifted, but his gaze only darkened.

"Cal…" she breathed, though she didn't know where the fuck she was going with it.

He closed his eyes, rolling away until he was lying on his back. "I'm fifty-five."

"I know. I googled you." Maggie turned too, staring up at the dark ceiling. "I'm twenty-seven."

"I know. I checked your file." His voice was pinched, pained. "I'm your boss."

"I'm your assistant."

"It's a cliché."

"A bad idea all around."

"Exactly." Cal blew out a long, shaky breath.

She knew they weren't wrong; it was a terrible idea. But she wanted him with a fever she'd never felt for Nathan, for anyone. If she didn't get his hands on her soon…

Maggie moved back onto her side until she was staring at his perfect side profile, his gray hair and beard flecked with silver moonlight. "Cal?"

She watched his chest rise and fall before he turned to face her, an expression of resolution that she was sure matched her own. "Yeah?"

"Are you ever going to kiss me?"

She bit her lip and his eyes fell to her mouth, emerald with desire. "I think that would be breaking my pinky promise." Still, he leaned in a fraction of an inch.

"Oh, well," Maggie managed, her voice raspy. "I guess you'll have to stop fucking up my spreadsheets."

Cal raised his eyes to meet hers, a smile spreading over his face. God, he was perfect. "Guess so, love."

And he finally closed the space between them and captured her mouth with his.

CHAPTER EIGHT

Maggie

His lips were like silk on hers, sending shivers down Maggie's spine. She reached up to cup his face, his beard soft beneath her fingers. Cal gripped the back of her thigh, his touch firm and flaming hot. She gasped as his fingertips grazed her skin, and he seized the chance to slip his tongue between her lips.

Maggie moaned as she finally tasted him—citrus and mint and the culmination of six long years of pretending she didn't want this. They barely broke for breath as Cal devoured her, his heart racing where it was pressed against her chest.

Maggie released his face, running her hands up the back of his t-shirt and Cal gently rolled them until she was lying on her back and he was kneeling over her, one knee on either side of her leg. Her head fell back against the pillows and she whimpered. Cal pulled back enough to turn his attention to her jaw, littering kisses across her skin and into the hollow of her throat.

"*Cal.*"

He stilled as his name slipped from her tongue, no longer able to hold it back. Cal sat up, towering over with an expression she thought might turn her to flames, panting. He trailed a finger over the strip of bare skin between her shirt and shorts. "Tell me to stop, love. If you don't want this... please." His voice cracked, pleading, but betraying just how badly he hoped she wouldn't.

He was a man tortured, nailed to the cross of her body, but Maggie knew he would pull himself away if she asked him to. And she *should* ask him to. She should take one for the team and walk away, take the elevator down to the first floor and curl up in the lounge. She should preserve her ability to walk in here on Monday morning, look her boss in the eye, and not think about how his fingers felt teasing the waistband of her shorts.

But Maggie had been doing what she was supposed to for so long. For once, she wanted to do what she wanted. What she needed.

"Please don't stop," she said, her voice barely above a whisper. "I just... I need... One night, please." For a moment, she wasn't sure he'd heard her over the din of the storm. Until he dragged that godforsaken finger down her shorts, between her legs, brushing her over the thin fabric and snapping something inside her.

Maggie's back arched off the bed, her eyes fluttering close and her thighs threatening to close.

"One night," Cal repeated. He shifted, both knees

now between hers, pushing them apart, and Maggie opened her eyes to find him staring down at her with reverence. "You're sure?" he asked, his voice gentle, contrasting with the edge of danger playing around his irises.

Maggie nodded and released her hold on the sheets to extend her pinky. "Pinky promise."

A smile split Cal's face as he twined his pinky with hers, then used it to tug her hand to his mouth and kiss every one of her fingers. Maggie's head fell back as he trailed his lips over the inside of her wrist, her blood rushing in her veins. He continued his descent down her arm, across her collarbone, but avoided her chest all together; instead, he skipped down to her stomach, and hooked his thumbs in the waistband of her shorts.

She didn't wait for him to ask. Maggie lifted her ass from the bed with more enthusiasm than she'd shown for anything in years. A soft curse fell from Cal's lips as he pulled them down her legs, leaving her only in basic black underwear. Maggie trembled as he ran a finger across the cotton—it was too dark for him to see how wet she was, but there was no way he couldn't feel it. He tugged it down, and she opened her eyes to see him toss it aside before focusing entirely on her.

Cal didn't move, just stared down at her, his mouth parted and eyes hungry. Maggie sat up enough to tug her t-shirt over her head and unclasp her bra. She began to pull it off, but stilled when Cal lightly grasped her wrist.

"Let me," he murmured, and she nodded, dropping

her hands. She expected him to take his time, to slowly pull it from her body and savor it.

She didn't expect him to lean in and wrench it away with his teeth. It was so much better.

He caught her nipple in his mouth, toying with the silver bar, and Maggie whimpered. They weren't kidding when they said nipple piercings made your nipples more sensitive, but she'd never had anyone pay such close attention to them. Cal's tongue was soft, but his teeth weren't, and he dragged them across her skin like he was trying to get her off with them alone.

Maggie writhed in the sheets, unintelligible words falling from her lips and pressure building from everywhere. Just as she thought she might scream from the heat covering her, Cal dragged his lips down her torso and stilled. He sat up a little and Maggie watched, tense, as he parted her thighs further with his hands.

"Oh, Maggie," he whispered as he took her in. But he drew his gaze up every inch of her body, meeting her eye, before dragging a finger through her center and pressing lightly on her clit.

Maggie cried out, her hips threatening to jump from the bed, but Cal held them down and smiled a wicked smile, drawing whisper-light circles over her clit. It was a barely there touch, but Maggie was sure she was going to explode. His other hand pressed lightly on her torso, twitching as if he wanted to grip her harder. And fuck, she wanted that.

The pressure of his finger increased, bringing her right to the edge before he pulled away. But the pressure didn't dissipate; it lingered in her blood, eddying through her and stealing her breath.

"You're so fucking beautiful, Maggie," Cal told her. "But your pussy... Christ, it's gorgeous."

Maggie didn't have time to process *that* before he pressed two fingers inside her, curled them, and the pressure boiled over. Her vision went black for a split second before every color of the rainbow burst behind her eyelids, and she gripped the silk sheets just for something, anything, to hold on to as her body shook with the force of her orgasm.

Cal's fingers massaged inside her, coaxing her through it. She could feel herself soaking him, but it was hard to care when it felt so fucking good. "That's my girl," he murmured, gripping her thigh with his free hand, and she opened her eyes to look at him.

His girl.

Holy. Fucking. Shit.

Her vision was hazy, but she looked down to see his fingers inside her and whimpered, clenching around him.

"Tell me what you want, love. Tell me what you like."

"I want... *fuck*," she cried, as he increased the pressure inside her.

He stilled. "Tell me."

Maggie tried to focus, to steady her breathing. What did she want? What did she like? Nathan had never really given her the chance to try anything. Sure, she'd seen movies and read books, and she had ideas, but Cal wouldn't want...

He stared down at her expectantly, his fingers still inside her.

"I want it to hurt a little."

Cal's eyes widened a fraction in surprise, but he didn't voice it. He gripped her thigh harder and slid a third finger inside her, curling them roughly. Maggie cried out, struggling to grip the bed.

"Is this what you want, baby?" he asked. *Baby*. She was going to be replaying that in her head for the rest of her damn life. "You want me to be rough with you?"

He pushed her thighs further apart roughly, baring her further to him, his eyes glued to his fingers as he fucked her with them, slowly. The contrast, she knew, was intentional—the slow drag of his fingers with his rough grip on her thigh.

"Yes," she cried out, twisting in the sheets, desperate for more; more friction, more strength, *more*.

"Yes what, love?"

Maggie blinked through the haze of the orgasm already building within her. Her brain was empty, save for thoughts of how good he felt inside her and how much she wanted to feel all of him inside her. "Um, yes... Daddy?"

Cal stilled as the word slipped from her lips before she could stop it, shocking her like a fucking defibrillator. Her mind cleared up fast enough for the mortification to hit, her cheeks turning scarlet as she realized what he'd meant.

She squeezed her eyes closed, her hand flying to her

forehead. "Oh my God. Oh shit. You were going for please. Oh my—"

"Say it again."

Maggie sucked in a breath and opened her eyes. Cal's expression was unreadable, between the low light and her still hazy vision. "What?"

She whimpered as Cal leaned in and gripped her chin with his free hand. "Say it again, love."

Up close, she could read the lust and desire etched in every line on his face. Somewhere along the way, she'd mussed up his usually flawless hair and beard. She bit her lip, and Cal brushed it with his thumb, holding her chin tighter.

"Yes…" she trailed off, her voice weak, and cleared her throat. Maggie swallowed and watched Cal's eyes trail down her throat before landing back on her face. "Yes, Daddy," she whispered and his eyes shuttered, the hand holding her chin twitching.

He opened his eyes and looked down at her, a wicked gleam in the darkest green. "Is that what you want, love?" He dragged his lips across her jaw. "To be daddy's baby girl?"

His teeth lightly grazed her skin as she tried to think through the fog. She'd never considered anything like that. Nathan wouldn't have even entertained her. *Did she want it?* It felt a little unhinged, and completely out of fucking character, like the kind of thing that *only* happened in books and movies. The thought of it should have disgusted her, should have been degrading, being referred to as his *anything*, but… Maggie surprised herself with how much she liked the idea of handing over that kind of control.

She couldn't have done it with just anyone, but she trusted Cal enough that the thought of it didn't scare her —it excited her. *Find the thing that excites you, love.* She was sure he hadn't meant she should find it lying beneath him, calling him *Daddy*, but fuck, she wanted to.

"Yeah, I… I think I want that," she said, her voice small, like she was scared of her own decision.

Cal sat back on his knees, shuffling backwards a little, and Maggie wanted to protest the loss of him. Shit, she'd taken it too far.

He swallowed and laid a hand on each of her spread thighs. Her skin pebbled beneath his touch. "Yeah, fuck it," he said under his breath. "I'm going to hell."

Maggie frowned. "What—oh, *fuck*." She had no time to think before he leaned in and ran his tongue over her pussy. His mouth closed around her clit, his teeth grazing the sensitive skin. Her thighs strained against Cal's grasp on her, but he held her open to him with firm hands.

Maggie's head fell to the side, her body trembling with the force of the electricity shooting through her. Cal ran the flat of his tongue over her clit and pulled back just enough to mutter something that sounded suspiciously like, "God, this fucking pussy."

But then his tongue was inside her, and Maggie stopped listening. Every thought left her head in a rush as the orgasm ricocheted through her. Cal continued fucking her with his tongue, releasing one of her thighs and using his free hand to press firmly on her clit.

Maggie's newly released thigh had a mind of its own, pressing against Cal's face, but he didn't seem to mind. Her cries mingled with the howling wind as she peaked and began crashing down, almost suffocating him. Cal pulled out of her, laughing wickedly against her pussy like he was drunk on her. His tongue was relentless, lapping her up, savoring her. And just as Maggie caught her breath, the dregs of the orgasm leaving her, he bit down on her clit and she bowed off the bed, her hand knotting in his hair and his name tumbling from her mouth like a sob.

Cal pulled back, his fingers replacing his mouth, rubbing much gentler circles on her clit to coax her through the orgasm. He hovered over her, pressing his lips to her cheek. She could feel his cock pressing into her stomach and she moaned, desperate. "You're doing so good, baby," he said, his voice hushed. "You're so fucking beautiful when you come."

His breath tickled her skin, and she leaned her head back, exposing her neck. Cal brushed a kiss on her neck and murmured, "I wish I could mark you here."

Maggie whimpered at the idea of being branded by him, and he looked up, capturing her lips with his and whispering over them, "Do you want that, baby? Do you want Daddy to mark you?" He pressed his thumb into the spot his lips had been moments before.

She had the brief thought that she would regret this come Monday morning, but that didn't stop her from nodding. "Please, Daddy," she moaned and Cal all but growled as he sank his teeth into her neck, before sucking on the spot.

Maggie's cries grew louder. She needed more of him. She tugged at his t-shirt until he sat back, his eyes glued to the mark he'd left behind. "Gorgeous," he whispered.

"Cal," she pleaded, fisting his t-shirt. "I need you inside me."

"I like it when you beg, love." His eyes danced as he tugged the t-shirt over his head. Maggie gasped, taking in his naked torso for the first time. She'd only been dreaming about this moment for six years.

She brushed a hand across his abs, firm yet soft in all the right places. He worked out four days a week religiously, but he was still a fifty-five-year-old man, and he had a little less muscle around his stomach to show for it. His chest was hairless, his shoulders somehow broader bare, and despite Maggie's desperation for more of him, she couldn't help but think that he must give amazing hugs. Six years, and that was a boundary they'd never crossed. She'd had his mouth on her pussy before she'd even hugged him.

But that was a problem for later. Maggie pulled her eyes back to Cal's face and found him watching, something like nerves on his face. Was he really worried about what she'd think of him? She couldn't have that.

"You are fucking devastating." She reached up to hold the side of his face. "I don't know how I survived six years without crossing every damn line."

Relief flashed in Cal's eyes, and he loosed a gravelly chuckle, leaning down to kiss her. He threaded their hands together, holding hers by her head. "Need I remind you that you were in a relationship for almost that entire time, Miss Burlington," he pointed out, and Maggie rolled her eyes.

"Maybe," she leaned in close to his ear to whisper, "But what if I told you that your name slipped out of my mouth by accident a few too many times when I was with him to be a coincidence, Mr. Michaelson?"

Cal's eyes flashed, his grip on her hands tightening. "Are you serious?"

"Deadly."

He moved abruptly, springing from the bed and walking across the lobby and into his office. "Where are you going?" Maggie grumbled, sitting up as she heard him opening his desk and rummaging around.

He walked back to the bed, tossing a box beside her. Maggie peered at the box and laughed.

"You keep a box of condoms in your desk?"

"Better safe than sorry." Cal leaned down to catch her lips roughly with his. "If I don't get inside you within the next sixty seconds, baby, I'm going to explode."

He pulled back, and Maggie nodded, swallowing. She grabbed a foil packet from the box and ripped it open with her teeth, her eyes glued to Cal as he pushed his sweatpants and underwear to the floor.

She let her gaze fall down his body and whimpered, her legs spreading of their own accord. Cal kneeled between them, and her hand shook as she rolled the condom over the thick length of him. He groaned, his forehead falling against hers. "Fuck, baby."

He dipped a hand between her legs and dragged his fingers over her clit. Maggie's body tensed, already so sensitive from her previous orgasms. Cal's fingers were lazy, building the pressure up slowly. She let herself fall back onto the bed, back arching.

"Maggie, love." She half opened her eyes and looked up at him through her lashes. "How rough do you want me to be?"

He increased the pressure of his fingers, and she fought to hold on to her focus. "Hmm?"

Cal pulled his fingers away, instead leaning in and dragging his cock across her pussy. She pushed her hips towards him, begging. "You said you wanted it to hurt a little." He stilled, the head of his cock barely pressing against her pussy. When she tried to wriggle closer, he held her down. "How rough do you want me to be, baby?" he repeated.

Maggie growled in frustration. "Like you've been waiting six years for this, and you can finally do whatever you want with me," she panted, and Cal's eyes gleamed. He released her thighs, and leaned over her, moving her hands above her head and holding them there with one of his, his grip firm. She was completely at his mercy.

"Promise me you'll tell me if it's too much."

"Pinky promise."

He caught her bottom lip in his teeth and captured her gasp with his tongue as he finally, *finally*, pushed into her.

Cal entered her in a hard stroke, then stilled, giving her body time to adjust to the sheer, perfect size of him. His body pressing into hers, a guttural groan falling from his lips. Maggie whimpered, her body stretching to accommodate him, the beautiful burn clearing her mind enough for it to really sink in that this was *Cal*. Her boss Cal, who she'd been lusting after for six excruciatingly long years, was inside her. And *holy shit,* she'd never felt anything like it.

"Six years is a long time to make up for in one night," he murmured against her mouth, his voice breathy.

Maggie thrusted her hips towards him and they both cursed. "I guess we'd better make the most of it, then." She wrapped her legs around him, pushing him deeper into her.

"I guess so," he agreed, holding down harder on her wrists and giving her a wild smile. She had no time to consider the ramifications of that smile before he pulled out of her and propelled her into the mattress with the force of his hips. Maggie cried out, flames licking at her body. Her nails bit into her palms as she tried, unsuccessfully, to pull her hands away so she could hold on to something. Cal held her down, his body playing with hers like a twisted dark symphony.

An orgasm fluttered at the tips of her toes, the top of her head, and Cal ravaged her mouth with his tongue, catching every moan and gasp and cry of his name. He pulled back, still pounding into her with deep thrusts, and groaned as his eyes fell on the spot they were joined. "You take Daddy's cock so well, baby." *Holy shit*. How was she going to make it through her workday going forward, knowing how fucking filthy that tongue could be? "Look how perfect we look together."

He didn't make it easy for her to sit up, holding her hands into the mattress, his hips unrelenting as they beat against her. She struggled against him, and he must have liked that because he growled and somehow found a deeper spot inside her. But when she managed to pull her body up enough to look between them, to watch Cal's cock disappearing inside her, glistening with her desire, the sight stunned her.

Her orgasm ripped through her, the strength of it catching both of them by surprise. Maggie fell back, shaking and clenching around Cal's cock as she sobbed his name and writhed around in the sheets. He faltered, his grip on her wrist slipping and his body falling forward. He caught himself with a hand by her face as he came with a gravelly moan, and her name had never sounded better.

Maggie didn't know what possessed her to lean into his arm and press a gentle kiss to his wrist as the aftershocks rippled through her, but Cal groaned and collapsed onto her, painting kisses on her shoulders, her neck, and finally her lips.

They broke apart panting, Maggie's thighs still shaking as she tried to unclasp them from around Cal. She finally managed, her legs falling to the bed like Jell-O, and Cal winced as he reluctantly pulled out of her. He was in no rush to move, though, stopping his weight from pressing into her with strong forearms as he continued placing lazy kisses all over her.

"So fucking gorgeous," he whispered against her ear before pressing a kiss behind it and rolling away to toss the condom. Maggie's eyes fluttered closed as she let herself enjoy the moment while she could.

Because the worries were already creeping into her mind. This was supposed to be a one-time thing; a get it out of their systems fuck so they could move on in a professional capacity. Maggie didn't know how Cal felt, but already she was craving more. Maggie tugged the covers up.

"Hey." She opened her eyes to find Cal watching her, his lips down-turned at whatever he saw on her face. He ran a finger over her cheeks, leaving a trail of warmth in its wake. "Don't go getting shy on me now, love. I've been waiting six years to cuddle you."

Her responding smile was automatic; the thump of her heart when Cal smiled back was problematic. But she snuggled into his waiting arms and breathed away every drop of tension as she fit perfectly against him.

CHAPTER NINE

Cal walked into work on Monday with more enthusiasm than he ever had before. It had been two days since he'd seen Maggie, two days since he'd kissed her goodbye in the parking garage, watched her drive off, then sat in his car for twenty minutes, absolutely fucking stunned.

They'd woken up in the middle of the night to the crack of thunder, and Maggie had sleepily straddled his hips and blown his mind again. When morning had dawned, and they'd woken well aware that their expiration date had arrived, they'd dragged it out as long as they could. Cal had been determined to make her come enough times to make up for six years of wanting her, and she'd walked down to the parking garage on shaky legs when they could no longer hide from the daylight.

She'd made it clear it was a one-night thing, so why

was he walking through the office, counting down the minutes until he saw her like a lovesick teenager?

He waved good morning to everyone as he passed them, heading straight for the elevator. He had to get his head back in the game. That had been the unspoken agreement of Friday night—one night to get them both back on track. But never in a million years of fantasies could he have dreamed up how incredible it would be.

I want it to hurt a little. Yes, Daddy. Please, Daddy.

She was a fucking dream come true, and he craved her more now that he'd touched her than he had before. Cal's tastes had always run a little on the depraved side, but he met those needs with relative ease at the club, with strangers he didn't have to face at work on Monday. He'd never, in his three decades in the legal world, mixed business and pleasure. But then, he'd never been with a woman half his age or had a woman call him *Daddy*, either.

Daddy. He knew he was fucked in the head for loving it so much. He was an actual father, for Christ's sake.

Cal shook himself as he stepped out of the elevator, his gaze snagging on the couch outside his office. He would be treating it with the reverence of holy ground going forward.

Maggie hadn't shown any indication that she had struggled to walk away on Saturday morning. Perhaps *getting it out of their systems* had been all she'd needed, but she was so hard to read. He just had to figure out if she wanted more. If more was even an option.

Cal sank into his desk chair and groaned. A mess,

that's what it was. A fucking mess. He turned his computer on and paused as a flashing red light on his answering machine caught his eye. Very few people had his direct line; even calls from his family went through Maggie (a necessity, after his dad kept calling during meetings to update him on rugby scores he'd never asked for.) The only exceptions were Liam and Eliza, who knew only to call in case of emergencies.

Cal pressed the button on the answering machine. "Hey, it's me." There was a pause. "Maggie, obviously." A smile spread over his face. As if he wouldn't recognize her voice. He heard a rumble as her car started. She was probably running late. "I'm so sorry. You know I never do this, but I have a family emergency and I'm not going to make it in today." Cal's smile melted away.

"I went through the inbox first thing this morning and there's nothing urgent. I've left Josie a list, so she'll make sure you get your coffee and—*you have a blinker for a reason*—get the Stintson meeting set up for you. I've got my phone on me, but I might not be glued to it, so if you need me, just text me—what am I saying—leave a voice-mail and I'll call you as soon as I can. I don't know how long I'll be, but if I'm back in the city early enough tonight, I'll—*for fuck's sake, this is the fast lane*—drop in at the office and do whatever needs done. I'm so sorry, Cal."

Maggie continued to apologize for sixty whole seconds, though some of that was road rage, sounding more and more harried as the call went on. She hung up with a stressed goodbye, and Cal stared at the machine for a while before sitting back in his chair.

Family emergency was vague. And unlike her. Hell, taking time off at all was unlike her. She'd already been grumbling about the office shutting for a week over Christmas and New Year, as she did every year. Was something really wrong, or did she just not want to see him after Friday night?

She'd sounded stressed, and she had been driving *somewhere*. But Maggie didn't half-ass shit; if she'd wanted to fake an emergency to explain her absence, she would make it convincing. She'd pinky promised to tell him if she was uncomfortable, but had that promise extended beyond Friday night?

He buried his face in hands, groaning. While he'd been thinking of how to talk to Maggie about wanting more, she'd either been dealing with a family emergency, or potentially trying to find another job. He didn't like either option.

Cal looked up as a knock sounded. "Come in." Christ, he sounded rough.

Josie poked her head in the door, smiling and holding up a coffee cup. "Morning, boss," she said, crossing the office and placing the cup down on his desk.

"Thanks," he said, gratefully, immediately pulling the cup towards himself. He could have easily managed making coffee himself, but Maggie would never let her absence be enough to disrupt his day. What the fuck was he going to do if she left?

"Everything okay?" Josie asked, frowning at him. "You look a little stressed."

"Yeah, everything's fine. Just didn't sleep well thanks to the wind," he lied, and Josie nodded in sympathy. Though the weather had calmed considerably, the city was still dealing with severe winds.

"And Maggie—is she okay? It's not like her to take time off."

Cal sipped the scalding coffee before answering. "She's fine. She just has a family thing today."

Relief shone on Josie's face. "Oh, good. Everyone was so worried about her when we got in this morning. She really keeps us all going."

"Yeah," Cal agreed softly, something like a lump in his throat. "She's pretty great."

"That she is. Well, just give me a shout if you need anything today." Josie waved and left him alone with Maggie's face burned in his mind.

He wondered if she knew how much she meant to the whole team, how valued she was. Cal tried to create the kind of work environment where his team didn't dread coming to work; ultimately, they were here for a paycheck and would rather be with their loved ones. He wasn't naive to that, but he had always promised himself he'd do everything he could to make his employees happy and show them how much he appreciated them. He knew every employee by name, and made himself accessible to anyone who needed him; everyone was paid above the market average, and he made sure they all took every day of their paid time off (including Maggie, even if she protested every step of the way.)

But day to day, it was Maggie who set the atmosphere in the office. It was Maggie who took the calls when people were sick, who arranged flowers when relatives died; she ordered the birthday cakes and planned the parties, organized the monthly happy hours but never attended, because she was, for all intents and purposes, his second in command and she wanted the team to feel comfortable enough to let their hair down.

She'd spent countless hours planning the company New Year's Eve party for the following month, waving away Cal's suggestion to hire an actual planner, and just as many researching and ordering personalized holiday/appreciation gifts for every single member of staff (and not just his staff—she hadn't wanted Ben's team to feel left out.)

Maggie was the heart of the office, and if he'd fucked things up with her, he'd never forgive himself. Cal blew out a breath, pulled his phone from his pocket, and slowly typed out a message.

Maggie.

Maggie rubbed her eyes and sighed as she leafed through the pile of paperwork on the desk. Where the hell had she gone wrong? Her system was flawless. She knew every penny coming in and going out of Burly's business account. Since she'd taken over the cafe's finances at sixteen, by sheer necessity since her parents refused to learn how to manage them themselves or hire an accountant, they'd never missed a rent payment, never been late paying their bills or supplier invoices. So why had she woken up to a panicked call from her dad that the power had been shut off?

She'd assumed, at first, that it was an aftereffect of the weekend's storm, but one call to the power company later and her heart had fallen into her stomach.

"We haven't received a payment since May, Miss Burlington. Your account is thirty-two hundred dollars in debt, plus a three hundred dollar late fee. We sent several warning letters to the business address."

Warning letters her parents hadn't opened or passed on to her. Upon further digging, the customer service representative had informed her that their auto-payment had been canceled after June's payment bounced. Which made no sense, because there was always plenty of money in the business account. Or so she'd thought.

Her parents refused to open an online banking account—they didn't trust technology. But Maggie worked during banking hours, so it was the one aspect of the business they were forced to handle. She gave them explicit instructions when payments had to be made at the bank, and every month, when she knew they'd received their monthly statement, she called for an up-to-date balance. All they had to do was open the statement and read it out.

But they'd lost April's statement, so they'd made a

figure up, not wanting to admit it. And they'd left it at the cafe in May, so they made it up again. Come June, they decided just to give her any old figure, assuming they'd at least be close to the account balance. And Maggie, seeing nothing awry in the figures, hadn't questioned them or asked to see the statements.

Now that they were on the desk in front of her, she could see the problem clear as day: her parents. They'd spent far more than they'd let on, dipping into the business account for personal expenses.

She fought the urge to pull her hair out. "You spent twenty-two thousand dollars of business cash to buy a personal vehicle? You can't do that." They'd lied and told her they were financing the used Subaru now sitting outside the cafe.

"We use it to pick up deliveries," her dad protested, and she scoffed, exasperated.

"You already have two cars. And the twenty-five hundred you spent on the kitchen at home?"

"Your mom tests recipes at home when she's not working."

Maggie cursed under her breath. "You drained the account, Dad. There's no money left. I had to pay almost four thousand dollars from my own savings just to get the power back on."

"Well, you can afford it. You've been spending a fortune decorating that house of yours."

"I'm not *decorating*," she said through gritted teeth. "I'm renovating. I need to get the entire house rewired next month, not to mention the landscaping costs I'm going to have come Spring. I don't have four thousand dollars to spare."

"We'll pay you back, darling," her mom piped up from the corner. She, at least, had the decency to look a little guilty.

"How the hell are we supposed to afford that?"

Maggie glared at her dad. "You can start by selling the Subaru. And canceling your Florida trip in a couple of months. The deposit is non-refundable, but you'll get the rest back and you can pay the business back for your kitchen stuff." Thank God she'd made them spring for insurance.

"We were so looking forward to that trip," her mom whined, her lip wobbling.

"The cafe won't make it through the winter if we can't recoup some of this cash." They wouldn't get it all back, she knew that. The Subaru's value would have dropped in the six months they'd owned the car, and most of the withdrawals her parents had made were for smaller things here and there. They all added up, though. She knew she was never seeing the money she'd spent to get the power back on again, but she'd settle for getting the cafe back in the black. "And you need to ask me before you use the business account to pay for anything in the future. Okay?"

Her dad sniffed. "Fine."

"I'll see what I —" Maggie cut off as her phone chimed with an incoming message and the contact name stopped her in her tracks.

Calahan Michaelson
(1) New Message

She swiped the message open and scanned it, her heart racing.

> I hope everything's okay with your family, love. Please let me know if you need anything and don't worry about today. Josie and I have it all under control.

Cal had... texted her? He never texted. She was sure the message was supposed to be reassuring, but she was more alarmed by the fact it existed than reassured.

"Everything okay, Mags?"

She looked up at her mom, then back down at her phone. "Yeah, just... I'll be back in a second. I need to check on something at work."

She fled the back room, darted through the cafe, and began pacing back and forth beside the cafe to keep warm before dialing.

"Hello?" They really had to work on his work phone greeting.

"You texted me," she said, a little out of breath, forgoing any pleasantries.

"Hey, love. How are things?"

"Cal. You texted me. You never text me. Is something wrong?"

"What?" he spluttered. "No, nothing's wrong. I knew

you'd be worried about what's going on here and wanted to put your mind at ease."

"By texting?"

"Maggie, love, I *do* know how to text. I just prefer to call. I like to hear your voice."

The breath rushed out of her, opaque in the freezing air. "Oh."

"Yeah." She could hear him smiling down the phone. "How are things going with your family?"

Maggie groaned and rubbed her face with her icy hands. "Getting there. It's a long story, but I'll tell you about it all tomorrow. Everyone is, at least, alive." She glanced back at the cafe. "For now anyway. Still considering killing my parents."

"Well, if you do, I have legal connections and we can definitely get you off." She stilled, suddenly too warm in the thick turtleneck she'd chosen because it was the only sweater she owned that covered the massive hickey on her neck. "I heard it the second I said it. Sorry," Cal added.

Maggie snorted and leaned back against the rough stone wall. "I think we're probably past the innuendo stage considering a couple of days ago I was calling you—"

"Maggie?"

She cursed under her breath as her dad walked out looking for her. "I'm on the phone, Dad." His timing was comical. Maggie heard Cal cursing softly through the phone, and could just picture his cheeks glowing pink.

"What's taking so long?" he grumbled.

She counted to three in her head. "You realize I had to call out today with zero notice to come and fix this, right?" she asked, and he just rolled his eyes.

"Come on, Mags, you're just an assistant. They probably don't even notice when you're not there."

Any hope she had that Cal *hadn't* heard her dad died instantly when she heard his sharp intake of breath.

"I'll be inside in a second. Okay?"

Her dad grumbled under his breath, frowning, as he walked back into the cafe and Maggie sighed.

"Maggie—"

"We're just not going to address that," she said firmly.

"But—"

"Nope. I'm okay, Cal. Really." Never mind the fact that she would have killed for a hug.

Cal sighed, and she knew this wasn't the last time she'd be hearing about it. "Okay, love. We'll talk tomorrow, yeah?"

"Yeah, of course."

"And if you need anything—anything at all—you'll call me?"

"Promise."

"Pinky promise?"

Her smile matched the one she could hear in her voice. "Pinky promise."

CHAPTER TEN

Cal leaned against the desk in the lobby and tried to look casual. Well, as casual as one could look in a five thousand dollar suit while waiting for his assistant, who he couldn't stop thinking about, to walk through the door.

"Morning, Cal."

"Morning."

"Hey, Cal!"

"Morning, Demi."

"Nice to have a bit of sunshine for a change, huh?"

"Sure is."

He smiled and small talked, and held himself together as nine a.m. drew closer, and he waited for Maggie to walk in. She was usually the first in the office, but she must be exhausted after whatever she'd been dealing with the day before. Maggie rarely spoke about her family, and if her dad's comment was anything to go by, he understood why.

You're just an assistant. They probably don't even notice when you're not there.

He couldn't have been more wrong. And Cal was determined to prove it; while he'd initially planned to work his ass off so Maggie could come back and know they could handle shit if she took time off, that comment had caused him to pause. He'd done just enough, and asked just enough of Josie, that Maggie wouldn't have extra work upon her return, but not so much that she'd think they hadn't missed her.

Cal glanced at the clock above the desk. Eight fifty-eight. Was she not coming? Maybe there was a voicemail waiting for him on his answering machine. He'd been waiting in the lobby since eight fifteen just in case. His heart sank at the thought of her spending another day dealing with whatever was going on.

He was half ready to cancel his afternoon appointments and drive up to Marysville himself to see what he could do to make her life easier, when the parking garage door opened and she stepped into the lobby, her dark hair a glossy curtain shielding him from view. Relief coursed through him—she was here. She was okay.

Cal looked at the clock, then back at Maggie. Eight fifty-nine. As if she would ever be just on time. Even running later than usual, she had to make it before nine.

Maggie looked up as she approached, a smile curving her perfect mouth. Her eyes lit up, a little hesitant, a little tired, but she seemed mostly happy to see him. "Hey."

"Hey, love. You're here," he all but breathed as she paused just short of him.

"I told you I'd be back today," she reminded him.

"Yeah." Cal nodded, swallowing as he took her in. Her dark hair was unstyled, just curling slightly at the ends. Her skin was December-pale, but her cheeks flushed pink—from the wind or him, he didn't know, but Cal wanted to brush his lips across them. Maggie always wore some variation of a skirt and a shirt or sweater to work, perfectly put together. As always, she had a bag over her shoulder and not one, but two, of those ridiculously large drink cups she loved. Today's turtleneck hugged every curve like a dream, and Cal's mouth was dry as his eyes looked her over. "Have you eaten?" he asked.

"No, not yet. I brought a smoothie." She nodded towards the extra cup tucked in her arm, but her eyes widened when she looked back at him and took in whatever she saw on his face. "That I can drink later?" she asked, and he nodded, relief flooding him. He needed to talk to her, to make sure she was okay. And that they were okay.

"Ethel's?" he asked, and she moaned, the noise going straight to his cock.

"You have no idea how good waffles sound right now." He knew how good they sounded from her lips, at least. "Can you give me like five minutes to run into the office and check on things?"

"Sure thing, love." Cal plucked the two cups from her arms and followed her into the office.

Maggie's absence hadn't gone unnoticed, nor did her arrival. Everyone looked up and offered her smiles, *good mornings* and well wishes as she walked through the room towards her desk. She returned every greeting, every smile, but Cal noticed it slipping as she turned away from the room and focused on her computer. Whatever had happened with her family must have exhausted her.

Her tongue poked through her teeth as he watched her scroll quickly through her inbox. She pulled her tablet from her purse and opened it to her to-do list—already a mile long—scribbling a couple of additions at the bottom.

"I'll just be a few minutes," she said before darting around the office at lightning speed, her to-do list clutched in her hand, checking on cases, handing out reminders and assignments, and noting any questions and follow-ups on her list.

He wasn't sure how she made it through the whole office in less than five minutes, and still looked like she was paying attention to each individual, but she did. Cal thought he'd seen efficiency before, but he'd never seen Maggie working the office like this. Did she do this every morning? It shouldn't have turned him on as much as it did, but these days it seemed like everything Maggie did was his kryptonite.

She finished up writing down a vacation request and made her way back to her desk. He couldn't take his eyes off her. She looked up, catching him staring, and blushed. "What?"

"Nothing," he said quickly, but she tilted her head like

she didn't believe him. Cal gestured to the office. "It's just that I don't really get to see you work like this, in the office, you know? Keeping everything and everyone under control."

Maggie lifted a shoulder in a shrug. "It's kind of my thing."

"You're unbelievably good at it," he said, appreciatively, and Maggie seemed to stand a little taller, smiling under the praise. *Yeah. He needed to do that more often.*

"Thanks." She opened her bag but hesitated, her tablet hovering over it. "Is this a working breakfast?" she asked, softly enough that no one at the surrounding desks would hear.

"If I say no, will you change your mind about coming?" She thought about it for a moment, uncertainty clear in the depths of her blue eyes and the way she bit her lower lip, but slowly shook her head. "In that case: no. It's not."

"Okay." She dropped the tablet gently in her desk drawer and locked it before taking a deep breath. "I'm ready."

"I'll do the peanut butter and jelly parfait, please," Cal said, setting his menu down and smiling at Ethel. The diner was almost empty. They'd missed the breakfast rush, and they had hours until the surrounding businesses descended on Ethel's come lunch time. Soft jazz played in the background, loud enough to offer some privacy, but quiet enough that they could talk.

"Not a problem. And for you, dear?"

Maggie stared at the specials board, chewing her lip in indecision before saying, "What are the banana crumble waffles like?"

"Oh, they're delicious," Ethel assured her. "They do have peanut butter, though. We could swap it for syrup?"

"Sounds good, thanks," Maggie replied, tucking her menu into the stand.

Cal looked between Maggie and Ethel. "You don't like peanut butter?"

"I've never tried it," she replied with a shrug. "I'm allergic."

"Oh." Cal frowned before turning back to Ethel. "Can I change to the strawberry mango parfait?"

"Sure."

"You don't have to," Maggie interjected, wide eyed. "My allergy's not that severe. It's only a problem if I get it in my mouth."

Cal's eyes fell to that perfect mouth before he looked up at Ethel, who was watching them both with an unexpectedly knowing expression. "The strawberry mango, please."

"You got it, hon." Ethel walked away, laughing, leaving Cal and Maggie staring at each other, tension stretched thin between them. Cal wondered if her mind was whirring with memories of Friday night too, if she also had to physically stop herself from reaching across the table for his hand.

He looked away first, clearing his throat. "Is everything okay with your family?"

Any tension on Maggie's face was replaced by outright aggravation. She blew a piece of stray hair out of her face and cupped her hands around her coffee. "They're still alive for now and I more or less fixed everything yesterday. Or at least started to." She took a sip of the coffee, and Cal couldn't help but smile at the flicker of pleasure on her face as she breathed it in. "I told you they own a cafe, right?"

"Yeah."

"Burly's," she continued. "They opened it when I was thirteen and just about stayed afloat at first. They'd both been working in cafes and restaurants since college—it's how they met—so they had a decent amount of kitchen and front of house experience, but knew nothing about running a business. And they refused to learn." She scowled.

"Burly's almost went under when I was sixteen. They'd put every penny into it so we would have lost everything. I looked online to see if there was anything we could do, and discovered I was pretty good at going over the financial stuff, the spreadsheets, managing everything. I just kind of took over. They worked in the cafe, but I ran it behind the scenes."

"When you were sixteen?" Cal asked, blinking in surprise. It didn't shock him to know Maggie had picked it all up so quickly, but she'd been in high school.

She shrugged. "Yeah. It was exhausting. I still had school, and it was a couple of years before we could afford to hire extra help, so my parents worked seven days a week and I helped after school and at weekends. But I also had to look after my siblings. I did homework with them, dinner, kept the house clean, that kind of stuff."

That kind of stuff. It sounded like she'd done everything.

"I thought, naively I guess, that I would get a break when I went to college. We'd turned things around by then and hired a few extra pairs of hands, but my parents were totally unwilling to learn any of the business side of things, so I had to run things remotely when I moved closer to UW for college. Then when you hired me for the internship, I told them I wouldn't have as much time, but they refused to listen. And when I officially got the job…" she trailed off, running a finger around her cup. "Well, you heard what my parents think of it."

Cal's blood still boiled at her dad's words. *Just an assistant.* Maggie wasn't *just* anything. And hearing about everything she'd done for them? The need to protect her from everyone who'd ever taken advantage of her roared in her chest like a monster.

"You're still running the business," he said, and she nodded. "You work forty hours a week, officially—I know you check your inbox from home," he added with a wry smile, when she started to protest. "Plus, how many hours on the business?"

"Ten on a good week, but probably closer to fifteen."

"Plus at least a few hours a week renovating, right?"

She nodded, and Cal did the math in his head. How the hell did she find time to sleep?

"Since I broke up with Nathan and started working on the house, I haven't been as focused on Burly's," she admitted, guilt shining in her eyes. "Which explains yesterday, I guess. I haven't been up to Marysville as often, and when I do go, I have so much to do that I haven't been properly going over the finances. I got a call yesterday because the power was out and, with a little digging, found out that the business account was basically empty and the power company cut us off because the payments bounced."

She took a deep breath, as if steeling herself. Cal still wasn't prepared for her to say, "My parents blew fifty thousand dollars of the business funds on personal expenses. In eight months."

His jaw dropped. "Fifty thousand? Christ."

"Tell me about it." Maggie shook her head, her dark hair glittering with flecks of gold from the overhead lights. "I had to pay out of my own savings to get the power back on—four thousand dollars." Cal winced. "But I made a plan to recoup some of the money they spent. I can probably get at least half back, so that should help keep things going until their busy season in the summer. I don't want to, but I think we'll have to let one or two of the part timers go."

She said it matter-of-factly, but Cal could see the responsibility of the decisions she was being forced to make weighing on her. How could her parents not see it? Or did they just not care?

He and Eliza had promised since day one that they would never put too much pressure on Liam. He'd seen it happen, time and time again, where parents tried to force their kids into becoming miniature versions of themselves. It was all too common in the legal world. They'd been a little worried when Liam had chosen a creative field, though they'd never put those worries on him, but he was far happier as an art curator than he ever would have been as a lawyer or optometrist.

It wasn't fair for Maggie to be juggling so much, and it sure as hell wasn't fair for her to be spending her savings bailing her parents out.

"You know, I—"

"No," she said, firmly, cutting him off, and he paused, frowning at her.

"You don't even know what I was going to say," he protested.

"I do, and thank you. But no." She shook her head, but smiled nonetheless. "I've got it under control, I promise. And besides, even if I was to put every penny of my savings into Burly's, it would just be a band-aid. Throwing money at them won't fix the wider issue. I just... I don't have it in me to deal with that right now." She drummed her nails anxiously on the scratched table.

Fuck it. Cal leaned forward and threaded his fingers through hers. "You're doing so well. They might not see it, but I do. And not just me, for the record. All anyone could talk about yesterday was how much they missed having you around. Everything you do, it doesn't go unnoticed."

Maggie stared at their hands, her cheeks stained crimson. "Thank you. And I promise," she added, quickly, her hold on his hand tightening a fraction. "I love my job, and I try really hard to make sure nothing interferes with it. Yesterday was… It's not acceptable. I'm so sorry, it won't happen a—"

"Maggie, baby. Breathe." She took a shaky breath, her eyes uncertain. "It's okay. I'm not here as your boss right now—though, if I *was*, I'd be telling you it's okay and you need to take more time off anyway. I just… I care about you, you know. And I'm worried."

"I'm fine," she said, instantly. Too quickly, like it was automatic to default to *fine*.

"You do a lot. And it kind of seems like you aren't really doing anything for you—the house doesn't count, when it does things like leave you without running water." He added the last part as she opened her mouth to protest.

She opened her mouth and closed it twice before finally saying. "Friday. That was for me."

Cal's heart thundered in his chest. "That was just one night," he pointed out, wondering just how obvious it was that he hoped it would become more than that.

"I suppose it was," she agreed, looking away. "But —"

"One strawberry mango parfait, one banana crumble waffles." They looked up at Ethel, their hands falling apart as she set their food on the table. "Can I get you two anything else? More coffee?"

Maggie shook her head. "I'm good. Thanks, Ethel."

"Me too," Cal agreed and Ethel told them to call her over if they wanted anything before walking away.

He watched Maggie pick up her silverware, waiting for her to finish her sentence. She hesitated, staring at her food but neither eating nor speaking. "But what, love?"

Maggie dragged her fork through the banana caramel topping on her waffles, biting her lip, before looking up at him. "Does it have to be? Just one night, I mean."

Cal remembered the feel of every inch of her, the sound of every breathy moan and every *please* and *Cal* and *yes, Daddy*. That night would be branded in his mind forever. Yet, it wasn't enough.

He held her gaze and shook his head. "No. It doesn't have to be just one night."

"Oh. Well, that's… good. That's good," Maggie said, a smile twitching at the corner of her lips. "I mean, we're both really busy, and our work is stressful. I have no interest in starting to date again anytime soon, and you don't really seem to date at all, so it might be nice to have a casual, regular stress relief kind of thing. We should probably figure out the logistics of whatever this is. A plan, you know. Set some ground rules and…" she trailed off. "Am I being too much?"

Cal shook his head, smiling as he picked up his spoon and pulled his parfait closer, trying to play it cool while his heart thudded in his chest and his brain screamed something that sounded a lot like *holy shit, she wants to do this again*. He cleared his throat. "You're never too much. I like watching you in planning mode."

"Oh," was all she replied, digging into her waffles, the tips of ears turning pink.

"Do you want to come over tonight? We can order dinner and figure everything out."

"That sounds nice," Maggie agreed, and Cal had to resist the urge to lean across the table and kiss the smile on her face. "Is tonight..." She searched around for the word and Cal laughed.

"I'd like you to stay over, if you're comfortable with that," he said and she hesitated for only a moment before nodding. Thank God he'd spent the weekend cleaning up his apartment. He liked things tidy at home, but he wasn't as organized as she was.

Maggie was going to be at his place tonight, for more than a flying visit to drop something off or pick something up. She was going to be in his bed tonight.

How the fuck was he supposed to make it through the next seven hours?

CHAPTER ELEVEN

Maggie

Maggie wasted no time in running up to the second floor and hiding in an empty meeting room upon their return to the office. She had a mountain of emails to go through, paperwork to check and file, clients to call, and appointments to set up, but there were more pressing matters.

She locked the door, as if one tiny metal mechanism would make the slightest difference to the already sound-proofed room and had the phone to her ear, ringing, before she'd even sat down.

"This better be important. I was sle—"

"I had sex with Cal," she interrupted her grumbling best friend.

Jazz took a sharp inhale. "What the fuck? It's not even eleven a.m. How did you squeeze sex with your boss in to your morning?"

Maggie leaned back in her chair, squinting under the fluorescents. The lighting in these rooms was far from ideal. Calmer lighting equaled happier clients. She should speak to Cal about upgrading them. "Hello? Earth to Maggie."

She groaned. "Not this morning." Though she wouldn't have complained if their breakfast plans had ended that way, they had to talk first. "We got stuck here overnight on Friday because of the storm."

"Oh shit. At the office?"

"Yeah."

"You were supposed to be meeting Rebekah on Friday, weren't you? Shit, I forgot. I'm the worst best friend," Jazz cried, but Maggie just laughed. She'd forgotten Rebekah existed the moment Cal's lips had touched hers.

"It's fine. Don't worry about it."

"I'm guessing you canceled with her in favor of fucking your sexy older boss?"

She wasn't wrong with the description, even if it made Maggie roll her eyes. "I canceled because of the storm, but yeah, that was the result."

"Damn," Jazz said dreamily.

"Tell me you're not picturing me and Cal having sex, Jazz."

"Can you blame me? He's fucking gorgeous, and it's my biggest regret that you and I never fell in love with each other." She sighed dramatically, and Maggie could perfectly picture her lounging across her bed, blankets askew, with her arm over her face, shielding her eyes from the sun because she refused to buy curtains. "I can't believe you didn't tell me about this."

"I'm telling you now," Maggie replied weakly, as Jazz scoffed.

"Please. You should have called me the second you got home—no, you should've called me on the drive home."

Maggie waved as one of the senior attorneys passed by, peering in curiously at her. When she'd passed, Maggie stood up and pulled down the blinds. "I wasn't sure I was going to tell anyone," she admitted.

"I'm not anyone," Jazz protested.

"True. I would always have told you." She sat back and kicked her shoes off before resting her legs on the table.

"So?" Jazz prompted.

"So what?"

"How was it? And are you going to do it again? Please tell me you're going to do it again. You really need some way of calming the fuck down on a regular basis and you won't do yoga with me anymore."

"You banned me from doing yoga with you," she reminded Jazz, though her best friend had had a good reason; Maggie hadn't been able to stop herself from checking her email mid-class. For three classes in a row.

For years, Jazz had tried to help her *find her zen.* In addition to yoga, she'd tried meditation, tarot, hiking, swimming, ice water baths, and even fire walking, all to no avail. She liked to work out, but it didn't help her switch off. The only thing that did was cleaning, which Jazz said didn't count because it was still work.

"Maggie, babe, answer the fucking question. How was it?" Jazz whined.

"It was… a little unhinged and completely life changing," she replied with a sigh. "It turns out I have a daddy kink. And apparently, so does he."

"Oh, that's hot."

"Mhmm. And yeah, I'm going to do it again."

"Damn. Is it just sex, or are you dating again?"

"I'm not dating again," Maggie said quickly. She had no interest in dating, in giving up a single shred of the independence she'd clawed back from Nathan. He had been so sure she couldn't manage on her own, but Maggie was proving every day that she could. Maybe one day she'd be ready to start dating again, but she was in no rush —and even if she was, dating her boss was a bad idea. People already didn't respect her job as an assistant; she hated to think what people would say if she started dating her boss. Even the people she worked with, as much as they respected the hard work she did, would probably take issue with her being with Cal. But it was a moot point. "It's just sex," she reiterated to Jazz. "Hopefully a lot of it, starting tonight. That's kind of why I'm calling. You're not working today, right?" She had more or less memorized Jazz's work schedule, but she sometimes swapped shifts.

"Nope. You want me to swing by your place and bring you an overnight bag?"

"That would be amazing, thank you," Maggie said.

That was twice in the past week she would have benefited from keeping an overnight bag in her car. "And some nice underwear—I'm wearing comfy underwear, and while I don't plan on it staying on for long…"

"Say no more," Jazz said, and Maggie heard a rustle as she, presumably, sat up. "Why don't I pick up food and come by at lunchtime? Subs in your car?"

It was a ritual they'd had in college when they'd worked together. Whenever their shifts crossed over and they could, they'd hide out in Maggie's car, eat, and debrief on the previous night's debauchery. That had been before Maggie had met Nathan and handed in her party hat. They'd kept the tradition up, though these days it was mostly Jazz's debauchery fueling them.

"Sounds good. You're a lifesaver."

"I'm going to want a step by step, *detailed* recap, for the record," Jazz pointed out. "And I'm going over to your place now so I can have a nice long soak in that glorious tub before I pack your bag."

Jazz loved Maggie's tub almost as much as she did. Maggie wondered if Cal was a bath kind of guy… She shook herself. She was already too distracted. "I picked up a new bubble bath this weekend—frosted juniper or something. It's on the top shelf of the linen closet."

"Fancy, and exactly where all of your bubble bath is, because your house is impeccably organized." Jazz said it in a jokey-scolding way, but she thrived on chaos where Maggie loved order. "Okay, I'll be there for one. Text me your sub order."

"On it," Maggie said, standing and rolling the blinds

back up. She began pushing the chairs back in neatly around the table and paused. "Oh—Jazz? You know those cozy over the knee socks I love?"

"Sure."

"Can you pack a pair?"

"Oh my *God*," Jazz all but squealed. "Are you telling me sexy Irish boss man has a *foot fetish*? Shut up."

"It's not feet. It's thighs," Maggie replied primly.

Jazz sighed. "That's so much hotter. Alright, I'm on it. See you at one."

She hung up before Maggie could say goodbye, presumably running off to terrorize Maggie's house. Jazz wasn't wrong, though. It *was* hotter.

Maggie had no idea how she was going to make it through the next six hours.

Four hours until he got to take Maggie home. Officially. Realistically, it would probably be closer to five, given that Maggie liked to be the last one in the office, and it would look pretty suspicious if he whisked her away at five p.m. on the dot.

He'd hardly seen her since they'd gotten back, which wasn't a surprise. Although he'd made sure she wouldn't be coming back to a mile long to-do list, she'd still managed to put one together. It might have been impressive if he hadn't seen the weight of it on her shoulders.

Cal stepped into the lobby and paused at the sight of a familiar redhead leaning against the wall. "Jasmine?"

Jasmine straightened, a smile lighting up her face. "Cal! It's good to see you again. You know, Maggie's suiters usually call me Jazz," she added conspiratorially and, though Cal barely knew her, it felt like a test to see whether he would protest and pretend there was nothing between him and Maggie.

"Oh, well. Jazz then," he said, and even if it was only to Jazz, warmth spread through him as he publicly declared there *was* something between them. Jazz leaned back, a pleased look on her face. "Are you here to see Maggie?"

"Mhmm. It seems we have a lot to catch up on," Jazz said, and Cal laughed.

"I guess you do." He was glad Maggie had someone she could run to when she needed to talk; it didn't sound like her family was much of a support system. *You're just an assistant.* He hadn't stopped being pissed off about it since he'd overheard her dad.

"Hey, what's your sign?"

"Cancer," he replied warily.

"June or July?"

"Does it matter?" Jazz simply raised an eyebrow. "July." She wrinkled her nose, her lips twisting. "Is that bad?"

She shrugged, lounging back against the wall. Jazz had the air of someone who was just comfortable wherever she went, like she walked into the room and the room adjusted to fit her, not the other way around.

"Cancers are a little possessive and protective for my taste. But that's exactly what Maggie needs in her life. Just remember, though." She poked him in the chest with a turquoise tipped finger. "You'll never be as possessive and protective of her as I am."

"What are you doing?"

They both turned around to see Maggie staring at Jazz like a deer in headlights.

Jazz gave her best friend an unabashed grin. "Just catching up with Cal here."

Maggie groaned, stopping beside them and looking up at Cal with apologetic eyes. "I'm so sorry for literally everything she said."

Cal laughed, unable to resist reaching out and rubbing a hand across her back. "I like her."

Jazz let loose a noise of triumph. "See!"

Maggie rolled her eyes, but she smiled, and Cal's stomach did somersaults. "She's alright, I suppose."

"Are you two going to lunch?" he asked, forcing himself to look away from Maggie's smile. It was quickly becoming a problem, how hard he found it to look away.

"If by going to lunch, you mean sitting in my car eating subs, then absolutely," Maggie said.

Jazz nodded. "Yep. It's a ritual. I'm getting a recap —"

Maggie forced her keys into Jazz's open hand, her smile gone. "I'll meet you in the car," she said through gritted teeth, and Jazz pouted but headed for the door that led to the parking garage.

"Lovely seeing you again, Cal."

"Likewise. Enjoy your lunch," he said, trying not to laugh as Maggie's cheeks burned.

"Oh my God," she groaned, when Jazz had left the lobby.

Cal's blood warmed as her bright eyes landed on his. "You're cute when you're flustered, love."

"I'm pretty much always flustered around you these days," she admitted with a sigh, though it had no weight behind it.

"That explains why I'm so distracted all the time."

Maggie rolled her eyes, and God, he couldn't wait to get her in his arms later. "You want me to run and grab you some lunch before I head off?"

"I'll be fine, don't worry. Go have fun with Jazz."

"Thanks. Oh, we got an update on the McKinnish case, by the way. I can come up just after two and go through it with you."

"Sounds good." Like he'd say no to spending more time with her, even if the McKinnish case gave him a headache. Maggie turned to leave, lifting a hand in good-bye, and he just wanted to take it and—"Maggie, wait."

Maggie stilled, turning back to face him with a confused expression. Cal looked around the lobby. Their receptionist was absent, and he didn't see anyone lingering when he peered through the door into the hallway.

"What are—"

He reached for Maggie's hand and tugged her in, brushing a gentle kiss on her lips, breathing in the surprised gasp that escaped them.

They broke apart, and she looked up at him, eyes wide and cheeks rosy. "What was that for?"

Cal brushed a finger down the side of her cheek, swallowing as her eyelashes fluttered. "I just couldn't wait. But I won't keep you from Jazz. Go enjoy your lunch, love."

She hesitated to drop his hand and turn away, as if weighing up how badly she wanted her lunch with Jazz, but she did, leaving with a soft smile and a wicked gleam in her eyes that felt like a promise.

CHAPTER TWELVE

Maggie

Cal's apartment building made the apartment Maggie had shared with Nathan look like a hovel. She wouldn't do her house the disservice of comparing it. Even the parking garage screamed money, impeccably clean with a marble wall by the elevator, and plants that surely couldn't be thriving underground. And that didn't even touch on the cars. Maggie hated parking here; she wasn't a bad driver, but parking had never been her strongest skill and she had nightmares over accidentally bumping one of the cars that cost more than the down payment on her house had.

So when Cal offered to drive, she didn't hesitate to say yes. Before Nathan, she'd always had a rule about taking her own car on dates and to hook-ups, in case she needed a quick getaway, but this was Cal. She knew she was safe.

He'd kept his hands to himself since that surprise kiss in the lobby. *I just couldn't wait.* She'd wanted to abandon her lunch plans with Jazz, pull him up to his office and forget all about talking it out. But she needed a plan; she needed ground rules and boundaries and some idea of how she was going to make it out of this alive, and with her job, before he got her out of her clothes again.

But when he offered her a hand to help her out of his car, she threaded her fingers through his. And when both of her feet were steady on the smooth concrete, neither one of them made any move to let go. Maggie sidled closer to him in the elevator, and Cal hesitated for all of a second before wrapping both arms around her and tugging her until her back was flush against his chest.

Maggie glanced up in the mirror and found him watching her with dark eyes and a hint of a smile. She swallowed.

"Sushi for dinner?" he asked, resting his chin on top of her head.

"Mmm, that sounds good," she murmured, unable to take her eyes off them. She couldn't deny they looked good together; the contrast of Cal's gray hair with her dark brown, his gray suit and her cream sweater, green eyes and blue, earth and water.

The elevator doors opened into Cal's penthouse, and he pulled her into the apartment.

It was exactly how she remembered, swathed in the glow of Seattle through the floor to ceiling windows that covered one wall of the open plan living room and kitchen. A plush suede couch sat in front of a fancy electric fireplace with one of those picture frame TVs above it. It wasn't homey—it wasn't Cal—but it was lux. He must have hired someone to design the place. Most of it wouldn't have looked out of place in the apartment of any millionaire bachelor in the Pacific Northwest, but Maggie could see him in the small things; the face down fantasy book on the coffee table, the open bag of his favorite coffee beans on the kitchen counter.

The place screamed money, and she didn't want to think about how much the penthouse, let alone the interiors, had set him back. But Cal *was* a millionaire, no matter how easy it was to forget.

He led her to his bedroom, and Maggie smiled as she quickly scanned the room. Cal was written all over his room. Though the furniture and finishings were just as lux as those in the main room, a bookshelf sat against one wall full of creased spines and worn out hardbacks. The dresser by the window was littered with discarded cufflinks, pens, and papers. A wrinkled suit had been tossed over the back of the chair in the corner, a pair of navy slippers sitting beside it, and the whole room smelled of citrus and mint and Cal.

"I'm guessing you have comfy clothes in here," he said, setting her bag gently on the bed.

Maggie unzipped the bag and pulled out the matching cozy shorts and sweater set that Jazz had packed for her. "I can't believe you thought you didn't know me that well a couple of weeks ago."

"I'm pretty sure we have clients who know how much

you love cozy shit. You keep a blanket in your desk drawer," he said, eyes crinkling. "I'll order dinner while you get changed. Do you have any sushi preferences or should I just order a mix?"

"I like everything except celery."

Cal stared at her in horror. "Where are you getting sushi with celery in it?"

Maggie laughed, holding the fluffy set to her chest. "Jazz likes to make sushi, and she's really into vegetables. I think I forget sometimes that a whole head of broccoli with lemon juice and a slice of American cheese isn't actually a meal, it's just Jazz."

"Somehow, I'm still surprised every time I learn something new about Jazz," Cal replied, shaking his head with a smile. "I'll just be in the living room. Shout if you need anything."

She made quick work of stripping out of her work clothes and plain underwear—and *holy shit*. She was naked in Cal's bedroom. His bed, while not as big as hers, was impressive. The crisp white sheets were wrinkle free, and she almost groaned as she ran a finger across the buttery soft fabric. She couldn't wait to climb inside.

Because somehow, her life had taken a wild turn, and she was sleeping at Cal's place tonight. *Her boss*, Cal. She shook her head at the bed, nerves settling in her belly.

Jazz had done her well, packing a delicate pink lace lingerie set that she'd bought post-Nathan, when she'd been under the illusion that she was going to break out of her shell. The fuzzy lounge shorts were the shortest she owned, and, even with the over the knee socks she loved so much, most of her thighs were still exposed.

She pulled her hair up into a messy, but intentional, ponytail and spun in front of the floor to ceiling mirror that faced his bed. It was effortlessly casual, and she knew it was going to drive him wild. She freshened up quickly in the en suite and walked back into the living room.

Cal had his back to her, standing in front of the tall windows and staring out at the Seattle skyline, his phone pressed to his ear. Of course he called the restaurant instead of ordering online. Maggie found it more charming than she should have. She let herself take it all in: Cal, where she was, what she was doing here.

Cal looked like he'd stepped straight off the pages of a romance novel and, though she knew it wasn't a fairy tale romance they wanted from each other, the situation still didn't feel entirely real.

She dropped her own phone on the coffee table as he hung up. "It should be about an hour. Do you want—" Cal stopped in his tracks as he spun around, his mouth falling open and his eyes immediately zeroing in on her thighs. Any nerves she had melted away at the look of awe on his face, boldness taking their place.

She crossed the room, taking the spot beside him and staring out at the glowing city. "God, this view is even better at night," she murmured, hiding her smile at his reaction. She looked up at him. "Do I want what?"

Cal dragged his eyes back up to her face with what seemed like great difficulty and cleared his throat. "Wine.

We have saké coming, but I can open a bottle if you want a glass now." His eyes were flooded with black, just a ring of emerald green around the edges.

"I don't mind waiting."

Cal took a deep breath in and looked away, his chest rising and falling faster than it had been before she'd changed. "Alright. I'll, uh, go change. There's a blanket on the back of the couch—I know how much you love blankets—"

"Cal?" she cut him off and he turned back to her, eyes somehow darker.

"Yeah?"

"I know the whole reason I'm here is because we need to talk and figure everything out, and I also know the only reason we're doing that at all is because I like everything to be ordered and organized, but the suit? It *really* does it for me. And I've been watching you wear these suits for six years." She took a deep breath, before slowly sinking to her knees before him. The hardwood was slippery beneath her socks, but they were worth it for the way Cal's eyes kept flicking to them. "So I was wondering if I might cross this off my list before you get changed."

"*Fuck.*"

Maggie dragged her tongue along his cock before

opening her mouth and taking him inside. Cal's knees buckled, every nerve in his body lighting up like fireworks. He wrapped Maggie's ponytail around his fist and fought the urge to push his cock further down her throat. Her mouth was fucking heaven, soft and warm, and she looked up at him with eyes like glittering sapphires. She fisted the base of his cock, taking as much as she could between her lips and humming before pulling away and releasing him with a pop, saliva pooling at the corner of her mouth. She was the picture of sin. Cal brushed a thumb across her lower lip, his vision hazy.

"Cal."

"Yeah?"

"Stop holding back and fuck my mouth until I cry." His thumb twitched on her lip, fire flooding his veins. "Please, Daddy."

The words had barely left her mouth when he snapped, forcing himself between her lips. He almost came immediately as Maggie's eyes lit up like starlight, excitement shining on every inch of her face. Cal hesitated for all of a second as he neared the back of her throat and she growled around him, forcing her own head down until she gagged, gripping the back of his legs. He threw a hand out, slamming it against the glass window while the other clung to her hair, furiously fucking her mouth and watching tears pool at the corners of her eyes.

Maggie moaned and whimpered and gagged around his cock, the sounds spiraling around him, mixing with his own gasping breaths and cries of her name. He was teetering on a cliff's edge, just a step away from flying. A single mascara-streaked tear ran down Maggie's cheek, and she looked up at him through fluttering lashes with an expression of sheer bliss.

"Fuck, baby, I'm—"

Maggie cut him off as she relaxed her throat and took him somehow deeper. Cal didn't so much step off the cliff as stumble, knees buckling as he came, Maggie humming and drinking him down happily.

"God, baby, you did so good. That's my girl," he groaned as she pulled away, swirling her tongue around his cock as if she didn't want to miss a drop. She sat back on her knees with a happy sigh, her cheeks streaked with black, a pleased smile on her lips.

Cal pulled her to her feet, grasping her face and claiming her mouth with his. He could taste himself on her tongue and groaned into her mouth before pulling away, panting.

"Thank you," she murmured against his lips and he leaned back enough to stare down at her, blinking.

"What—You're thanking *me*?"

Maggie shrugged, licking her lips clean. "I've wanted to do that for a really long time."

"I'm… actually a little speechless," Cal said, running a finger down the tear tracks on her face. As it touched her lips, she opened them and sucked it into her mouth, moaning. Cal didn't think he'd ever gotten hard so quickly again since he was a teenager. "Christ, Maggie. Where the hell has this side of you been all my life?" He paused, wincing. "Okay, maybe not *all my life* considering—"

"I wasn't alive for half of it?" Maggie asked, fighting a laugh.

"I can't be held accountable for what comes out of my mouth right now," Cal said, holding his hands up. He had to physically force himself to step away from her and pull his boxers up but, if he didn't, they weren't going to make it to the talking part of the evening. "No one could after experiencing that." His eyes caught on her outfit again, if you could even call it an outfit. "Those fucking socks," he murmured, his cock already straining against his boxers.

"The faster you get changed, the faster we can get to talking, and the faster I get to wrap them around you," Maggie pointed out. Cal was halfway out of the room before she'd finished speaking.

CHAPTER THIRTEEN

H e wasn't going to fucking survive this. Everything she did made him want to touch her. Watching her eat the sushi was a lesson in self control he didn't know he had, and the second she put her chopsticks down, he couldn't help but reach for her hand. His racing heart settled as she happily twined her fingers with his, leaning back into the plush couch and resting her feet in his lap.

She'd forgone the blanket, and while he didn't think she'd done it purposefully to torture him, the effect was the same. If they were going to talk coherently, he had to get it together. He pulled the blanket from the back of the couch and laid it over her legs.

Maggie snuggled into it almost instinctively, but raised a brow in question.

"We're supposed to talk and I can't… I…" He took a deep breath. He couldn't remember the last time he'd been so flustered. He was too fucking old for that. "Thighs," he said, finally.

Maggie laughed, but pulled the blanket further up her body. "If I'd known it was this easy to rile you up, I might have dressed a little differently over the summer."

"You didn't break up with Nathan until September," he pointed out and she wrinkled her nose.

"Would it make a terrible person to say I might have done it earlier if I'd known *this* was an option?"

It wouldn't make her a terrible person, but it did make his pulse race and his breath catch in his chest. That wasn't something he could unpack, though. "Not even a little," he said instead. "I have to ask, though. How the fuck was Nathan not all over you when you're like—" He waved a hand towards her, "—this."

"I wasn't really like this with him," she said, toying with the blanket fringe. "I mean, I was when we were in college, I guess. We were more fun in college—everyone was more fun in college," she added with a wry smile.

"Tell me about it." He'd gotten Eliza pregnant on the last day of their junior year. They'd been young and stupid and practically strangers, but they'd certainly been fun.

"I think, once Nathan realized he *had* me, once we graduated and got our grown up jobs, he just lost interest. He isn't a bad guy. He wasn't violent or abusive, he didn't cheat. But he also isn't very nice, and I don't think he ever respected me. And I think I started to believe the shit he said about me over the years." Shadows clouded her face, and Cal had the sudden urge to get in his car, find Maggie's ex and… That was probably the saké talking.

"Anyway, over time, I learned that if I just got on with the shit I didn't like, he would leave me alone for the stuff I *did* enjoy. And sex was like that, something I just had to force myself to do, like spending time with his God awful parents or making a stupid pot roast every Sunday, even though I don't like even like pot roast. A chore I had to get out of the way so I could get to the fun stuff—and, trust me, I learned to take excellent care of myself over the years."

Anger coiled in Cal's gut for the man who had dulled Maggie's spark so much that she'd forced herself to have sex with him just so she could be left alone. She said it so matter-of-factly, like it was completely normal to her. He'd made her believe she owed him something before she could find her own joy, made her believe she was anything less than a fucking miracle.

He tried to remember what she'd been like when she'd first walked into his office, twenty-one and determined as hell. His assistant at the time, Zhara, was a law school grad who had failed the bar exam twice, and decided she didn't really want to practice anyway. She'd been his assistant for a decade, and Cal knew long before she told him she wouldn't be coming back after her maternity leave. It had been Eliza's idea to hire an intern to work under Zhara, in the hopes that he'd have a decently trained assistant at the end. He'd planned to hire another law school grad or hopeful, someone who had some kind of legal experience. He even had his candidate all but picked out when Maggie arrived for the final interview.

She had zero legal experience, had never worked as a PA, and Cal hadn't been sure why the firm he used to recruit had bothered to put her through the next round. Until Maggie had walked into his office, sat down and answered every question with more passion than he'd expected, given her resume. She surprised and impressed the hell out of him, but that didn't leave him any less confused.

"Are you planning to go to law school after UW?" he'd asked, running a finger over her resume. Her class choices didn't suggest law school, but they didn't rule it out either.

"No," she replied, a twitch of her fingers on her skirt the only sign of nerves. *"Would that be a problem?"*

"Not a problem, just surprising," Cal answered, setting the resume down. *"If you have no interest in law, why do you want to work at a law firm?"*

Maggie looked around the room, her eyes snagging on the piles of paperwork, half open filing cabinet, and the broken pen on his desk. She cleared her throat. *"I like results. I like starting a task and following processes, going through every step thoroughly, and seeing it all work out perfectly. A lot of industries are process and result focused, sure, but law follows really specific processes with high stakes. I'll be honest, I've had enough of college so you're not going to catch me doing another three years, and, frankly, I cry during arguments so I wouldn't be a good lawyer anyway. But I'm helpful, and organized, and great at keeping things under control. And you're the best in the city. You get results. So, I'd like to be a part of that, however small."*

Her eyes lit up with excitement as she spoke, and Cal recognized the hunger. His path to law had been born of a love of results; of the buzz he got after spending hours preparing for his first debate in debate class, and the winning result. It had never been the external validation —the congratulatory claps on the back upon winning a case had never done much for him—but the knowledge that he'd put in the work and reached the desired outcome was better than whiskey.

"Thank you for coming in today, Maggie," he said, standing and shaking her hand as she mirrored him.

"No, thank you."

Maggie turned to leave, and Cal's eyes fell to the resume on his desk. She didn't make sense for the firm, but... "Maggie?"

She turned back to him, a wrinkle between her brows. "Yes?"

"Our onboarding process is usually pretty quick, but as long as the background check goes through with no issues, can you start on the thirteenth?"

She blinked, eyes wide. "Yes, absolutely."

"Excellent. I'll get Zhara to email you with your contract and the background check details. Welcome to the team, Maggie."

Cal watched her try and fail to fight the smile threatening her face. "Thank you, Mr. Michaelson. Just... thank you."

He hadn't seen that excitement in a single other candidate—entitlement and expectation, but never excitement. "Call me Cal."

"Thank you, Cal," she said softly, the smile finally splitting her face as she turned away and left his office.

Prior to Friday night, Cal couldn't remember the last time he'd seen that hunger in her eyes. Somewhere along the way, Nathan had stolen it and Cal hadn't even noticed. Now he knew what her life looked like thanks to her parents using her to run their business, he understood her love of results. Pieces were clicking into place on the Maggie-shaped puzzle before him. From working far more than she could, to teaching herself to renovate an entire house alone, she still had that fire to prove she could get results.

"Don't look at me like that," Maggie said, frowning and shifting uncomfortably.

"Like what?"

"Like you feel sorry for me. I'm not—"

"Love, this isn't my *feeling sorry* expression. This is my *thinking worryingly violent thoughts about your ex* expression."

"Oh." Her eyes widened. Fuck, he should've kept his mouth shut. Maggie tilted her head, considering. "Why is that kind of hot? I was a fucking idiot for sticking around for so many years."

She absentmindedly dragged her foot over his thigh and he caught it in his hand. "He was a fucking idiot for letting you go."

"Both things can be true," Maggie said with a laugh.

"Anyway, I thought we were supposed to talk about *us* tonight, not Nathan."

Cal recognized that she'd shared enough for the day, and he couldn't blame her. She'd been more vulnerable with him in the past twenty-four hours than she had in six years, and that made his stomach do somersaults even more than hearing her emphasize *us* did.

He sat back, drumming his fingers gently on her ankle. "I know that, even if it's not intentional, there's a pretty big power imbalance here. And I never want you to feel pressured, or obligated, or stuck because I'm your boss."

"Honestly, I'm not worried about that. I'm not saying the power imbalance doesn't exist—it does—but I trust you. You would never lean on it. And my pinky promise still stands, to let you know if I'm uncomfortable," Maggie said, wrapping a tassel around said pinky.

"Does it change anything if I broke mine with the spreadsheets yesterday?" he asked and snorted when she winced.

Maggie winced. "We're having a really nice night, so I'm going to let that slide for now, and I'll deal with it tomorrow," she said with a sigh. "I guess we should set some ground rules."

"Shoot," he replied, knowing she likely already had a mental list.

"I'm not naive enough to think that we're always going to be able to keep our hands to ourselves at work or in public, but we should still be… discreet. It's probably not a good look if people find out we're sleeping together." She wrinkled her nose.

"That makes sense," he agreed, nodding and swigging from his glass.

"And like I said earlier, I'm not interested in dating right now and I know you don't really date, but if either of us meets someone or wants to call this off for whatever reason, we just need to be honest and not make things weird."

If either of us meets someone. Cal's stomach twisted at her words, but he wasn't going to start unpacking that. It wouldn't lead anywhere good. He knew she was right; it wasn't like they even could date. He was twice her age and her boss. She wasn't interested in dating anyway. And neither was he. He just had to try a little harder to remember that. When Maggie *was* ready to start dating again, she would be looking for someone she could have a long life with, and Cal would support her in that.

But he couldn't lie to himself; his feelings were already a tangled, messy knot, and he had to get them in check. Or at the very least, keep them to himself. They could be friends. They could spend time together and enjoy this for what it was while they could.

"Do you have any ground rules?"

Cal hesitated before saying, "We should hang out." At Maggie's confused expression, he added, "I mean, if we only spend time together when we're sleeping together, it might feel a little…"

"Cheap," she finished for him with a nod. "I agree. And I like hanging out with you, so that sounds nice."

His breath caught in his chest. "Yeah?"

She nodded, the blanket slipping down her torso with the movement, exposing her midriff. "I was worried it might feel a little awkward, me being here, but it doesn't at all." Maggie looked at home, stretched out on his couch. "And I liked having you at the house. Well, other than trying not to be all over you anyway."

"You can do that next time I'm over," he pointed out, smiling at the thought.

She sat forward, her eyes lighting up. "You can try out the bath."

Cal laughed, leaning closer to Maggie and twirling a loose strand of her hair around his finger. "That bath has been torturing me since I called you."

"You want to know a secret?" He nodded, the blood rushing to his cock as her eyes darkened and her voice took on a husky edge. "After we hung up, I closed my eyes and imagined it was you touching me instead of myself."

His body ached with the need to pull her in closer. "After we hung up, I got in the shower and did the same. But…" Cal caught her chin between his fingers, tilting her face up towards his. "The reality is so much fucking better."

He gave her no time to agree, but he saw it all over her face as he leaned in and pressed his lips to hers. Her tongue met his greedily, and Maggie pushed up onto her knees until she could push him back and straddle him. She sat back, pressing her ass into him and groaning into his mouth, rolling her hips as if she needed the friction so much she just had to take it.

Cal couldn't still his hands. They roamed over her body, desperate to feel every inch of her. Her skin was silky smooth and pebbling beneath his touch. He buried his face in the crook of her neck, breathing her in, honey and vanilla and something so unmistakably *Maggie* that he snapped. He needed more.

He sat up, gripping Maggie's ass firmly, and stood with her. She squealed, wrapping her legs tightly around his waist and gripping his shoulders for dear life.

"Some warning would have been—"

Cal cut her off with a kiss, carrying her through the penthouse and dropping her gently on his bed. Her dark hair fanned around her, over the cotton sheets like curling smoke. His mouth went dry as she slowly peeled her fuzzy cropped sweater over her head and rolled the matching shorts down. She kicked them off, leaving her in only those fucking socks and two scraps of pink lace that could barely be called underwear. Her fingers brushed the edge of the socks and he stilled them.

"Leave them on."

He kneeled down, pressing kisses up her thighs and watching her fall back with a content sigh.

"Maggie?"

"Hmm?"

"Are you particularly attached to this underwear?" he asked, slipping a thumb in the band.

She peered down at him, frowning in confusion. "Not really. Wh—oh *fuck*."

He didn't let her finish before tearing through them easily with his teeth and diving tongue first into her pussy with a groan. Four days he'd gone without tasting her, and it was four days too fucking many.

He slipped his tongue out of her and pressed it flat against her clit, curling his fingers inside her pussy. Maggie's thighs trembled around his head, her hand sinking into his hair and holding him to her. He bit lightly down on her clit as he fucked her roughly with his fingers and she screamed his name, twisting and fisting the covers, flooding his tongue.

Cal stood on wobbly legs, drunk on the taste of her. He leaned down to litter her face with kisses. "You taste so fucking good, baby girl," he whispered against her lips and she whimpered into his mouth, shaking from the comedown.

Maggie tugged at his t-shirt and he pulled it over his head, stepping out of his pants and kicking them in the direction of Maggie's shorts. She eyed him hungrily, her chest rising and falling. He turned around to rummage in his nightstand, dropping a handful of condoms on top and ripping one open before turning back to her just in time to watch her rolling onto her stomach and looking back at him with a heady expression.

She sat up on her knees and unclipped her bra as he kneeled behind her, rolling the condom over his cock. He wrapped his arms around her, one hand tugging at the silver bar through her nipple, the other cupping her pussy, as he watched them in the floor-to-ceiling mirror that faced his bed. Maggie's head fell back against his chest, a sigh falling from her lips.

"Is this how you want it, love?" he asked softly against her ear. "You want me to hold you down and fuck you hard from behind?"

"Yes," she hissed as he dragged a finger across her clit. She took a gasping breath. "I want to watch you ruin me, Daddy."

The words were his undoing, his cock begging for her. "Then you better open your eyes, baby girl," he said before wrapping her hair around his fist and entering her as he pushed her down on the bed.

Maggie cried out, her eyes snapping open and focusing, hazy, on their reflection in the mirror. Her pussy was beautifully tight around his cock, squeezing him with every vicious thrust. Maggie threw her head back, exposing her throat, and Cal couldn't resist bracketing it with his hand. She gasped, her eyes landing on his in the mirror, wide and bright.

"Is this okay, baby?" he asked, panting, squeezing her throat lightly, and Maggie moaned.

"Yes. *God*, yes. *More*."

Cal growled and pressed more of his weight into her, pounding mercilessly into her, gripping her throat, watching and feeling her come undone beneath him. Maggie's arms gave way as she snapped, and she took him with her, crashing to the bed and over the edge as fireworks exploded between them. He let go of her throat and buried his face in her back, hips unrelenting, gasping her name against her skin. Maggie whimpered into the bed, writhing and shivering and, as soon as he had the strength, Cal sat up and tugged her gently onto his lap, cradling her to his chest.

"Deep breaths, baby. Are you okay?"

She murmured unintelligible things but nodded, a sleepy smile on her lips as she leaned into him and took deep breaths.

"Good girl," he said, rubbing her back. She opened one eye and looked up at him.

"You can't call me that right now. I'm too tired to come again," she whined and, fucking hell, his cock took notice. Of course Maggie liked praise; she practically glowed when someone complimented one of her spreadsheets. Despite her protests, she moaned as she felt him harden beneath her, wiggling around on his lap.

"You're going to be the death of me, love," he groaned, shifting her from his lap and standing up to toss the condom. Her gaze burned him every step of the way into the en suite and back. He lay down beside her, and she licked her lips as her eyes zeroed in on his cock. "What happened to being too tired?" he asked, shaking his head and smiling.

Maggie sat up and straddled his hips, leaning across him and grabbing a condom from the nightstand. The foil crinkled in her hands as she ripped it open and looked down at him. "I think I have one more in me."

"Good girl."

CHAPTER FOURTEEN

Maggie

S he was *supposed* to be emailing a picky client who insisted on working with one specific attorney (who was on paternity leave for at least the next two weeks). Instead, she glanced at her computer for a second and then at the pile of perfectly printed and stacked paperwork on her desk. Cal didn't technically *need* it until tomorrow, but she supposed it wouldn't be unreasonable to take it up early. She did like to be prepared, and maybe... maybe she just wanted to see him.

Maggie sighed and opened the email and typed a firm, but friendly, reply. She sent it and sprang from her desk, gathering the paperback and rushing to the elevator to avoid being stopped by anyone along the way. The elevator spat her out into the lobby outside Cal's office, and she frowned as she spied him through the open door.

He was hunched over the desk, his tie askew and

brow furrowed, his passport clutched in hand. Cal looked up as she approached, only some of the tension falling from his face. She stopped and set the paperwork on the edge of his desk. "What's wrong?"

Cal rubbed his face and pinched his brow. "Hungry."

Maggie fought a smile at his rough tone. "*Growly*," she corrected. "You want me to go grab you something?"

Cal hummed, considering for a second before standing up. He reached for her, taking her hand and dragging her around the desk. "Sit," he said, nodding to the chair.

Maggie dropped into the supple leather and looked up at him, confused. "What are you—*oh*."

Cal sank to his knees before her. *Hungry*, indeed.

He took his time with her, bringing her to the edge over and over before finally letting her fly. By the time he was done with her, she was a shaking mess and he pulled back, his face glistening with her. Cal licked his lips and plucked her from the chair, ignoring her squeak of protest, carrying her to the couch in the lobby and holding her on his lap.

"If someone comes up—"

"We'll hear the elevator in plenty of time, love," he murmured against her forehead, pressing a kiss to her skin.

He seemed happier, at least, whatever bad mood he'd been in disappearing as she'd come all over his face. She pulled away enough to look him over. "You want to tell me what's really going on?"

Cal frowned, hesitating before finally saying, "What are you doing next weekend?"

She didn't have to think; her weekends remained free until Jazz called her, usually on Saturday morning, with a hare-brained scheme. "I'll probably just be working on the house. I need to pick out paint colors for the dining room, but I'm really torn between staying neutral or going dark and moody. I was thinking maybe jewel..." she trailed off at his impatient expression, trying not to smirk. "Why?"

"Do you have a passport? Or a criminal record?"

She blinked at him. *Not* having a criminal record was kind of a requirement to work at a law firm. "I have one of those things," she replied with a raised brow.

"Assuming it's a passport—"

"It is."

"—you know I'm going home for my parents' sixtieth anniversary party, right?" he asked, uncertainty creeping into his eyes.

"Yeah." He'd planned the trip himself, but she had his calendar memorized.

Cal swallowed, tapping her waist, almost nervously. "Come home with me."

Surprise flooded her. She'd expected him to ask her to pick up some extra work or deal with a client while he was away, not go with him. How would they explain it to his family?

"Why would you invite your assistant to a family party?" she asked carefully, and Cal frowned at her.

"I'm not inviting you as my *assistant*, Maggie," he

said, as if it was obvious. And it was, but he clearly hadn't thought it through.

"No, I know that," she replied, rolling her eyes. "But when you introduce me—"

"I don't want to introduce you as my assistant." Shadows crossed his face, this clearly bothering him more than he was letting on. Oh.

Maggie paused before brushing her thumb across his cheek. "But I *am* your assistant," she said gently, as he covered her hand with his own. "And I've spoken to half of your family on the phone, so they already know who I am." Besides, even if they didn't know her and he introduced her as a friend or girlfriend, how would his very Catholic parents respond to him taking a twenty-seven-year-old home?

Cal looked away, his throat bobbing. "I know, I know. But I want you there."

Maggie knew they were tiptoeing around dangerous territory here, but she desperately wanted to wipe that expression of defeat from his face. "When's the party?" she asked, chewing her lip.

"Saturday night. I fly out on Friday afternoon and back on Monday morning."

It was Thanksgiving week, and the office was closed Thursday through Monday. Maggie drummed her fingers on the edge of the couch. "I suppose if there was a work call you absolutely couldn't miss or reschedule on Saturday morning, it wouldn't be totally out of the question that you might need your assistant with you to set it up," she suggested. Cal turned back to her, brow raised uncertainly, but a glimmer of hope shone in the depths of his emerald eyes.

"I don't think any of our clients are going to be up for a call at that time on a Saturday, love, given the time difference."

"No one said it had to be a real client," Maggie answered with a mischievous smile. "Jazz would do it for the chance to ask you questions that are entirely too personal and watch me blush." Besides, Jazz's sleep schedule was so nonexistent that she'd probably be awake.

Cal sat up straighter, the hope outshining the disappointment on his face. "I can handle that. So you'll come?"

It was a terrible idea—a world away from the arrangement they'd made. *Hanging out* meant lunch at Ethel's, or introducing Cal to the wonders of reality dating shows and five-dollar bottles of rosé after work one day. It didn't mean flying six thousand miles across the world to meet his parents.

"Of course I'll come," she said, despite all the reasons she should say no. "If you want me there, I'm there. Is this why you were in a mood earlier?"

"I wasn't in a mood," he denied. She gave him a look that immediately wiped the protest from his face. "Okay, maybe I was. I just didn't want to spend a whole weekend away from you."

Maggie's breath caught in her chest. That wasn't something people who were just sleeping together said, so why did she like hearing it so much? *Dangerous.* She looked away, closing her eyes and leaning her head on his shoulder, rather than feel the weight of his gaze. "It'll give me even more of an excuse not to go to my parents for Thanksgiving." Maggie had already lied to her parents and told them they weren't closing this year so she wouldn't be forced to sit through a too-long Thanksgiving day. She could easily add on an emergency work trip; they knew so little about what she did, that they had no basis to question it.

"How about I come over on Thanksgiving and help you paint your dining room? I'll make us dinner, and we can talk about just how thankful we are for that giant bed of yours," Cal suggested huskily, running a finger down her throat.

"You're offering to paint my house, cook for me, *and* give me mind-blowing orgasms? How could I say no?"

"You just agreed to meet my nine siblings, love. I'll give you anything," Cal said, chuckling lightly. Maggie grimaced. She'd forgotten he had so many siblings; he was smack dab in the middle of ten, and the only Michaelson sibling still living stateside. "I can't cook you a Thanksgiving dinner, though. I'm not American enough for that shit. Sweet potatoes with fucking marshmallows? Christ."

"I don't think I've ever seen you so disgusted," Maggie said, shaking with laughter at his wrinkled nose and curled lip. He was still so fucking gorgeous. "I didn't know you could cook."

"Liam went through a phase of wanting to be a chef when he was six. Eliza and I didn't know how to cook, and she hadn't met Danisha yet. There weren't any kid cooking classes in the city, so I took the adult classes and reenacted them for him a couple of days later. It was kind of fun, honestly."

Maggie had never wanted kids, but something about Cal taking cooking classes to teach his six-year-old how to cook made her stomach flutter. Of course, Liam was in his thirties now, and she hadn't even been conceived when he was six, but it was still cute.

"So what are you making me?"

Cal hummed. "I'll have to think about dinner, but right now..." He pushed up the edge of her skirt, his fingers trailing along her thigh. "I was thinking I might make you come again."

Maggie almost said yes, but her phone chimed with a reminder and she jumped off his lap before she got sucked back into him. "Sadly, *some* of us do work around here, Mr. Michaelson," she chided, smoothing her skirt down and watching his eyes flash wickedly.

He stood and pressed a soft kiss to her forehead, smacking her on the ass as she turned towards the door. "Brat."

Maggie winked at him over her shoulder, her blood singing as she knew she was going to pay for that, in the best way, later. "I'll take a raincheck on that orgasm."

She heard him cursing as she stepped into the elevator, smiling to herself.

M aggie had just finished rolling the last sweater and placed it in her suitcase when she heard the door open and Jazz's dulcet tones echoed up the stairs.

"In my room," Maggie shouted back.

Jazz waltzed in and collapsed onto her bed with a groan. "Did I mention I fucking hate Thanksgiving?"

She was dressed as *Jazz Lite*, as she called it—the Jazz she was for her parents—in a plain black dress and loafers, her choppy orange bob tied back in a tiny bun. She didn't see her parents often, just major holidays and life events, which meant she detested all major holidays and life events. Where Maggie's parents were unmotivated and content to expect her to pick up the slack, Jazz's family was the kind that tried to outdo each other at every turn. She'd long ago given up trying to meet her parents' impossible expectations, trying to compete with her brother and sister, but she dragged herself to every event with her head held high.

"You might have mentioned it a time or two," Maggie snorted, pushing her suitcase aside so she could lie down beside Jazz.

Jazz peered at the suitcase, spotting the empty half and the pile of Maggie's things beside it, ready to be packed, and laughed. "Tell me you're not doing the domestic split packing thing with Cal."

Maggie frowned. "It's the most efficient way to pack. And the safest." She always insisted on splitting her and Jazz's things between both of their bags when they traveled. That way, if one went missing or was stolen, they'd each have enough to get by until they could replace anything they needed.

"I don't think you need to worry about losing your luggage in first class, babe."

"What? We're not—" Maggie stared at Jazz in horror. "Holy shit. Do you think we're flying first class?"

"You mean you haven't asked him for every single detail of the flights yet, so you can make sure you're at the airport six hours early?"

"I've been trying to play it cool!" Maggie replied, sounding decidedly *un*cool. Traveling was a perfection-ist's worst nightmare. No one navigated airports, jet lag, and menus in foreign languages *perfectly*. Every trip had some kind of fuck up, no matter how small.

"I can't really picture Cal flying coach. Can you?" Jazz asked reasonably, and Maggie shook her head with a sigh.

"I can't let him pay for me to fly first class," she protested. "I never even let Nathan—"

"He probably used his airline miles. You said he has a shit ton, right?" Jazz interrupted.

"Yeah, because he never spends them. He lets Liam use them."

"Well, there's a big difference between Nathan and his trust fund and Cal. Cal's a literal *millionaire*. Besides, unlike Nathan, Cal would never let you fly coach while he drank complimentary champagne in first class." Jazz scowled at the audacity of Maggie's ex. Maggie didn't disagree; traveling with Nathan was a masterclass in compromise. As in, she compromised everything she wanted so he wouldn't complain anymore.

"That's true," she relented. "But it still feels weird to let a man—"

"Maggie, babe. Come on. You can be a strong independent woman on Tuesday. For now, let your sexy older millionaire boss whisk you away in first class to his parents' castle in the Irish countryside and give you multiple orgasms every time he so much as looks at you."

"Well, when you put it that way," Maggie grumbled.

"What time is he coming over today?" Jazz picked up one of her perfectly rolled shirts and fluffing it out to inspect it.

Maggie snatched it back and checked her phone for the time. "Could be any minute. He and Liam were doing food deliveries for a shelter this morning, but they should be done." Because of course they were.

"Fucking hell. Tell me about baby Michaelson. Is he as hot as daddy? Single?" Jazz had a dangerous twinkle in her eye that Maggie recognized all too well.

"First of all, *baby* Michaelson is older than both of us. He is single, recently-ish."

"You missed out the most important part," Jazz said pointedly and Maggie scrunched up her face. A few months ago, she wouldn't have hesitated to call Liam hot. As hot as Cal? Maybe. Cal was more her type, but Liam *had* inherited his dad's devastating dimples and piercing green eyes. "Interesting," Jazz said, reading the conflict in her eyes.

"Nothing is interesting."

Her best friend didn't bother to fight her shit-eating grin. "You can't tell me if you think Liam's hot because you're falling for his dad. I'd call that pretty interesting."

"I am *not* falling for his dad," Maggie insisted, but Jazz knew her well enough to see her conflicted feelings a mile away.

"Sure you're not."

Maggie ignored her. She wasn't falling for Cal; she was just having fun. Finding her excitement. Not that *Cal* was the thing that excited her... "We're just having fun."

"Mhmm."

Maggie glared at her, but opened her phone and searched through Instagram until she found Liam's profile. "Here. That's what he looks like."

Jazz raised her eyebrows and grabbed the phone. "Damn. That mustache is a *choice,* but he's gorgeous. In that kind of slightly nerdy, pretentious way, like he takes people to museums on dates, then fucks them in the shadows of the alien exhibit, you know?"

Maggie stared at her friend with concern. "Do you really think museums have alien exhibits?"

She shrugged, swiping liberally through Liam's profile. "How would I know? I haven't been to a museum since I was a kid."

"Clearly. Well, I can't speak for what he gets up to in the shadows, but you were right on the money with the museum. He's the head curator at the Seattle Art Museum. He—What are you doing?" Maggie said, as Jazz did something that looked suspiciously like a double tap.

She tried and failed to snatch her phone from Jazz's hand but saw, to her horror, that she'd not only followed Liam from Maggie's account, but had liked several of his pictures. "Jasmine Elisabeth Cannon, what is wrong with you? Why the fuck would you do this?"

"You've met him, right? It's not weird."

"Yeah, I've met him. At work. Where I'm his dad's assistant," she emphasized, and Jazz raised a brow.

"His dad's assistant, who he's taking home to meet his family," Jazz said skeptically.

"They think it's a work thing. And give me my phone back."

She grabbed for it and Jazz stepped out of arm's reach, smirking and continuing to scroll through Liam's feed. Maybe it was the nerves about the trip to Ireland, or maybe it was the Thanksgiving mimosa she'd started her day with, but Maggie tackled her.

Jazz squealed, laughing as Maggie grappled for her phone, only a little aware that she was risking liking even more pictures in the fray. "Give it back."

"No." This wasn't the first time she'd had to do this; she knew better than to give Jazz her phone. She managed to pin one arm, but all Jazz had to do was pinch her in the side and Maggie squealed.

"What am I watching here?"

They both turned, in slow motion, to see Cal standing in the doorway, an amused expression on his perfect face, his keys dangling from his hand.

Maggie untangled herself from Jazz, her cheeks burning, as Jazz whisper-squealed, "He has a *key*?"

Maggie ignored her. "Jazz stole my phone and followed Liam on Instagram."

"And he followed you back," Jazz piped up. Maggie took the opportunity to pluck her phone out of Jazz's outstretched hand, leaving a pout behind on her best friend's face.

"Okay," Cal said, dropping his bags by the dresser and squinting. "Is there some kind of social media etiquette thing I'm missing where that's a problem?"

Maggie had tried to explain Instagram to Cal after his sister's wedding the year before when he'd wanted to show her the pictures. They'd given up after an incredibly frustrating hour, and waited for his mom to email them.

"It would be considered unusual for your dad's assistant to follow you on Instagram, yeah," she explained as Cal crossed the room and captured her mouth in a chaste kiss, thanks to Jazz sitting beside her. Maggie tried not to frown as he drew away too soon.

"But you're not *just* my assistant," he said.

She sucked in a breath through her teeth. *How many times…* "Oh my God. Yes, again, *I* know that," she said. "But no one outside of this room knows that."

"Well, actually…" Jazz said quietly, a guilty look on her face.

"Who did you tell?" Maggie asked, taking a deep breath. As much as she loved Jazz, she had the world's loosest lips.

"Just a couple of the girls at work. Oh, and you know my landlord, Betty." She turned to Cal. "None of her family visit because she left her church and started dabbling in witchcraft in her sixties. She makes a mean mojito. Hey, when's Liam's birthday?"

Cal blinked at the quick change of subject, but didn't question Jazz before answering. "March twenty-second."

Jazz raised her brows, whistling. "An Aries. Hot."

"I don't know what that means. And I don't think I want to," Cal added quickly when Jazz opened her mouth. "So, this Instagram thing *isn't* a problem?"

"Nope. Not a problem," Jazz confirmed before Maggie could explain why it was.

"Well then," Cal said, taking her at face value.

Maggie crossed her arms and looked between them. "I'm not a fan of this little alliance you two have going on." But she was lying. She was a *big* fan of seeing someone she was interested in treating Jazz with kindness and respect. Sure, Cal looked permanently shocked around her, but he didn't seem to mind how absolutely unhinged Jazz was.

"Tough," he said simply, taking a seat beside her and slinging an arm around her shoulders. "Are you staying for dinner, Jazz? I'm making Italian."

Jazz looked at Maggie, impressed. "He cooks too?"

"Apparently." But all Maggie could think about was that Cal had invited Jazz to join them, making it clear that he didn't mind spending time with her best friend. Nathan hadn't even liked Maggie having Jazz over at their apartment when he wasn't around.

"Damn. Sadly, I must go home and listen to my family compare their achievements for the last quarter." She pressed a kiss to Cal's cheek, leaving him shell-shocked once again, before pulling Maggie into a tight hug. "Have the best time, babe. And go easy on him," she leaned in to whisper in her ear. "He's not Nathan, okay?"

Maggie didn't bother to protest that what she had with Cal was nothing like what she and Nathan had been. She just nodded as Jazz pulled away, smiling. "Alright, you two, please give me a chance to get out the door before you pounce on each other. And send pictures this weekend!" She shouted her goodbyes as she ran down the stairs, the front door slamming behind her.

Maggie blew out a long breath before turning to face Cal. "Hi."

"Hi, love." He smiled, his dimples on full display. "So… can I pounce now?"

"Please do."

CHAPTER FIFTEEN

"Okay, I see the merits of first class now," Maggie panted, rolling onto her side to face him. She was cast in shadows by the low airplane lights, but her cheeks still burned scarlet. Her hair was tangled from his hands, and he knew she was going to give him shit for it later when she caught herself in the mirror, but she was gorgeous, and he liked when she gave him shit.

Cal hadn't told her they were flying first class, because he'd known she would protest. And protest she had—until the seatbelt sign was switched off and the flight attendant had asked if they'd like the bed made up. When he'd finished turning their seats into one double-bed, complete with pillows, a comforter, and a big screen to watch movies, if they wished, he left an open bottle of champagne and closed the floor to ceiling curtains behind him.

Maggie had stared around the suite open-mouthed until he'd beckoned her towards the bed, and pulled her into his arms.

He reached out and smoothed her hair down, brushing the errant strands from her face. "You know, this was a first for me."

"Sex on a plane?" she asked, eyes lighting up, as if she liked the idea of being his first for something. He nodded, and she hummed happily. "Do I get a rating?"

"Full marks, every time." His heart was still attempting to jump clean out of his chest. Physically, Cal didn't feel old. He worked out, got regular massages, and remembered to take his vitamins most days, but he hadn't worked his body so hard since before Liam was born. Every part of him ached, a constant reminder of what he and Maggie got up to pretty much every day.

Maggie smiled, stretching out like a cat in the sun before cuddling into him. "This wasn't my first time on a plane, but this is much nicer than a Delta bathroom. Also a much better partner." She pressed a kiss to the hollow of his throat and Cal shivered.

"How did Nathan squeeze his ego into an airplane bathroom?" he asked, and Maggie snorted. He'd never met the asshole, but Christ, he fucking hated him. Even the fact that he'd never met him was a red flag; they had a company New Year's Eve party every single year, and everyone brought their families. Maggie had never brought Nathan.

"It wasn't Nathan. He wouldn't even have couch sex. He was strictly a bed guy. Jazz and I went to Cabo for

Spring Break our freshman year. We were both still a little drunk on the flight home, and our seat buddy was very friendly. He wanted to squeeze both of us into the bathroom, but Jazz is a terrible flier, so he settled for me." She shook her head at the memory. "When we got off the plane, I watched him walk straight into the arms of his wife and kids while Jazz threw up in a trash can."

"Holy shit," Cal said, not sure whether to laugh or not.

Maggie wrinkled her nose. "I'm still not entirely sure how we survived the first couple of years of college."

"Were you and Jazz always just friends?" He knew Maggie was bi, like he was—she had a bi flag sticker on her laptop—and he assumed Jazz was queer too, considering who she'd left the sex club with.

"We tried to see if there was something more there, but it was like kissing my sister, so we swiftly moved on. I'm pretty sure that's why Nathan hated her so much." Maggie tilted her head. "Well, either that or the fact that she called him a boring asshole like two weeks into us officially dating. Who could say? Were you and Eliza always friendly after you split?"

"It took us a year or so to become friends, but we'd been fighting for so many years by that point that I think we just forgot how to have a conversation without screaming at each other. I stayed in Stanford the first year after we split, and she moved back to Seattle to be near her parents. I flew up every couple of weeks to see Liam, and things settled between us when I moved back too. Liam was only three when we divorced, so he only remembers us being friends." They were a cautionary tale of not getting married just because you had a kid. Neither of them had wanted to really—hell, neither of them had wanted to keep Liam—but both of their parents had insisted, and neither of them would change a single thing about it all now.

"You must be so proud of Liam," Maggie said with a smile, and he nodded.

"We are. He turned out alright, all things considered."

"How come he's not coming this weekend?"

"He said he couldn't get off work, but I'm pretty sure he's just avoiding telling my parents that he and his ex broke up. Eliza says he hasn't taken it well, which is probably true since he's just flat out refusing to discuss it," he replied with an eye roll.

"Ah, avoiding your feelings. I'm familiar with that one."

"Yeah. Same," Cal replied, thinking of his constantly racing heart these days. Maggie's face softened, her tongue darting out to lick her lips as if her mouth had gone dry.

"Tell me about your family," she said in a hurry. "So I know what to expect."

The subject change was for the best. So Cal lay back, and with the hum of the plane as background noise, told Maggie about his family.

In a word, the Michaelson family was chaos. Cal loved them dearly, but he didn't mind living six thousand miles away, either. His parents had never intended to have ten children, but they'd never tried not to, either. Nine of the ten had been born within the first decade of their marriage, with Cal's mom finally saying enough was enough after the triplets had been born. Owen had been a surprise a few years later, but there were still only twelve years between him and Cal's eldest brother.

His parents had made it work though, and, for the most part, they'd been good kids. The biggest drama had been Cal getting Eliza pregnant out of wedlock while they were in college. He knew his parents had spent years dealing with whispers at the church he'd given up on attending when they'd moved to Washington. His mom had cried for a week straight when he'd told her, and, though they loved Liam more than he could ever have hoped, he knew it wasn't the life they'd imagined for him.

It wasn't the life he'd imagined for himself either. Cal had grown up watching his parents and dreamed of a marriage, a love, like they had one day. Sixty years together, and they still looked at each other like they had when he was a kid. It was the kind of love most people never experienced, all he'd ever wanted, and something he'd given up on long ago.

"Dad still wakes Mom up every single morning with a cup of tea in bed, and they can have full conversations with just their eyes."

Maggie's eyes lit up as he told her about them, a longing smile settling on her face. "That's what I want."

She deserved it; to love someone for sixty years, still just as excited about them so many years down the line. Someone she could grow old alongside, someone she would want to say yes to when they got down on one knee.

If Cal couldn't have a long love like his parents did, he hoped she would.

It would be unfair of him to even consider letting his feelings grow any further. He was her boss, and twice her age. He'd been married and divorced before she was even born, for Christ's sake. Cal had had his chance. And Maggie wasn't interested in more anyway. He would do everything he could to build up the confidence her ex had destroyed until she was ready to find the love she deserved and then, no matter how it killed him, he would let her go.

Cal pulled the rental car into the driveway of his parents' home and stared up at the massive house. It was twice the size of the one they'd grown up in. Most people downsized when they retired, but James and Helen Michaelson had ten kids, thirty-four grandkids, and six great grand-kids. They needed the space.

The driveway was already full to the brim with cars, and Cal sighed as he jumped out of the car and grabbed their bags from the trunk. He hated this part. It wasn't like he never visited. He was here at least once a season, but his homecoming was always such a fanfare.

They made their way up the gravel driveway, and Cal looked over at Maggie, expecting to see her gazing up at the castle-like house in wonder, but her eyes were on him. "What's wrong?" she asked, stopping in her tracks, her face full of concern.

"Who said anything's wrong?"

"I did," she replied with a touch of sass. "I know you, and this—" she gestured to him, "—is not the calm and collected Cal I've basically been spending every waking moment with lately."

"I'm rarely collected around you," he pointed out, but she leveled him with a stare and he sighed. Was it seriously only four weeks ago that they'd sat together in the club and talked about not knowing each other that well? So much had changed in such a short time. "I get nervous, coming home," he admitted, dropping their bags gently on the ground and rubbing his face.

"To see your family?" Maggie asked, with more understanding that he liked. Her reasons for being stressed around her family were vastly different. His family, at least, didn't treat him like free labor.

"I always do. I don't know. I guess it's just old shit coming up. I am *technically* the family fuck up, you know."

Determination flashed in Maggie's eyes—the same determination he'd seen when she was hyping up one of their interns before the bar exam. "Are you kidding me? Okay, sure—you had a kid out of wedlock, then got divorced three years later. So what? You co-own the top business and corporate law firm in the Pacific Northwest, you're *literally* a millionaire, and Eliza and Liam are both doing well too. I seriously doubt your family is still thinking about what you were doing in your twenties. And if they are? Fuck them. You're Cal fucking Michaelson. You have nothing to prove."

She knocked the breath from his chest and Cal couldn't help but lean in and catch her lips with his as the last word left them. She squeaked, but grinned against his mouth, pressing her hands to his face and brushing his cheek with her thumb.

Cal was weighing up staying out here all night, lost in each other, and getting back in the car to find a hotel when an entirely too familiar voice sounded.

"Oh my."

Horror filled Maggie's face as they broke apart. "Oh no."

They turned slowly to see, not just his mom and dad in the doorway, but at least half of his siblings gathered around them, identical expressions of shock on their faces.

"Jesus Christ," Maggie whisper-groaned as he retrieved their bags and ushered her forward. Cal fought a smile. Had she noticed how quickly she was picking up his turns of phrase?

Maggie schooled her face into friendly neutrality, but her blue eyes were still full of panic. Cal inspected his family warily for any signs that they were going to give her shit. But among the raised eyebrows and open mouths were curious eyes, tentative smiles, and... was that approval? Cal had so rarely seen it on his parents' faces that he wasn't quite sure he recognized it.

He cleared his throat as they stilled at the foot of the stairs. "Everyone, allow me to introduce you to Maggie. My..." He glanced at her, wondering how they were going to do this since his family had just seen him all but devour her. Maggie winced. He'd already told them he was bringing his assistant with him, and she hadn't been kidding when she said she'd spoken to half of them on the phone before. His mom called at least twice a week, just for a chat. "My assistant," he finished lamely.

There was a beat of silence before his mom rushed forward, ignoring him entirely, and swept Maggie into a tight hug. Maggie looked at him over her shoulder like a deer caught in headlights. "It's *so* nice to finally meet you, Maggie. And put a face to the name! Well, I've seen pictures, of course, but it's not the same. I feel like I know you already."

"It's lovely to meet you, Mrs. Michaelson," Maggie managed and his mom tutted.

"Helen, please. Oh, aren't you just darling? Cal talks about you all the time, but he didn't do you justice." His mom pursed her lips and frowned accusingly as she turned towards Cal, while Maggie just blinked, looking as confused as he was. Did he really talk about her so much that his mom considered it *all the time*?

"Good to see you too, Mom," he said dryly, as she gave him a hug with half as much enthusiasm as she'd given Maggie, but there was no mistaking the glint in her eye as he took her in up close: it was, indeed, approval.

The rest of his family descended upon them, Dom reaching them first and gathering Maggie in another bone-crushing hug, all but knocking the wind from her. A curse fell from her lips and she winced, but Dom laughed, releasing her and clapping her on the back. "Och, you'll be grand around here with a mouth like that, sweetheart.

Welcome home, you two," he said, with a wink to Maggie and a knowing smile to Cal.

They were ushered inside, every one of his siblings offering Maggie a hug or a clap on the back. Owen planted a kiss on her cheek, just to fuck with him. Little shit.

By the time the racket fell to a less overwhelming level and everyone had been introduced, Maggie was struggling to keep her forced smile in place. Cal wasn't close enough to take her hand or rub her back, but his mom, standing closest to her, must have noticed because she shushed his siblings and took Maggie's hand herself, leading her out of the fray to his side.

"You two must be exhausted. It's a long travel day," she said with a frown. His mom considered anything beyond the two-hour drive from Bray to Cork to be a long travel day, but even in first class, nine hours on a plane was just about Cal's limit.

"We're pretty exhausted," Cal agreed, and Maggie gave him a grateful smile.

"Well, I have your room all set up for you. Owen, take them up, will you? They're in the room next to you." She pulled them both into a gentler hug. "I'll bring some food up in a bit when you're settled so you can eat in peace," she said quietly, shaking her head towards the rest of his siblings with an exasperated smile.

"Thanks, Mom." Cal gave her an extra hug. He never realized quite how much he missed his parents, or quite how old they were now, until he saw them in person.

"Thanks, M—Helen," Maggie said, before bidding

his siblings goodnight. Cal did the same, and Owen led them through the living room and up the winding staircase to the top floor. He chatted away, but Cal was too ready for peace to take in what he was saying.

He paused outside an open door. "You two get the room with the fire. Oh, to be the prodigal son," he said, dramatically, but his eyes were all mirth. "Sleep well."

He left them with a wave and Maggie leaned against the doorway, taking in the bedroom, and the massive fourposter bed, with wide eyes. She tilted her head, turning to look at him with a furrowed brow.

"Cal."

"Yeah?" He carried their bags into the room and set them beside the bed, sinking onto the plush mattress and kicking his shoes off.

"What exactly does your family think this is?" Maggie asked, following behind him and gesturing between them.

"What do you mean?" he asked. "They know you're my assistant." She'd been there when he introduced her all of ten minutes ago, though he couldn't blame her if she'd blocked out the descent of half a dozen Irish folk upon her.

"Yeah, no, I know that, but..." she trailed off, staring pointedly at the bed. Cal looked between her and the bed until it dawned on him. The bed. One room, one bed.

"Huh." His mom, though less devout than she once had been, hadn't allowed him, or any of his siblings, to share a room with the opposite sex before they were married. And that wasn't an old trait; Maeve had only been married a year, and her now-husband had been forced to room with Dom for Christmas before they'd been married.

When Cal had called his mom to let him know he was bringing Maggie along, he'd offered to get them a hotel, but she'd insisted there would be enough room. It hadn't even occurred to him they wouldn't be in separate rooms. Sure, he'd planned on sneaking Maggie into his room or vice versa, but this... Cal had made it clear she was coming for work. There was no reason for his mom to suspect anything more between them.

I've seen pictures, of course. Cal talks about you all the time.

She *had* asked for pictures of Maggie years ago when Cal had been telling her how well she'd handled the Heminger West case. And, sure, she asked how Maggie was getting on whenever she called, and he sent her pictures from their New Year's Eve party, but his mom had never given any indication that she thought anything of it.

But then, he had mentioned she'd broken up with Nathan. And he'd told his dad all about her house renovation. And it was possible he'd mentioned they were spending Thanksgiving together...

"Ah," he said, his cheeks burning. He kicked off his shoes and swung his feet up on the bed, leaning back against the pillows. "I think I see what's happened here." Worry coiled in his gut.

Maggie shed her sweater and climbed up to nestle in the spot between his legs. He wound his arms around her instinctively, and she hummed. "Care to share with the class?"

He was a fifty-five-year-old man; he had no excuse for blushing so much. "I, uh, I think I kind of talk about you a lot."

She turned her neck to look at him, curiosity on her face. "Yeah, your mom mentioned something about that."

"I've always talked about you when I talk about work, but I mean… it's possible that recently you're basically all I talk about. And I don't mean in a work capacity," he admitted, and his heart raced, because he knew he'd crossed whatever casual lines they'd drawn between them without even meaning to.

"Oh." A line appeared between Maggie's brows as she let the words sink in, and Cal braced himself for her to tell him he was taking this too far. But she didn't—her face melted into a soft smile and she wrapped her arms around his neck, brushing a gentle kiss against his lips. "Well, that's fucking cute."

Relief flooded him. She didn't mind; hell, she even seemed to like that he'd been talking about her. Cal didn't know how to begin unpacking that. "You're fucking cute," he replied, and she glowed.

"So, what do they think we are?" Maggie asked, and Cal shrugged.

"I have no idea. And regardless of what she thinks, unless she thinks we secretly got married behind her back…" Cal trailed off as *that* image flashed through his head. Fucked. He was absolutely fucked. "It's still not like her to let us share a room."

He filled her in on how his siblings' significant others had been treated pre-marriage and she chewed her lip. "I don't know what to make of that."

"It might just be because my mom likes you so much," he suggested, thinking of her expression earlier, the same one mirrored on his dad's face. His parents not only thought there was something going on between them, but they approved. Did they not realize how young she was?

"I won't complain that you're not going to have to try to sneak into my room," Maggie said, shrugging nonchalantly, though her eyes were still wary. "I mean, I was never going to let you but—"

"What do you mean you weren't going to let me?" he protested, and she snorted.

"I was absolutely not going to let you sneak into my room in your Catholic parents' home." At his clearly pouty expression, she added, "I'm not a saint. I was going to get you to drag me into the woods when no one was paying attention, obviously."

If Cal's family wasn't downstairs, likely gossiping about them, he would be dragging her out there now. He settled for rolling onto his side and tucking her into his chest, his arms wrapped around her like she might disappear at any moment.

"I'm really glad you're here, love."

CHAPTER SIXTEEN

Maggie

S he wasn't entirely sure how she'd found herself at a table full of Cal's sisters, but Maggie's head swiveled back and forth as she tried her best to understand a single word they were saying. Cal's accent had softened somewhat in the four decades he'd been living stateside. It thickened in mere minutes in his family's presence, but it still wasn't as strong as his siblings and she at least had some idea of what he was saying.

How Cal's parents had managed ten kids in such a short space of time, and lived to tell the tale, she didn't understand. As adults, the ten of them, and their partners, were fucking loud. She couldn't imagine what they'd been like as kids. But she liked them; they spoke to each other with a fondness she'd never known from her own siblings, and seemed genuinely happy to see Cal.

They'd pulled her into every conversation, however

little she understood them, but, so far, hadn't grilled her. As the youngest of the Michaelson daughters turned to her with a twinkle in her green eyes, Maggie realized that luxury was about to come to an end.

"So," Claire began, clasping her hands primly on the table in front of her. "What's going on between you and our brother?"

Maggie glanced subtly around the room, looking for said brother, but Cal had been pulled away by a cousin the second they'd stepped into the party and was still nowhere to be seen.

"I'm his assistant," she said, giving up and settling her gaze back on the keen-eyed Michaelson women. She knew it wouldn't be enough, but she still hoped they'd drop it.

"And does Cal usually kiss his assistants with so much… vigor?" Claire's triplet, Maeve, asked, wrinkling her nose with the word *vigor*.

"Well…" Maggie wanted the ground to swallow her whole. "His last assistant was married. And a lesbian. So probably not." She picked up her much needed glass of wine.

"So it's not in the job description?"

Maggie choked. "Nope. And I'm not sure that would hold up anyway, from a legal perspective." Not that she needed a knight in shining armor, but if Cal wanted to show up and whisk her away, now would be an excellent time.

The Michaelson sisters exchanged a look that clearly said, *we have to push more*. Maggie drained the wine.

"So you're his assistant and his girlfriend?" Deirdre, the oldest of the sisters, and by far the most intimidating of Cal's siblings, asked. She was the spitting image of their dad, her eyes darker than her siblings' and narrowed to slits.

"Uh, no. I'm not. We're friends, I guess, but I'm not his girlfriend."

"Friends with benefits?" Deirdre asked immediately.

Maggie sighed. Was there any point in trying to say otherwise at this point? They'd all seen Cal practically devouring her, and they were sharing a room. "Yeah."

Deirdre hummed, eyes still narrowed, and Maggie swallowed. "How old are you?"

"Twenty-seven."

"And you've been Cal's assistant for how long?"

"Six years," she offered. "Well, I was an intern for a year, and I've been his assistant for five." Deirdre's expression melted into one almost of concern, her sisters sharing the worry. "Oh, this has only been going on for like a month. Not since I started," she assured them, and relief flitted between them.

"Twenty-seven. Christ," Siobhan said with a sigh. "That feels like a lifetime ago. That's got to be younger than Liam, doesn't it? How old is he now?"

"He's thirty-four," Maggie supplied, and the sisters tutted, as if they couldn't quite understand how their first nephew had gotten so old.

Deidre focused back on Maggie, and she braced herself. "So, do you like him?"

She blinked at her. "What? Liam?"

Deirdre waved a hand. "No—Cal. I mean, we haven't really seen him with anyone but Eliza, but he seems pretty smitten with you."

Maggie's eyes widened in surprise. "Of course I like him. But we really are just friends—and colleagues, I guess."

Fiona's gaze drilled into her. "So what's in this for you?"

"What's in *what* for me?"

"Sleeping with Cal. Are you trying to get ahead in your career? Is it the money?"

"No, of course not," Maggie said quickly, blanching at the accusation. "Are those really the only two reasons you can think of that someone would be with him?"

"We're not saying that's what *you're* doing, Maggie, love," Claire cut over her older sister, frowning at her. "It's just that he's twice your age. It's hard to imagine what you see in him." Maggie understood why they'd think that, but it didn't make it sting any less. This was why they had to be discreet; if people found out, especially at work, they would think she was using Cal for some nefarious purpose.

Speak of the devil, Maggie spied Cal across the room just as he turned and spotted her. His face lit up, and he mouthed something that looked a lot like, *You okay?* She nodded, but she must not have convinced him, because his lips fell into a frown. He made to walk towards them, but was pulled away by someone she didn't recognize.

Maggie turned her attention back to his sisters. "He's a good man—a gentleman. He's kind, and funny, and ridiculously intelligent. And sure, he's fifty-five and struggles to open a PDF without help, but he makes me laugh, and feel safe, and I like spending time with him."

The sisters shared another look, and Maggie was no closer to understanding them than she had been when she sat down. She and her own sisters had never had an unspoken language.

Finally, they turned back to her, and Fiona tilted her head before saying, "Those don't seem like the kinds of things you'd say about someone you're *just* sleeping with."

"Well, I didn't think you'd want to hear the more personal details."

"Christ, no," Maeve said, wrinkling her nose. "And you don't have to prove yourself to us. We're just checking you and Cal are both okay. We're tough on family. You'll get used to it, love." She winked, and Maggie felt a flood of warmth rush through her.

The conversation settled on lighter ground as she learned about the sisters. She'd quizzed Cal on their lives, jobs, kids, spouses, but it was better to hear it from them. She told them about Jazz, absolutely sure that she would fit into the Michaelson family with no problems, and they excitedly asked to see pictures of the progress on her house.

"That color is stunning," Claire gushed, as she showed them the newly painted dining room.

"Right? We only painted it on Thursday, so I haven't had the chance to see it with any furniture, but I'm so excited to finish it."

Claire raised a brow. "We?"

"Well, Cal did the bulk of it. I did the detail work," she said, neglecting to add that it had taken her twice as long as usual since Cal had decided painting without a shirt was the most efficient way to do it.

"He's helping you with the house?"

Maggie nodded at Fiona's question. "Oh yeah, he's been a huge help." She told them about how he'd shown up to fix her water and showed them pictures of the floating shelves he'd hung in the kitchen. His ability to hang something perfectly straight with very little effort turned her on to a concerning degree, but she didn't tell them *that*.

"That's interesting," Fiona replied, drumming gold glittered fingernails on the table.

"Interesting how?" Maggie asked, frowning as she set her phone down. "He said your dad taught all of you how to do that kind of thing."

"Oh, he did," Deirdre said, laughing. "We had tools in our hands as soon as we could walk. But Cal always hated it, even when he was really young. He got a weekend job as soon as he turned sixteen so he didn't have to work for Dad anymore."

Shit. He'd never indicated he minded helping—hell, he'd offered—but she didn't want him to resent coming over to the house or feel obligated to help. She'd been managing just fine on her own, running water aside. Maggie didn't know how to respond to his sisters, guilt coursing through her. This is what happened when she accepted help.

"Do you have an Instagram or a TikTok for your house progress?" Maeve asked, leaning in, and Maggie shook her head.

"I watch a ton of home reno stuff, but I hadn't thought about making it," she said and Maeve's eyes lit up.

"You definitely should. Short form video content is the way forward. I've been trying to convince Cal to look into it for the firm." Maeve launched into an excited tirade about what TikTok could do for Michaelson and Hicks, and for Maggie if she posted about the house. Like Maggie, she'd majored in marketing, but, unlike Maggie, she'd actually made a career out of it. A career she clearly still loved three decades down the line, despite how much marketing had changed since she'd gotten started.

By the time Maggie excused herself to the bathroom, she almost believed Maeve that setting up a social media presence for the house was a good idea. If nothing else, it wouldn't hurt to get feedback and tips from the people in the DIY space. She spent more time crippled with indecision when trying to decide between paint colors and finishings than she did actually getting shit done these days.

She finished up in the bathroom and went in search of Cal. Dom and Conor mentioned seeing him heading into the garden, so Maggie stepped out into the freezing November night and looked around, hugging herself tightly. She followed the house around until she spotted a familiar black dress shoe peeking out of the gazebo and crossed the grass.

Cal was mostly hidden by the vines creeping up the

gazebo walls, but a cloud of smoke billowed through the foliage. Maggie raised a brow as she stepped into the gazebo and found Cal sitting on the concrete ground with a cigarette in his mouth and a pint in one hand.

Fuck, she'd thought the glasses were lethal, but the sight of Cal with a cigarette in his mouth made her want to drop to her knees and fucking worship him. She really had to get a handle on herself.

"Since when do you smoke?" she asked, sitting across from him and tucking her feet in his lap. She might have hesitated to put outside shoes on a suit that probably cost thousands of dollars, but he was sitting on the ground and he immediately laid a hand on her leg, so she didn't think he minded.

He blew a stream of smoke away from her before saying, "I know it's a shitty habit, but I only do it when I'm around my family."

"Your family is great," Maggie said, and he shrugged, but a smile played around his mouth.

"They are, but Christ, there are a lot of them."

Maggie laughed and leaned across to pluck the cigarette from his fingers. "There are. I think I've only remembered about twenty percent of their names." She brought the cigarette to her lips and inhaled the bitter earthy smoke. Cal's eyes darkened as she blew it out, his tongue darting out to lick his lower lip. Maggie was purely a social smoker, usually when she was drunk, and though Jazz would choose a joint over a glass of wine any day, Maggie rarely joined her. But with Cal reacting like that… She might have to reconsider.

She handed the cigarette back and Cal took a drag before asking, "Were my sisters interrogating you?"

"They were," Maggie answered, but offered a smile so he didn't worry. "They wanted to know that everything was above board between us, and I told them you're a perfect gentleman."

Cal's eyes twinkled. "Is that what I am, love?"

She considered him, taking in every inch of him in the silver glow of moonlight, from the still perfectly neat hair, to the tail end of a cigarette, the somehow still wrinkle free suit, to the wild look in his eyes.

"You are," she said, running a finger along his shin. "Okay, you're really unhinged in bed—which I love, obviously—but normally, you're a perfectly respectful, kind, and just a generally nice man. Honestly, I don't understand how you're still single. You're a fucking catch."

Cal's face melted into a soft curve of a smile and he stamped out the cigarette before holding a hand out. "Get over here and let me thank you properly for that, baby."

Maggie shuffled closer until she could sit in his lap and Cal pressed a tender kiss to her lips, lightly holding her face. "I'm serious," she murmured against his lips. "Why are you still single?"

Cal huffed out a breath and screwed up his face. "I have tried to date since Eliza and I divorced, but it was hard at first, being so young with a kid. Liam has always been my priority. I did date someone when Liam was seven—Andrew. He was a nice guy, and he really liked Liam. We dated for two years, but he didn't like me being so close with Eliza and that was a non-negotiable for me." Cal shrugged. "By the time Liam was older and didn't need as much attention, the firm was up and running and I'd made a name for myself. It became difficult to know who was in it for the money and who was in it for me, you know?"

"It's not a problem I have personally, no," she said with a wry smile, coaxing a laugh from him. "But I get it. You know that's not something you have to worry about with me."

Cal gave her a look of mock surprise. "Oh really? I wasn't sure how you felt about me spending money on you, after you shouted at me at the airport for booking first class."

"I did *not* shout at you," she protested.

"Well, you glared at me very aggressively."

"I'll show you aggressive," she growled, thankful for the floaty skirt that allowed her to straddle his thighs. She pushed lightly on his chest so that his back was pressed against the wooden post behind him.

"Oh no. Whatever will you do with me?" Cal said huskily, his lips against her jaw.

"The aggressive thing would be to do nothing," she quipped, and he chuckled, pulling back and looking up at her with eyes darker than the night sky beyond.

"Maybe, but that wouldn't be much fun."

"I suppose I *am* supposed to be finding the thing that excites me," Maggie replied with an exaggerated sigh, and Cal caught her mouth with his, the taste of tobacco and beer on his tongue.

"I like being the thing that excites you, love," he said softly, as they broke apart, and Maggie's heart raced.

Those don't seem like the kinds of things you'd say about someone you're just sleeping with.

Neither did that. But they *were* just sleeping together, even if she was craving more.

CHAPTER SEVENTEEN

Maggie

I n Cal's youth, Sundays in the Michaelson household had been reserved for worship, but the day after the party saw only three of the Michaelsons attending church. Cal's mom had invited Maggie to attend, but she'd politely declined.

Though she had been baptized, her family had never been religious and the closest she got to church these days were the trunk sales in her neighborhood where she liked to buy girl scout cookies. Cal had pulled her back into bed once his mom left to practice a much more unholy kind of worship.

The day had passed in a flurry of cups of tea and card games with more cheating than Maggie had ever seen in her life. The Michaelsons who lived locally dropped in and out, often bringing children and the odd grandchild with them. Maggie found herself holding a baby whose name she didn't even know, handed to her by a Michaelson she didn't even know, three separate times. They welcomed her into the fray like she'd been one of them forever, and Maggie had forgotten that this was what a family could look like.

Once upon a time, when she'd been too young to resent her eldest sibling role, she'd had fun with her family. There had been days with board games and jigsaw puzzles, greasy pizza from the place by the laundromat, and karaoke on the neon machine Cassie got for her fifth birthday. Young Maggie could never have known that, in a few short years, her weekends would be spent doing laundry, making dinners, and trying to get her siblings into bed at a reasonable time, so they wouldn't be too tired for school on Monday.

"Are you okay, love?"

Maggie started as Cal slung an arm around the back of her chair, his voice hushed against the din of the dinner table. How they'd squeezed so many people around it, she had no idea.

She nodded, letting herself lean into him a little. "I really like your family."

Cal's eyes warmed, crinkling at the corners. "I think the feeling is mutual."

Maybe it was the wine, or maybe the fact that Cal's family didn't seem to care about the weird situation they'd stumbled upon, but Maggie felt bold enough to rest her head on his shoulder, her wine in one hand and his hand clasped in her other. They were on dangerous ground; she'd gotten too used to holding his hand and hearing him call her *baby* for what they were, and they would have to steady themselves before they returned to work on Tuesday. But for now, among the twinkling music playing from Cal's parents' old speakers and a family that felt like a family, Maggie found it hard to care.

As the night wore on, the table was cleared of plates and people drifted off to other areas of the house. Cal was pulled away by his dad to look at his new train set, and Maggie found herself alone in the Michaelson's giant dining room. She breathed in the quiet, trying to force it into her mind and pounding heart to no avail. So she did the only thing that ever helped; she started tidying.

Maggie gathered the glasses left scattered across the table and piled the cloth napkins over her shoulder. She balanced them precariously on her walk to the kitchen, pausing in the doorway as she spied Cal's mom humming to herself as she stacked dishes by the sink. Helen stopped and turned to face Maggie as she heard her footsteps, smiling widely.

"Oh, thank you, love. It's always such an ordeal, bringing everything through after the big family dinners."

Maggie crossed the room and set the glasses down gently beside the sink before dropping the towels on the island. "Can I help you clean up?" she asked, and Helen waved her away.

"You're a guest, Maggie. Don't even think about it."

"I don't mind. I like cleaning," Maggie offered, and Cal's mom pursed her lips but, finally, nodded.

"Why don't you wash and I'll dry and put away?" she

suggested and Maggie nodded, rolling the sleeves of her sweater up.

She filled the sink and swirled her hands in the warm, soapy water. As much as she loved her dishwasher, there was something so relaxing about the ritual of washing dishes. She grabbed the glasses first, she and Helen washing and drying in a comfortable silence.

"You don't have kids, do you?" Helen asked out of the blue, causing Maggie to almost drop the glass in her hand.

"Oh God, no," she replied immediately, then winced as she realized how disgusted she sounded. Maggie liked kids; they were funny and cute, but they weren't for her. "Sorry," she offered Cal's mom, who just laughed, her twinkling eyes so similar to her son's that Maggie had to look away.

"Don't worry about it. That might have scandalized me thirty-odd years ago, but things change."

"I bet," Maggie replied with a wry smile.

"I assume Cal has told you how his dad and I reacted when we found out Eliza was pregnant?" Maggie nodded, and Helen sighed. "I wish I could say that seeing them become such great parents and figure out how to make it work after divorcing was enough to make me a little less… judgmental, I suppose is the best way to put it, but it took me longer than I'd like to admit."

"What changed?" Maggie asked curiously, and Helen's face softened.

"Eliza. We were never close—civil, yes, but I think she always resented us a little for pushing them to get married. James and I weren't the only ones, mind, but it was easier to blame us than her own parents, I suspect. We were surprised when the invitation to her and Danisha's wedding showed up. We thought it would be rude not to go, so we did. And when we got there…" Helen trailed off, setting silverware in the drawer.

"Eliza's parents didn't show up. They'd promised to, but they couldn't bear to watch their daughter marry a woman, so they left her a voicemail and said they didn't want to be a part of her life anymore. For all our differences, Eliza was a good friend to Cal and a wonderful mom to Liam. And everyone deserves to have a mother on their wedding day. So I helped her get ready, and watched Cal and Liam be so happy for her and Danisha, and something about it just gave me the perspective I'd been lacking."

"I can't even imagine how much that must have meant to Eliza," Maggie said. She knew her own mom would never step up like that for anyone.

"It meant a lot to me that she let me help," Helen replied with a smile. "And let me tell you, I'm much happier now than I was looking at the world through such black and white glasses. I haven't always gotten it right by my kids, Cal especially, but it's never too late to learn."

"He's always spoken very highly of you—and his dad," Maggie offered. "He lights up whenever I tell him it's you calling, and I know how much he loves coming home to visit."

"That's all you can hope for as a parent, really—that

your kids will want to come home. Do you want them? Kids, I mean."

Maggie scrubbed at the casserole dish in her hand and considered her word choice. "Um, no, I don't think so. I have younger siblings and my parents were busy growing up, so I more or less raised them. I think that's about as much of motherhood as I'd like, to be honest."

"Hmm," Helen replied interestedly. "You know, Cal doesn't want more kids, either."

She didn't know, though she wasn't surprised. Who wanted to start over with a new family when they had an adult child? "Well, they already did such a good job with Liam. It would be hard to top that," Maggie said, for lack of anything else.

"He's a great kid," Helen agreed with a proud smile. "Have you ever been married?"

Maggie hid her smile, looking out the window into the dark night. As much as Helen softened it with smiles, this was, without a doubt, an interrogation. And though she knew exactly what Cal would say at the thought of his mom interrogating her, she didn't mind. With Cal's history, status, and money, she would have been surprised if his parents weren't concerned about her intentions.

"Never married, no, but I was in a long-term relationship that ended in September after six years," she explained, and Helen nodded in recognition.

"Of course, Cal mentioned that. I'm sorry, that must have been rough."

Maggie waved a hand. "Thank you, but it's fine. Really. It was my choice to end things."

Helen raised a brow. "Well, now I'm just being nosy, but what happened?"

Maggie laughed and gave her a summary of the disastrous proposal, and the boring ex-boyfriend attached. Helen's brows inched higher and higher until it seemed they might slip right off her face.

"Sounds like you're better off. Best to end it while you're young, if you're not sure, anyway, or you might end up saddled with them for sixty years," she replied with a wry smile, but her eyes shone with love for her husband.

Maggie set the last plate on the drying rack and dried her hands before turning to face her. "What's it like? Getting to love someone for so long."

Helen considered as she reached for the plate and ran the ragged dishtowel over it. "There's a sense of peace in knowing exactly your place in the world, when your place is beside someone else. But every day with him is just as exciting as it was the day he first held my hand, even if we're just sitting at home watching the world go by."

"That sounds like magic," Maggie said. It almost didn't sound real.

"Not magic, Maggie, dear," Helen said, patting her face like only a mother could. "Love."

Cal

Cal carefully set the suitcases Maggie had repacked three times before deeming them organized enough in the trunk of the rental car and turned around at the crunch of gravel.

His parents crossed the driveway, bundled up in the same coats they'd been wearing for a decade, his dad in the tattered bobble hat Maeve had knitted him when she was seventeen.

"What time do you have to leave for the airport?" his dad asked as Cal leaned against the car.

"In about twenty minutes. Our flight isn't until eleven, but Maggie will spiral if we're not at least three hours early." Even he could hear the fondness in his voice. How was he supposed to go back to playing just her boss at work? Whatever lines they'd once danced around no longer existed.

"Cal," his mom said gently, and Cal knew what was coming.

He looked at the ground before replying. "Yeah?"

"What are you doing here?"

Cal refused to look up. "What do you mean?"

His mom sighed, frustration etched on her face. "You know exactly what I mean. According to your sisters, Maggie is under the impression that whatever is going on between you is… casual." She kept most of her disgust out of her voice. "And obviously you're both adults, so you can do what you want. But you brought her to meet us—and don't pretend it was work related—and then introduced her as your assistant."

"She is my assistant," Cal said, finally looking up. Though his mom's expression was one of concern, his dad wore an all too knowing smile. "And we're friends, I guess, outside of work. But that's all it is."

"Then why do you look at her like you're in love with her?" his dad asked, and Cal swallowed, not letting the words penetrate his brain. It was denial, it was survival. Maybe he was falling for her, and maybe he didn't know how to stop his descent, but he wouldn't, couldn't, think about it. Because at some point, he was going to crash and Maggie couldn't know. He wouldn't put that pressure on her.

He sucked in a shaky breath. "She's twenty-seven," was all he said in response, and it should have been enough, but his mom rolled her eyes and waved a hand as if it was irrelevant.

"So what? She's an adult woman who is perfectly capable of knowing what, and who, she wants. Don't infantilize her because you're scared of how she makes you feel."

Cal's mouth opened and closed stupidly. He settled on frowning at his mom. "I'm not... She's not..." He sighed and pinched the spot between his brow as it pounded. "All my life, all I've wanted, all we've *all* wanted," he amended, nodding to the house where his siblings were. "Is what you have. We've been so lucky to watch the two of you being so ridiculously in love, and that's what

Maggie deserves—someone who can give her sixty years, not thirty." And he was being generous with thirty.

"Oh, love," his mom said, pulling him into a tight embrace. Over the years, her already small frame had thinned, and Cal was struck by how fragile she felt in his arms. He hadn't woken up one day and realized they'd all gotten so much older. He'd watched every year tick by with a sinking feeling in his stomach that he was wasting the time he had left.

Sure, he had his dream job, an incredible kid, and more money in the bank than he could possibly spend before he died. But he spent all day at work to go home to an empty apartment. Or he had before he'd had Maggie anyway.

Liam had his own life, and they weren't as close as they were before he graduated college and met his now ex-girlfriend. He saw him every couple of weeks, Eliza and Danisha once a month, if that, and his family four times a year. Half his friends had moved away over the years, the other half he'd fallen out of touch with. He tried to trace back through the years to figure out when he'd become so fucking lonely, but he couldn't remember a time he wasn't. The past month with Maggie was the most time he'd spent with another person in years; it was the first time he'd taken the time to really get to know someone—and wanted someone to really get to know him.

"Cal," his mom continued, pulling back. "If your Dad and I could have had only sixty days together, let alone sixty years, we'd still do it all again."

"And you never know how long you'll get with some-one, son. Your plane could crash on the way home, or you could be hit by a bus tomorrow—"

"That's not helpful, James," his mom chastised.

"I'm just saying—don't waste the time you have."

Cal chuckled, shrugging and crossing his arms as he squinted in the winter sun. "It's a moot point. Regardless of what I feel, I don't think Maggie is looking for anything more than this anyway. Especially not with her boss." He knew she was already nervous about her job, even though he'd assured her he wouldn't let this thing between them impact it.

"Did she tell you that?"

Cal frowned. "Well, no."

His mom pursed her lips and raised a brow. "I see."

"You see what?"

"I don't know Maggie very well yet, but I can't imagine she would be very happy to hear that you've decided how she feels and what she needs without asking her."

"Probably not," he relented with a grumble. In fact, he was pretty sure she wouldn't speak to him for the whole journey home if she knew.

He was saved further interrogation as the front door opened and his siblings and their partners streamed out onto the driveway, Owen talking an overwhelmed-looking Maggie's ear off. He was amazed how well she'd fit into his family, especially considering the much smaller one she hailed from, but she must be exhausted.

Still, her eyes landed on his and lit up, her shoulders relaxing.

"Time to head to the airport, love?" he asked, and she nodded, checking her purse for what he was sure was the millionth time to make sure she had their passports.

They were pulled into more hugs than he could count, clapped on the back and told to have a safe flight a dozen times over, but they finally made it into the rental car. Closing their doors was another story; Maeve hovered by Maggie's open door, rambling on about social media something or other.

Cal's mom leaned into the driver's side to give him one last hug.

"Be safe," she murmured in his ear. "And Cal?"

"Yeah?"

"Next time you bring Maggie home, you better not introduce her as your assistant."

CHAPTER EIGHTEEN

Cal jumped as Maggie lay her hand atop his on the gearshift, his parents' house disappearing in the rearview

"Sorry," she said quickly, pulling her hand away, but Cal tugged it back. "Are you okay?"

He looked over at her for the split second the road allowed him and smiled. "You just gave me a little fright, love. I'm fine."

"I don't mean about that," she replied, and he could hear her rolling her eyes, though his own stayed on the road. "It has to be hard to leave your family when they're so great."

"It is. I love it here. I love Seattle too, but there's something about the stillness here. I guess it wouldn't be the same if I lived here all the time," he admitted. "But I do miss my family, even if they are complete chaos."

"You're lucky," she said, so softly he almost missed it. He allowed himself a glance towards her, but she was staring out the window, her mouth in a thin line.

"Family events aren't like that for you, huh?"

"Not at all," she replied with a mirthless laugh. "We don't go all out for special occasions anyway—mostly because I'm always left to organize them and I don't have time to go over the top. We do the big ones, and I always do a little something for their birthdays."

"What about your birthday?" Cal asked. Maggie arranged a party in the break room for every birthday in the office, and he always did something when hers rolled around. Not a party—she would have hated the attention —but he always had everyone sign a card and ordered cupcakes, instead of a big cake, so Maggie didn't have to do the blowing out candles moment. He'd tried, her first year as his assistant, to convince her to take the day off, but he'd since learned not to bother.

Maggie leaned back in her seat. "This year was the first year I've really celebrated my birthday since I was a kid, and only because Nathan didn't know how to take no for an answer. To the party at least. He took the no to the proposal pretty hard," she added drily.

Cal frowned, drumming his fingers on the wheel. "You don't usually celebrate? Not even with Jazz?"

"Jazz always asks if I want to do something, but I really don't like my birthday, so she usually just leaves me alone. I went over to her place a couple of times to watch movies and get takeout since Nathan didn't like her coming to our place." Christ, Cal hated him.

"Why don't you like your birthday?" he pressed, and she was silent for a moment, staring intently at her lap.

"It's really stupid."

"Well, now I just have to know more," he said, squeezing her hand on the gearshift.

Maggie laughed softly and cleared her throat. "For my twelfth birthday, I really wanted to go to the Pacific Science Center. They have a planetarium, tide pools, dinosaurs, everything, and I'd never been. I talked about it for months. My parents have always been super disorganized, so they liked that I always knew exactly what I wanted. They told me we would go, and I told everyone at school. I was so excited." She paused, and when Cal looked over, her face was cloudy.

"You didn't get to go?"

"No. My parents made an appointment with the bank the morning of my birthday, to see about a loan for the cafe. They left really early, so I didn't see them, but they left a note telling me to look after my siblings. I figured they would be back in plenty of time, but they got approved for the loan and went out to celebrate after."

"Christ. Did they at least apologize when they got home?" Everything Cal learned about the people in Maggie's life, save for Jazz, infuriated him.

Maggie blew out a breath. "Nope. They realized, three months later, when they had to take me to the hospital for a broken elbow and give my date of birth, that they'd forgotten my birthday completely. They promised to make it up to me, but I'd learned not to hold my breath by that point."

She should have sounded bitter, angry, hell, fucking furious at how her parents had treated her—still treated her. But it was the way she said it, so matter of fact, that almost had Cal pulling off the road to hug her. How often had she been let down for her to say it so nonchalantly?

But Cal knew her well enough to know she wouldn't appreciate the sympathy, so he pulled himself together and took a deep breath. "Did you ever go? When you were older, I mean."

"No," she replied with a shrug. "I always meant to, but never got around to it. You know how it is. Oh, I have a question for you," she added, a clear subject change. It was becoming routine when they had these kinds of conversations, but Cal would never complain as long as she kept letting him in, at least a little.

"Shoot."

"Your sisters told me you hated helping with your dad's construction business—that you hate DIY shit."

He took the exit for the airport. "That's not a question, love."

"Alright, fine, I guess it's not a question, it's a statement. You don't have to help me with the house. I appreciate it, of course, but I love doing it, and I promise I manage just fine on my own."

He turned into the car rental place, pulled into a space, and cut the engine, before turning to her. "I didn't like being forced to help with my dad's business because I was a moody teenager. It wasn't the actual work, just the fact I had to be there at all. I love helping you with the house. I know you can manage on your own, but I like spending time with you. So let me keep helping you, please."

She chewed on her bottom lip, but nodded. "Okay. I suppose that would be… okay. Thank you."

"You don't have to thank me. I enjoy it," Cal assured her, but she shook her head.

"No, not for that—although, yes, thank you for that too—but thank you for bringing me here. For sharing your family with me."

Cal's heart warmed. He leaned across the center console and brushed his lips across hers. "Pretty sure you have an open invitation to the Michaelson family now, you know. They all loved you. What was Maeve talking about before we left? Something about a clock?"

Maggie scrunched her nose up. "You know, every now and then I forget how old you are and then you say something like that," she teased, tapping his lip when he scowled. "She was trying to talk me into setting up TikTok and Instagram accounts to make videos about renovating the house. Renovation videos are pretty popular online and obviously I have a lot of free time," she joked.

"That sounds perfect for you," Cal offered. He really had no fucking idea if it did or not, but Maggie's eyes were sparkling with excitement, and anything that made her face light up like that was a good idea is his book. "So you're going to do it?"

She pulled her lower lip in between her teeth and bounced her knee, like she always did when she was thinking something through. "Yeah," she said, finally. "I think I will. It's something different and exciting and it shouldn't require a ton of extra time on top of what I'm already doing. Maybe it'll be fun."

Cal brushed his thumb down her cheek and over her bitten lip. "It will be. I'm really proud of you, love. Although, you know what this means, right?"

"What?" she asked, warily.

"You're going to have to teach me how to use these things so I can—How do people support you on them? Commenting? Sharing?"

Maggie pressed her lips together, fighting a laugh, but nodded. "Alright, I'll try to teach you. Thank God for long flights and inclusive Wi-Fi."

"Don't forget the all-inclusive alcohol," Cal reminded her. They were almost certainly going to need it.

Maggie

Ireland had been cold and windy, but at least it had been dry. Maggie stared out the window of Cal's Tesla, watching the rain pound the pavement, and wished they were still curled up in front of the fire at his parents' house.

"What do I have to do to convince you to come back to my place?" Cal asked as he pulled out of SeaTac.

Maggie opened her mouth to respond, but closed it as soon as the phone in her hand rang. She'd been back in the country for less than an hour. "Kill my parents, apparently," she replied with a groan, silencing the call. She already knew they would want her to go over.

"Don't tempt me," Cal grumbled. "They're on thin ice after the birthday story."

Sure enough, a moment after she declined the call, a flurry of messages from her parents flashed up on her phone. She scrolled through them and sighed. "I have to head up to Marysville. They got locked out of the safe. Again."

Cal's grip tightened on the wheel, but she knew it had everything to do with how much of her time her parents demanded, and how little thanks she got for it, rather than for the fact she couldn't stay with him

"You want me to come?" Cal asked, and she stared at him in surprise. "We could head straight up there now and be back in the city before it gets dark."

Maggie sat back and let herself consider it. As much as she would love the safety blanket of having Cal with her while sorting out whatever shit her parents had left for her to deal with, it wouldn't go down well.

"Thank you, but I don't think my parents would be as understanding of me bringing you to meet them as your parents were."

Not that they would ever guess there was something going on between Maggie and Cal. Maggie's parents had told her time and time again that they didn't understand how she'd gotten *someone like Nathan*. They would never believe a man like Cal would show any interest in her. If she said that, though, she knew Cal would take the choice out of her hands and drive to Marysville, whether she liked it or not. So, instead, she said, "My dad thinks lawyers are assholes."

"I think your dad's an asshole," Cal said without missing a beat, and Maggie almost choked on her own saliva. "But yeah, most of them are. Sorry I called your dad an asshole," he added, almost as an afterthought.

"In the interest of being a good daughter, I'm just going to say *no comment.*"

"And in the interest of not making the *daddy* thing weirder than it already is, I'm not going to touch the *good daughter* comment," Cal said with a chuckle, and, despite the stress and anxiety that just seeing her parents' names brought on, Maggie calmed a little at the sound.

Cal pulled up outside Maggie's house and carried her bags while she struggled with the lock, rushing to get in out of the rain. Maggie wrinkled her nose and sighed as she took in the house from the hallway. As hard as she was trying, it wasn't homey yet.

Cal carried her bags into the kitchen and set them beside the dining table. "I can't believe we have to go back to work tomorrow," he said with a mournful sigh as he spotted Maggie's work bag by the table.

Maggie nodded in agreement, rummaging through her key drawer for the spare key for her parents' safe. "I'm going to say this once and then you're never going to hear me say it again," she said, turning back to Cal.

"Okay," he said, an amused smile playing on his lips.

"I can't wait to have a week off at Christmas."

Cal's mouth dropped comically, and he crossed the room, cupping her face with his hands and inspecting it as if he might find something awry. "Who are you and what have you done with my Maggie?"

My Maggie. Maggie's heart thundered in her chest, her mouth going dry. Oh no. Oh shit. She shouldn't like that so much. She shouldn't like that at all.

"Are you actually going to take time off or am I going to wake up at seven a.m. and find you answering emails in bed?" Cal added, and Maggie forced herself to smirk nonchalantly, despite the blood rushing in her ears.

"No comment." He hadn't even hesitated to assume they'd be spending their Christmas week off together, and neither had she. Was that why, for the first time in six years, the thought of a whole week off didn't fill her with dread?

"What are you doing on Christmas Day?" he asked, absentmindedly running his fingers through the ends of her hair.

"My mom makes a mean Christmas dinner, no marshmallows in sight, so I'll head over there for the day." It wasn't a lie, it just wasn't the whole truth, either. Her mom did make a good Christmas dinner, and she would head over in the morning, but she wouldn't stay. She'd show face in the family room and watch her siblings enjoying their morning with the weight of zero responsibilities on their shoulders, then make an excuse to leave before they'd even stepped foot in the dining room. She didn't want to resent them—it wasn't their fault—but it was too hard to stay.

"You don't stay over on Christmas Eve?" Cal asked, frowning.

"Absolutely not. I value my sanity over watching my siblings tear open their presents at five a.m. like zoo animals," she said with a shudder. She'd hated the chaos of Christmas as a child, but she'd tried her best to hide it for the sake of her siblings.

Cal's lips lifted in a mischievous smile. "I bet you're the kind of person who unwraps your presents excruciatingly slowly, then sets aside the wrapping paper and says they're going to reuse it but never actually does," he said, hitting the nail a little too hard on the head.

"Excuse you," she protested. "I *always* reuse it. What are your Christmas plans?"

"Liam and I usually stay at his moms' place on Christmas Eve. Eliza goes all out for Christmas, and Danisha is the best home cook I've ever met. I'd choose to eat at their place over any restaurant, seriously." He was practically drooling just talking about it.

"I like that you all still do holidays together as a family."

Cal shrugged like it was no big deal, but even Maggie's friends with amicably divorced parents had been forced to travel between them for Christmas growing up. "I'm not sure Liam will be up for it this year, but we'll figure something out. Can I steal you the day after Christmas?"

"It's not stealing if I enthusiastically agree," Maggie said, giving him a kiss and stepping away before she got distracted and didn't make it to Marysville.

"Excellent. Speaking of enthusiastically agreeing," Cal said, in the tone he used whenever he knew he was going to say something she wouldn't like. Maggie groaned, shouldering her bag. "Can I convince you to enthusiastically agree to letting me take care of you tonight? Please?" It was instinctive to interrupt him, to protest, but he looked so hopeful that Maggie bit her tongue. "It's a two hour round trip to Marysville and your parents stress you out. You're going to be exhausted by the time you get home."

"So?" she asked, warily. She knew she would be exhausted; the drive always tired her out, and her parents were always a nightmare. Especially when they hadn't spoken in a few days.

"So," Cal said, gently cupping her chin. "Let me stay here, make dinner so it's ready for when you get home, and hold you while you fall asleep."

That wasn't the kind of thing you did for someone you were just sleeping with. And fuck, she knew better, but Maggie didn't have it in her to say no. "That sounds nice," she said, and Cal's eyes lit up.

She made it out of the door and into her car, after a very enthusiastic goodbye kiss, and pulled out onto the quiet Seattle street. Maggie waited until she made it onto the I-5 before calling Jazz, the phone ringing loudly through the car's Bluetooth.

"You're home!" Jazz squealed as she picked up. "How was Ireland? Did you fall in love with an Irishman?"

Maggie loosed a strangled laugh. "I am in so much fucking trouble, Jazz."

CHAPTER NINETEEN

Maggie

"I'm so sorry, Mr. Klein, but I'm afraid we don't handle civil cases."

For the first time in her life, Maggie was counting down to a week off work. *Five days to go.* And she didn't want to spend another second of those five days listening to Peter Klein, the owner of a Seattle-based insurance consultancy firm, who was well known for his infidelity, talk about his impending divorce.

"I know you don't usually," he droned on. "But I was hoping you might make an exception. It's so hard to find a trustworthy attorney these days, and we've been working with Calahan for years."

Maggie rolled her eyes. Cal rarely said a bad word about any of his clients, but she watched his face fall every time she told him Mr. Klein had scheduled a meeting. "I'm afraid we don't have anyone on staff who would be suitable. But what I can do is speak to Mr. Michaelson and ask him who he would recommend. He does have a lot of contacts outside of the firm."

"Oh, yes, that would be helpful. Calahan has..." Maggie stopped listening to Mr. Klein as Cal himself walked into the office, his eyes landing straight on her. Cal crossed the room and squeezed her shoulder gently as he set an Ethel's Diner coffee cup on the desk before her. He smiled and headed back out the door.

Maggie felt the weight of a dozen eyes flicking between the two of them as he left, and she looked down at the coffee cup with a frown. She got coffee for Cal; it was literally in her job description. He'd never brought her coffee at work. Every morning for the past two weeks, while she worked on emails in either his bed or hers? Absolutely. But at work... He was her boss, and she was his assistant. And as Maggie looked up and saw several of the team exchanging raised brows, she knew it hadn't gone unnoticed. Maggie pushed down the panic that was blooming in her gut.

"Maggie? Are you there?"

Maggie shook herself. "I'm sorry, Mr. Klein. I've been having some trouble with my phone today. What was that?"

"I said Calahan has gone through a divorce himself, has he not?"

"He has," Maggie replied, pulling the coffee closer to her and breathing in the chocolate and peppermint.

"Perhaps the attorney he used," Mr. Klein suggested, and Maggie rolled her eyes, wondering how quickly she could get out of this conversation.

"Well, Mr. Michaelson got divorced over thirty years ago, Mr. Klein, so I'm not sure if his attorney would be available."

"Ah, three decades of freedom. He has the right idea!"

Maggie forced a laugh. She didn't know if Mr. Klein had ended things with his wife, or if she'd left him, but either way, good for her. "I'll speak to him and get back to you this afternoon. Is there anything else I can help you with in the meantime?"

"Excellent, you're always so helpful, Maggie. Actually—" He paused and Maggie braced herself. "Are you seeing anyone at the moment?"

Just once, she'd like to get through a work week without a client hitting on her. "I'm afraid we're not allowed to discuss personal matters with clients, Mr. Klein. I'm sure you understand."

Mr. Klein tutted, but didn't argue. She promised again to be in touch by the end of the day and hung up, taking a long drag of the sweet coffee. She looked up from her desk just in time to see a cluster of people look quickly away from her, trying to look busy, and sighed. So much for *discreet*.

Maggie gathered the coffee and her tablet in her arms and crossed the office quickly. She leaned against the mirrored wall of the elevator and closed her eyes.

She wasn't ashamed of what she and Cal were doing, but fuck, she didn't want to have to explain it to anyone. Even Jazz, who went with the flow more than anyone she knew, had started to ask questions that Maggie didn't want to answer.

Both she and Cal knew there was an expiration date on this; even if they dodged the conversation. Calling them friends with benefits didn't feel quite right, but they weren't dating. And as much as her feelings were growing, it didn't matter. Sure, Cal had invited her home to meet his family, but it didn't mean he wanted to date her. In six years, she'd never known him to go on a single date. It was what it was, and it was working for now, but they couldn't keep it up forever.

If people found out, it would only make the end more difficult. Not to mention how it might look to the rest of the office.

She stepped out of the elevator and frowned at the open door into Cal's empty office. He had nothing scheduled, but he often used his free time to check in on his senior attorneys. Unlike the juniors, they didn't have regular check ins, but he still liked to keep up to date with their cases.

Maggie set her coffee and tablet on his desk, running her eyes over the office to see what needed to be done. She was perched on the edge of the desk, warring with the plastic packaging holding a new ink cartridge for the printer, when Cal's phone rang.

"Michaelson and Hicks, Maggie speaking. How may I

direct your call?" So few people had Cal's direct number that it was almost certainly an internal call, but Maggie answered on autopilot. Sometimes, she even answered her cell phone with her Michaelson and Hicks greeting.

"Hey, Maggie, it's Eliza."

Maggie stilled in surprise. Cal's ex-wife rarely called the office. "Hi, Eliza. How are you?"

"Oh, you know how it is, just trying to get through the holiday rush. How are you?"

Did ophthalmologists have holiday rushes? It didn't seem like they would, but how would she know? "I'm good, thanks," she replied politely. "Are you looking for Cal? He's not in his office right now and I'm not sure when he'll be back, but I could take a message for you."

"I do need to speak to him, but I was actually hoping to speak with you too. Is now an okay time?"

Maggie frowned. Why would Eliza want to speak to her? "Um, of course?" It sounded more like a question than she would have liked.

"How was your trip to Ireland?"

"It was great. Cal's family is so nice, and Bray is gorgeous. It went by too quickly," she said, wishing she was still tucked in Cal's arms in the world's comfiest bed.

"It's amazing, isn't it? Such a shame you had to work while you were there." There was something in Eliza's voice that set Maggie on edge, as if she was leading her towards something.

"We only had to work for a few hours on Saturday, so we still had a good time."

"Ah, I see. I guess you work a lot of extra hours, huh? A lot of late nights in the office."

Maggie set the ink cartridge on the desk and paused. Did Eliza know? She supposed it wasn't out of the question that Cal's parents might have mentioned something if she'd spoken to them—or Cal himself. But, on the off chance she didn't know, Maggie wasn't going to just spill.

"I probably stay later than most people at the office, yeah," she admitted. "But most of my extra work I can do from home, so it's not too bad."

Eliza hummed. "What does your boyfriend think of you working so much?"

Confusion flooded her. If Eliza did know about Cal and Maggie, that was a weird question. "I don't have a boyfriend," Maggie said, hoping her voice didn't betray her confusion.

"Oh, I swore you were seeing someone. He worked in marketing or something?"

"Ah, Nathan," Maggie said, wrinkling her nose. At what point, post-breakup, would she get to stop talking about him? "We broke up a few months ago."

"That's good, that's good," Eliza said, almost absent-mindedly, and Maggie blinked in surprise. She heard the soft rumble of the arriving elevator seconds before Cal stepped into the office and lit up at the sight of her perched on his desk. "How old are you, Maggie?"

Cal dropped into his desk chair and raised a brow in question.

"*Eliza*," she mouthed, before turning her attention back to the call. "Sorry, what was that?"

"How old are you? You must be around thirty, right?"

What a weird conversation. "I'm twenty-seven," she said.

Before she had a chance to focus on Eliza's response, Cal's hands closed around her waist, lifting her onto his lap. Maggie squeaked, unable to stop the sound from escaping.

"Everything okay?" Eliza asked, concerned.

"Ye-yeah, everything's fine. Just a bird flying into the window, but I think it's okay," she lied. She turned to glare at Cal, but it melted off her face as she spied the devilish gleam in his eyes.

Maggie's heart thundered as he nudged her thighs apart with his knee and, without hesitation, shredded through her tights.

Maggie's head fell back against his shoulder as he cupped her pussy, her eyes fluttering closed. He could hear the tinny tones of Eliza chatting away, and he lightly tapped Maggie's nose in a warning.

She opened her eyes and bit her lip as he mouthed, "*Pay attention*," towards the phone, before sliding a finger inside her underwear.

Maggie's breathing hitched as she answered Eliza's question, but he didn't hear a word she said as he dragged his finger over her clit, fighting a moan at how wet she was. He circled her, almost lazily, wishing he could feel her flooding his tongue. God, he was so fucking addicted to the taste of her.

Maggie writhed in his lap, her body twisting and pressing into his cock torturously. Her knuckles were white, holding onto the phone and the arm of the chair for dear life, her fingers twitching as if she was desperate to reach out and touch him. She was always so perfectly, beautifully, in control, even when she was trying not to be.

However dominant he was, however much she begged and gave her body over to him, it was all an illusion; Maggie had always been the one in control here. There was nothing she could ask for, nothing she could demand, that he wouldn't give her.

He slid a finger inside her, his thumb brushing her clit, and she bit down hard on her lip. Cal curled his finger, and a tiny moan slipped from Maggie's lips, but she turned it into a cough at the last second. He knotted his free hand in her hair, tugging it to pull her head back gently so he could drag his tongue along the hollow of her throat. Maggie's pussy clenched around his finger and he pressed harder against her G-spot. She shuddered, her back arching, forcing her ass in to his cock even more, as her mouth fell open in a silent scream.

He stroked her gently, bringing her down slowly, while she forced her voice to steady as she answered

Eliza's questions. For the first time, Cal tuned in and realized that Eliza was asking Maggie about... Maggie.

Maggie ground out an answer about her house as she opened her hazy blue eyes and focused on Cal. He withdrew his finger, her eyes following it as he brought it to his mouth and licked it clean. *Fucking delicious.* Maggie bit her lip, dark pupils swallowing her ocean blue eyes.

"Cal's here now, Eliza, if you still want to talk to him," she said, nestling back against him, clearly with no intentions of going anywhere. Cal tucked an arm over her torso, pulling her closer. "Yeah, of course. I'll see you then. Bye."

Maggie breathed a soft sigh of what he could only assume was relief as she dropped the phone in his hand. "Hey. How are you doing?"

"I'm good," Eliza replied. "Is this an okay time to talk?"

"Yeah. Why were you interrogating Maggie?" he asked, curiosity getting the better of him.

"That's actually what I wanted to talk to you about," Eliza replied and Cal stilled.

"Oh?" Did she somehow know about him and Maggie? He hadn't told her, but he *had* been talking about Maggie more than usual lately. And he already spoke about her more than most people spoke about their assistants.

Not that he was hiding anything, but how exactly was he supposed to explain what was going on between them? Whatever it was, they weren't just sleeping together, but they weren't dating either. And how could he justify being with her anyway? He was twice her age, and she deserved so much more than him. It was easier if no one knew, even if he wanted nothing more than to scream at the sky how fucking obsessed with her he was.

"Yeah, I was just thinking. You know Liam's not having a great time right now, after everything with India and Bart," Eliza continued.

"Yeah, he still seems really cut up about it." Liam had just dropped thousands of dollars on an engagement ring for his girlfriend, India, when he'd gone home to find her in bed with his best friend of twenty-five years. *Cut up* didn't really scratch the surface.

"Exactly. So what do you think?"

"Of what?"

"Setting him up with Maggie," Eliza said, and Cal could all but see her rolling her eyes as if he'd missed something obvious.

He stiffened, his grip on Maggie tightening until she opened her eyes, her satisfied smile slipping into one of concern. "*You okay?*" she mouthed, and he nodded, though the blood pounding in his head said otherwise. Cal forced himself to relax his hold on her and leaned back into the chair, taking a deep breath.

"I don't think that's a good idea," he replied, surprised by how level his voice sounded.

"Why not? Maggie seems like a good girl."

Christ, let the ground swallow him up now. "She is," he ground out. "But I just don't think they'd be a good match."

Eliza hummed, and the sound of a gurgling coffee

maker started up in the background. "Well, you know Maggie best. They'll see each other at the New Year's party, so we can keep an eye out for a spark between them. They'll both need someone to kiss at midnight, after all." Cal bit his tongue in case he was unable to stop himself from canceling the whole party.

What was it Maggie and Jazz had said about Cancers? *Possessive and protective.* Yeah, there it was.

Cal hurried through his goodbyes with Eliza and, before Maggie could even ask him what was wrong, he picked her up, sat her on the desk, and claimed her mouth with his.

Maggie wrapped her legs around his waist and pulled him closer into her, like that was where he was meant to be, but he needed to be closer; he needed to feel her bare skin on his.

Cal tore at her cardigan and tossed it aside, tugging Maggie's shirt out of the waistband of her skirt and pulling it towards her head.

"Hey, hey," Maggie said breathlessly, pausing him with a hand on his chest. "Not that I'm not a big fan of this, but where are you at right now? What's going on?"

"I just… I need to be close to you right now," Cal panted.

Maggie searched his face before nodding and pulling her shirt off the rest of the way. She set it aside and brushed a finger over his cheek. Cal's eyes fluttered closed, his forehead falling onto hers. "I'm all yours," Maggie murmured.

Cal didn't know if she'd heard enough of the conversation to understand the jealousy coursing through him, or if she was just guessing, but it was exactly what he needed to hear.

He stripped off the rest of their clothes and left only long enough to lock the door. By the time he got back to her, Maggie had the condom open. She rolled it down his cock and he groaned, electricity zinging across his skin. She wrapped her arms around his neck and kissed him softly, gasping as he pushed into her.

Fuck, she was so tight and wet and *his*. Even if just for this moment, she was his. Cal pushed her down until her back was flat against the desk, trapping her hands on either side of her head.

"You feel so fucking good, baby girl," he growled, pounding into her pussy as her heels dug into his back, drawing him in closer. He leaned over her, his lips ravishing the hollow of her shoulder. "Your pussy is so fucking perfect."

"Yours," Maggie groaned as his teeth grazed her skin. He wanted to mark her, claim her.

"This pussy is mine, huh?" he asked, pulling out slowly and slamming back into her.

Maggie's head fell to the side, her mouth falling open with a whimper, legs quaking. "Me," she said, as the orgasm ripped through. "I'm yours. Right, Daddy?"

She met his gaze with hazy blue eyes and Cal lost it, his heart pounding in his chest as he fell apart, crying out. "Fuck, yes. You're mine, baby girl." His elbows buckled, and he almost collapsed on top of Maggie as flames rushed through him.

Cal fell back into his chair, tossing the condom in the trashcan beside his desk, and pulling Maggie into his lap. Her skin was almost cool against his, he was burning so much. He brushed a soft kiss against the underside of her jaw, ran his fingers through her tangled hair, and felt her body relax into his.

The gravity of the past half hour crashed into him; Cal was a fifty-five-year-old man. He didn't do jealousy. He sure as hell didn't do jealousy involving Maggie, who he had no claim to, and his son, who hadn't shown a lick of interest in her. What the fuck was wrong with him?

"I'm sorry," he said, still catching his breath. Maggie opened one eye and frowned at him.

"Sorry for what?"

"For being so…" he trailed off, searching for the right word. "Manic, I guess."

Maggie leaned in to kiss him and pulled away with twinkling eyes. "I liked it. Does Eliza know? About us, I mean."

"No," Cal replied, shaking his head. He opened his mouth and closed it. Did he want to tell Maggie that Eliza wanted to set her up with Liam? He should warn her, but what if she… No, she wouldn't want that. "Eliza wants to set you up with Liam at the New Year's Eve party."

Understanding dawned in Maggie's eyes as she realized why he'd acted how he had. "Oh. Well, obviously, that's not going to happen," she assured him, threading her fingers through his and squeezing his hand.

"But we won't be able to kiss at midnight. Will we?"

Maggie's face dropped. He was asking too much of

her, of their arrangement. "That doesn't mean I'm going to kiss Liam instead. I've survived without a midnight kiss at the New Year's party for six years. It's fine. We can make up for it when we get back to your place, and it's just the two of us."

"We could sneak off."

"You always give a speech right before midnight," Maggie reminded him with a laugh. "Besides, I don't think sneaking off would go unnoticed." She took a deep breath, worry creeping onto her face. "What happens if people find out about this?"

"What do you mean?"

She looked away, swallowing. "I mean, people are noticing that we're spending more time together. You brought me coffee this morning."

"I'm not allowed to bring you coffee?" Cal asked, missing the problem.

She sighed, rubbing her already rosy cheeks. "No, it's not—that's not what I said." Maggie turned back to look at him, her lip caught in her teeth. "I'm your assistant. I get you coffee every morning. It's literally in my job description. But you've never brought me coffee at work —you've never brought anyone coffee at work. You're the boss. So, when you do something like that, as much as I love and appreciate it, people notice."

Cal's heart fell into his stomach. "People noticed today?"

"Yeah," Maggie said softly, nodding. "Everyone was staring and whispering. And I can take that, it's fine—"

"You shouldn't have to," Cal interrupted. He wasn't

sure who he was more mad at; his team for staring and whispering, or himself for making things more difficult for her. "It's technically not against any rules. I don't think it is, anyway, and I should probably know," he said, wracking his brain.

"There's nothing about it in the employee handbook —I checked," Maggie confirmed. Of course she'd checked.

"So, would it be so bad if we told people?"

Maggie's face fell, her body tensing up. "If we told people what? What are we doing here, Cal? What is this?"

Cal had no answer for that. They'd been hovering around a crossroads since he'd taken her home to his family; hell, since he'd asked her to go with him. He wasn't ready to take any road except one that meant he got more time with Maggie, but it felt like that road was getting shorter and shorter.

"I don't know," he admitted, running a hand across her bare back. "It's not what it was the night we got stuck in the storm, though."

"No, it's not. But whatever it is, if the whispering today was any indication of how people would react—"

"Anyone who starts shit can kiss goodbye to their jobs, love."

The corner of Maggie's mouth lifted, and she shook her head in exasperation. "You can't fire people for being mean to me."

Technically, he could fire anyone for anything. And he would know. "According to state laws, I—"

"Cal."

"It's a moot point. Everyone here loves you, and they all know this place would fall apart without you. No one would treat you badly if they found out."

Maggie nodded, blowing out a breath. "I don't want you to think I think there's anything wrong with what we're doing, for the record. I'm not ashamed at all, it's just—"

"I know, love. It's okay. It's just complicated," he assured her and her body relaxed a little. "Why did you come up here anyway? You have your tablet, so I assume it's sadly work related," he added, nodding to the tablet teetering on the edge of the desk. They'd made quite a mess.

"Oh, yeah. I need a recommendation for a divorce lawyer," she replied, reaching for the tablet.

Cal quirked a brow. "You'd think declining the proposal would get you out of that."

"It's for Mr. Klein," she said, rolling her eyes. "He doesn't trust any other firms, apparently, but will take your recommendation. He specifically asked for the attorney you used for your divorce."

"Christ, I got divorced thirty years ago. Derek died a decade ago."

"You got divorced before I was born," Maggie said, shaking her head in jest. "God, you're so old."

Mischief lit her eyes, and every drop of Cal's blood rushed to his cock. He lifted her smoothly by her hips until she was balancing precariously over his knee, his palm flat against her ass. "You want to take that back, baby girl?"

Maggie wiggled her ass. Thank God he'd splashed out on soundproofing when they'd bought the building. "Absolutely not."

CHAPTER TWENTY

T he light shining through Maggie's living room
window confirmed what Cal had suspected when
they'd discussed their Christmas plans; she'd had no
intention of spending a full day with her family.

Also, as he'd suspected, Liam hadn't been in the
mood to celebrate. Instead, he'd spent the morning
frowning at his phone while he scrolled through pictures
of India and Bart's romantic Christmas getaway, and
made an excuse to leave as soon as Danisha's delicious
lunch had been cleared from the table.

Cal couldn't blame him. Liam would come to them
when he was ready, but the holidays were hard on broken
hearts.

December had passed in a flurry of snow and busy
work days as they prepared to take a week off at the end
of the year. Most evenings saw Cal and Maggie at the

office until well past closing, then stumbling back to her house or his apartment and falling asleep in each other's arms. Some nights, they were too tired for anything more than a chaste kiss goodnight, but neither one of them suggested going back to their own places.

Cal hadn't realized, until he'd kissed Maggie goodbye on Christmas Eve and headed to Eliza and Danisha's place, that he hadn't spent a night without her in almost two weeks. Alone in their guest room, he'd hardly slept a wink.

He grabbed his bags from the trunk and made his way to Maggie's front door, his heart racing at the thought of seeing her. She'd given him a key weeks ago, but he didn't want to just walk in if she wasn't expecting him. He knocked and heard the creak of the old wooden floors as she padded down the hall.

Maggie cursed as she warred with the lock—it had taken everything in him not to just change the thing— then wrenched the door open. Any frustration melted from her face, her blue eyes lighting up like Christmas lights as she took him in. Warmth spread through Cal at the sight of her in her baggy crewneck and Christ, the socks. They'd been apart for less than twenty-four hours, but it had been too long. He was so fucked.

"What are you doing here?" she asked, pulling him inside before he had a chance to answer. He dropped his bags on the bench and tugged her into his arms, claiming her mouth and breathing Maggie in. She stood on her tiptoes, clasped his face, and sighed happily against him.

"Merry Christmas, love," he murmured as they broke apart.

Maggie smiled up at him through dark lashes. "Merry Christmas. Aren't you supposed to be with your family?"

"Et tu?" he replied with a raised brow.

Maggie just rolled her eyes and led him further into the house. "We both knew I was lying about that. Let's not pretend."

The living room had been used largely as a storage room since Maggie bought the house, but she'd started working on it the previous weekend and, already, it was homey. Like most of the house, she'd swathed the room in jewel toned green and blush pink, the dark wooden floors shining after the hours she'd spend sanding and refinishing them.

Though she may have bought the fixer upper on a whim with zero experience, Maggie had a real knack for design—and for putting it into practice. Cal could tell she was exhausted, but he thought that had more to do with trying to juggle fixing up the house with work and managing her parents' cafe. And him, he supposed. He took up a good chunk of her time these days, but it was hard to feel bad about that when it was the only time she actually relaxed.

"Liam wasn't feeling it?" she correctly guessed as they sank onto the velvet couch and she lifted her feet onto his lap.

Cal shook his head, giving her a rundown of his morning. She winced as he told her about Liam scrolling through his ex's pictures. "Shit, poor Liam. Eliza and Danisha didn't mind you leaving?"

He shook his head. "Danisha got Eliza a fancy new hot tub. They were itching to give it a shot. Your parents were okay with you not going?"

"I went over this morning to give them their presents," she replied with a shrug. He didn't dare ask if they'd actually gotten her anything; he wasn't sure he could handle her saying no. "But my dad said he had a list of stuff for me to look over and I didn't want to deal with it today, so I told them Jazz needed me to pick her up somewhere. I stayed for an hour, at least." A two hour round trip, just for her to stay for an hour. Christ.

He was proud of her for walking away, though. "Well, I won't complain about getting you to myself," he said, holding a hand out to her. She took it and he tugged her into his lap.

"I…" she hesitated, her cheeks turning pink and her teeth catching her lip.

"You what?"

Maggie took a deep breath. "I missed you last night. It was weird, sleeping without you."

Cal's heart soared. *She'd missed him.* "I missed you too," he told her, tightening his hold on her. "I didn't sleep much."

"Me either." She punctuated it with a yawn. No wonder she was exhausted after driving for two hours on hardly any sleep.

"We should go to bed early tonight."

Maggie's eyes twinkled. "Not to sleep, I assume?"

"That depends how tired you are, love."

"I have coffee," she replied, springing out of his lap and disappearing into the kitchen at lightning speed.

Cal laughed, trailing behind her, unwilling to let her out of his sight yet. He grabbed the bags he'd left in the hall, set the bag of groceries on the kitchen table and unloaded them while Maggie set the coffee to brew and grabbed the Christmas creamer from the fridge. Cal had always been a black coffee guy until Maggie had declared it *fucking boring* and offered him her fancy Christmas latte a couple of weeks ago. He'd been missing out.

"You're making dinner?" Maggie asked, spying the groceries.

"Enchiladas," he confirmed, and her face lit up. It might not be a traditional Christmas dinner, but it was Maggie's favorite.

"You're literally a dream. I'll be back in a second," she said, setting their cups on the table. "Your presents are upstairs."

Cal looked around the kitchen when she left, then crossed the hall to the living room and frowned as he took it in. Maggie didn't have a Christmas tree. Her first Christmas in her new home, and she didn't have a tree? How had it taken him this long to notice?

She skipped down the stairs, a gift bag dotted with shiny gold trees in hand, and found him frowning. "What's wrong?"

"You don't have a tree."

"Oh, well, no." She shifted uncomfortably.

"Why don't you have a tree?"

"I have one in storage in the basement, and ornaments and shit. I just didn't get around to putting them up," she explained. "After putting up the decorations at my parents' house, the cafe, and the office, I just couldn't be bothered by the hassle of it here."

Guilt flooded Cal. For as long as he'd known her, Maggie had loved Christmas. She went all out with the office Christmas decorations every year, set up a secret Santa among the team, and even organized daily deliveries of Christmas treats the week before the office closed. She showed up in Christmas sweaters, with a smile on her face, and he'd never once stopped to consider that she was doing it all on top of the mountains of work she did every day. So much so that she was too burned out to even decorate her own home.

"Hey, don't do that," Maggie said, stepping forward and wrapping her free arm around his middle.

"Do what?"

"Feel bad about me decorating the office. I love doing it. At least people actually get to enjoy it there. It's just me here. Well, us," she corrected with a smile, and Cal's body relaxed more than it should at the two-letter word. "Quit worrying." And with that, she smacked him lightly on the ass and stepped into the living room.

Cal shook his head but smiled as he grabbed their coffee and the bag of presents from the kitchen. He joined Maggie on the couch, stomach fluttering nervously as he handed her the presents. "You open first." If he had to wait any longer, he might combust.

Cal had given Maggie birthday and Christmas gifts

over the years; small things, appropriate for someone to give their assistant. But now, he wanted her to see how well he knew her.

Maggie carefully pulled the tape from the candy cane striped paper, gasping as her fingers grazed what lay inside. "Oh my God. Is this what I think it is?" She tore the paper away and squealed, hugging the forest green bedding to her chest and groaning. "This is the softest thing I've ever felt. Thank you."

She was just as excited when she tore into the matching towels, already gushing about the first bath she was going to take before wrapping herself in the fluffy towels.

"I have one more for you. I know you love practical things," Cal said, nodding to the towels and bed sheets. "But I wanted you to have something pretty too."

"I already have you, and you exceed the pretty quota by a long shot."

He held out the black leather box, and Maggie eyed it suspiciously. "Just open it, love."

She gingerly took the box and opened it, her mouth dropping open as she took in the necklace. Cal didn't know much about jewelry, but he knew her eyes were like sapphires, so that's what he'd told the people in the store. And when the sales assistant pulled out the cluster of sapphires and diamonds, Cal had all but salivated at the thought of the necklace around Maggie's neck.

"Oh my God. Cal." She looked up at him, her eyes wide, as a finger traced the necklace. She swallowed.

"This is gorgeous. I... I love it. Thank you. Will you put it on me?"

She stood up, holding a hand out to him and leading him forward so she was facing the mirror. Cal's fingers trembled with the need to touch her as he fastened the platinum chain around her neck. He laid a hand right below the sapphires and diamonds, Maggie's chest rising and falling as she met his gaze in the mirror. As expected, the necklace only made her blue eyes sparkle more. She was radiant.

"It's beautiful. Thank you," she whispered.

"You're beautiful." Cal pressed a kiss to the back of her neck and Maggie shivered.

"Your turn." She tugged him back to the couch and handed him the shiny gift bag. "There's kind of a theme."

"Of course there is," Cal replied with a laugh; no one loved a theme like Maggie. He pulled out the first gift, perfectly wrapped with a green ribbon and an honest-to-God sprig of holly.

He set the decorations aside and pulled the paper off to reveal a nondescript brown box. Before he'd even opened it, the scent of home immediately hit him like a ton of bricks; the sweet, salty air of the Irish sea and smokey driftwood permeated the room. It all made sense when he slid an amber jar from the box. The candle was aptly named *The Coast of Bray*, and Cal recognized the logo from the church craft fairs his mom often dragged him to when they coincided with his trips home.

He brought it to his nose and breathed it in, his eyes falling closed. They'd nailed the scent. "Holy shit. It's like I'm there. Did you get this when we were home?" he asked, and Maggie nodded.

"In that little store beside the coffee shop we went to on Sunday. Fiona dragged me in while Owen was showing you his bike."

Cal's heart warmed with the familiarity in which Maggie spoke of his family, the fondness that lit up her face. "I love it. Between this and the constant rain, it's going to feel like I'm back in Bray. Thank you, love."

"Keep going," she said, practically bouncing.

It took two more gifts, both of which he loved as much as the candle, before Cal got the theme; a noise machine, programmed to play the soft sounds of a quiet beach, and a box stuffed full of different kinds of short-bread, and his parents' favorite Irish breakfast tea, that was impossible to find stateside.

Maggie had recreated home for him here in Seattle, for days when he missed being back in Ireland.

The fourth gift was the softest blanket he'd ever felt, knitted in Bray with a heather gray yarn that felt like clouds as he ran his fingers over it. The fifth stole the breath from his chest. He'd seen Maggie taking pictures around his parents' place for Jazz, she'd said, but she hadn't shown him any of them.

The panorama she'd taken of the view from the back patio captured his parents' home perfectly, and he had to swallow a lump in his throat as he spotted his parents, mid-embrace, in the gazebo.

Cal brushed a hand across the photograph. He missed Ireland, but he missed being there with Maggie more.

"I thought you could hang it in your reading nook, in your bedroom," Maggie explained. "And then with the candle, the sound machine, the tea, and the blanket, you have all five senses covered if you're ever feeling homesick."

How lucky he was to have someone know him so deeply. But Cal never felt homesick when Maggie was around. Whether they were in Ireland, at her house, his apartment, the office, or even the hardware store—he felt like he was exactly where he was supposed to be, as long as he was with Maggie.

Cal set the picture down gently before reaching for her, pulling her into his arms and holding her tightly. "This is the best, most thoughtful gift anyone's ever given me. Thank you, love."

"There's something else," she said, her voice muffled against his chest. "But I'll put it on for you later."

Cal's eyes widened as he imagined taking whatever it was *off* later and all the blood in his body ran south. She was perfect—completely and utterly perfect.

Maggie

Maggie sighed and let the water rush over her body. Cal had ushered her up the stairs and into the bath to relax while he made dinner, but his fingers had lingered on her neck as he unclasped the necklace and it had taken everything Maggie had not to pull him in with her.

They had all night for that; hell, they had a whole week before they had to go back to the real world again. Though Maggie was sure she wouldn't be able to resist checking her emails or working on the Burly's finances during their week off, it didn't seem so bad to do it at home with Cal.

Once her fingers and toes were pruny, Maggie begrudgingly drained the bath and wrapped herself in one of her new towels with a sigh. She was trying not to think about how much money Cal had spent on her—the necklace alone made her shudder to think—and just enjoy herself. Cal wasn't Nathan, who'd given expensive gifts, usually things Maggie had no interest in, just to prove that he could. Cal had truly thought about what she'd like —he'd picked out her favorite colors, and even pre-washed the towels and bedding so she could use them right away.

And the necklace… It was fucking gorgeous, and Cal had noticed that she was a silver jewelry kind of person, not yellow gold. The engagement ring she'd declined had been yellow gold.

Maggie toweled off and slipped into Cal's other Christmas present; scraps of barely there nude mesh, embroidered with sapphire and silver moons and stars with a matching bejeweled garter. The garter was the main event, but the set had worked out better than expected, perfectly matching the necklace he'd given her. She carefully fastened it around her neck, the diamonds and sapphires cool against her skin.

Maggie checked herself out in the mirror, sparkling

like some kind of sapphire fairy. She was going to drive Cal crazy, but they had to get through dinner first. She shrugged on her fluffiest robe, slid her feet into slippers, and skipped down the stairs.

Twinkling caught her peripheral vision as she turned towards the kitchen, and she spun back to the living room, her breath catching in her chest.

Cal was clutching the overpriced silver star she'd splurged on at a Christmas market a couple of years ago, standing beside a fully dressed and glittering Christmas tree, watching her reaction warily.

"I realized about halfway through that you're probably really specific about where everything goes, so you might hate this, but it's your first Christmas here and you should have a tree," he said, all in one breath.

Tears threatened Maggie's eyes, but she blinked them back, not willing to address the emotion coursing through her.

"It's perfect. Thank you," she murmured, crossing the room and leaning into his side.

"Well, almost." Cal handed her the star and lifted her by the waist so she could set it on the top branch. "There. Now it's perfect."

He didn't release her, just slid her down until she was lying in his arms bridal-style. "I love it," Maggie told him.

Cal opened his mouth to respond but stilled as she shifted, and the robe fell open enough to expose a sliver of the garter. "What is that?" he asked, his expression pained.

His voice was low, causing heat to spread over

Maggie's body. "I did promise another present," she said, pushing the robe and exposing more of her thigh.

Cal groaned, his pupils swallowing any shred of green in his eyes. "Dinner can be reheated. We're going upstairs."

"Uh-uh," Maggie said, licking her lips. She wiggled her hips until he gently set her on her feet, an eyebrow raised in confusion.

Maggie pulled a thick quilted blanket from the back of the couch and set it on the ground in front of the tree, before sinking to her knees beneath the sparkly lights. "This is technically a present, so I think that means you have to unwrap me."

Cal hummed, placing a finger under her chin. "And what if I want to do the opposite?"

Maggie raised a brow. "You want to wrap me up?"

He reached behind her, dragging something silky over her shoulder. Maggie tried to look down, but he held her chin firmly. She only realized what was in his hand when he brought it into her line of sight: the green ribbon she'd wrapped around his gifts. He brushed his thumb across her lower lip.

"I want to tie you up."

CHAPTER TWENTY-ONE

Maggie

Maggie's heart raced as Cal drew the soft ribbon over her skin, leaving sparks in its wake.

"Yes. Please." Her breath caught in her throat as Cal tugged on the knot holding the robe together and pushed it over her shoulders. His eyes darkened as they lingered on the garter, but it was the complete and utter adoration on his face when his eyes met hers that made Maggie's stomach do somersaults.

Cal tapped the underside of her chin. "Up."

His voice was soft but commanding, and Maggie rose, leaving the robe behind her under the tree. Cal wound his arms around her middle, hugging her close to him. The ribbon dangled from his fist, tickling the back of her legs. "Are you sure you want to do this?"

"Positive."

Cal searched her face, as if confirming that she was

sure, and, finally, nodded. "Promise me you'll tell me if it's too much and you want to stop."

Maggie held up her pinky. "Pinky promise."

Cal wound his pinky around hers, then tugged her hand behind her back and spun her so her back was pressed against him. He pressed a feather-light kiss in the crook of her neck and Maggie shivered as heat spread across her skin. He pulled her other hand behind her back and wound the ribbon around her wrist—once, twice, three times—before securing it with a knot.

He gently nudged her forward until she was standing in front of the arm of the couch. Cal hooked his thumbs in the sides of her underwear and pushed the embroidered mesh down. "These are too pretty to tear off," he said, sounding almost sad that he couldn't shred the fabric. He didn't unhook her bra, just pushed it down until her breasts spilled over the cups, his thumbs brushing her nipples and teasing the metal bar. Maggie's back arched against him, her body already demanding more.

"Bend over the couch, baby girl." Cal held onto her wrists, keeping her steady as Maggie obliged. He leaned over her, the weight of his body pressing her against the velvet, and littered her skin with kisses, dragging his lips down her body before stepping away.

She heard a rummaging sound somewhere behind her, but with the way her body was positioned, Maggie couldn't peek to see what he was doing. Every one of her senses was on high alert as she felt him kneel behind her and loop another length of soft ribbon around her ankles. "Feet together, love," he murmured.

Maggie squeezed her feet together, and Cal pulled the ribbon, tying it in a tight knot. She didn't need to test it to know it wouldn't budge; with her hands tied behind her back, and her ankles tied together, Maggie was entirely at Cal's mercy.

She spent every second of every day trying to keep everything in her life completely under her control, but this? Handing control of her body over to Cal felt better than she could have imagined. There was no one else she would trust to do this, but she and Cal were so in tune with each other that she knew he would stop if she so much as tensed.

Maggie heard the crinkle of a packet and Cal leaned over her, his beard tickling her shoulder and his lips teasing her skin. But it wasn't his cock he pressed inside her—it was his fingers. She gasped as he curled them, pushing up on to her tiptoes, trying to press him deeper. Cal groaned as she clenched around him, a whimper falling from her lips. Every stroke of his perfect fingers felt like the strike of a match, and Maggie was burning up.

"Promise me again, love," Cal said, his voice low and gravelly. "Promise me you'll tell me if you need to stop."

She needed the opposite of stopping; she needed him inside her. "I pinky promised. It's legally binding," she managed between moans.

"Binding, huh?" Cal tugged on the ribbon around her wrists, pulling her closer to him as he withdrew his fingers and wasted no time replacing them with his cock. Maggie cried out, her body screaming with the urge to reach for him, but she couldn't move her hands. She was pinned beneath him, completely immobile, and every thrust was like a flaming whip against her skin as her body stretched around him. Her vision blurred at the edges as Cal groaned her name, using the bindings around her wrists for leverage, pulling her roughly onto his cock.

"You're so fucking pretty when you take my cock like this, baby girl."

Maggie's thighs shook with the force of Cal's thrusts and her nipples rubbed against the soft green velvet. She whimpered, tightening around Cal's cock at his words.

Cal ran a light finger down her spine, in perfect contrast to how firmly he held her wrists. "Do you like this, love? Do you like letting me take control?"

"*Fuck*," Maggie cried out as he pulled his finger away from her back, only to spank her hard across the ass. The smack reverberated around the room, breaking through the sound of Maggie's blood rushing in her ears. "I love you being in control, Daddy," she gasped, and Cal rewarded her with another smack, the soft ribbon tugging hard enough against her ankles and wrists that she knew they would leave marks—marks she knew Cal would kiss better when they climbed into bed. Marks she knew he would absentmindedly rub while they watched Christmas movies and drank hot chocolate, snuggled up against each other like it was the most natural thing in the world.

And it was that thought—not the bindings, or the dirty talk, or the spanking, or the electric feel of Cal's cock inside her—that tipped Maggie over the edge.

Kaleidoscope colors flashed before her eyes as fire

ripped through her. Maggie struggled against her bonds, but Cal held her firmly, coaxing her through the orgasm with a soft, "Fuck. You feel so good, baby girl."

Maggie cried out Cal's name and felt the moment his control slipped. His knees buckled, his thrusts becoming faster and harder, and Maggie wasn't ready for the second orgasm that rolled through her. Cal's fingers dug into her hips, his breathing ragged as Maggie tightened around him. He came with a soft groan of her name, his upper body collapsing on top of her.

The steady weight of him was better than any blanket Maggie had ever snuggled under, and she whined in protest as he pulled away. Cal chuckled, pressing a gentle kiss between her shoulder blades, before crossing the room and returning a moment later. She felt him sliding something hard between the ribbon and her wrists, and then heard a slice as he cut it off. It slipped down her legs, tickling her skin, and Cal kissed her tender wrists before kneeling to cut the ribbon from her ankles. He stroked his thumbs over the sore spots, then lowered his head to kiss her ankles like he was worshiping her, and Maggie's heart skipped.

"You did so well, love," he murmured as he stood, gently pulling her body up and kissing her forehead. Her cheeks were flushed, his eyes bright, and his hair somehow mussed, despite the fact she hadn't touched him. They collapsed onto the couch, still panting. They turned to face each other at the same time, a sleepy smile stretching over Cal's face.

"Best Christmas ever," Maggie said, her voice hoarse.

"Best Christmas ever," Cal agreed, reaching for her hand and pulling it into his lap so he could rub the red marks circling her wrists.

"**W**hat about Maggie Makes Over?" Maggie wrinkled her nose at the hundredth username idea she and Cal had come up with.

It was the day after Christmas and they'd spent the morning brainstorming ideas for her home renovation TikTok account. They'd even made her first video, editing together before and after clips of some of the finished spaces to a trending song. Well, Maggie had made it—Cal had kept her mimosa topped up, handed her mini pastry bites, and pointed out all his favorite parts of the video.

"It feels unfinished. Maggie Makes Over what?"

"True. M isn't the best letter for home renovation alliteration," Cal said with a sigh, and Maggie laughed.

"It doesn't have to be alliteration."

"I like alliteration," he protested. "It's catchy."

Maggie scoffed, scrolling through yet another list of DIY related words for inspiration. "That's what my parents said when they named me Margaret Mary."

"Your middle name is Mary? It's a good thing you didn't tell my mom that. She would have never let us leave."

Maggie snorted. "What's your middle name? I didn't see one when I was google-stalking you."

Cal hesitated before sighing and saying, "Uilliam. It's the Irish version of William—we got Liam's name from it."

"Huh." Maggie frowned, rolling the word around her brain. "Wait. How do you spell that?" Cal said nothing, but his cheeks turned pink and he was suddenly remarkably interested in his own phone. "Holy shit. Your initials are CUM?"

"We're supposed to be talking about your name," Cal grumbled, and Maggie bit her lip to stop herself from laughing.

"It suits you," she offered, and Cal gave her a look that made it clear she was going to pay for that in bed later.

"Home," he said, changing the subject. At her confused look, he added, "Maggie Makes Home. That's what you're trying to do, right?" It was, but Maggie was finding it harder and harder not to think that Cal was doing a better job of it just by being there, than she was by ripping out the baseboards.

"Maggie Makes Home," she said, tasting the words and letting them wash over her. "Yeah. I like it. Alright, let's do it."

Cal tapped his lap. "Come here. I want to watch."

"You want to watch me set up the account?" she asked with a laugh, but obliged him and settled herself on his lap.

"Hey, if you're going to become a big internet star and leave me, I want to watch it all."

Maggie rolled her eyes. "Neither of those things is going to happen."

Cal wrapped his arms around her and she let herself sink into his chest, his chin on her shoulder, peering down at her phone as she typed in her details. She uploaded her profile picture—a candid shot Cal had taken a couple of weeks ago of her painting the living room. It was blurry, as was the case with most of Cal's pictures if she was being honest, but she'd slapped a hazy filter on top and it almost looked intentional.

"That's it. Now I just need to upload the video."

"Do it," Cal said, his eyes twinkling with a mixture of pride and excitement.

Maggie was, at her core, a planner, and she'd spent the weeks since deciding to start the account researching trends and hashtags. She already had a list of them ready to go, so she slapped them in the caption and watched the bar tick towards a hundred percent as her first video uploaded. Her profile refreshed, showing the single video, and she let out a breath.

"It's up?" Cal asked excitedly, and she nodded. "How do I like it? I want to be the first." His eyes twinkled in the glow of the blinking Christmas tree lights, pride lacing every inch of his perfect face.

Maggie's heart hammered steadily in her chest, thumping stronger than she thought it ever had. *Oh no.* She was falling in love with him. It wasn't the first time the idea had teased the edges of her mind, but it was the first time she'd been unable to stop it from taking root.

It was, without a doubt, the worst idea she'd ever had.

There was no way that this wasn't going to destroy her when it ended—and it would end. She had no intention of losing herself to another person ever again, even if that person *was* as kind and supportive as Cal. Once upon a time, Nathan had been kind too.

"Love?"

Maggie blinked, Cal's voice pulling her back to the present, his phone clutched in his hand. "Huh? Oh. You just start by opening TikTok. You should still be logged in from when we set it up the other day."

"Are you okay?" he asked, eyeing her with concern instead of looking at his phone as he punched his pass-code in wrong—twice.

Maggie held the phone up, so it recognized his face, and nodded. "Mhmm. Fine. Yep."

Cal narrowed his eyes, but didn't press. He never did, even though she knew he saw through every lie she told. Not in the sense that he didn't care, but like he was waiting for her to come to him when she was ready. She wanted to say that was the kind of emotional maturity that came naturally after fifty years, but her parents still acted like fucking teenagers half the time, so maybe it was just Cal.

And maybe she should never compare him to her parents ever again. *Jesus.*

Cal bit his tongue in concentration as she directed him to her profile and showed him how to follow her and like the video.

"There," she said, watching her follower count tick from zero to one. "You're officially my first follower."

"As it should be, since I am your number one fan," Cal pointed out, a proud smile on his perfect face. "So what's next?"

"Finishing the house, I suppose," Maggie said with a sigh, looking around the living room with a sigh. "Not today, though. I'm exhausted." Though she'd tried to sleep in—and sometimes managed when Cal tired her out enough—she'd been woken up before the sun by her mom, calling to ask if Maggie knew where the spare handset for the cafe's landline was. She didn't, and her mom had wanted her to drive up to find it, but Cal had rolled over in his sleep, the blankets slipping to reveal his naked torso, and Maggie had had no intention of going anywhere. She'd ordered a couple of spare handsets with two-day shipping to the cafe, told her mom she'd have to wait, and pounced on Cal the second she'd hung up.

"Let's have a quiet day," Cal agreed, kissing her temple. "Why don't I go make some popcorn, and you head up to bed and queue up *LoveStruck*."

"You know, we could watch something you like for a change," Maggie suggested, laughing at Cal's instant protesting head shake. Though he'd only agreed to watch the trashy reality dating show begrudgingly, and with a drink in hand, he'd been hooked by the end of the first episode.

"Are you kidding? I need to know what Lila does when she finds out Kai and Maren hooked up—quit laughing at me."

Maggie darted out of reach just before he swatted her ass, but he caught her at the foot of the stairs with a crushing kiss. "You're sure you're okay?" he asked when they broke apart and Maggie didn't hesitate before nodding.

Even if he didn't buy her lies, she wasn't giving up so easily; even if it was written all over her face, she had to keep it in. Cal couldn't know exactly how she was feeling, because she didn't want to know what he would think of it.

Maybe it was one sided, and he'd let her down gently, ending their arrangement because she couldn't keep her fucking heart in check. Or maybe it wasn't, and he wanted more—more from them, more from her. But Maggie didn't have any more energy to give; between work, Burly's, and the house, she was already stretched thin enough that she was bursting at the seams. What she and Cal had worked because it didn't add any extra pressure to her life. She couldn't handle *more*, even if she couldn't always pretend she didn't want it.

"Of course I'm okay." She mustered up the most convincing smile her racing heart allowed and pulled out of his grip. "Don't forget the pretzels," she called down the stairs as she skipped up two at a time.

CHAPTER TWENTY-TWO

Cal stared around the function room and shook his head. Where the hell had she found time to do all this? He hadn't questioned the parties Maggie had organized over the past five years, just handed over the company credit card and told her to do whatever it took to give the team the night they deserved. But now that he spent so much time with her, and had become more aware of just how much she did at the office, he couldn't figure out how she'd done it all.

The theme was midnight, and Maggie had nailed it. Swathed in sheer silver streamers that gave off a moonlit effect, and hundreds of twinkling stars hung from the ceiling, the room was magical. The cocktails had swirling blue glitter and tiny gold moon sprinkles, and the buffet looked like something out of a magazine. Though she hadn't set the party up herself, he'd seen her pouring over her tablet, working on mood boards and sketches to send to the venue coordinator, and they'd done an incredible job bringing Maggie's vision to life.

It was their third year celebrating in the penthouse venue, the floor to ceiling windows making it the perfect spot to watch the fireworks when the clock struck midnight. Cal stood by the window, staring down at the blurry skyline through the thin film of raindrops that covered the glass. He wasn't avoiding everyone, he was just… waiting. And it would have been sad to stare at the door until Maggie arrived, so he'd chosen the window instead.

"Hey, Dad."

Cal turned away from the rain and smiled as Liam, Eliza, and Danisha approached. He pulled Liam into a hug. "Hey. How are you doing?"

Cal took him in, surprised. The purple smudges that had become a permanent feature of his son's face recently had faded, and he was finally wearing something other than his collection of classical art sweatshirts.

"I'm good, yeah," Liam said, and, for the first time in a while, he sounded like he meant it.

Relief flooded Cal. It was something he hadn't been prepared for, when he'd become a father—just how much you worried, even when they were all grown up. Not that he'd been prepared for anything when he'd become a father, but Liam had turned out well despite his and Eliza's struggles.

He hugged Danisha and Eliza, rolling his eyes when

his ex-wife greeted him with, "Is Maggie here? I can't see her."

"Not yet, but she's coming," he assured her, tamping down the jealous monster threatening to rear its head in his chest.

Jazz had kicked him out of Maggie's house, insisting that them getting ready together on New Year's Eve was a tradition even if they didn't get to spend the night together anymore. Not that Maggie hadn't tried to convince Jazz to come to the party instead of putting herself through a night with her family—who sounded worse than Maggie's, if that was possible—but Jazz had said no, while downing half a glass of wine.

Cal glanced around the room and then at his watch. He frowned, wondering how clingy it would look if he texted to check on her. It looked like Maggie was the last to arrive, and, even though she was far from late, he knew how much she would hate that.

"You know, Eliza," he started, quietly so that Liam couldn't hear. "I still don't think it's a good idea to—"

"Isn't that her?" Danisha interrupted, and Cal's head snapped up. Sure enough, Maggie was standing in the doorway, unbuttoning her coat. She shrugged it off, handing it to the attendant with a smile, and turned towards the party.

Cal almost moaned. If he'd thought the venue captured midnight well, it was nothing on Maggie. Her navy blue dress shimmered silver in the light as she walked into the room, a long slit in the skirt exposing one leg. Thin chain straps held the dress up, and the sapphire necklace he'd given her shone around her neck. She sparkled like the night sky, her eyes lined with smokey blue and so much glitter that he knew Jazz must have done her makeup.

Her gaze swept over the table and decor, checking that everything was perfect. Her shoulders relaxed, and a smile settled on her maroon lips. She looked onto the dance floor, eyes searching, and Cal's breath caught in his throat as he realized what she was looking for: him.

"Oh. Well, *that* explains it."

Cal pulled his eyes from Maggie to Eliza, who was watching him with an all-too-knowing expression.

"I have no idea what you're talking about." He had no issue with Eliza knowing there was something going on between Maggie and him, but he still had no idea how to explain it. And he wasn't sure how Liam would take it, given that Maggie was almost seven years younger than him.

"Really?" Eliza replied, fighting a laugh. Liam and Danisha were, thankfully, lost in conversation about Liam's job. "So I suppose you won't mind if I suggest to Liam—"

"No."

"Noted." She sipped her whiskey sour and shook her head—at least she was smiling. "Is it mutual?"

"Yeah, but it's complicated."

"Because she's your twenty-seven-year-old assistant?"

Cal furrowed his brow, and Eliza quickly added, "No judgment! It's just… twenty-seven? God."

"Tell me about it," Cal replied with a sigh. He knew Maggie couldn't care less about how old he was, but he couldn't let himself forget that she had her whole life ahead of her and that life didn't include him.

"What's she doing?" Eliza asked, frowning at the circle of people who had surrounded Maggie.

Her smile was still firmly in place, but it was a world away from the relaxed smile he'd been lucky enough to live with for the past week; Maggie was back in work mode. Two days early.

He hoped she was telling the half dozen employees around her that she'd deal with whatever they were asking when they were back in the office on Tuesday, but Cal knew her better than that.

"Fucking hell," he cursed, as she took a deep breath and pulled her tablet from her purse.

Eliza followed as he crossed the floor towards the little group. Maggie looked from her tablet as they approached, her eyes lighting up as they landed on him. Cal looked pointedly at the tablet, and her expression morphed into one that clearly said *guilty*.

"Put it away, love."

"But—"

"Away."

Her eyes flashed, and Cal knew that, as much as she loved it when he got a little bossy with her, she hated that she couldn't answer back—and reap the rewards—when they were around other people.

She huffed out a breath, the movement making the

diamonds around her neck sparkle. It was torture, being so close to her and not being able to kiss her.

"It's just a couple of things," she said, and Cal turned towards the group crowding her.

"What's so important that you need Maggie to do it before Tuesday?" he asked, and they exchanged looks.

"Well, I accidentally locked myself out of my emails," Eric Nowak, a junior attorney who locked himself out of his emails at least once a month, piped up.

"Do you really need your emails before Tuesday?" Cal asked, and he shrugged, shaking his head. "Perfect. Tech can sort it on Tuesday."

"I'll set up an appoint—"

"Put the tablet away, Maggie," he implored. "Anyone else?" He breathed a sigh of relief as, one by one, his employees shook their heads. "Good. This is the only week of the year we force Maggie to take time off, so let's leave work at the door. If anything is urgent, come to me."

The group mumbled apologies and split off, back to their friends and families. Cal turned back to Maggie, who was still clutching the tablet, and held a hand out. He really had to find a way to stop her from taking on so much work.

She sighed and rolled her eyes, but placed the tablet in his hand anyway. "Excuse me," he said, stopping a passing waiter. "Would you mind please dropping this at the coat check under Maggie Burlington?"

"Of course."

He rushed off with the tablet and Cal finally let himself step closer to Maggie. "Hi."

"Hi."

"You look beautiful, love," he told her, her cheeks and chest turning pink.

"Thank you. You do too," she replied, quietly, eyes brighter than the disco ball rotating above them. She looked up, suddenly spying Eliza. "And you, Eliza—you look incredible. It's good to see you again."

It was impressive how quickly she slipped from the Maggie she was when it was just the two of them, to the Maggie who wore a mask for the sake of everyone else. Cal fucking hated it.

"Hey, Maggie. You too. That necklace is gorgeous," Eliza offered and Maggie lifted her hand, brushing the necklace.

Maggie's smile softened, and Cal's blood warmed in response. "Thanks. It was a Christmas present."

She didn't so much as glance at him, far better at being discreet than he was, but Eliza whistled anyway. "There's no way you picked that yourself," she told him, and Maggie's mouth popped open, her eyes wide.

"Eliza knows," he explained.

"Yeah, I got that."

"And I did pick it," he told Eliza. "With the help of three store associates, sure, but I *did* pick it."

Maggie and Eliza both laughed. Maggie smiled up at him and said, "Well, you did a great job. I love it."

"I didn't plan on it matching the theme," he said, gesturing to the party. "But..." He ran his gaze over her midnight themed dress and the matching necklace, watching Maggie swallow as it branded her. "Wow."

"You two are cute," Eliza said with a sigh. "And also kind of hot. Am I allowed to say that? I'm saying it anyway."

"Are you allowed to say what?"

The three of them started, spinning around to find Liam and Danisha staring at them curiously.

Eliza didn't hesitate before responding, "That I miss that heatwave we had in July."

"You're absolutely not allowed to say that," her wife replied, frowning. "It killed my hydrangeas."

"And you complained every day for a month straight," Liam chimed in. "Hey, Maggie."

"Hi," Maggie replied with a smile, and Cal wondered why he'd bothered to let the jealousy take root; Maggie smiled at Liam like she did at everyone, but she smiled at him like it was just for him. He had nothing to worry about.

Liam looked out over the dance floor and tilted his head before looking back at Maggie and taking a deep breath. "Do you want to dance?"

"Oh." Maggie hesitated for a split second, but Cal knew her mind worked so quickly that she was likely searching through it for an excuse to say no. And apparently coming up empty. "Sure."

Liam grinned as she took his offered hand, leading her out onto the floor where half the office was already dancing. Maggie glanced back towards Cal, her expression a little sad, and the jealousy swelled in his chest, but not for the reasons he expected it to: Liam could ask her to dance and hold her on the dance floor without worrying about what people would say. He could kiss her at midnight and no one would bat an eye, and maybe he couldn't quite have sixty years with her, but he could have a hell of a lot longer than Cal could.

It wasn't about Liam. He knew, regardless of how and when things ended between him and Maggie, that she would never move on with his son. But she would move on, and there would be someone who could do all that and more with her. And he would be left behind.

Maggie

"How are you doing?" she asked Liam as he twirled her around the floor. He looked better than she'd imagined, based on how Cal had described their Christmas morning.

Liam looked more like Eliza than he did Cal, with dark wavy hair and olive-toned skin, but he was tall, like his dad, and he had Cal's dimples when he smiled. And, of course, the lethal emerald eyes. "I'm good, yeah. Busy with work and shit, but surviving. How have you been? My mom mentioned you and your boyfriend broke up?"

Ah, yes; she'd forgotten that Eliza had planned on setting them up. "Oh, I'm fine. Better than, actually. Best decision I've ever made. How are you managing everything?"

She didn't need to specify that she was talking about *his* breakup. Liam shrugged and, though his eyes still had an edge of sadness, his expression was one of sheer determination. "I've been a bit of a wreck, but I don't want to go into the new year like that, so I figured I'd better get my shit together."

"That's a good attitude."

There was no spark between them, no heat where his hand sat on her waist or his eyes lingered on her skin. She liked Liam; he was a nice guy and, even if she felt weird saying it since she was sleeping with his dad, he *was* gorgeous, but he wasn't Cal. Not for her.

When the song ended, she excused herself to the bar, pausing every few steps to speak to someone new. She wracked her brain to remember the name of every friend and family member who had attended previous parties, and filed away the new faces for next year.

As she chatted with Grant and his parents, she wondered what it was like to like your family enough that you voluntarily invited them to spend time with you. If Maggie didn't text the family group chat at midnight, she would never hear so much as a *Happy New Year* from a single member of the Burlington family—and she would text them, even if it pained her. She'd already asked her parents and siblings about their plans for the night, but they hadn't bothered to ask her.

She didn't avoid Cal as the night wore on, she just didn't seek him out. She was always perfectly aware of exactly where he was standing in the room, his presence drawing her in like a magnet, but it was hard to be around him with alcohol in her system and keep her hands to herself. Their week of playing house had spoiled her, and she'd forgotten what it was like to pretend she wasn't crazy about him at work.

He found her standing by the ravaged buffet table, recharging her social battery in the shadowy corner. "Hey love."

Cal glanced quickly around the room before reaching out and threading his fingers with hers. Maggie could have groaned at the touch—it had only been a few hours, but after a week straight of touching him, it had been killing her. She was pretty sure most people would call that withdrawal but, like the way she ignored how she couldn't function without three cups of coffee a day, she wasn't addressing it.

"I have to give my speech soon," Cal said, wrinkling his nose. "Almost midnight. Will you come stand with me?"

"Of course." She always stood with Cal when he made his end-of-year speech. For someone who was so comfortable standing up in court, he hated public speaking. Still, better him than Ben Hicks (who spent his Christmas vacation in the South of France every year, and hadn't attended a single one of the company New Year parties since she'd joined Michaelson and Hicks, despite being the one to implement them a decade ago.)

"Thanks." Cal sighed, running his thumb across the back of her hand. "I really don't want to let go."

Oh. "Me either," she promised, softly. "But just a few hours to go and then we can go back to your place."

"True." He squeezed her hand once before dropping it, and Maggie wrapped her arms around herself, fighting the sudden chill.

She followed him to the front of the room where the DJ was working. Cal leaned into the booth and said something too quietly for her to hear, but the DJ nodded and handed him a microphone, gradually lowering the volume of the music.

Maggie offered Cal a reassuring smile as he cleared his throat, schooling his expression into one that didn't make it obvious he hoped the ground would swallow him up.

"Good evening, everyone," he began, his voice smooth. Already, the room hung onto his every word. He really had no idea how devastating that accent was. "It's so good to see you all here tonight. It's been another incredible year for Michaelson and Hicks and we couldn't have done it without you. I won't bore you all with stats—especially since I know Maggie has spent hours making an end-of-year recap presentation for next week's company meeting."

It was true; Maggie loved statistics almost as much as she loved a PowerPoint. Cal had hovered over her shoulder and watched in awe as she'd done the bare minimum of slapping a design template on the presentation, as if she'd hand painted the thing.

"But something that's been really nice to see in the office this year is how many firsts we've had. From first-time parents—" He nodded to Brett Kennedy and his husband. "To first-time marathon runners—" Twyla.

"And first-time homeowners." His smile settled on Maggie. "And so much more. I'm so happy and proud to see you all doing so well."

He thanked the venue, and Maggie for planning the party, and handed the microphone back with a sigh of relief. A projector buzzed to life, shining the countdown to midnight on the wall as Cal and Maggie walked across the room towards his family.

She hated this part, where everyone gathered in groups of their favorite people and counted down to new beginnings. Maggie was used to standing alone, since Nathan had refused point blank to attend the parties and Jazz could never get out of her parents' parties. It wasn't that she wasn't friendly with everyone at the office, she just wasn't friends. Though her job title was Cal's assistant, the role itself was more like an office manager and the team were never completely relaxed around her. Or maybe she didn't know how to be relaxed around them; hell, did she know how to be relaxed period?

At times, she was calmer than she ever had been these days, in the quiet hours when she and Cal weren't working or tearing each other's clothes off. She'd learned to relax into his lilting laugh, to let the way he absent-mindedly toyed with the tassels on her favorite blanket while they watched TV soothe her ever racing mind. But it was also too easy for those moments to turn into more than she could let them, and with the rush of feelings for Cal came the wave of panic, cresting over her but never crashing. Maggie knew she couldn't avoid the swell forever, but for now…

"Cheek."

She started, looking up at Cal in confusion. He was standing closer to her than he should be at a work event, his sleeve a hairsbreadth from her arm. "What?" she asked.

"I don't think it would be totally inappropriate for me to kiss your cheek at midnight."

It would be, and they both knew it. Cal would never kiss another employee's cheek, even if they were both alone at a New Year's Eve party. But they were standing at the back of the crowd, with only Eliza and Danisha standing close enough to notice. Liam had disappeared, and she didn't blame him; as glad as she was sure he would be to say goodbye to the year, he probably didn't want an audience to do it.

"I think that would be okay," Maggie replied softly, and Cal's face lit up.

The room began chanting, counting down from ten, but Cal's gaze didn't leave Maggie's. Midnight struck, cheers and fireworks sounding, and he ducked his head to brush his lips across her cheek.

"Happy New Year, baby," he whispered against her skin, and Maggie breathed in the closeness of him, her lips lifting automatically. It was the closest they'd been to *them* outside of their homes or his office, and fuck... Maggie could get used to that.

CHAPTER TWENTY-THREE

Maggie

Maggie stared from the blaring phone clutched in Cal's hand, to the man himself, engrossed in the videos swiping along the screen, to the table full of employees just trying to enjoy their lunch hour.

"What are you doing?" she asked, and Cal looked up, smiling widely at the sight of her.

"Just TikToking. Did you know people talk about books here? I'm getting so many recommendations."

Despite the note-taking capability of the twelve-hundred dollar phone he was holding, he pulled an honest-to-God slip of paper from his pocket and showed her the list of book titles printed in his perfect script. It was fucking adorable, even if everyone else in the room side eyed him a little.

Maggie pulled out the seat beside him and sat down. "That's great. But, uh, you shouldn't really have the volume on if you're looking through TikTok around other people."

Cal frowned. "But no one else is watching anything."

"Right. That's true, but…" Maggie glanced around the room, but apparently no one was up for helping her out. Josie hid her smile behind her coffee cup, and Grant was adamantly avoiding making any kind of eye contact with her as he fought a laugh. "You're just going to have to trust me on this one. It's an internet etiquette thing," she finished, and Cal shrugged, turning the volume down.

"I'll take your word for it. This thing is addictive," he added, with a sigh, swiping through his feed.

"Tell me about it," Josie chimed in. "I swear I open my phone after dinner and suddenly it's bedtime."

"Same," Grant agreed, and Cal leaned forward.

"You guys are on TikTok?"

"Cal," Maggie warned, knowing exactly where this was going.

As expected, he ignored her as Josie and Grant nodded. He held his phone up. "You should follow Maggie. She posts about her house renovation." He turned his phone around to show them, and Maggie's cheeks burned.

Since she'd started the account, Cal had taken every opportunity to promote it. Not only had he put the link in the Michaelson family group chat—which Maggie had, much to her confusion, been added to—and told his siblings to share the account with all their friends, but she'd come back from the restroom at Wholefoods a few days ago to find him showing her page to the barista making her matcha. He'd done more to promote it than she had.

She'd racked up a couple thousand followers in her first week posting clips from around the house, and she'd already had some great advice on refinishing her stairs. It only took an hour a day to film, edit, post, and comment —no small feat with her level of perfectionism—but she was enjoying figuring out something new.

"This is amazing, Maggie," Josie said, eyeing the videos on Cal's phone appreciatively. "Did you design all this yourself?"

"Thanks. Yeah, but a lot of it is just bringing out the house's original features and making them shine."

"It looks amazing. I bet you could do this for people —design and organize things," Grant suggested. "You're the most organized person I know."

"You'd do a better job than the guy who designed my apartment, that's for sure," Cal said, shaking his head and standing up, coffee cup in hand. "The place looks like a show home."

He wasn't wrong; Maggie was itching to make it more homey.

Cal leaned in towards her, then stilled, as if realizing he'd almost kissed her goodbye at work. Maggie leaned back with a jolt, her heart thundering. *What was he doing?* Cal's eyes widened a fraction, but he recovered, pulling back and pushing his chair under the table. "Enjoy the rest of your lunch, everyone. And make sure you follow Maggie," he added before waving and exiting the kitchen.

Maggie watched him go, unable to hide the smile on her face.

"It's nice that you two are so… close."

She turned to look at Josie, who was fighting a smile of her own. An all-too-knowing smile.

"I wouldn't say we're close," she replied, carefully. "But we spend a lot of time together, sorting through things and waiting for clients. We're not closer than anyone else is here." And now she was protesting too much. *Shit.*

"You're definitely his favorite," Grant said. "I don't know how you survive him calling you *love* in that accent. Now me? I'd have keeled over the first time he did it."

"He calls everyone love. It's an Irish thing."

"Nope. Just you," Demi, who had mostly been keeping to herself in the corner, piped up.

Maggie's brow knit together. "That's not true."

She wracked her brain, trying to remember him calling some else at the office *love*, but came up blank. She had to be misremembering; Cal had called her *love* since her first day, and she'd always just assumed it was common in Ireland. His family used the pet name on the phone, and in person.

"I've worked with Cal for twenty years," Josie said, that dangerously knowing smile in full force. "And I've never heard him call anyone else *love*. You're definitely his favorite."

Well, fuck. That was a lot to unpack.

"He doesn't have favorites," Maggie said, gathering her stuff and standing up. "And it's just a nickname."

Josie's answering *sure* followed her as she all but ran out of the kitchen. She dropped her cup and tablet on her desk and sank into the plush seat, letting her head fall onto her hand as she loosed a breath.

Cal had shown zero interest in her before they'd run into each other at the club. It wasn't like he'd been harboring some secret crush on her for the past six years. Hell, he was fifty-five; he didn't get *crushes*. Sure, he'd always been kind to her, but he was kind to all his employees. Maybe he'd organized cupcakes for her birthday, and sent flowers when she'd closed on the house, but that was just because she usually organized shit like that for everyone else. It didn't mean anything. It was just a nickname.

Maggie shook herself. She was spending too much time muddled in her feelings these days, and she was too busy for that. She opened her to-do list and was three pages deep into a client file, checking that they'd submitted everything they'd been asked to, when her phone chimed with a message from an unknown number.

Maggie frowned at it—aside from Jazz, Cal (who had finally given in to texting), and her parents when they wanted something, no one texted her. It was a little sad how surprised she was by an unexpected message.

She opened the message and sat back in her chair as she scanned the message, shock rippling through her.

"What the hell?" she whispered to herself.

> Hey Maggie, it's Liam. It was good to
> see you at the weekend. If you're
> around tomorrow night, I'd love to take
> you to dinner. Hope you're having a
> good day.

He'd almost kissed her in the middle of the fucking kitchen, in front of half a dozen people. The panic that flashed across her face as she leaned away from him had felt like a punch to the gut. Maggie had enough to worry about, and he didn't need to add to it. Cal was slipping closer and closer to the flimsy lines they were trying desperately to uphold.

Despite being back at work, they were still spending every night together. They went back and forth between Maggie's place and his, never stopping to talk about what that meant.

He'd been struggling since the party, the sight of her with Liam burned in his brain. It wasn't about Liam; it was the thought of Maggie dating anyone who wasn't him, even though he knew, ultimately, that's where this was going. They were approaching a crossroads, and he was going to have to walk away, but until then, he was letting himself enjoy every moment. A little too much, if the almost-kiss in the kitchen was anything to go by.

Cal hoped they would stay friends when it ended,

even if he wasn't sure how to be *just* friends with her after this. He would figure out how to make it work, and he'd make sure she would never know how much it killed him.

The elevator sounded, and Cal looked up. Maggie appeared in the doorway, biting her lip and drumming her nails against her tablet.

"Hey, what's wrong?" he asked. Maggie stilled before his desk, but said nothing, as if having to think. "Are you worried because I almost kissed you in the kitchen? Because I don't think anyone noticed."

"No," Maggie said, shaking her head. "And they did —well, Josie did at least. But that's not it."

Of course Josie had noticed. Cal searched Maggie's face and found lingering traces of panic in her eyes. Christ, he'd fucked up.

Maggie dropped into the chair across from him and set the tablet on her lap. "Did you give Liam my number?"

"My Liam?" he asked, and Maggie nodded. Confusion settled over Cal. "No, but I gave him my phone on Sunday night to call a cab when his died. Why? Did he call you?"

"He texted me." Maggie looked away from him, staring out the window, her knee bouncing. "He, uh, he asked me out for tomorrow night."

Something like fire flared in Cal's chest, burning hot enough to make him hold his breath. "Oh. And what did you say?"

Maggie turned back to him, her face set in a frown.

"What? I mean, I haven't replied yet but considering I'm his dad's... I don't even know what to call this—employee with benefits?—I'm obviously going to say no."

Employee with benefits.

It wasn't anything but the truth, but Cal was crushed under the weight of the words. He couldn't blame her, no matter how much it hurt. It was what they'd agreed to, and it wasn't her fault he was doing such a shitty job of holding up his end of the bargain. Discreet. That's all she'd asked for, and he'd fucked it up. Cal couldn't stop replaying that flash of panic in his head.

They hadn't been friends before this, and she'd never implied she wanted anything more from him than sex. He was the one that had added the *hanging out* stipulation to their arrangement, and he'd never been under any illusion that they would keep doing this forever.

She deserves better. She deserved someone like Liam —someone she didn't have to be *discreet* with, someone who would give her a long, happy life and treat her better than Nathan had.

Maybe the almost-kiss in the kitchen was a sign that it was time for them to end things, before Cal's feelings messed things up beyond the point of salvation and she didn't feel comfortable working with anymore.

"You should say yes." The words didn't sound like his own.

Maggie's face fell. "I'm sorry. What?"

Cal looked down at the paperwork on his desk, gripping the edge of his chair like a vise. He cleared his throat. "Liam's a good guy and you're a... You would be good together. It's not like this was ever going to go further between us, anyway, so… You should say yes."

Maggie recoiled, her back pressing into the back of the chair as if trying to get away from him. Cal's fingers twitched, desperate to reach for her.

"Are you being serious? What the fuck, Cal?"

"Yeah. It's probably for the best anyway." Every word was like ash in his mouth.

"I guess that means this—" she gestured between them, her hands shaking slightly. "—is done?"

It felt like dragging his head through mud when Cal forced himself to nod.

"Right." Maggie's voice was steady as she stood to leave, her face the picture of neutrality. Only her eyes betrayed her, the blue dull with a mix of confusion and sadness. The sight was like a knife in his chest, but Cal didn't let himself waver. There was no point in delaying the inevitable and Maggie deserved better, even if she couldn't see it right now.

Maggie turned towards the door, each step shattering some piece of him beyond repair. He couldn't let them leave it on such treacherous ground.

Work. Maggie would feel better if he pulled them back into colleague territory.

"Maggie."

She stilled, but didn't turn around, just looking at him over her shoulder. "Yeah?"

"Do you know if Jazz is still looking for a job?" She'd spent two hours complaining about her boss when she'd come over to Maggie's for dinner the week before.

"I think so, yeah. Why?"

"I'm thinking of hiring a new assistant. You know, someone to take appointment calls, sort out paperwork and stuff. I was thinking Jazz might be a good fit."

Maggie spun around, eyes wide. "But that's my job," she stammered. "Is this because... Are you firing me?" Her voice cracked and every fiber of Cal's being demanded he pull her into his arms. But he couldn't, not anymore.

"What? No, of course not. You just have so much on your plate. You're juggling too much. The new assistant would be *your* assistant, to free up your time for everything else you do." Which was everything, pretty much. He would reevaluate her contract at her yearly review; she needed a pay rise, and probably a title promotion, considering all that she did.

Maggie's shoulders slumped in relief. "Oh. That's not necessary. You don't have to—" she cut off, clearly realizing that it was a done deal in whatever she saw on his face. "Thank you. Do you want me to set up an interview?"

"I can do that," he said. "Can you forward her details over?"

"Sure. Thank you." Her voice was stiff and too formal.

"You're welcome," he replied. "And, uh, have fun tomorrow. With Liam." *Why the fuck did he say that?*

Maggie said nothing, but the mask slipped, and her eyes flared. She spun on her heel and left the room, pulling the door closed behind her with more force than usual.

Cal let out a long breath when he heard the elevator close, rubbing his forehead. *What a fucking mess.*

When his phone pinged with Jazz's contact details, he tried not to look up the text thread at the messages he and Maggie had sent that morning; promises of bubble baths and wine, theories about the stupid reality show she'd gotten him hooked on. Nothing to suggest that a few hours later, whatever bubble they'd surrounded themselves with would implode.

He closed out of the messages and punched Jazz's number into the phone on his desk.

"Hello?" she answered after a few rings.

"Hey, Jazz. It's Cal—Maggie's Cal." It slipped out before he could stop it. It was unnecessary—how many Irish Cals could Jazz possibly know—and untrue, acrid on his tongue.

"Oh my God, is Maggie okay?"

Cal winced. "Oh, yeah, she's fine. Sorry, I didn't mean to worry you."

"Thank God," Jazz replied with a laugh. "So what's up?"

"Are you still looking for a job?"

"Are you kidding me? My boss made me buy flowers for his wife *and* both of his mistresses this morning. I'm definitely looking."

Despite himself, Cal chuckled. Jazz was one of three personal assistants to the owner of a luxury department store, and he sounded exactly like most of the rich business owners on the Michaelson and Hicks' roster.

"Well, I'm looking to hire an admin assistant—an assistant for Maggie, essentially—and I know the two of you worked together in college, so I wondered if you wanted to come in for an interview?"

"Oh, wow. Yeah, absolutely. Thanks for thinking of me," Jazz replied, surprise lighting her voice.

"Of course. Are you around tomorrow afternoon? Say two?"

"Yeah, that works for me."

"Perfect. I'll email you the details." He would have to figure out how to set up a calendar invite, but he'd been getting better at that kind of shit since he and Maggie… Cal shook himself.

"Thanks. I'll see you then," Jazz replied, and they said their goodbyes before hanging up.

Sending the invite was far easier than he'd expected, and Cal looked at the clock with a sigh once it was done. There was still an hour in the day, but what was the point of owning your own firm if you couldn't leave early once in a while? He turned off the computer, shouldered his bag, and locked the office door behind him.

It wasn't until he was sitting in his car, Maggie's lilac perfume lingering in the air, that he realized he was going home alone for the first time in a long time.

CHAPTER TWENTY-FOUR

Maggie

M aggie glared at the Christmas tree, twinkling in the corner like nothing had changed. She and Cal had planned to order from his favorite Indian restaurant, get a little wine drunk, and take down the decorations over the coming weekend. Now it was just a reminder that she'd be sleeping alone.

"Stop staring at it like that," Jazz said, nudging her with a Halloween sock covered foot. "You'll set it on fire if you're not careful."

Jazz had texted her as soon as she'd hung up with Cal.

> Why didn't you tell me your secret sex buddy was hiring?????

> Because he's not mine anymore.

Maggie had pressed send, swallowing back something suspiciously close to tears.

> I'll be at your place for six. I'll bring ice cream!!!

Jazz had responded instantly, and Maggie's heart was soothed a little knowing that, even if she didn't have Cal anymore (had she ever really had Cal?), her best friend would always be there.

Maggie groaned, burrowing into the couch so she didn't have to look at the tree. They usually did Jazz's breakup ice cream nights in bed, but Maggie wasn't sure she could face the wrinkled sheets she and Cal had slept in just last night yet.

"Just so I'm clear: you're going out to dinner tomorrow night with Liam?" Jazz asked.

"I don't want to talk about it," Maggie grumbled. Even hearing it hurt. "But yes."

"Hmm."

Maggie turned her glare on her best friend. "What?"

"I think you know what. But let's pretend Liam *isn't* Cal's son for a moment—where are you going and what are you wearing?"

"Some new Italian place near the office," Maggie replied with a sigh. "Liam suggested it. And I'm going straight from work, so I was just planning on wearing my work clothes. They're fancy enough."

Jazz eyed the discarded pencil skirt and lilac sweater Maggie had stripped off and folded on the armchair as soon as she'd walked into the house and seen the fluffy new PJs Jazz had brought her. "That's being generous, but okay. Nice underwear?"

"I'm not sleeping with him," Maggie said quickly, grimacing.

Jazz tried and failed to fight a laugh at her expression. "Why not? You were always a sex on the first date kind of girl before Nathan."

"Yeah, well, people change."

"Sure. Or maybe, and I'm just throwing it out there, the thought of sleeping with Liam makes you look like you want to throw up because you're in love with—"

"Jazz," Maggie said sharply, cutting her best friend off. She didn't need to hear that right now. "It's just dinner. It'll be fine. I can muster up a smile enough for one meal."

"If you don't want to go, you don't have to."

"I agreed to go. It would be rude to back out."

Jazz threw up her hands in frustration, almost knocking over the pint of strawberry ice cream balancing precariously on her lap. "Why did you agree then?"

"Because Cal told me to!" Maggie shouted back, and Jazz's eyes widened.

"And what? You're just doing what you're told by some guy now?"

"He's not just some guy," Maggie protested. "He's my... He's Cal." Just Cal. Not her anything.

"Maggie—"

"We weren't dating. I don't even know if we were

friends," Maggie interrupted. "I just... I don't want to talk about it. Okay?"

Jazz looked like she might protest, but shook her head, thinking better of it. "Do you want to help me prep for my interview?"

Work. Maggie could do work. "Absolutely."

Maggie threw herself into prepping Jazz for her interview with Cal, giving her a rundown of the history of the firm and how the different departments functioned. Like Maggie before her internship, Jazz had little to no legal knowledge, let alone business law. Cal wouldn't be expecting any, but it calmed Maggie's racing mind to give Jazz the basics.

Maggie strongly suspected Cal wouldn't ask about anything they'd prepped; in fact, she was pretty sure Jazz already had the job. For her. It might have bothered her if it had been anyone else, but, as chaotic as her best friend was, Jazz was a damn good assistant. She'd been working for the same asshole CEO for years, and she deserved a work environment that didn't make her want to tear her own hair out.

Maggie and Jazz had always worked well together. They'd been best friends since middle school, got their first jobs together in high school, and when Maggie had become Jazz's supervisor during their college stint as baristas, it had been easy. Though Jazz liked to take the reins in her personal life, she didn't mind handing them over at work.

So even if Cal was all but giving her a job, Maggie knew she would prove she deserved it in no time.

Jazz left as the moon crested the Seattle sky, but Maggie didn't go to bed. She dragged her heels back into the living room, took a deep breath and, blinking back tears, took down the Christmas tree.

Cal pretended to scan Jazz's resume while she glanced around his office. Her eyes lingered on the couch sitting outside the door and Cal looked down.

He hadn't seen Maggie, but he knew she'd been in his office bright and early before he'd arrived. Her lilac perfume had settled on every surface of the room, but that wasn't the biggest giveaway; the place was spotless. Not just his office—the first floor offices, the kitchen, even the bathroom supply closet. Everywhere Cal had been over the course of the day was just a little neater, a little more organized than it had been when he'd left the night before. He didn't want to think about what time she must have arrived.

There had been a three-page detailed schedule for the following week printed and waiting for him on his desk when he'd sat down, and a copy in his email inbox. He and Maggie usually spent their Friday mornings making the schedule together, but she was avoiding him. There was no other explanation.

"Cal?"

He looked up, suddenly remembering that he wasn't

alone. "Hmm?"

Jazz's eyebrows drew together. "Did you have any questions for me?"

Shit. This was an interview. Cal sat up straight. "Uh…" He looked from Jazz to her resume and back, and sighed. "Honestly, this is just kind of a formality. The job's yours if you want it."

"Because of you and Maggie?"

It didn't seem professional to say *there is no me and Maggie*, nor did Cal think he could stand to hear it. "No," he said, and Jazz raised a brow. "Indirectly, I guess. You'll be working under Maggie and she told me you've worked well together in the past. Besides, Maggie loves her job too much to be okay with you coming on board if she didn't think you'd be a good fit."

"That's true," Jazz mused. "Well, alright then. I'm in."

That was easy. Cal opened his desk drawer and pulled out the contract he'd prepped before she'd arrived, sliding it across the desk to Jazz with a pen. "Welcome to the team."

She ran her eyes over the first page, which listed the salary, benefits, vacation days, and start date, and picked up the pen without looking through the rest of it.

Jazz held the pen to the signature line and paused, leaning forward. "Since I haven't officially signed anything yet, can I be Maggie's friend instead of your employee for a second?"

"You're technically not an employee for two weeks," Cal pointed out. "But go for it." Not that he expected Jazz would stop being Jazz when she *was* working.

"Why did you tell Maggie to say yes to this date—with your son, of all people—when neither one of you wants her to go?"

She didn't want to go? Of course she didn't. He'd practically forced her to say yes. She'd had every intention of letting Liam down gently before he'd acted like an asshole.

Cal wasn't sure what he'd been hoping to achieve by pushing her away; yes, she deserved the world, but she would never have that with Liam considering everything that had gone on between her and Cal. She'd only said yes because he'd pushed her, and he'd only done that because he was beating himself up for almost kissing her in the kitchen. It was a panic response, plain and simple.

It had taken Cal all of ten minutes after leaving the office to realize that he hadn't been thinking straight when he'd told her to say yes, and he'd been regretting it every second since.

"That's a great question," he replied, tapping his pen on the desk. "But I have no idea. The closest I can come up with is that I'm a fucking idiot."

"Ah, I see we're on the same page." Jazz smiled and shook her head, signing the contract in loopy cursive, a tiny heart above the I in *Jasmine*. She slid it back to him and Cal dropped it into his drawer.

He shouldn't ask her about Maggie, but he couldn't stop himself. "She really doesn't want to go?"

Jazz didn't hesitate. "Of course she doesn't, Cal. She's crazy about you."

Cal's heart thundered. It was the confirmation he'd desperately wanted, right after he'd fucked it all up.

"I have no idea what I'm doing here," he admitted, his voice raw. "She's twenty-seven. You know I'm fifty-five, right? And her boss. She deserves someone more... just more."

Jazz sighed, sympathy shining in her hazel eyes. "What I know is that Maggie has seemed happier and more excited in the past two months than she did in six years with Nathan. But Nathan really fucked her up. She gave up so much of herself just trying to make herself small so she didn't bother him." Jazz glared at the pen in her hand like he imagined she wanted to glare at Nathan. "Like the house. Yeah, she has no experience actually renovating, but did you know she spent hours watching HGTV in high school and playing with house simulators? She fell in love with designing when she organized a renovation at Burly's when she was sixteen and gave it all up the first time Nathan told her it was lame."

"I had no idea," Cal said, though it explained why she had such an eye for putting things together.

Jazz shook her head, her eyes sad. "I don't think she even remembers how much she loved it. I mentioned one of the simulator games to her when she bought the house and she'd completely forgotten about it. She dulled herself for him, but I've seen pieces of who she was before since you two started... whatever it is we're calling this. I really think you're good for her."

She was good for him too. Maggie wasn't the only one who'd needed to find her excitement; Cal hadn't realized how dull his life had become until she'd turned it on its axis. Until he no longer dreaded the quiet of an empty apartment after work. Christ, he missed her already.

"I have to fix this," he said and Jazz nodded, breathing a sigh of relief.

"You really do. I'm rooting for you, if it helps." She handed the pen she'd used to sign the contract back to Cal and stood up.

"Thanks," he replied, dropping the pen on his desk. "You know you shouldn't sign contracts without reading them first, right? You have no idea what you just signed." It was a fairly standard employment contract, and he was fair to his employees, but he'd seen far too many people screwed over because they hadn't read what they were signing.

Jazz just shrugged and picked up her bag. "You're in love with my best friend, so I'm pretty sure you're not going to fuck me over."

Cal raised a brow, heart hammering. "I never said I was in love with her."

"You didn't have to, boss," she replied with a wink, calling, "See you in two weeks!" as she skipped out of his office.

Cal smiled despite himself, sinking back in his chair and pulling out his phone. He opened it to his text thread with Maggie and took a deep breath. Cal knew if he asked to see her, she would agree out of obligation, and he didn't want that.

He stared at the screen, trying to figure out what to say.

> I'm sorry about yesterday. I panicked and acted like an asshole. It wasn't okay. I didn't actually want to end things and I understand if you don't want to talk about it, but I'm here if you do.

He sent the message, leaving the ball in her court, and sat the phone on the edge of his desk, where it stayed silent for the rest of the workday.

Cal unclasped his watch and dropped it in his pocket so he'd stop looking at it. He knew it was long past the time he should have left the office, and he knew Maggie would be on her way to meet Liam for dinner—he didn't need to obsess over it.

He should have ducked out early, but he hadn't been able to bring himself to leave in case Maggie replied. When she hadn't, he hadn't wanted to leave his office in case he ran into her getting ready for her date, since he assumed she was going straight from work. So he'd hidden away and watched the clock, and now he couldn't bring himself to leave just for an empty apartment and a Friday night alone because he'd fucked up.

The elevator chimed, and Cal looked up, expecting the office cleaner, Marie. But it was Maggie who stepped into the doorway of his office, stealing the breath from him.

She stepped into the room, her coat folded over

her arm.

"Shouldn't you be on your date?" he asked, and he sounded defeated to his own ears.

Maggie's eyes softened. She dropped her coat on a chair and rounded the desk. Cal rolled his chair out so he could look up at her, hair blowing lightly in the A/C like some kind of goddess.

"I canceled," was all she said, hesitating, as if she wasn't sure where to go from here.

"I'm so sorry, baby. I was an asshole," Cal said, his voice thick.

"You were," she agreed. She sighed, before sitting on his lap and cuddling into his chest. "But I forgive you." Tension melted from every one of Cal's muscles as he wrapped his arms around her, the breath rushing from him as he breathed in the sweet lilac scent of her. His heart raced in response. "We have to talk about it, though. What brought this on?"

"I almost kissed you in the kitchen and you... Fuck, you looked so panicked, love. The one thing you asked of me is that we keep this discreet, and I didn't do that. I've been struggling to keep my feelings in check for a while, and I have no idea how to keep this casual anymore."

Maggie's brows knitted together. "I'm sorry—I knew you were upset yesterday, and instead of staying and talking to you about it, I walked away. It wasn't fair to you or Liam. I've been struggling with my feelings too," she admitted.

"I'm not good enough for you, Maggie." She opened her mouth to protest, and he placed a finger on her lips.

"No, I know what you're going to say, and I'm not being self-deprecating, I swear. You know that all my life, I've wanted something like my parents. Sixty years with someone. It's too late for me to have that, but you could. I'm too old. And I know you don't care how old I am, but I can't get that out of my head."

"You're right. I don't care how old you are," Maggie said. "This, who you are now, is who I want. Your age doesn't play a part in that."

Cal pulled back so he could face her, taking in every perfect inch of her face. What was he doing? Why was he stopping himself from taking a chance on something beautiful just because he was older than her? His dad had been right; they could die tomorrow for all he knew. But whether he died tomorrow or in thirty years, he wanted to know he'd at least tried.

"I want to take you out," he said, and Maggie scrunched her nose up in confusion.

"We go out all the time."

Cal rolled his eyes, running his fingers through the ends of her hair. It was knotted, which meant she'd either gone out into the stormy day for lunch, or she'd spent the day fussing at it. Maybe both.

"We go to Ethel's, the grocery store, and the hardware store," he corrected. "I want to take you out on a date. A real date."

They'd never even had dinner together outside of his apartment and her house, and as much as he loved takeout at home with her, she deserved a proper dinner.

Maggie bit her lip, her face guarded. "Are you asking,

or just wishing for something that can't happen?"

"I'm asking, Maggie," he replied, brushing his thumb across her lips. "Let me take you on a date."

Maggie caught her lip between her teeth and took a steadying breath, as if trying to stop herself from panicking again. "Okay."

"Yeah?" Cal asked, almost not believing her. "You're not just saying yes because—"

"I'm saying yes because I want this and I'm tired of fighting it." Maggie cupped his face, her eyes bright. "I want to go on a date with you. Tonight?"

He shook his head. "I want to plan something special for you. Saturday?"

"You don't have to—"

"I want to, love. And I have the perfect idea." He just had to find a way to make it happen on short notice.

Maggie narrowed her eyes. "Are you taking me to the sex club for our first date? I'm not against it, I just need some notice so I can actually plan my outfit better this time."

"Definitely not," Cal said quickly. "If I take you to the club, I'm going to want to play this time." He ran his thumb across her jaw. "And, as it turns out, I'm a possessive, jealous asshole, so I'm not convinced I can handle anyone else seeing that."

Maggie sighed. "What's wrong with me that I like that so much? Are you still going to take me home with you tonight?"

"Obviously," he responded without hesitation. "I'm fucking obsessed with you. But before we go, I want to talk about something you said yesterday. You called yourself—"

Maggie winced. "Your employee with benefits."

"Yeah."

"I'm so sorry. That was a shitty choice of words on my part. I don't think of us like that at all, I just… I think I've been a little lost about what I should think of us as."

He should have known how difficult it would be for Maggie not to have a label for what they were. She liked things organized, physically and mentally.

"I won't lie, I didn't like hearing it, but I understand. I need you to know that I've never thought of you like that. You've always been more to me than that, and I'm sorry for not making that clearer. I suppose now that I've asked you on a date and you said yes, we're… dating?" he offered, and her eyes lit up like sapphires.

"I suppose we are."

She jumped out of his lap and held a hand out to him. "Come on. Last night was torture and we have a whole night of missed snuggling to make up for."

"Just snuggling?" he asked, following her from the room and turning the lights out as they left.

"Well, I don't know what your policy is on sex before the first date," she quipped as the elevator doors closed behind them.

"With you?" Cal said, pushing her against the cool glass and trapping her face between his hands. "As often as possible."

"I think we can make that happen," she replied, and Cal crushed his lips against hers.

CHAPTER TWENTY-FIVE

Maggie

A brisk wind whipped Maggie's hair around her face, but Cal wrapped his arms around her from behind, cocooning her in his warmth.

"Cal?"

"Yeah?" His breath tickled her ear, and Maggie ached for his lips.

"Can I take the blindfold off now?"

Cal made a strange noise, his arms tightening around her. Was she surprised that her first date with Cal involved a blindfold? Not in the slightest, even if it *wasn't* intended in a kinky way. She didn't think it was anyway. He'd pulled the black silk ribbon from his pocket and tied it around her eyes before driving off, hoping to surprise her with the location he'd chosen.

Maggie didn't like surprises—hell, it had taken everything in her to hand over the reins and let Cal plan the date at all—but she did like the blindfold.

"What's wrong?" she asked, when Cal didn't answer her question. She could feel his heart racing against her back.

He blew out a breath. "I'm worried that I've seriously miscalculated and this is a terrible idea."

Maggie's stomach dropped. "Us going on a date?"

"What? No, of course not, love," Cal replied quickly, then pressed a gentle kiss to the top of her head. "I mean specifically bringing you here. You might hate it. Fuck, we should've just done a movie or something."

Maggie had never heard him so nervous. She placed her hand over his and squeezed. "I'm sure I'm going to love it. But if we're not having a good time, we can leave and go to one of the millions of movie theaters in the city instead. Or go back to your place and pretend to watch a movie. We've got options, and I really don't mind what we're doing if I get to do it with you."

Cal released her from his viselike grip and spun her around until they were pressed chest to chest. His fingers were gentle, brushing her cheeks as he pulled the blindfold from her face.

Maggie's eyes zeroed in on the view behind him, but it gave nothing away; a nondescript parking lot, empty of all but a handful of cars, cast in twilight shadows. She had no time to look for any other defining features as Cal tipped her chin and met her mouth with a groan.

It was less a kiss than a claiming, Cal's tongue meeting hers with a fever, like it wasn't enough to kiss her—he had to consume her. They were both panting when they broke apart, Maggie's lungs burning almost as much as the heat spreading through her body.

"What was that for?" she asked with a breathy laugh.

Cal's eyes glimmered. His face was cast in shadows, but the glow of the moon reflected silver in his hair. "Obsessed with you, love."

Maggie had half a mind to suggest skipping the date all together, or at least sneaking off to Cal's car beforehand, when he spun her around and she took in the buildings looming before them.

She sucked in a breath, tears flooding her eyes, blurring the blue and green lights emanating from the sky-high illuminated arches.

"Oh my God," she managed, her voice watery. "Holy shit, Cal. We're going in?"

She looked up at him, and his shoulders relaxed. "Nah, I just brought you here to see the parking lot," he joked with a relieved smile. He caught an errant tear with his thumb. "Of course we are. We have the whole place to ourselves tonight."

Maggie's eyes widened. "How the hell did you manage this on such short notice?"

"You don't want to know."

God, she hated to think how much he'd dropped to book the whole place out on a Saturday night with two days' notice. She took a deep breath and let it go as she blew out.

"This is amazing. I can't believe you did this. Thank you." She reached up on her tiptoes to kiss him.

Then finally, fifteen years later than she'd first hoped, Maggie stepped into the Pacific Science Center.

C al hadn't just booked the venue; he'd gone all out.
A private guide showed them around the empty science center, and Maggie clung to every fun fact she shared. Even Cal seemed interested, though he spent more time watching Maggie's reactions than he did looking at the exhibits. His gaze was a brand on her skin, and Maggie was grateful that their tour guide disappeared now and then, giving them time to themselves. Time she used to show him just how much she appreciated him making her childhood dreams come true.

After enjoying drinks and appetizers in the planetarium and watching a short documentary about Perseus and Andromeda and their immortalization in the starry skies, they were led to the laser dome for dinner.

A fluffy white rug covered the center of the room, with plush cushions and an ice-filled champagne bucket. Cal had arranged for an honest-to-God private chef to cater their magical picnic, and every course was better than the last: focaccia with sweet fig jam and rosemary, the most pillowy gnocchi Maggie had ever eaten, dressed in a divine pumpkin and sage sauce, and sweet tiramisu that tasted even better on Cal's tongue.

When their plates were clear, Cal lay down on one of the soft pillows and tugged Maggie down until she was lying nestled on his chest. They watched the ceiling, the twinkling star-like lasers, and a calm settled over Maggie. She didn't remember the last time she'd felt so present, like the world outside ceased to exist as she breathed in the warm, honeyed scent of Cal and, for once, let herself be swept up by the feelings that were getting harder to ignore.

How could she ignore them when Cal had done such a beautiful thing for her?

"Tell me something I don't know about you," she said, tilting her head to kiss the sharp edge of his jaw.

"That's tough. I'm pretty sure you know more about me than anyone else at this point," Cal replied with a chuckle, his chest vibrating.

Maggie knew that wasn't true. No matter how much attention she paid—and she paid a lot—she'd only known him for six years. His older siblings had known him since birth. "Then tell me something no one knows about you," she amended, and Cal hummed.

After what felt like an age, watching lasers shoot across the ceiling, he said, "I'm scared of the dark."

Maggie blinked at him in surprise. "Seriously?"

Cal nodded, staring at the ceiling rather than at her. "Yeah. It's why I don't have curtains or blinds. I usually sleep with a lamp on, but the city lights are enough if I can't."

"Huh. I assumed you didn't have them because… well…"

"Because I'm a man?" Cal asked, raising an amused brow.

"I was going to say because you're a bachelor,"

Maggie corrected, rolling her eyes. "Why didn't you tell me? My house gets really dark at night." Her bedroom window faced onto the back of her house, and the giant pine in the yard blocked most of the light.

"It's fine. I've gotten more used to it, and it's easier when you're there," Cal replied with a shrug.

Maggie frowned, sitting up so she could look at him properly. Pink tinged his cheeks. Oh. "Cal. You don't need to be embarrassed. I'm pretty sure darkness is one of the most common fears. You've really never told anyone?"

"I mean, when I was a kid, sure. But people just assume you grow out of it. I think I just assumed I'd grow out of it—I didn't expect to be fifty-five with a fear of the dark, that's for sure."

Fifty-five years was a long time to be holding onto that kind of secret. Maggie threaded her fingers through Cal's. "Thank you for telling me. We can leave a lamp on at ho—at my place." She'd almost called it home, as if they both lived there.

"I don't want to disrupt your sleep," he protested.

"I sleep so wrapped around you these days that I don't think I would notice if every light in the room was on."

"That's true," Cal agreed, his dimples making an appearance. "Okay, your turn."

Maggie wracked her brain for something no one knew. She had plenty of options—she wasn't exactly an open book—but most of them opened her up to questions she didn't want to answer. Sure, she regretted her college degree—a waste of money and four years, when she could have gotten started learning on the job earlier—and she sometimes wondered if she'd made a mistake in saving Burly's from bankruptcy at sixteen, but she didn't want to put a damper on their date.

So, instead, she said, "I want a cat."

Cal raised his brows, surprise written all over his face. "A cat?" Maggie nodded, and he pressed his lips together as if trying not to laugh. "I didn't take you for a pet kind of person—or for a pet hair and toys strewn across the house kind of person, I guess."

"That is a con," she agreed. "But I grew up in a house with messy siblings and messier dogs—we had five at one point—so I can probably manage a cat or two. I would love to be one of those over the top cat moms who takes their cat out on a harness or in a stroller and buys ridiculously overpriced cat trees and fresh salmon, you know?"

"You'd be a great cat mom, love," Cal replied. There was a flash of uncertainty in his eyes as he asked, "Do you want human children one day, or just cat children?"

"Just cat children," she answered quickly, and she could have sworn relief flashed in his eyes. "Definitely not human children."

"So what's stopping you?"

"I'm going to do it," she said, all too aware that she sounded a little defensive. "I just... I don't know, the house is a lot to manage already, plus work is always so busy, and adding a cat on top of that? I don't want to look like I can't handle it."

Cal quirked a brow. "Interesting."

"What is?"

"You're more worried about looking like you can't handle it than not being able to handle it," Cal replied and it both unnerved and pleased Maggie that he saw through her so easily.

"Well, I know I can handle it. I can handle everything," she replied stubbornly. "Even if I don't always look like it."

"You do, love," Cal said, sitting up and cupping her face. "But, and I know this is a radical suggestion, maybe you don't always have to handle shit on your own." His emerald eyes drilled into her, and Maggie shivered under his gaze.

But Cal didn't know what he was suggesting. He hadn't met her parents—and wouldn't, if she had anything to do with it. He didn't feel the crushing weight of everything Maggie struggled with. As much as he wanted her to let him in, it was too much, too soon, and he didn't understand just how terrifying that was for her.

She couldn't say any of that, though. They were having a perfect night, and Maggie had no intention of ruining that. "Maybe," she lied through her teeth, and Cal's face lit up like it was the best thing he'd ever heard.

"Cal," she screamed, her thighs locking around his head until he chuckled, the vibrations causing her back to arch. He spread her thighs wider, running his tongue over every inch of her, like he couldn't get enough of her. Maggie twisted in the sheets, sparks flashing in front of her eyes.

"Please, Daddy," she whimpered as Cal brought her to the edge again and pulled away. He kissed his way up her body, stubble dragging along her belly, her breasts, her jaw.

"You want to come for Daddy, baby girl?" he purred against her ear, his breath sending goosebumps over her skin. He didn't wait for an answer before brushing a finger over her clit. Maggie's hips jumped from the bed but, trapped beneath Cal, it only pressed her closer to him.

"I need your cock inside me," she begged. Cal cursed and bit down on her earlobe before pulling away.

Best first date ever, Maggie thought as he slid open his nightstand and rummaged around.

"Fuck." He pushed it closed. "I'll be back in a second, love."

The mattress shifted as he stepped off and walked to the bathroom. Maggie stretched out, luxuriating in the feel of the soft cotton against her sensitive skin. A moment later, she heard the bathroom cabinet close and opened her eyes to see Cal walk back in, empty-handed.

"Tell me you have a condom in your bag." His voice was pained, like he already knew the answer.

Maggie winced and shook her head. "We used the last one in your office yesterday." They were going through condoms at a rapid rate; Maggie hadn't had to replenish her stack so often since college.

Cal groaned, kneeling between her legs. "I don't

suppose the pull out method has magically become more effective in the thirty-five years since it failed miserably for me?"

Maggie snorted, reaching out for his hand and tugging him closer. "No, but I *do* have an IUD, so you don't actually have to pull out."

Cal's eyes glazed over, his pupils swallowing the green. He leaned over her, his mouth hovering over hers. "Are you sure, love?"

Maggie nodded, so desperate to have him that, stupidly, she might have said yes to the pull out method even *without* the IUD. "I got tested after Nathan and I broke up, but we always used condoms anyway."

Somehow, the realization that Maggie hadn't let Nathan fuck her without a condom caused Cal's eyes to get even darker. "I get tested every few months," he confirmed, though Maggie already suspected that, considering she saw the quarterly medical appointments on his calendar. What else would he be visiting like clockwork for?

"Cal."

"Hmm?" He was too busy running his lips over her throat to see the desperation she knew was written on her face.

"I need you inside me. Now." She wrapped her legs around his waist, pulling him to her.

"Fuck," he cursed, lifting her legs and spreading them until she was wide open to him. "Baby girl, you're going to be the death of me."

He pushed into her slowly, and Maggie's head fell

back against the pillows, a whimper escaping her lips. How was it possible for him to feel even better every time?

Cal's eyes fluttered close, his jaw going slack. "Fucking hell."

Maggie's legs shook in his hands and he held them up, stretching her and leaving her entirely at his mercy. "Please, Daddy," she gasped, trying to wiggle her hips but unable to move in his hold.

"Hold on to the headboard, baby girl," he ground out, and Maggie barely had time to grasp the iron bars before he was driving into her relentlessly. The headboard banged with every thrust, but Maggie hardly noticed her knuckles scraping against the wall.

Her back arched almost painfully, every inch of her body alight with flames, electricity zapping over her from head to toe with every thrust.

Cal pushed her legs back further, shifting until his cock hit a new angle and Maggie's mouth fell open, her cries piercing the air.

"Tell me, baby girl," Cal panted. "Where do you want my cum?"

He trailed a trembling finger over her face, across her breasts, over her stomach. But Maggie wanted more.

"Please, Daddy. Please, I want..." she trailed off, begging unintelligibly.

"What do you want?"

"I want... inside me. Come inside me, please," Maggie pleaded. Cal cursed, his cheeks flushed and eyes wild. She tightened around him, her orgasm hitting her like a tidal wave, sending shocks all over her body.

Maggie watched with hazy eyes as Cal came inside her and an expression of sheer bliss took over his face, her name falling from his lips like a prayer. Cal had never lost control so quickly, and the realization that she'd done that, *her* pussy had done that, made her clench around him again, her hands flying from the headboard. Her nails raked down Cal's back while he thrusted one last time, seeing her through the orgasm and pulling out with a panting breath.

His gaze was glued to her pussy, and Maggie looked down to see his cum leaking out of her. Cal moaned softly, almost to himself, and before she could so much as blink, he ran two fingers between her legs, then pressed them into her pussy, forcing the cum back inside.

Maggie gasped, her pussy spasming around him. Cal released her legs, nudging her thighs apart with his knee. He curled the fingers inside her until they were pressed firmly against her G spot. He rolled them, and Maggie could feel his cum lubricating her from the inside.

"You took my cum so well, baby," Cal said, his voice low. He leaned in and pressed a whisper of a kiss against her lips. "Such a good girl."

"Yours," Maggie gasped, while he fucked her slowly with his fingers. She could feel his cum leaking out of her with every movement, hot against her skin. It was filthy and beautiful and she was on the edge of shattering again already.

Cal's face softened. "My good girl, huh?"

"Yes, Daddy."

He sat back and laid a hand flat across her pelvis. "I think you deserve to be rewarded for that."

He pressed down firmly on her pelvis while he teased her with his fingers, the pressure of his hand heightening every movement. His fingers pushed and swirled against her G-spot torturously slowly until she was begging him to go faster, harder.

Cal, the beautiful, perfect god of a man that he was, obliged with a low laugh. His fingers slammed inside her mercilessly, his hand holding her hips to the bed and pressing down firmly on her pelvis. The orgasms built within her so quickly that Maggie couldn't tell where one ended and the next began. Her whole body trembled, her legs twisting.

A pressure stronger than she'd ever felt swelled inside her and her head fell to the side, sobs spilling from her lips. "Cal," she cried, fisting the covers. "I… I can't."

"You can take it, baby girl."

His fingers were unrelenting, but Cal shifted and bent his head over her. Maggie teetered on the edge of an explosion, the pressure filling her. Cal closed his lips around her clit and it burst. Maggie's cry died in her throat, her body lifting from the bed, as she felt herself drenching Cal's face.

It felt like she was cycling through time, wave after wave of pleasure rippling over her body. Cal licked at her lazily, his fingers slowing down to bring her down from the highest high and onto steadier ground.

When she could finally breathe again, Maggie opened

her eyes. Cal was looking up at her like she was the most incredible thing he'd ever seen, his face honest-to-God dripping.

Maggie had gotten very good at taking care of herself over the years, and before Nathan, she'd had years of pretty good sex. But no one had ever made her squirt before.

"I... Fuck," she said, unable to find anything else to say in her short-wired brain. Cal laughed, pulling back and scooting up the bed to gather her in his arms. She burrowed into him, pressing her face against his, too tired to care that he was soaking wet and dripping all over her freshly washed hair.

"You're so fucking beautiful," Cal said, holding her tighter.

"And I'm pretty sure you're some kind of god. No human man could do *that*." She gestured to the bed, forcing one eye open.

It was carnage; the bedding was half off the bed, twisted in knots. Not to mention the stickiness...

"We made a mess."

"I'll deal with it tomorrow," Cal said, waving it away. "We can take a nice long soak in the bath and sleep in the guest room."

"That sounds nice." Maggie pressed a kiss to his shoulder and stilled as she spied red marks creeping down onto his back. "Sit up a second."

Cal did, and Maggie gasped, her heart racing.

"What?"

"I hurt you," she said, swallowing as she ran her

finger across the deep scratches on Cal's back. Two of them had bled—she couldn't even remember doing it.

"Hey, it's okay, love," Cal replied, cupping her face gently. "It doesn't hurt, I promise. And I like being covered in your marks."

He replaced the hand on her jaw with his mouth, and Maggie sighed happily. "I like being covered in your—"

"Don't finish that sentence if you're too tired for the consequences," Cal warned. Maggie's eyes flicked down and, sure enough, he was already hard again. Weren't longer recovery times supposed to be a thing as men got older? Clearly Cal hadn't got that memo.

Her body was spent, every muscle aching, and a long soak in the tub sounded incredible. But Maggie was a masochist; there was no other explanation for the way she opened her mouth and didn't hesitate to finish, "—cum."

CHAPTER TWENTY-SIX

Maggie

Maggie spent the two weeks leading up to Jazz's first day preparing to train her. She had the benefit of knowing how Jazz learned best, and Jazz had the benefit of knowing how Maggie liked things done. But by the end of Jazz's first week at Michaelson and Hicks, Maggie had to remind herself why she loved her best friend so much.

The fact that they were so different was one reason they worked well together; Jazz's scattered, creative brain complimented Maggie's focused, logical brain. Maggie liked structure to her day; Jazz liked to do things when they *felt right*. Together, they struck a harmonious balance—it just took a little while to sink in.

They survived it only because Maggie escaped to Cal's office three times a day—and Cal massaged the tension from her shoulders every night before bed. She was well distracted when they left the office—whether to his place or hers, or going out for a date night, they hadn't spent more than a few hours apart since their first date. That, at least, was going perfectly.

By the midpoint of Jazz's second week, Maggie no longer wanted to wring her neck. In fact, Jazz had taken over the email inbox, filing, and most of the reports, things that had usually taken up most of Maggie's week. Maggie had more time to handle appointment calls, setting up meetings, arranging case paperwork, and managing the team's schedules. For the first time in her five years as Cal's assistant, she had a little breathing room.

Jazz wasn't Cal's only plan to improve things at the firm: inspired by Maggie's success on TikTok, and his sister Maeve's constant badgering, he'd finally given in and decided to hire someone to fill the empty head of marketing role. Their head of PR had been juggling Michaelson and Hicks' outdated social media pages for the past decade.

Though still a small fish in a big pond, Maggie's TikTok had taken off overnight, after a sixty-second video showing her fancy new fillable paint roller had gone viral. She'd gone from five thousand followers to fifty thousand in twenty-four hours and, a week later, crossed the hundred thousand mark. It wasn't without its downsides—it seemed a large proportion of the internet hated every single thing she'd done to her house—but Maggie was letting herself enjoy the buzz that came with every new post.

Maggie yawned and drained her coffee while Jazz took her through an email from an unhappy client. It had been a long couple of days of interviews for the marketing role. Cal had tried to keep as much of it off her plate as he could. He'd hired a recruitment agency to arrange interviews and had handled the list of applicants himself. Maggie's only job was to welcome them and take them to Cal's office, but meeting a dozen new people in two days had drained her social battery. They only had one more to go, and then she and Cal were heading out for a much needed night of Mexican food and bottomless margaritas.

Maggie tuned Jazz out—the client in question was never happy, and she was well used to their complaints—so she didn't notice when her best friend stopped talking. She did, however notice, when Jazz stood up and said, "What the fuck are you doing here?"

Maggie's head snapped up, her mouth opening to tell Jazz to watch her language at work, but the words died on her tongue when she saw who Jazz was talking to. Maggie didn't stand up. She just stared at the man standing beside Demi, and the resume clutched in his hand, in horror.

"What are *you* doing here?" Nathan sneered at Jazz. "Did you finally get yourself in some legal trouble?"

"I work here, asshole. What's your excuse?"

Nathan held up the resume with a smirk. "Looks like we might be colleagues soon. I have an interview for the marketing job."

Maggie pushed back from the desk and stood up as

calmly as she could muster. "No," she said, grateful that her voice didn't wobble.

"No?" Nathan asked, flicking his eyes up and down her body and curling his lip.

"No," Maggie bit out, significantly *less* calmly. "You're not working here, Nathan. Why do you even want to work here? All you've ever done is talk shit about this place." Though she tried to keep her voice as low as possible, Jazz had already drawn attention to them.

Nathan rolled his eyes. "I have no problem with the firm, Maggie. I had a problem with the fact that my girlfriend was a glorified secretary." He smirked at her. "And I don't think it's up to you if I work or here or not. Let's see what your boss has to say. Cal, isn't it?"

"You know," Grant interjected from the desk beside Maggie's. "I actually think we'd *all* like to see what Cal has to say about his gi—your ex boyfriend being here." He rushed the last sentence and Maggie's mouth popped open as she realized he'd almost said *girlfriend*. She glanced around the room, and no one else looked surprised. Had they all figured it out? Were they talking about them behind their backs? Maggie and Cal were dating now—she knew they wouldn't be able to keep it to themselves forever—but they hadn't talked about how they were going to handle things at work yet. She couldn't deal with that just now.

Maggie sucked in a breath and squared her shoulders, ignoring Grant and the curious eyes that felt like they were closing in on her. "Fine. Follow me," she told Nathan, pushing past him and out of the office.

She slammed the button to open the elevator and stepped in, closing it as soon as Nathan was inside.

"So how have you—"

"My job is to escort you to your interview. Not make small talk," she ground out, staring at the doors.

"You're awfully pissed off, considering *you* broke up with *me*. Regrets, Maggie?"

She ignored him, holding her breath until she could get more than two feet away from him.

Cal looked up and smiled when she knocked on his door, but it slipped from his face as he took in whatever expression was on hers.

She cleared her throat and gestured to Nathan. "Your ten o'clock—Nathan Finch."

"Thanks, love," Cal replied, clearly not recognizing Nathan's name. "Do you want to stick around?"

He liked when she sat in on interviews, often noticing things he didn't and vice versa. But for this one… Maggie shook her head. "No, thank you."

She caught a flash of confusion in Cal's eyes as she turned on her heel and practically sprinted out the room. When the elevator doors finally slid shut, she leaned back against the glass and closed her eyes, taking a shaky breath.

Cal watched the door close behind Maggie with a

frown. Something was wrong with her, but he couldn't exactly leave his interview to check on her. He just had to focus on the man before him for the next hour, and then he would be all Maggie's.

"Thanks for coming in." He stood to shake the man's hand; he'd forgotten his name already. "Take a seat."

Cal gestured to the seat across his desk, and the man sat down.

"Thanks. I have a copy of my resume here, if you need it." He handed the paper over, and Cal took it gratefully. The recruitment firm had emailed all the resumes over, but there were so many, he hardly remembered them. He quickly scanned the resume before double-checking the man's name.

"This is an impressive resume you've got here, Nathan," he said, smiling at the man. He had slicked back blond hair and a clean-shaven face that was oddly familiar to Cal. "An MBA in marketing from UW, four years as the head of marketing at Culverstone..." Cal trailed off, frowning slightly at the resume. Why did that ring a bell?

He dragged his eyes back up to Nathan's full name and address: *Nathan Finch, 1415 Russell Avenue, Ballard.*

Ballard... Hadn't Maggie lived in Ballard before buying her place in Ravenna?

Cal looked up at Nathan, and everything clicked into place; Maggie's reaction, why the company he worked for was familiar. Maggie's ex, who he'd been dying to knock down a peg, had wandered right on into his office.

"So, Nathan, how did you hear about us?" Cal asked, setting the resume down. He'd already made up his mind; he wouldn't be needing it.

"Oh, well, Maggie's my ex-girlfriend," Nathan confirmed, and Cal reminded himself he couldn't actually punch the asshole in the face. "She talked about work all the time, so I feel like I already know the firm so well."

"I thought your name was familiar. Maggie's spoken about you a lot too," Cal replied pleasantly, and he didn't miss the flash of worry in Nathan's eyes. "Do you think that would be a concern for you? Should you be successful, I mean."

"A concern?" Nathan asked uncertainly.

Cal clasped his hands on the desk. "Working with Maggie."

"Oh." Nathan laughed and shook his head, like Cal had said something hilarious. "No, not at all. I mean, she's just an assistant, so it's not like we'd be working together."

Cal's jaw clenched. He reached for his coffee cup, because if he didn't do something with his hands, he might reach for Nathan's neck.

There were those three words again. *Just an assistant*, dripping with derision. Sure, Maggie did more than your average assistant, but even if she didn't, what the fuck was wrong with being an assistant? He could only assume Nathan, and Maggie's dad, were the kind of people who supported pitiful wages for *unskilled* work, then complained when their fast food servers didn't go above and beyond.

Cal cleared his throat. "Well, yes, Maggie is *my* assistant. She works directly under me, and Jasmine works under her." Nathan barely hid his look of annoyance when Cal mentioned Jazz. "Maggie is, for all intents and purposes, my second in command. She runs the office and more or less manages everyone within the Michaelson half of Michaelson and Hicks."

Nathan blinked in surprise. "I had no idea she'd been promoted."

"Oh, she hasn't," Cal replied with a forced smile. "This is what she's been doing for the past five years. I assumed you'd know, since she spoke about work so much."

Nathan scratched the back of his neck, his cheeks flushing pink. "Ah, well, you know how it is. Women talk so much; sometimes you just have to smile and nod."

Fucking asshole. Cal counted to three in his head. "Right. Well, you would be reporting directly to Maggie in this role. You'd be running everything by her so she could sign off on it. Would that be an issue?" Cal had no intention of giving Maggie that kind of extra work, but he enjoyed watching Nathan's face fall.

"That wouldn't be an issue. I'm used to Maggie telling me what to do—she used to nag me all the time to do more around the house." The joke fell flat, and Cal no longer had it in him to hide the anger from his face. Nathan's eyes widened, and he swallowed, before adding, "Mr. Michaelson. Sir."

"Great," Cal replied dryly. "So. Tell me about your current role."

CHAPTER TWENTY-SEVEN

Maggie

Maggie scrubbed the sparkling coffee cup, her hands bright red and screaming from the scalding water. He wasn't supposed to be here; work was her happy place. Or it had been, anyway, before the whole office was gossiping about her and Cal behind their backs.

She hadn't been able to face anyone, even Jazz, after depositing Nathan in Cal's office. Her best friend had stood to greet her, but Maggie held a hand up and said, "Not now," before walking straight into the kitchen and closing the door. She couldn't stop people from talking about her and Cal, or, apparently, Nathan from showing up here, but she could scrub the kitchen within an inch of its life.

She'd cleaned the table and counters until she could see her reflection—and promptly looked away—wiped down the chairs and cabinet doors, and was halfway through the dishes when the kitchen door creaked open.

"I'm not in the mood, Jazz. I'll call you later."

"It's after five," the clipped voice of her ex-boyfriend replied. "Everyone is gone."

Maggie looked over her shoulder at him for a brief second before turning away and taking a deep breath. "Not everyone, clearly."

"Ouch, Mags. I don't remember you being so pissy." Nathan crossed the room to stand entirely too fucking close to her.

"Things change, Nathan."

"No shit," he replied with a humorless laugh.

She set the plate she'd been washing onto the drying rack and turned to look at him. He looked... fine. He wasn't a bad-looking guy; she was just seeing him through a different lens than she once had. Besides, after spending three months with Cal, it was even more apparent just how dull Nathan was.

"How was your interview?" she asked with an attempt at civility.

Nathan sniffed and lifted a shoulder in forced nonchalance. "I did well, but I don't know about the role. I'm overqualified."

"I'm sure." Maggie couldn't help but roll her eyes.

"What's that supposed to mean?" he spat.

Maggie sighed, picking up another plate. "Nothing. It doesn't matter."

"So what, you think I'm not good enough for this place?" Nathan's eyes flashed with ire.

"I never said that," she protested, her temples throbbing. "Can't we just forget—"

But Nathan had already made his mind up. She didn't know what had happened in Cal's office, but whatever it was must have bruised his ego, because he was straight onto the offensive. "That's rich coming from you. You wasted your degree, tried and failed to get your parents' cafe off the ground, gave up on the best relationship you'll ever have, and for what? To be a quote unquote *assistant*? You're cleaning fucking dishes, Maggie. You're twenty-six without a single achievement to your name. At least with me, you might have been something. You can't do a damn thing on your own." He shook his head, disgust dripping from his curled lip.

Maggie stilled, gripping the plate in her hand with more force than necessary. "Twenty-seven," she said finally.

"What?"

"I'm twenty-seven, remember? You proposed to me at a party full of all the people who only care about *you* and now you're acting like an asshole because I said no," she said, her voice surprisingly steady. "I don't need you to make something of myself, Nathan. I don't need anyone. I'm doing just fine on my own." She relaxed her grip, her fingers cramping. "And I'd like you to leave now."

"You can't—"

"Ah, Nathan. You're still here." They both turned to find Cal leaning in the doorway. Maggie didn't know how much he'd heard, but there were shadows in his eyes as he leveled Nathan with a look. "I'm afraid I need you to head out so I can lock up."

Nathan threw her one more look of loathing over his shoulder as he followed Cal out of the kitchen. Maggie loosed a breath, falling forward until the water and soap suds tickled her elbows.

She counted to three, breathed in, counted to three, breathed out. Three times, until she was sure she wasn't going to scream, and then picked up a bowl. She didn't need Nathan. She didn't need anyone. She managed just fine on her own.

"This place is spotless."

Maggie jumped, the bowl slipping from her grasp and splashing into the sink.

"Shit, sorry, love. I didn't mean to scare you."

"It's okay," Maggie replied, inspecting the bowl and confirming it was crack-free.

"Do you want to tell me why you've cleaned this place so much it looks like it's never been used?" Cal asked, crossing the room and standing beside her.

Maggie didn't like how much her anxious heart calmed at the mere proximity of him. *You can't do a damn thing on your own.*

She blocked out Nathan's voice. "Marie's daughter went into labor six weeks early. She's fine, and so is the baby, but Marie has been staying with them now that they're home from the NICU and she's exhausted by the time she gets here. I've been trying to pick up some of the cleaning, so she has less to do."

Her voice wobbled, and Cal sucked in a breath. "Look at me, baby."

Maggie tried to stop her lip from trembling as she turned to face him, but God, she was so fucking tired.

"Fuck, baby." Cal reached a hand out to rub her back, and her eyes fluttered closed. "He's an asshole. He has no idea what he lost."

"He is an asshole," she agreed with a sigh. "But he's good at what he does. And he has a lot of experience," she admitted, opening her eyes.

Cal tilted his head, raising a brow. "I don't care. I'm not fucking hiring him."

"You can't not hire him just because he's my ex." Maggie had no idea why she was arguing; she sure as hell didn't want Cal to hire Nathan.

"That's not the reason—I'm not hiring him because he's an asshole. If you had a *nice* ex…" Cal trailed off, then shrugged. "Actually, I still wouldn't hire them. You bring out a jealous streak in me, love."

Maggie laughed softly. "You're welcome. So, who are you hiring?"

"Shaylee, I think. She doesn't have as much experience as the other candidates, but she double-majored in marketing and business studies, so she seems to understand our client base better than the others," Cal said and Maggie nodded her agreement. She'd liked Shaylee.

"Good choice."

"You know you don't have to do this, right?" Cal said, gesturing around the kitchen. "I can give Marie paid leave to take care of her daughter and we can bring an agency cleaner in for a while."

"I like cleaning," Maggie said, firmly.

"I know, but—"

"It calms me down," she interrupted, her voice sharper than she wanted it to be. "And there's nothing wrong with that. Just because it's a traditionally feminine task, which is bullshit, for the record—"

"Maggie, baby. Breathe. Of course there's nothing wrong with cleaning. As long as you don't feel obligated," Cal said gently.

"I don't feel obligated," she confirmed, taking a deep breath and, though he searched her face for any trace of a lie, he finally nodded.

"I didn't know—about Marie's daughter."

"I'm sorry. I meant to tell you, but I forgot." Worry coiled in Maggie's gut; she didn't forget work stuff. Ever. "She had to leave early last week, but I handled it. We sent a gift—a play mat for the baby, a gift card for a meal delivery service for Mom and Dad, and flowers for Marie."

"Thanks, love. Where did you learn to do all this shit?" Cal asked, sounding impressed.

She peered up at him. "It's a little late to be asking for my qualifications, is it not?" she asked, her voice steadier. She even managed a smile.

Cal rolled up his sleeves and grabbed the dishtowel hanging over the cabinet handle. He swatted her on the ass before picking up a plate from the drying rack and drying it. "That's not what I mean, and you know it. You didn't go to school for this—you majored in marketing too, didn't you?"

"Yeah. I didn't know what I wanted to do when I was in college, so I just picked a major that I thought would help with the cafe." It had, to an extent. Burly's issues lay with her parents' shitty management, not a lack of marketing.

"So how did you learn all this... assisting?" Cal asked.

"Practice, I guess," she replied with a shrug. "That first year after I graduated, when Zhara left and I became your official assistant, not just an intern... I spent a lot of time googling shit. And I took a few online courses for PAs when Nathan wasn't home. Over time, it just became second nature."

"He didn't approve." It wasn't a question, but Maggie nodded anyway.

"He always thought being an assistant was beneath me, like my parents. Apparently he still does."

"What do you think?"

"I think," Maggie began, setting the last dish on the rack, draining the sink, and grabbing a second towel to help Cal dry, "that there's nothing wrong with being an assistant, and I don't understand why people act like there is. I also don't give a shit what they think about my job. I love it here, and I'm good at it."

Cal frowned at the glass in his hand. "But you work too much."

"Isn't that why you hired Jazz? To take some of the pressure off?"

"Yeah, but… fuck, Maggie, you work more than I do."

Maggie snorted, standing on her tiptoes to place a stack of bowls in a cabinet. "I think that's the benefit of being a CEO and having people to do shit for you."

"That doesn't seem fair," Cal grumbled, and she raised her brows at him.

"Is this your first time hearing about capitalism?"

He dropped his towel on the counter and pushed her back against the sink, trapping her with his legs on either side of her. "Brat."

"What are you trying to do? Are you trying to convince me I don't want to work here?"

She reached up to cup his face, and he held her hand to his cheek.

"I don't know. I just… I don't know."

"I like my job," she promised. "You're a good boss— and I'm not just saying that because I know I'm going to enjoy paying for being a brat later. Everyone here likes you. We're all paid well, and the workload is fair. Everything extra I've done has been on me, not you."

"I just want what's best for you."

As soft as his expression was, as caring as his eyes were, Maggie couldn't help but blanch. *You can't do a damn thing on your own.* No matter what was going on between them, Cal didn't get to decide what was best for her.

"*I* know what's best for me. I know what I'm doing."

Cal held his hands up in defense. "I didn't say that you didn't. But I care about you, and I'm allowed to worry."

Maggie looked away from him, pushing down the instinct to fight him on it. Shame curdled her blood. That was exactly what she'd done for six years with Nathan—pushed down the urge to fight.

Cal wasn't Nathan, but Maggie wasn't the girl who kept her mouth shut anymore. She didn't need him to worry about her—she was managing just fine on her own.

"Can we just go? It's been a long day."

Cal opened his mouth like he wanted to argue, but thought better of it and closed it. "Yeah. Let's go."

Maggie followed him to the parking lot, bristling as he opened the car door for her. It wasn't anything new—he always opened the door or pulled out her chair—but with Nathan's words ricocheting through her, the gesture left a sour taste in Maggie's mouth.

CHAPTER TWENTY-EIGHT

Cal gripped the desk, white-knuckled, watching Maggie swirl her tongue around the metal straw sticking out of her godforsaken cup, her head buried in her tablet.

"Maggie, love."

She didn't look up. "Hmm?"

"If you don't stop doing unholy things to that straw with your mouth, I'm not going to get anything done this afternoon and I'll throw your whole weekly schedule off."

Her mouth stilled, her gaze flicking up to his; hungry. "I suppose we could make a little space in that schedule."

She didn't need to say it twice.

"Get over here."

Maggie took her sweet time setting the tablet down and rounding the desk. She hitched her skirt up and straddled his lap, leaning in to brush her lips against his jaw. After Cal had ruined a dozen pairs of her favorite tights (he *had* replaced them), she'd given up and started wearing thigh highs instead, which felt like more of a reward than a punishment for his being so destructive.

She rolled her hips, her pussy separated from his cock by nothing more than a few thin scraps of fabric, and Cal barked out a curse. He grappled with her shirt buttons while Maggie unzipped his pants and wrapped her hand around his cock. She didn't bother with taking her underwear off, just pushed it aside and slid down on his cock with a breathy moan.

"Fuck, baby girl," Cal ground out as her pussy hugged him tightly, clenching around him. They hadn't used condoms since their first official date, and he would never tire of the raw feel of her. He buried his face in her breasts while he gripped her ass, bouncing her on his cock.

The silky fabric of her bra threatened to tear as he wrestled it with his teeth, so Maggie took pity on him, pushing it down enough to expose herself to him. He gave thanks by wrapping his mouth around her nipple, running his tongue along the silver bar that drove him fucking wild.

Maggie's pussy tightened around him, her breaths coming short and fast. Cal increased his grip, holding her ass so tightly that he was sure he'd leave fingerprints behind. He was so fucking close. At home, he could spend hours coaxing orgasm after orgasm out of Maggie, taking his sweet time wrapped around her like he might never let her go. At work, they were hurried— tight grips and bitten lips, rushing to the finish line like someone might walk in at any minute.

He bit down on her nipple, and Maggie trembled. Cal pressed his lips against hers to catch her cries as she crumbled, her pussy spasming around him, claiming his orgasm for herself. He came with a gasp, clinging to Maggie like he might never let her go.

She captured his mouth in a searing kiss before pulling back and pressing her forehead to his, a soft whisper of, "Fuck, Cal."

Cal wrapped his arms around her, holding her to his chest, memorizing the weight of her. They stayed like that, pressed so close together he could hardly tell where he ended and she began, until a knock sounded at the door, and Maggie pulled back, wide-eyed.

Cal frowned at the door. Thank fuck they'd closed it. "Do we have an appointment today?"

Horror crossed Maggie's face. "Oh my God. Shit. *Shit.* I forgot. It's Robert Sanderson—I haven't prepared anything."

She was hyperventilating, on the verge of tears. Cal tightened his hold on her. Since Nathan's interview last week, she'd been constantly on edge, ready to tip over at any second. Anytime he tried to talk to her about it, she shut down. He had no idea how to help.

"Maggie, baby, it's okay. It'll be fine."

A second, more insistent, knock sounded, followed by Twyla's voice. "Mr. Michaelson? Are you in there?"

"Fuck." Maggie jumped off his lap, tugging her skirt

down, and Cal tried his hardest not to notice the cum leaking down her thighs. He buttoned his pants, shifting uncomfortably, as she ran for the door, buttoning her shirt. There *were* pros to condoms. Maggie's skirt was long enough that no one would notice, but Cal couldn't imagine she would be comfortable sitting through the meeting.

She pulled the door open. "Mr. Sanderson, it's so great to see you." If Cal hadn't witnessed her almost-panic attack all of thirty seconds ago, he would never have suspected a thing. Her voice was perfectly smooth and professional, and she welcomed their long-term client into the room with a friendly smile. "Thank you for bringing him up, Twyla. I'm so sorry I wasn't downstairs to meet you—we've been having some computer problems this morning. Technology is great when it works, huh?" She punctuated the perfect lie with a sweet laugh that had Robert Sanderson eating out of the palm of her hand. It was incredible how easily she took control of a situation.

"Don't you worry your pretty little head, Maggie. How are you, sweetheart?" he said, clapping her on the shoulder.

Maggie was as much of a hit with clients, if not more, than he was. At least he didn't have to worry about Robert hitting on her—the old man was pushing eighty-five, still running a successful restaurant chain, and more likely to offer her a caramel and a twenty-dollar bill than ask her out.

"I'm very well, thank you. How have you been?" she

replied, leading him to the desk and stepping back so he could take the seat she'd been working in earlier. She picked up her tablet and rounded the desk, taking the empty seat beside Cal, crossing her legs.

"Can't complain," Robert replied. "And yourself, Cal?"

"I'm good, thanks, Robert. Good to see you again."

Maggie swiped open her tablet and leaned forward. "I'm afraid we haven't been able to print anything out, because of the computer problems." She didn't have to explain further. Robert's eyes glazed over at the mere mention of technology. "But I have everything here." She held the tablet up. "So let's get started, shall we?"

Maggie

A shrill ringing woke Maggie with a start. She opened her blurry eyes to find Cal, feeling around the nightstand until his fingers closed over the ringing phone. The glowing red clock read three forty-two a.m.

"Hello?" he answered gruffly.

Maggie yawned and sat up, the light from Cal's bedside lamp enough for her to see Cal's expression of confusion at whatever the person on the other line said. He pulled the phone away from his ear and winced as he took in the green case. "It's yours, baby."

She took the phone from him and checked the caller

ID, her heart racing. *Dad. Shit.* She held the phone to her ear. "Dad? What's going on?"

"There's been a break in at the cafe. They smashed the place up," her dad replied, panic in his voice.

"Oh my God, are you okay? Were you there? Did you phone the police?" Maggie jumped out of bed and wedged the phone between her ear and shoulder while she searched the floor for her pants.

"We're fine, yes. We weren't here—Ricardo from across the street called us. We haven't called the police. I don't know what to do, Mags. That's why I'm calling you."

Maggie paused and took a deep breath. Somehow, he still surprised her with how fucking useless he was when it came to Burly's. "You have to call the police, Dad. I live an hour away. They'll get there faster."

"But you're always the one to deal with these kinds of things," he protested. Sure, Maggie handled any complications with the cafe, but that didn't mean she could single-handedly handle criminal activity.

"I'll be there as soon as I can, but call the police while I'm on the way, okay?"

"Yeah, sure," her dad replied with a sigh. "Maggie?"

"Yeah?"

"Who was the man that answered?" he asked with an air of suspicion.

Maggie's eyes flicked to Cal, who was watching her with concern.

"You seriously want to talk about that now?" she

asked her dad, looking away from Cal and sitting down to pull her socks on.

"He sounded Irish. Isn't your boss Irish? I thought you wanted to be on your own and that's why you left Nathan." She didn't have to see her dad's face to imagine the look of disapproval; it was written all over his voice.

"We're not talking about this right now. Call the police—I'll be there soon."

She hung up and tossed the phone on the bed, grabbing her sweatshirt from the floor. "Someone broke into Burly's," she told Cal, her voice muffled as she pulled it over her head.

"Shit, is everyone okay?"

"Yeah, they're fine. Apparently whoever it was fucked up the cafe, though. I have to drive up there."

"I can drive you," Cal said quickly, and Maggie turned away.

"No, it's—"

"Please, love. It's three a.m. You're stressed and you have no idea what you're walking into."

Maggie took a deep breath. It was the same argument they had every single time her parents called her these days. She knew Cal just wanted to help, but she couldn't ignore the voice in her head—that sounded suspiciously like Nathan—telling her he thought she couldn't handle it on her own. God, seeing him again had fucked her up.

"I'll be fine," she said, tossing her phone into her purse.

"You don't even have your car, Maggie," Cal protested.

"I'll get a cab to the house and drive from there."

Cal pushed the comforter back and stood up, moonlight catching his bare chest. "If you think I'm going to let you get a cab at three a.m.—"

"Let me?" The words sank their claws into her skin, so reminiscent of how Nathan used to act. Maggie knew Cal wasn't Nathan, but that didn't stop her from seeing red. "You don't *let me* do anything, Cal. I'm my own fucking person and perfectly capable of making my own decisions." He didn't get to decide things for her—no one did. She hadn't finally made it out from under Nathan's thumb just to fall into someone else who thought he knew what was best for her.

She stormed out of the bedroom, and Cal trailed behind her, groaning her name. "You know that's not what I meant, love. Can we talk about this, please?"

"I don't have time for this right now." She perched on the edge of the couch, tugging her shoes on.

"So what, you're seriously just going to walk out of here right now? At least let me drive you to your place and you can drive from there."

"I'm *fine*."

Cal loosed a growl of frustration. "I know you're fine, Maggie. But I'm here and—"

Maggie didn't mean to raise her voice, but what came out was suspiciously close to a shout. "I can do this on my own."

"And I'm saying you don't have to," Cal replied, and she could tell he was forcing his voice to sound somewhat calm. He reached for her as she crossed the room towards the hall.

Maggie pulled herself out of his grip, her blood rushing in her ears. "I don't need you, Cal," she shouted, and Cal stepped back as if she'd punched him in the stomach, his face falling. "Fuck, that's not what I meant. I…" Maggie trailed off, her stomach in knots. She needed to get out of here. She was so tired, and she had to clear her head. "I have to go."

She stepped into the elevator and slammed the button to close the door before Cal could stop her, but her name falling from his lips followed her down from the penthouse like nails on a chalkboard.

CHAPTER TWENTY-NINE

Maggie

Blue flashing lights lit up the Marysville street that played home to Burly's, but Maggie couldn't bring herself to get out of the car. The drive had passed in a blur, flashes of her fight with Cal blaring in the back of her mind.

She was still furious that he'd tried to tell her what to do, but she was just as angry at herself for reacting so badly.

Maggie jumped as there was a quick rap on the window, looking up to see a police woman peering in. "Everything okay, ma'am?"

Maggie nodded, though nothing was actually okay. She opened the door and the police woman stepped back, allowing her out of the car. "Hi. This is my parents' cafe."

"Ah. You must be Maggie. We've been waiting for you."

Great. Some small part of Maggie had hoped her parents might have worked with the police themselves, and there would be little for her to do by the time she got to Marysville. The officer led her into Burly's, where her parents were sitting with a further two police officers, waiting for her.

"Oh, Mags, thank God," her mom cried, jumping up as she spied her. "This is our daughter," she told the police. "She'll be able to fix this."

Maggie looked around the cafe in disbelief. Though the windows and doors seemed largely undamaged, everything else was trashed. Broken glass and smashed coffee cups crunched under her shoes; what looked like black paint had been splashed across the tables and walls; the glass pastry cabinet had a large hairline crack from, she assumed, the smashed espresso machine lying in front of it. Maggie wasn't sure she could fix this.

"Did you find out who broke in?" she asked, approaching the table. The officers exchanged a look that set her, somehow, more on edge. "What?"

An older officer cleared his throat. "It's Maggie, isn't it?" She nodded, and he gestured to the seat across from him. "Why don't you take a seat?"

She didn't want to take a seat; she wanted to go home. But she didn't feel like arguing, so she sank into the chair, the legs wobbling, and looked at the officer.

He clasped his hands in front of him. "It wasn't exactly a break in."

"What?" Maggie asked, looking at her parents in

confusion. Her dad's mouth was set in a thin line, but her mom looked a little abashed.

"Well, the door was left open, so it can't be classed as a break in. Trespassing, burglary, and destruction of property, yes, but not a break in," the officer explained, but Maggie struggled to listen after *the door was left open*.

"You left the door open?" she accused her parents, and, after what felt like an age, her dad gave a jerky nod. "What the fuck is wrong with you?" she shouted, pushing away from the table. "Tell me you at least locked the safe."

Their silence was deafening. "How much?" she ground out, but her parents just stared at the ground, saying nothing. "How much did they take?"

"We glanced over the sales record book. It wasn't totally up to date, but we estimate it to be somewhere around twelve to fifteen thousand from the safe," the officer who'd led her in interjected. "And around six hundred from the register."

"Twelve to fifteen thousand," Maggie repeated, shaking her head. How the hell had it all gone so wrong? "How could you be so stupid?" she asked her parents. "You're supposed to take the cash to the bank every couple of days. It's right down the street!"

"Stop shouting at us," her dad grumbled, and Maggie gaped at him.

"You just lost thousands of dollars and you're worried about me shouting at you? You realize that insurance won't cover any of this, right? All the repairs, replacing the equipment and lost money, none of it. Because you didn't lock the fucking door." The repairs and damaged equipment would cost tens of thousands alone.

"You can help us out though, Mags. Right?" her mom asked and Maggie felt a lump in her throat. Was that all she was good for to them? Someone to sweep in and fix things? Someone to finance their stupidity?

She had the money, sure, but she would need to more or less empty her savings to get Burly's back up and running again. Once upon a time, she might have just done it, but if she did, she would end up right back here a few months down the line.

"No. I can't."

Her parents' jaws dropped, panic flashing on her mom's face.

"What do you mean, you can't?"

"I don't have that kind of money. And I can't keep paying for your mistakes."

"Jesus, Maggie, why are you always so hard on us?" her dad shouted and Maggie flinched.

"Are you kidding me? Hard on you? I show up every single time you mess up—which is constantly, for the record. I've spent a goddamn fortune cleaning up your messes, not to mention the hours of sleep I've lost and the constant stress of trying to juggle managing you and everything else in my life." The words streamed out of her, like once she started, she just couldn't stop.

Her dad's answering laugh was mocking. "What life, Maggie? You should be glad you have the cafe to help with, considering how beneath you your job is. Four years of college to become some rich guy's assistant?

Though it sounds like that's not all you are."

"What the fuck is that supposed to mean?"

"Language, Maggie," her mom chastised, and Maggie ground her teeth.

Her dad sneered. "You know exactly what it means. You broke up with Nathan because you wanted to be independent and now look at you. You didn't even manage a year on your own before finding some other man to take care of you—and you say we can't handle shit."

"What's he talking about, Maggie?" her mom asked.

Before Maggie could respond, her dad jumped in. "When I called her to tell her about the breakup, her boss answered. Called her *baby*," he sneered.

Her mom shook her head, disappointment etched on her face. "Oh, Maggie. You know, I'm sure Nathan would take you back if you apologized. He could take care of you."

Maggie felt a crack going down her spine, her moms's words breaking something deep within her. She couldn't pretend this time that it didn't get to her.

She turned away from her parents, blinking back tears. "Is there anything else you need from us?" she asked the police officers, who were watching the display with wide eyes.

"We need the footage from your security cameras. Your parents didn't know how to access it," one of them piped up. "And a contact number for you."

Maggie pulled a piece of paper from her purse and scribbled her number down, handing it over. "The security footage is online. I'll download it onto a flash drive and drop it into the station tomorrow."

"That would be great, thanks," the officer said, offering her a reassuring smile. "Do you have any questions for us before we head out?"

"No. Thank you for coming. We really appreciate it," Maggie replied, waving the officers off and wishing she could walk out behind them.

She turned back to her parents, who were watching her with matching frowns.

"So what's your plan?" her dad asked with a shrug that put Maggie's hackles up.

"My plan?"

"How are you going to fix this? If you sell your house, that should be enough to fix things, right?"

Maggie stared, open-mouthed, at them. "I'm not selling my house. I live there."

Her dad threw up his hands in frustration. "How are you going to afford to fix this place if you don't sell your house?"

"What makes you think I'm going to be paying at all?"

"Who else is going to? It's always been your job to fix things, Maggie."

The words severed whatever patience Maggie had left and she snatched her purse up from the paint-splashed table. "No."

"No?" Maggie's mom repeated, her voice wobbling.

"No. I'm not doing this. I'm not giving you a penny,

and I'm not helping with Burly's anymore. Fix it your-
selves or sell it, I don't care. I'm done."

Maggie ignored her parents' protests as she stepped
out into the cool air, holding her breath. She slammed her
car door behind her and pulled out of Marysville faster
than was technically legal. Adrenaline rushed through her
like sugar in her veins; she'd finally done it. She'd stood
up for herself and stopped letting her family walk all
over her.

Maggie held her breath until she was far enough away
from Marysville that she could cry without the risk of
being recognized.

I cy air filled Maggie's house. She didn't bother
turning the heat on; what was the point when she had
to leave for work in a couple hours? Any hope of sleep
had died on the drive home. Even if she had the time to
sleep, the morning's events had thoroughly woken her.

She dropped into a chair at her kitchen table and let
her head fall into her hands. *What a mess.* At least she
finally knew where she stood with her parents. Sure,
she'd always known they didn't respect her job, but
they'd made one thing perfectly fucking clear: they didn't
respect her, either. After everything she'd done for them.

Why had she waited so long to say no? She didn't
know how to be her parents' daughter without taking care
of everything for them, just like she hadn't known how to

be Nathan's girlfriend without doing whatever he wanted and leaving nothing for herself.

Were her parents right? Had she just fallen into the same pattern with Cal? She'd fallen for the one person in the world she was contractually obligated to do shit for. It felt good to take care of everything at work so that he didn't have to worry—even if it annoyed him to no end that she did too much. She didn't do anything for him after work—the one time she'd tried, Cal had found her in his laundry room folding a dry load and told her in no uncertain circumstances that she was there to relax, not do chores—and he didn't seem to expect anything from her, but that didn't change how much she exhausted herself going above and beyond at the office.

How were they supposed to have a balanced relationship when she couldn't ignore the sense of obligation that she had to take care of him, and he didn't believe that she could manage on her own? He'd told her over and over that he did, but all evidence suggested otherwise—why else would he constantly try to take care of her?

Maybe he was right. Hell, maybe her parents were right. She and Nathan had broken up only two months before she started sleeping with Cal, and she'd fallen much harder and faster than she had when she met Nathan. Maybe none of it was real, and her heart had just seen something easy and safe to fall into. And if that was true, it wasn't fair to Cal.

She hadn't been fair to herself either; she'd wanted the chance to prove to everyone that she didn't need anyone to keep everything under control, and now everyone knew that she'd just jumped straight from Nathan to Cal. Her parents' disappointment, the whispers in the office…

I can do this on my own.

And I'm saying you don't have to.

Cal didn't understand. He couldn't. *I care about you,* he'd said, after Nathan's interview. *I'm allowed to worry.*

Maggie wanted to believe him more than anything. But she didn't. She'd tried her best to hold it together and keep a smile on her face, but she couldn't do it anymore. And that wasn't fair to Cal. He deserved better than a performance, but Maggie had nothing else to give him, which meant she only had one choice.

She took a deep breath, pulled the notebook from her bag, and carefully tore two pages from the middle. Maggie leaned over the table and willed herself not to cry as she penned two letters.

CHAPTER THIRTY

Exhaustion weighed Cal's shoulders down as he slumped against the elevator wall, but it had nothing on the worry weighing down his heart.

Maggie hadn't called or texted. He had no confirmation she'd even made it to Marysville in one piece. She'd walked out of his apartment and it had taken every fiber of Cal's being not to chase after her.

I don't need you, Cal.

She didn't; Cal knew that. She could walk away from him, head out into the world, and excel wherever she went. But he needed her. He hadn't realized how incomplete he'd been until Maggie filled the empty space just waiting for her in his heart.

He loved her. And he had no idea if she would ever let him.

Cal dragged his feet into his office. He didn't want to

look at his desk, scared he would see his answering machine flashing red with a message that could only be from Maggie. It wouldn't surprise him—she was probably still dealing with the cafe and, even if she wasn't, she must be exhausted. But Cal needed to see her. He couldn't stand to leave things how they'd left them that morning.

Cal breathed a sigh of relief as he spied the answering machine, free of flashing lights, and sank into his desk chair. He leaned forward with a sigh, his elbow sliding on a piece of paper, knocking it to the ground. Fuck knows where it had come from. He'd actually tidied his desk for once before leaving yesterday.

He reached down, grabbing the paper from the floor and stilled. Not paper. An envelope—two envelopes. The flawless cursive on the front of each was as familiar to him as his own; he even recognized the dark blue, almost black, ink, belonging to a familiar pen.

His heart raced as he set the envelopes side by side on the desk. One read *Mr. Michaelson*. The other, *Cal*. He brushed a finger over the latter before sitting back in his chair and swallowing the lump in his throat.

If it didn't open the letters, this wasn't happening. If he didn't open the letters, nothing had changed. He couldn't even let himself think about what the letters contained. It was too easy to guess, and that made things too real.

Cal didn't realize the world was still spinning, and time was still passing, until there was a loud knock at his door, and Jazz's voice shouted, "Are you in there,

Maggie? Because, as much as I support you spending your morning locked up in here, it would be helpful to know."

"It's open," he called back, his voice shaky, and Jazz stepped into the office.

She frowned as she clocked him sitting alone. "Where's Maggie?"

It was the giant tumbler in her hand that snapped him back to reality, a gift from Maggie to Jazz for her first day at the firm. It matched Maggie's perfectly, except Jazz's was turquoise and Maggie's was green.

"I…" He didn't know what to say, how to explain. Cal closed his eyes, pinching the spot between his brows. "She's not here."

"Okay…" Jazz drew the word out as she crossed the room. "What's going—what are those?" Her eyes zeroed in on the letters on his desk.

"Letters," Cal managed.

"From Maggie?" she asked, though Cal knew she recognized the handwriting as well as he did. He nodded. "What do they say?"

"I haven't opened them. I… I can't." His voice cracked and sympathy flooded Jazz's face.

"Oh shit. What happened?"

She sank into the seat beside his desk while he gave her a rundown of the morning's events. Jazz's eyes got wider and wider, wincing when Cal explained how Maggie had walked away.

"And she hasn't called or texted? At all?"

"No, just the letters."

"Do you want me to open it?" Jazz asked, and Cal nodded, handing her the one addressed to *Mr. Michaelson.*

She opened the envelope and slid a perfectly folded piece of paper out, scanning Maggie's handwriting. Her eyes narrowed as she processed the note until she set it down with a small shake of her head. "It's her resignation. Effective immediately. It's very… generic," she added with a wince.

Fuck. Cal had expected it—why else would she write two letters? One for him to file away in her staff file, and one for him to file away in his heart. He didn't have it in him to read the latter, but he needed to know. And he couldn't ask Jazz to read that one.

"Will you… Would you mind staying while I open the other one?" he asked and sympathy shone in Jazz's eyes as she nodded.

Cal's hands shook as he slid his letter open across the top of the envelope, freeing the letter inside. He took a deep breath and unfolded the paper.

> *Cal,*
>
> *I'm so sorry for leaving things like this. I know doing this via letter makes me a coward, but I don't think I could do it in person.*
>
> *It feels like years ago that you told me to do whatever it took to find the thing that excited me and, thanks to you, I did. It was you the*

whole time. The past three months have been the most beautiful, magical, exciting three months of my life, and I'm so grateful.

But seeing Nathan again and everything with my parents has just reminded me why I left Nathan, and I didn't do it to turn around and fall for someone else. I need to figure myself out, and I need to do it on my own.

I wasn't lying all those times I promised I loved my job, but I have to stop using it as an excuse not to get my shit together. Jazz might drive you a little crazy at first, but she's good at what she does.

It might not have been sixty years, but I'd do it all over again for those three months.

I'm sorry.

Maggie

Cal stared at the letter, blinking back the burning in his eyes.

"Cal?"

He started as Jazz said his name, then set the letter down on the table. He couldn't look at it anymore; the words had cleaved him in two. There was Cal from twenty-four hours ago, the Cal who spent every moment wondering what he'd done to deserve even the chance of a happy ending with Maggie, and post-letter Cal, who knew he never did.

"It's over," he replied, his voice raw. "She wants to be on her own. It's over."

"For fuck's sake, Maggie," Jazz muttered under her breath.

"What the hell am I supposed to do here? Do I just let her go?" Cal's voice cracked and Jazz sucked in a breath.

"No. Definitely not. You two are great together. She's just scared," Jazz assured him, patting him on the shoulder in what he thought was supposed to be a comforting way. "Maybe just give her some space for now. She won't want to see me today, but I'll talk to her and figure out where her head's at. It's going to be okay. This isn't the end."

Cal wanted to believe her, but Jazz hadn't seen Maggie's face when she'd told him she didn't need him.

"Cal. Listen to me. I've known Maggie for twenty years, and I've never seen her fall for anyone like she's fallen for you."

"But she didn't want to fall for me," Cal said, his voice cracking. "Isn't that the problem?"

"Maggie never wants to do anything that's good for her. It's why she never takes a break. Just give her some time, and it'll all work out. Oh, and this?" She tapped a finger on Maggie's letter of resignation. "Ignore that for now. She's not resigning. I'm not letting her. Can we just tell the rest of the team that she's taking some time off?"

"But if she gets another job—"

"She won't." Jazz seemed much more certain than he

was. She clapped her hands together and stood up with a deep breath. "Okay. I'm going to go deal with the rest of the team. You don't have any client meetings today, but you have a meeting with Carissa. She has a case she wants to go over with you, but don't ask me what it is. Are you up for it, or do you want me to cancel?"

Cal wasn't up for anything, but the team would notice if he checked out on the same day Maggie took unplanned time off.

"No, it's fine."

"Awesome. It'll all work out, Cal. Promise."

Cal tried to let her words sink into the depths of his shattered heart as Jazz skipped from the room; he tried to emulate the look of sheer determination on her face. But his office was too quiet, too empty, without the possibility that Maggie might make her way up the stairs at any moment, just to work beside him.

Maggie was built into the foundation of this place as much as he was, so why had it taken him so long to figure it out?

I'd do it all over again for those three months. It was eerily similar to what his mom had said back home, but Cal couldn't help thinking that his mom didn't know how much it fucking hurt to have something so magical just to lose it.

CHAPTER THIRTY-ONE

Maggie

Maggie put the phone down and looked around the room at what she'd created. She walked around the house, trailing her fingers over the furniture, the finishes. Not an inch of the place had been left untouched. She'd knocked down walls, refinished floors, painted, tiled, and designed the hell out of the place.

Maggie hated that her first thought was how proud Cal would have been. Tears she didn't realize she still had in her pricked at her eyes.

She paused in the hallway, staring up the stairs. She'd taken a house that was falling apart with the intention of making a home and made… a nicer house. It was beautiful, there was no doubt about that, but that didn't make it feel like a home.

Three weeks had passed since she'd quit her job,

given up on her parents, and walked away from Cal. She'd worked day and night to finish the house, not because she was in a rush, but she didn't know how else to fill her time.

For the first time in forever, she technically didn't have anything else to worry about; she'd quit her job and left Burly's behind her. That didn't stop her from worrying, of course. She still worried about everything: her parents, Jazz messing up her years of organizational work and the office falling apart, the clients she'd spent years cultivating relationships with forgetting her name, Cal.

Cal.

Cal clearing out the clothes she'd left in his closet. Cal turning on the sound machine she'd given him for Christmas and settling into his reading nook. Cal going to the club and bringing someone new home—

Nope. She wasn't going there; if she did, she might just throw up.

She'd forgotten how to sleep without him. She'd forgotten how to sit on the couch and watch TV, or make a nice cup of coffee to enjoy a quiet morning on the couch, how to lie in the dark without leaning over to what had been his side of the bed to switch on the lamp. She'd forgotten how to exist in a world where she wasn't Cal's, and he wasn't hers.

What a terrible time to realize that a beautiful house meant nothing when the person you wanted to share it with wasn't around anymore.

Maggie sat on the stairs and shook her head. Three weeks of trying not to think about him. Three weeks of lying through her teeth when Jazz asked if she was okay, resisting the urge to ask how Cal was. Part of her didn't want to know. She didn't want him to be miserable, but how could she be okay if he wasn't? How could she be okay if he'd found a way to live comfortably without her?

I don't need you, Cal, she'd screamed at him. She'd figured out how wrong she was too fucking late. What part of her brain had twisted things so thoroughly that she'd believed she needed to be alone to prove anything?

She knew now that he hadn't been trying to control her; he'd just cared about her and she hadn't appreciated it. Because no one had ever cared for her like Cal had, so Maggie hadn't been able to recognize it for what it was.

Walking away had never felt like this before. She hadn't shed a single tear over Nathan, and, though she'd been devastated when her high school boyfriend had broken up with her and immediately started dating one of her sister's friends, she'd never wondered if she would actually survive it.

Cal might have been the one to turn her into a lovesick mess, but she'd been the one to mess it all up. She had no right to be so sad when she was the one who'd called it quits—personally and professionally. For the first time in a long time, Maggie had no idea what she was doing.

She had no Cal, no job, and a house she didn't care about. How did she get it all so wrong?

Maggie had to get out of here. She grabbed her purse and keys from the hooks by the door and ran down the stone steps onto the tree-shaded street. A walk would clear her head.

It had surprised her how much she'd enjoyed reno-vating the house; getting a design on paper and bringing it to life with her own two hands. And her TikTok had been a saving grace through the last few weeks of loneli-ness. Her following had tripled as she'd started posting more, and she'd even started getting emails from brands offering to work with her. And pay. A lot.

The idea was appealing since she was technically unemployed and her savings wouldn't last forever, but she didn't see how she could maintain the platform now that the house was finished. She had a couple weeks of videos saved up and ready to post, but after that… Short of tearing the whole thing down and starting again (which she had no intention of doing), there was nothing left for her to work on.

If she hadn't stormed out of Burly's so hastily, she could have made renovating the cafe her next project, but she couldn't bring herself to regret the decision. That was just about the only thing from the past month that she didn't regret.

Maggie walked until she reached the nearest store that sold ice cream and wine; it was a cliche for a reason. Armed with a bottle of merlot and a pint of salted caramel ice cream, she walked back to the house in record time—melted ice cream did nothing for broken hearts.

She frowned as she approached to find a woman standing outside the house, her face pressed against the living room window.

"Can I help you?" Maggie asked, and the woman spun around, her cheeks coloring.

"Oh, I'm sorry. I can't imagine what this must look like—you're Maggie, right?"

Maggie took a subconscious step back. "Yes."

"I'm Nadia Anderson—the realtor who sold you the house? I don't think we ever actually met in person," Nadia explained, and Maggie took a sigh of relief.

"Right, your assistant showed me around."

Nadia nodded. "I was on third trimester bed-rest. You were my last sale before the twins were born, actually."

"Congratulations," Maggie offered. Now that she knew she wasn't in danger, she was just curious why her realtor was here.

"Thanks. And congratulations to you—I've seen your videos. The place looks great. Do you have much left to do?"

It felt bittersweet to open her mouth and say, "I just finished. Today, actually." She held up the wine and ice cream. "These are to celebrate."

Nadia's eyes lit up. "Wow, congrats!"

Maggie returned her smile, and then, before she could think it through, said, "Do you want to take a look?"

"Are you kidding? I'd love to! I was just heading back from an appointment and thought I'd sneak a peek in the window."

Maggie chuckled and pulled her keys from her pocket. "I think we can do better than that."

Jazz would be furious that she wouldn't be the first to tour the finished house, but if Maggie saved the wine and ice cream for her coming over, she was sure she'd be forgiven.

Nadia followed her from room to room, bright eyed and full of praise for everything Maggie had done to the place.

"You must be so happy with everything," she gushed as they finished up in the kitchen and Maggie poured her a glass of water. "And relieved to be done with it."

"Yeah," Maggie replied, wincing at the lack of enthusiasm in her voice.

Nadia quirked a brow. "You don't like it?"

"No, I do, it's just…" Maggie trailed off, leaning against the kitchen island. "I think I enjoyed renovating it more than I like the outcome. It's a beautiful house, but it doesn't feel like my home, you know? It's a little big for one person," she tacked on, so she didn't sound completely out of her mind.

"I get that," Nadia agreed, pursing her lips. "You know, you got a steal on this place, and I don't know how much you put into it, but if you wanted to sell it, I have no doubt you'd probably double your money at a minimum."

Maggie blinked at her. "Seriously?"

"Oh, yeah. There are a ton of fixer uppers around here. A lot of older houses have been neglected over the years, and need a ton of work, but the people desperate to buy are families and young professionals who are looking for finished homes. Most of them don't have the time, or inclination, to put this much work into a place, so the good houses are selling fast." She leaned in conspiratorially. "I had a house close less than four weeks after listing last month."

Maggie had no idea. She hadn't exactly researched the market before buying her house on a whim. "So what, I'd sell this place and buy another fixer upper to renovate?" she asked, and Nadia shrugged.

"I don't see why not. You clearly have an eye for design and a knack for following through on it. Not to mention your TikTok. There are people out there making a lot of money fixing up run-down houses. Not everyone is cut out for it."

Maggie blew out a breath, mulling it over. It wasn't like she didn't have any kind of emotional attachment to the house; it was where she'd moved after Nathan, seeking independence. This was where Cal had helped with her pipes and removed Margaret the spider, where he'd made her Thanksgiving dinner and helped paint the dining room before carrying her up to bed. This was where she'd realized she was falling in love with him. Hell, there was no point in lying to herself anymore; she hadn't been falling for a long time. She'd crash landed, head over heels, before he'd even asked her on a date.

But those memories were exactly why this house would never feel like a home to her. It had started to, but she'd given that up when she'd given up on her and Cal. Starting over might not be such a bad idea. And with another house to renovate, she could take some of those brand deals and stop blowing through her savings. Maybe it would all go terribly wrong, but maybe, just maybe, she could make a career out of this.

For the first time in weeks, Maggie let herself be a little excited. *Do whatever it takes to find the thing that excites you, love.* She'd found that thing, and lost it just as fast. But it was Cal's voice in her head, telling her to keep looking, that made her say, "Alright. Let's do it."

CHAPTER THIRTY-TWO

A knock on his office door dragged Cal's head from his hands. He was exhausted. Fifty-five days without Maggie; almost two months—not that he was counting—and he hadn't had a decent night of sleep since.

"It's open," he called, surprised when the door opened and Liam slipped into the room. "Hey. Is everything alright?"

"Yeah, it's all good," his son reassured him. "Just wanted to check in. I haven't really seen you since my birthday. How are you doing?" Liam took a seat across from him.

"I'm good. Everything's great, yeah," Cal lied through his teeth. "Sorry I've been so quiet lately. Things have been pretty busy around here."

"Ah, because Maggie's on leave?"

Cal swallowed. "Exactly, yeah."

"When will she be back?" Liam asked, and Cal physically ached.

"Uh, we're not sure yet. But she hasn't taken a proper vacation in six years, so it's about time."

"Hmm." Liam drilled his fingers on the arm of his chair, a tic he'd inherited from Cal. "I met Jasmine downstairs. She's great. Very... chatty." He gave Cal a weighty expression and Cal knew.

"Jazz told you about Maggie and me, huh?"

"Yeah."

Cal sighed, rubbing the back of his neck. "In her defense, I'm surprised she hasn't told everyone." For all he knew, she had, and he just hadn't found out yet. Jazz was an excellent assistant, but different from Maggie in every way. More things went wrong during their day-to-day operations than they had in the six years Maggie had been there, but Jazz had a knack for problem solving and fixing things so they worked even better than before.

"Why didn't you tell me, Dad?" Liam asked gently.

"I didn't know how," Cal replied honestly. "How do you tell your thirty-four-year-old kid that you fell in love with a twenty-seven-year-old?"

"Thirty-five, as of three weeks ago," Liam reminded him.

"Christ." It felt like he'd blinked and missed Liam growing up.

"It's a little weird, sure, but if she makes you happy, then that's all I want."

"She does," Cal said, his stomach churning. "She did."

Liam gave him a look of sympathy, fresh off a heartbreak of his own. "Are you busy for the rest of the afternoon?"

Cal glanced over his calendar. There were only a couple hours left of the workday, and he had documents he should be reviewing before leaving. But nothing was urgent.

He said as much, and Liam stood up. "Perfect. Grab your jacket and we'll go across the street to that ridiculously overpriced bar and you can tell me all about it."

Cal had never really had time to imagine fatherhood before it was thrust upon him, but he didn't think he could ever have anticipated drinking with his adult son in a bar and lamented their concurrent heartbreaks.

He started at the beginning, talking Liam through his and Maggie's chance meeting at the club (though he lied and said they'd met in a bar instead of a sex club), to the mess of him telling her to say yes to Liam, to their first date, and then watching it all implode right in front of his eyes,

Cal left out the unsavory parts, but he told his son about fixing her plumbing and painting the dining room, putting up her Christmas tree and the most thoughtful gift he'd ever been given. He told him about falling in love with her in the small moments, watching her laugh in his parents' living room, as his dad showed her blurry pictures of a funny dog he'd spotted; watching her breathe as she drifted off to sleep in his arms.

By the time he was finished, their glasses were empty and Liam was staring at him with a look of shock.

"So let me get this straight," he said. "Maggie left you because she doesn't believe she can manage on her own and wants to prove it to herself, and you've given her space for two months?"

"Pretty much, yeah," Cal agreed.

"What the fuck, Dad?" Liam punched him, not entirely lightly, in the arm.

"What?" Cal asked, bewildered. "Jazz said giving her space was the right call. She needs time to prove to herself that she's okay alone."

"Jesus Christ," Liam muttered, pinching the bridge of his nose. "She's been alone this whole time. Other than the few months you were together anyway. You don't have to be solitary to be alone. Sure, she might have been living with her ex or working with her parents but, from what you've said, she was doing everything on her own. Exactly like she did at the office. Maggie doesn't need to learn how to do things on her own. She needs to learn that you're going to show up and be there for her, even when she pushes you away."

Cal sat back, letting Liam's words wash over him. It's all he'd wanted, for Maggie to let him in enough to trust that she could lean on him. "I tried to help her," he said, tapping his fingers against his empty glass. "I tried to go with her to her parents. I hired Jazz to lighten her workload. Hell, I even tried to make her bed once—she didn't like that." The only thing she'd let him do without complaint was help her with the renovation, and even then she'd looked for the first excuse she could find to convince him he didn't have to. He said as much and Liam rolled his eyes, as if Cal was missing some massive point.

"She's spent her whole life serving people who have never appreciated her, Dad. It must have scared her shitless to have you suddenly trying to take care of her. It sounds like she was neglected as a kid, and her ex took advantage of her to get what he wanted and gave nothing in return. She probably doesn't know what it feels like to be taken care of."

Cal thought about how touched Maggie had been when his family had treated her like one of their own—how happy she'd been to see a family that acted like a family.

Maggie walked through life with her head held high, leaving a trail of perfection in her wake. It was hard to imagine a cracked shell below the surface, but Liam was right—no one could live through twenty-seven years of endless trying with no appreciation and survive unscathed.

"When did you get so good at this kind of shit?" Cal asked his son, and Liam's cheeks flushed scarlet.

"I've been reading a lot of romance books lately. I'm learning a lot."

All Cal's genre of choice had taught him recently was how to identify poisonous berries and sharpen a sword.

Maybe he should borrow a couple of books from Liam. "Huh. I don't suppose you know how I can fix this?"

"You need to convince her you want to fix it first. It sounds like she's been fixing everything for anyone else and has never had the chance to mess up before. She might not let you at first, but you just keep trying," Liam said, gesturing to the bar for another round of drinks. "You show up and you keep helping, even when it pisses her off. Over time, when she sees that you just want to care for her and don't want anything in return, it'll rewrite the part of her brain that tells her she only deserves to be loved if she works hard enough for it."

He could do that. Maggie was stubborn as hell, but Cal hadn't gotten where he was by giving up. He could meet her stubbornness head on and, no matter what it took, he could prove that he loved her for her.

"I'm going to fix it," Cal said resolutely.

"I believe you," Liam replied. "I don't think I've ever seen you so determined."

"She's the one, Liam. Seriously, I know she's young, and it's weird and will probably take a little adjusting to, but I never thought I'd meet someone who made me feel like this. She's... everything."

"I'm happy for you, Dad." And despite his son's own broken heart, Cal knew Liam meant it. Their drinks arrived and Liam picked up his glass, sipping his beer, before saying, "So tell me more about Jasmine."

C al's heart thundered in his chest as he leaned against his car, staring up at Maggie's front door. It was a sleepy Sunday morning in Ravenna, and he was sure she would be curled up on the couch with a cup of coffee, scrolling through her favorite design blogs, with a podcast or music playing in the background.

He'd driven all the way out here yesterday, just to drive straight past her house without stopping, convincing himself that Liam was wrong and he should stay away. But he'd woken up from another night of broken sleep and decided enough was enough. He hadn't told Jazz he was coming, and was regretting that as he walked up the stone path. What if he was making a terrible mistake?

Cal took a deep breath and knocked on the door, holding his breath as footsteps sounded down the hall and the lock clicked.

"Hi, can I help you?"

Cal's heart fell into his stomach as he took in the man in the doorway. For all the scenarios he'd gone over in his head on the drive over, he hadn't considered Maggie having... company. He cleared his throat. "I, uh, I'm looking for Maggie." His voice sounded weak.

Confusion lit the man's face. "I'm sorry. I think you have the wrong address. Actually, hang on." He turned his head and shouted up the stairs. "Babe, what was the woman we bought the house from called?"

Cal held his breath as a voice shouted Maggie's name

down the stairs. He took in the view over the man's shoulders—moving boxes were stacked in the hall. She'd sold the house?

"That's right. Sorry man, we've only been here a couple of weeks and I'm not sure where she moved to."

Cal thanked him and walked back to his car in a daze.

"She sold the house."

Jazz looked up from her desk, a croissant hanging half out of her mouth, as he walked straight into the office to find her on Monday morning.

"Good morning to you too, boss," she mumbled through a full mouth. "What was that?"

Cal dropped into the chair beside hers. He wouldn't usually talk about this in front of the whole office, but no one would hear them over the buzz of post-weekend conversation.

"Maggie. She sold her house."

Jazz swallowed the croissant with a gulp. "She did, but how do *you* know that?"

"Because I went over there yesterday and met the new owners."

"Shit. You went over there?" She whistled when Cal nodded. "Does this mean you're going to try to get her back?"

"Do you think I should?" Cal asked Jazz. The meagre fragment of confidence he'd had the day before had disappeared somewhere on the drive to his apartment.

"We all think you should."

Cal turned around slowly, eyes wide, looking for the culprit. He couldn't single out the person who'd shouted it if he'd tried; every eye in the room was trained on them. Shit.

"Yeah, we don't know what happened between the two of you, but you need to fix it. We miss Maggie," Twyla piped up.

"And we want you both to be happy," Josie added.

Cal raised a brow at Jazz, who held her hands up and said, "I didn't tell anyone! Josie already knew when I started."

Damn. He really thought they'd been discreet. "How did you all find out?" he asked.

"We started to suspect after Thanksgiving, when you took Maggie home to Ireland to work on a case no one had ever heard of," Grant said with a shrug. "And then there was the day you showed us your TikTok, and you were literally only following Maggie."

"But also, you were just terrible at hiding it, Cal," Josie added gently. "She was all you ever talked about, and you regularly made offhand comments about stuff you would only know if you were seeing each other."

Cal frowned. "Like what?"

"One time you told me that Maggie liked to listen to the band I was listening to when she was in the bath," one of the newer paralegals offered.

"And you showed me that picture of those fancy donuts you got for Sunday brunch in bed—Maggie was in the picture, Cal. In your bed," Twyla added.

"Wow. I officially no longer feel bad about telling anyone about this," Jazz said, shaking her head.

Cal covered his face with his hands. Had he always been this oblivious, or was it just that Maggie brought it out in him? Between his family already assuming they were a thing before they'd even arrived and this, he'd done a shit job of staying discreet.

"No one minds, if that's why you're worried," Grant added matter-of-factly. "I mean, I mind a little, but that's just because I'm jealous."

"I think what Grant's trying to say," Josie cut in, "is that we're rooting for the two of you. No one here cares that you're her boss. If she comes back and you are still her boss, that is."

Cal sat back with a shuddering sigh. He hadn't expected any of this.

He must have looked as blindsided as he felt, because Jazz took pity on him, shouting to the team, "Alright, I think Cal gets it. Back to work, everyone."

It didn't have quite the same effect as Maggie's business-mode voice, but, one by one, eyes returned to computers and paperwork.

"She finished the renovation," Jazz explained to him. "But she wasn't in love with the house and knew she was going to miss renovating, so she sold it and bought another fixer upper."

Jazz scribbled something down on the corner of a legal pad and tore it out. "That's her new address. Frankly, this constant pining from both of you is exhausting me, so please do me a favor and go fix it. But not today—you have a ton of work today, and Maggie wouldn't approve of you skipping it to go to her. Tomorrow's pretty empty."

Cal held the address to his chest and nodded. "Tomorrow then."

CHAPTER THIRTY-THREE

Maggie

The clawfoot tub had sold Maggie on the house, but the patio had sold her on the cottage. It wasn't the most sensible selling point, considering how often it rained in Seattle, but she had visions of an awning you could sit below to stay dry and watch the rain.

Unlike the house, Maggie had no illusions that the cottage was her dream home. With the huge yard and basement that would be a gorgeous living space once she finished it, it was the perfect home for a young family, and a new challenge for her to flex her design skills. The cottage was in significantly worse shape than her house had been initially, but she'd gotten an even better deal on it.

She was no less lonely now that she'd sold the house, but she had a new project to distract her, at least. And she had Jazz, who had been with her almost every night since she moved in a week ago, helping her unpack.

Maggie considered calling Jazz no less than three times as she locked the back door. She hadn't told her best friend what her plans were today, because she wasn't sure she was going to follow through. She wouldn't be sure until she stepped out of the elevator and into the office she'd called home for six years until she'd ungraciously walked away without even a goodbye.

For the first couple of weeks, her phone had chimed daily with messages from people at the office, reaching out to ask if she was okay, if she needed anything, but it was the *We miss you!* messages that brought tears to her eyes. She'd known most of the team for years and she'd just left them. In trying to claw back her independence, Maggie had apparently forgotten how to be a decent human being.

Though how she'd treated the team had nothing on how she'd treated Cal. Maggie didn't know if he would want to see her, but she had to apologize. Maybe going to the office during his workday to do it was a bad idea, but the office was where everything had started with them, and it felt right.

She struggled with the gate that led from the backyard to the front of the house—the front door was jammed and she hadn't had the chance to fix it yet, so she'd been using the back door to come and go. There was so much to do, but she couldn't make herself move on until she'd spoken to Cal.

Maggie unlocked her car and reached for the handle

just as a car pulled up on the street. She looked up and her heart stilled at the sight of the familiar Tesla.

Cal stepped out of the car and her chest swelled as she took in his face for the first time in two months. Maggie thought she'd gotten used to the uncomfortable ache in her heart, but it felt like she was breathing for the first time since she'd woken up to a ringing phone in Cal's bed.

"Hi," she said, her voice barely above a whisper.

"Hi, love." Cal's voice washed over her like the softest blanket, her body begging her to wrap herself up in it.

She glanced, confused, from Cal to her car door, shaking her head. "I was just coming to see you. What are you doing here?" If he was here at all, and she hadn't just fallen asleep on the patio again.

Cal's eyes widened. "You were coming to see me?"

"Yeah, I thought it was about time we talked."

Gravel crunched beneath his feet as he walked across the driveway toward her. "I thought so too." He held up two coffee cups from Ethel's. "I brought coffee," he continued. "And also, I miss you. And I couldn't stay away any longer."

"Oh." Maggie's eyes stung with tears. "Fuck, Cal. I don't... I don't even know where to start."

"We'll figure it out," he promised, his words soothing Maggie enough that she managed to pull air into her lungs.

"We can sit out back."

She led him back through the tricky gate to the outdoor table and chairs she'd bought before she even got the keys, dreaming of sitting outside and designing on her tablet when the days got a little warmer.

Cal took a seat opposite her and slid a coffee cup across the table.

"You sold the house." Maggie didn't miss the flash of hurt in his eyes. Though they'd split their time pretty equally between the house and his apartment, she understood why he would be sad to see it go. So many of their defining moments as Maggie and Cal, rather than boss and assistant, had happened within those four walls.

She took a deep breath. "I finished it, and it didn't feel like home after all."

Maggie told him about meeting her realtor; about putting the house on the market and getting offers within twenty-four hours. The couple that bought it in the end were moving to Seattle from Cleveland, and bought it without ever seeing it in person.

"The woman watches my videos," Maggie explained. She was talking too much, but it was easier to talk about this than what was to come. "So she wanted to buy it as is —furniture and everything. It was a really quick sale and, thankfully, I found this place pretty much as soon as I started looking." The cottage had been empty for a couple of years, but she'd still had to stay with Jazz for a few days before getting the keys. Since both Maggie and the couple buying her house were paying cash, the whole process had taken a little over three weeks—a new record for her realtor.

"It's nice," Cal said, looking around the yard. "The garden is amazing."

"That was the selling point for me."

Cal turned back to her. "So, do you think this place is it? Home, I mean."

Maggie bit her lip, shaking her head. "No, but I'm not expecting it to be this time. This place is a job. I loved renovating the house and my TikTok is going well, so I figured I might as well keep going." Something like pride shone in Cal's eyes, and she had to look away. She swallowed, her breath catching in her throat. "Home is, home *was*… you. I just realized that too late."

Cal sucked in a breath. But if she looked at him, she'd crumble. "I thought that letting myself have this, have you, meant giving up a piece of myself and losing it. I've gotten so used to people taking parts of me and treating them like they're nothing, and I've been punishing you for the things that Nathan and my family have done. I'm so sorry." Her voice cracked, and she heard the scrape of Cal's chair on the patio stones as he leaned forward and set his hand over hers.

A shiver ran down Maggie's spine at the touch. God, she'd missed him. So fucking much.

"I see it now," she continued. "I wouldn't really lose that piece of myself. I would just have been giving it to you to take care of. And I trust you. I know you would have treasured it and treated it with nothing but respect. I just realized that too late too."

"Maggie," Cal breathed. "Look at me, love."

Maggie's lip was trembling when she finally looked up and met his gaze.

"It's not too late. It could never be too late. If you

need to walk away a thousand times to figure shit out, I'll always be here for you to come back to. You're it for me, Maggie."

Maggie bit back a sob, covering her face with her hand. Did she really have another chance with him? With how badly she'd treated him, leaving him how she had, was he really willing to try again?

"I was awful to you, Cal. The whole time we were together, I didn't treat you how I should have."

"Maggie," he said, softly, gently pulling her hands away from her face and holding them. "You've spent twenty-seven years being treated badly by almost everyone in your life. And you *are* still only twenty-seven, even if you were forced to grow up way too young. You're still figuring shit out and you got scared. That's okay."

"I wanted to come back," she admitted. "Almost as soon as I left. But I didn't know if I could come back to you as Maggie without coming back to you as your assistant."

There was no judgment, no anger, in Cal's voice as he asked, "You don't want to come back to work?"

Maggie shook her head, a tear slipping down her cheek and landing on the bleached wood tabletop. "I loved being your assistant, but for all the wrong reasons. I threw myself into work because it was easier to take care of everyone else than myself. And if we're going to make whatever this thing is work, if that's what you want, then I can't do that anymore."

A soft smile lifted the corners of Cal's mouth. "Of

course I want to make it work. And my feelings aren't going to change just because you're not my assistant anymore."

All of it seemed too good to be true, and Maggie's face must have betrayed her uncertainty because Cal stood up and dragged his chair around the table, so he was sitting beside her. His sudden proximity was enough to make her dizzy, like she could get drunk on just his presence.

"I know it's going to take a while for you to believe me, but I'm not going anywhere," he continued, his eyes blazing. "You don't have to take care of me for me to love you."

Maggie was propelled back by his words, both the promise and declaration sinking into her bones and taking up residence in the very deepest parts of her. "You love me?" she whispered shakily.

"Quite desperately," Cal replied, his smile wider now, his dimples making her heart race. She'd missed that smile something fierce. "And that doesn't mean there's any pressure for—"

"I love you too," she interrupted, the words streaming out in a blur. Cal blinked in surprise, his mouth falling open. "I love you," she repeated more slowly. "So much that it feels entirely out of my control. And I know I usually hate things that are out of my control, but I don't hate this. I really, really love this. And I really, really love you."

It was different, she realized, than saying it to Nathan. The first time she and Nathan had exchanged *I love you*s, the lack of fireworks had surprised her. It had been matter-of-fact, something they'd done right on schedule, and Maggie wasn't sure she'd ever meant it if this was what love really felt like.

It was like soaring from the highest cliff knowing that you might crash and fall, but being thrilled by every second of the journey anyway. It was the feeling of placing the last piece in an incomplete jigsaw puzzle; of finally cracking the formula on a nightmare spreadsheet, pressing enter and watching everything fall into place; the first sip of fresh coffee in the morning, and taking your bra off at the end of the night.

And when Cal tugged Maggie into his lap and whispered, "I love you," against her lips before claiming them with a searing kiss, it felt like coming home.

CHAPTER THIRTY-FOUR

Maggie

They still had so much to talk about, but it was hard to talk with Cal's tongue in her mouth and Maggie had no intention of pulling away. She clung to him, making up for two months without tasting him, without feeling his arms around her.

"Inside," she gasped as they broke for a split-second breath. She wrapped her legs around Cal's waist as he picked her up and stepped back, pushing his way through the backdoor and into the kitchen.

Maggie pulled away for long enough to direct him to the bedroom, punctuating each instruction with a kiss to his jaw. Cal pushed into the bedroom and lay her back on the bed, sinking to his knees before her and running his hands up her legs. Maggie's head fell back against the mattress, a groan tumbling from her lips, as he hooked his fingers in the waistband of her leggings and pulled them from her in one sweep.

His beard had grown a little unruly since she'd last seen him, his face ticklish against her skin as he brushed his lips over her thighs.

"I've missed you so much, love," he murmured, his voice rumbly against her. "But fuck, I've missed this too."

Cal claimed her pussy with his mouth like a man starved, his tongue pressing into her and fucking her ruthlessly. Maggie twisted in his grip, the sheets silky and cool beneath her burning body. It had been a while since she'd even touched herself, unable to stop the memories of the man on his knees before her when she did, and she knew it wouldn't be long before she fell apart with the way he was consuming her.

"Cal," she gasped, grasping at his collar. "I want... I need..." Cal pulled back, looking up at her, his bright eyes shining with love. Maggie drew a long breath into her longs. "I want us to come together."

"Fuck, baby," Cal murmured, swallowing. He stood, shedding his clothes quickly while Maggie pulled her sweatshirt off and tossed it aside. Her mouth watered as she took him in, every inch of him calling to her. She reached for him, and Cal clasped their hands together as he pressed his weight on top of her.

"I love you, Maggie. So fucking much," he whispered against her mouth.

"I love you," Maggie replied and Cal pressed into her, her pussy clenching around his cock, welcoming him like it had missed him just as much as the rest of her had. Cal rolled his hips slowly, teasing her.

"Do you want soft and gentle, baby girl?" he whispered, his lips a hairsbreadth from her neck. Maggie gasped as his breath tickled her. "Or do you want me to fuck you like I've missed the hell out of you for the past two months?"

He cursed as Maggie squeezed her pussy around his cock. "We have the rest of our lives for soft and gentle. Fuck me like you missed me, Daddy."

Cal's pupils swallowed any trace of emerald in his eyes. "The rest of our lives, huh?"

Maggie nodded and bit her lip, but Cal stole it out from under her teeth, biting down lightly as he drove into her, drawing a cry from her throat.

His thrusts were rough as he used the mattress for leverage to hit the deepest parts of her. Maggie sobbed into his mouth, pleasure building faster than she could control. Neither of them was going to last long, and Cal's grip tensed on her hands as she tightened around him.

"Together, baby," he whispered, his lips feather light against the corner of her mouth. "I love you."

Those three words were her undoing and emerald stars flashed behind Maggie's eyelids as she snapped, Cal's name falling from her tongue with a worshipping cry. Cal came with a shuddering breath, filling her while her pussy spasmed around his cock.

His knees buckled, letting more of his weight land on top of her and, though he shifted to pull back, Maggie held him to her, not ready to let go of him.

Finally, when their breaths and hearts had settled down, Cal pulled out of her. She whimpered as he did so, the movement sending aftershocks through her body. Cum spilled out of her, down her thighs, making a mess of the bed. Maggie had no idea where the box of spare bedding was, but it was hard to care.

Cal ran a gentle hand through her hair, as if he couldn't bear to stop touching her. "You know, I did plan on us talking about everything before falling back into bed."

"But you did plan for us falling back into bed," Maggie pointed out with a laugh.

"Obviously."

"I guess we do still have shit to talk about." Maggie pouted as she rolled over to face him. They'd been too busy, too occupied with each other, when they'd come inside, but she really wished she had that coffee right about now. "Like you said earlier, I'm still twenty-seven, and I know that bothers you—"

"You being twenty-seven has never been my problem, love," Cal interrupted, squeezing her hands. "It was me being fifty-five. I thought you deserved someone you could have sixty years with like my parents, and I can't give you that. I mean, I don't feel old yet, but technically I am, and—"

"Cal," she interrupted, and he paused, sucking in a deep breath. "I know how old you are and I understand everything that comes with that. I still want you. I'm sure our ages are going to trip us up along the way, and people are probably going to mistake you for my dad whenever we go out—" Maggie wrinkled her nose, "—but that's a small price to pay for getting to love you."

Cal's cheeks flushed, his smile blinding. "I love you. More than anything, baby. Talk to me about work. This—the houses and your TikTok—you're going to make a go of it?"

"I think so, yeah." She gave him a quick rundown of how it would work, financially, based on how much she'd made from the house and her TikTok so far, and her budget for the cottage renovation. Cal raised his brows and whistled, impressed. "I guess ideally, if it goes well, I would look into designing for existing homeowners too," she explained. It was all part of a five-year business plan she'd written at three a.m. one morning when she'd woken up missing him and hadn't been able to get back to sleep. "None of it's guaranteed, though, which is fucking terrifying."

"This is you we're talking about, love. No one follows through on a plan like you do," Cal pointed out.

"That's true," Maggie agreed with a nod. "You're sure you don't mind me leaving? Officially, since I'm pretty sure you never actually processed my resignation."

"I didn't," Cal admitted. "I suggested it once, but Jazz shouted at me. And no, I don't mind. I'll miss having you around all day, but I'm so fucking proud of you, love. The rest of the office will probably be pretty mad, but I'll order lunch for everyone tomorrow and break the news gently. You have to tell Jazz, though. She scares me sometimes."

Maggie snorted. "I'll tell her. I'm sure telling her we

figured things out will soften the blow. One perk of being self-employed is that I'll be able to come by and see you when you're not busy," Maggie mused, and Cal's eyes lit up. "Although that might be weird for the rest of the office."

"Oh, they all know," Cal said, his cheeks turning crimson. "Apparently, I wasn't exactly being subtle about things and basically indirectly told everyone we were seeing each other months ago. They're all rooting for us, though."

Maggie was surprised by how much hearing that warmed her. Admittedly, she'd missed her office-family almost as much as she'd missed Cal. "I kind of feel like I've let them all down by leaving," she admitted, and Cal's fingers stilled their journey through her hair. He cupped her face, brushing her cheek with his thumb.

"You haven't let anyone down. They all want the best for you as much as I do, and everyone is going to be over the moon that you're doing something you love. As long as you come and visit," he added.

"Are you kidding? I'm going to bug you all so much you'll think I never left."

"We'll see how you feel after you see what Jazz has done to your spreadsheets," Cal replied with a soft smirk.

Maggie winced. "I'm going to choose to live in ignorance. Everything's going okay, though?"

"Yeah, everything's fine. We had a couple of growing pains initially, but Jazz thrives on the chaos. We'll look for a calmer assistant for her to balance her out," Cal said, shaking his head and smiling fondly about her best friend.

"She met Liam last week, and he didn't seem to know what to do with her."

Maggie frowned. "She never told me they met."

"Probably because that would have meant admitting she told him about us," Cal replied with a chuckle.

Nerves coiled in Maggie's belly. "Was he… How was he? About us, I mean?" Maggie held no illusions; Cal's son would always be the most important person in his life. As he should be. She wasn't trying to take that spot. They were all adults, but she knew it would matter to Cal what he thought of her.

"Are you kidding? Liam's the one who told me I was an idiot for giving you space. He's okay with this. Everyone is, love," he assured her. "Well, I assume your parents aren't based on what I overheard when your dad called."

"They didn't react well," she admitted, her stomach souring at the memories. "That's probably why I left how I did, to be honest. They had some pretty shitty things to say about me not being able to be on my own." She still had some hope, however small, that they might reconcile one day, but that day wasn't coming anytime soon. She needed time.

"Assholes," Cal grumbled. "Sorry. Has it been crazy? Sorting the cafe after the break in?"

"Turns out you can't call it a break in if the door was never locked in the first place," Maggie replied dryly, and Cal's jaw dropped. "But I don't know how it's been. I'm not really speaking to my family anymore."

She explained how she'd put her foot down, refusing to help them, and Cal's face shone with pride. "It took them a while to realize I wasn't kidding. They kept calling, asking me to look over things, or for money, and, fuck, it was hard, but I refused every time until they stopped asking. At first, I still called a couple times a week and even went up to Marysville to visit a few times, but they're not all that interested in me when I'm not doing shit for them."

"I'm sorry. They don't deserve you, love," Cal said, pressing his lips to her forehead.

"It's okay," she replied with a shrug. It had surprised her how little she missed them. She was sure it wouldn't always be so easy, but it hadn't stung all that much yet. "Really. I don't need them. They weren't contributing anything positive to my life."

"I'm so fucking proud of you, baby."

Maggie looked up at Cal, his face the picture of adoration. "Where do we go from here?"

Cal hummed, his eyes twinkling. "Well, I was thinking a summer wedding in Ireland, a giant party, the whole shebang. We can honeymoon in the south of France, and I bet if we try really hard, we could have a couple of kids by the time you're thirty," he teased, and Maggie rolled her eyes, pushing lightly on his chest.

"Shut up."

Cal's smile softened. "I want to move in together. For real. I know it's soon, but we practically did live together for a couple of months and I miss that."

Though Maggie's heart was soaring and flying, her

brain was struggling to keep up. "I can be difficult to live with."

"I already know all the parts of you that people consider *difficult*," Cal said. "And I love them all. We're not going to get sixty years. I know that. And I don't want to waste a single second of the time we do have."

The *yes* spilled from Maggie's lips before she could stop it, but it felt like the right decision even if it scared her shitless. Two months without him was enough. "Yeah. Let's move in together," she agreed, squealing as he scooped her up and cradled her to his chest, littering her face with kisses. "Here? Or your apartment?" she asked, and Cal pursed his lips, mulling it over.

"Not the apartment. You're scared of parking there. We could stay here," he said, slowly. "Or you could renovate this place for work, and we could get a new place that's all ours. That way, we can both leave work at work and come home to each other every night."

Maggie had no idea what leaving work at work looked like, but she didn't know what having a place to call home looked like either, not really. The minute she'd gotten close to calling Cal home, she'd run. But nothing sounded sweeter than a place they could call their own—somewhere they could hide away from the world and be *home*. She could worry about the logistics later; they had time.

"That sounds perfect," she murmured, and a smile stretched over Cal's face. "Cal?"

"Yes, love?"

"What if I fuck it up again? What if I give you this piece of me and I can't handle it, so I push you away?"

"You can push all you want. I'm not going anywhere," Cal said firmly. "I know you, and I love you for *you*, Maggie. You're not going to unlearn twenty-seven years' worth of shit overnight, and I'm not expecting you to. But we'll talk it out when we have to, we'll have space when we need it, and we'll *always* work it out."

Cal's conviction was catching, and Maggie wanted to let herself believe him one hundred percent. "You're sure?"

"Better than sure." Cal held up a pinky, hooking it through hers. "I pinky promise that whatever happens, we're going to work through it. Hell, I pinky promise that I'm going to love you forever, baby."

Maggie loosed a watery laugh. "And I pinky promise to talk to you when I get overwhelmed, instead of running away. And to love you forever and ever." And then some.

Cal shook her pinky once, leaning in to press his forehead against hers. "It's a promise," he confirmed, and Maggie let herself relax into the safety of his arms. Of home.

Of Cal.

"A pinky promise," she echoed, brushing her lips against Cal's and breathing him in, her lips upturned at the edges. "Those are legally binding, you know."

SEVEN MONTHS LATER

"God, it feels good to be back here." Maggie took a deep breath, like she was pulling the cool Irish air into her lungs. Cal closed the trunk of the rental car, their bags tucked safely inside, and Maggie leaned back against it. He stepped closer to her, trapping her against the cold metal with his body.

Heat spread over his skin as she reached for his face and brushed her thumb across his jaw. "It does feel good to be back," he agreed, leaning in and teasing her lips with a barely there kiss. "But you feel better." He nipped her bottom lip and Maggie whimpered, her head falling back and exposing her neck. Cal trailed his lips down her wind-chilled skin and kissed her throat, Maggie shivering against him.

"You have to stop or we won't make it to your parents' house before dark." Maggie pushed lightly on his chest and Cal stepped back. Her rosy cheeks and dark eyes made it clear she was pulling back begrudgingly, but she was right; they had to get on the road.

He rounded the car and opened the door for her, stealing one more kiss before closing it gently and getting into the driver's side.

"I'll text your mom and let her know we're on the way," Maggie offered as Cal started the car.

"Let her know we landed, but we're not going straight to my parents."

She peered over at him, confused. "Where are we going?"

"I booked a place for us for a few days as a surprise." He watched a thousand worries flicker over Maggie's face and reached for her hand, squeezing it reassuringly. "You'll like it, love. I promise."

Surprises for Maggie, Cal had learned, had to be *true* surprises. If he wanted to plan something, he had to do it without mentioning it to her at all until the last second, so she couldn't focus on not knowing exactly what was going on and panic. Maggie loved planning shit, but she worked ridiculously hard—harder, even, as her own boss than she had as his assistant—and she deserved nice things without having to work for them. Cal didn't surprise her often, but he tried to do little things here and there, and the therapist she'd been seeing for the past few months approved.

Maggie squeezed his hand back, swallowed, and deep breathed through the unknown. When she looked back at him, her eyes had calmed. "How far is it?"

"It's only an extra thirty minute drive. We're staying just outside of Wicklow and heading to my parents' house on Saturday. I wanted to have a few days just for us."

Maggie's lips curved. "That sounds nice."

Cal turned to rummage in the bag he'd stashed in the backseat, pulling out a blanket and setting it on Maggie for the drive. She snuggled into it while he connected his phone to the car Bluetooth—with surprising ease, considering he'd barely known how to turn Bluetooth on a year ago. He pressed play on the album Jazz had gotten him hooked on after playing it non-stop at work, and filling him in—in alarming detail—on the artist's tumultuous personal life. If asked, Cal would lie and say he couldn't care less about celebrity gossip, but he'd hung onto every word, and had even found himself defending the artist when he heard people in the office making offhand comments about her, ignoring Jazz's *I told you* so smile every time.

Jazz had settled into Maggie's former role well, though she was still as chaotic as ever. Her new assistant, Sierra, was the calm to Jazz's chaos, and between the two of them, Cal had no concerns about leaving the office for an extra couple of days to visit his family with Maggie. Sierra was even staying at his and Maggie's house, looking after their new baby. Maggie had cried when they'd said goodbye to Peach, their fluffy calico, and even Cal had struggled to close the door behind her, but she was in good hands with Sierra.

Maggie had been working so hard since officially setting up her business that she hadn't been able to come with him last time he'd visited Ireland, and the Michael-sons were dying to see her. Not to mention how much Maggie needed the break.

Maggie Makes Home had grown arms and legs in the seven months since Maggie had bought the cottage. Since she was working on it full time, Maggie had fully renovated the cottage in only six weeks, and it sold as quickly as her house had. She'd bought another fixer upper and, thanks to the success of her TikTok, she'd also been hired to design and renovate an apartment for a couple who loved her videos. A couple who, unbeknownst to her, had a big social media following of their own. They'd sung her praises online, and Maggie's inbox had been flooded with job inquiries and sponsorship opportunities. She was now renovating her fourth fixer upper, had three client projects under her belt, and a full schedule for the following year. And she'd done all of that while making their new house a home. But Maggie didn't seem tired or worn out like she had when she was dealing with her parents and working as his assistant; she was having the time of her life. She was even planning to look for an assistant of her own in the new year, and Cal was so fucking proud of her.

Daylight waned as they drove down to Wicklow, but it was still light enough for Maggie to get the full effect of where they were staying as Cal pulled into the shadow of the lighthouse. She leaned forward and peered through the windshield before turning to him with wide eyes.

"We're staying in a lighthouse?"

Call nodded, smiling at the excitement on her face. "It has a hot tub."

"We're staying in a lighthouse with a hot tub? Holy shit." Maggie squealed and jumped out of the car before Cal could blink. He chuckled as he followed her, opening the trunk to grab their bags.

"If I'd known we would be climbing so many stairs, I might have packed a little lighter," Maggie said.

Cal shouldered their carry-ons and grabbed one of their suitcases, while Maggie grabbed the other and her purse. "Don't worry. There's an elevator."

"What kind of lighthouse has an elevator?" Maggie asked as they locked up the car and headed up the gravel path towards the door.

"When I was a kid, it was just a regular lighthouse. We used to drive past it all the time on the way to my grandad's place, and when I was really young, I wanted to live here." Being a lighthouse keeper had seemed like a fun job at seven. "One of Conor's friends bought it a few years and converted it. He buys a lot of weird, unused buildings and makes them livable. I think he's working on a giant tree house at the moment."

Maggie's eyes lit up. "That's so cool." He'd known she would love it. She loved watching renovation shows, and her favorite houses were always the weirdest ones.

At first glance, as they stepped into the lighthouse, it looked like any other vacation home. The front door opened up into a living room, and Cal knew there was also a bedroom and small bathroom, in case someone found being high up too much and needed to sleep closer to the ground. But the main living quarters were just an elevator ride away, and even Cal's breath was knocked from his chest as the door slid open to reveal the view from the top floor.

The lantern room had been converted into a living room, with couches set up to look out of the floor to ceiling windows, facing the sea. Rain drizzled down the glass, and the November sea beyond was stormy, but the room was warm and cozy.

"This is gorgeous." Maggie walked straight to the windows, placing a hand against the glass and staring out at the sea. "This view... Can we sleep in here?"

Cal wrapped his arms around her from behind, breathing in the sweet lilac scent of her. "There's a bedroom downstairs, but there's a pullout couch up here so we can wake up to this view."

Maggie turned to face him, peering up at his face, her eyes twinkling. "A pull out couch, huh? Just like old times."

She grabbed his hand and tugged him onto the plush couch, the wind and rain hitting the windows the background music to their gasps and moans. *Just like old times, indeed.*

Maggie

They were bundled up in jackets and scarves, but the rain had stopped long enough for them to take their coffee outside to the gallery deck. Seals basked on sea-worn rocks in the distance, and Cal and Maggie passed binoculars back and forth, watching them and pointing out interesting birds.

If eighteen-year-old Maggie could see twenty-eight-year-old Maggie, she would have been horrified that this was her idea of exciting. But twenty-eight-year-old Maggie was pretty fucking happy.

Cal set his cup and the binoculars down on the weathered iron table in front of them and turned to her, his knee bouncing and his expression serious. Maggie set her cup down, worried butterflies fluttering in her stomach. "What's wrong?"

"Nothing," Cal assured her quickly, glancing at his knee and stilling it. "I just wanted to talk to you about something."

"That's ominous."

He rolled his eyes, his lips lifting enough for that fucking dimple to appear. *Still lethal.* "It's not ominous." He took a deep breath. "Do you want to get married?"

Maggie blinked in surprise. She hadn't been expecting *that*. Her shock must have shown on her face, because Cal bit his lip before continuing. "I mean, I know you didn't want to marry Nathan, obviously, but I wasn't sure if you just didn't want to get married at all."

"Are you asking, or are you *asking*?" Maggie said carefully, though she was fairly sure he was just asking. They'd only been together, officially, for seven months, but they owned a house together. They'd adopted a cat—Peach—and were the over-the-top cat parents Maggie had always dreamed of being. Marriage was, logically, the next step. It was a completely reasonable question, but not one she'd even thought about.

Cal's eyes were uncertain as he replied, "If I was *asking...* what would you say?"

Maggie's heart skipped. *Oh shit. Was he asking? Was this why he'd surprised her with a few days to themselves?* Maggie hadn't been surprised by Nathan asking her to marry him, just blindsided by the proposal itself. She'd thought about it often in the years leading up to him getting down on one knee, and every time she'd begrudgingly assumed she would say yes. She hadn't known until he'd been on his knee before her that she couldn't, wouldn't, marry him. The thought of tying herself to a life with Nathan had felt like a duty, like something she was just expected to do.

The thought of tying herself to a life with Cal felt like every day with Cal—just right. Like the first sip of coffee in the morning, tucked into his side; like waking up in the middle of the night and just watching him breathe for a while, because she couldn't quite believe he'd trusted her with his heart; like looking forward to coming home from work and days off because, as much as she loved her job, she loved him more.

Seven months with Cal had felt more like forever than six years with Nathan ever had. Her life was already tied to Cal, whether they had rings on their fingers or not. He was already her family, but thinking about making it official made Maggie's heart swell.

"Hmm," she said, drumming her nails against the

table. "I think you have to actually ask before I answer that."

Cal considered her, biting his lip, before taking a deep breath and disappearing inside for a moment. When he returned, he took a seat beside her, and Maggie swallowed at the green velvet box tucked in his hand. *Holy shit*. It was really happening.

"I've been thinking about this pretty much constantly, for much longer than I probably should have," he began, brushing his thumb over the box. "I was so sure I'd missed my chance—that I would never have anything like what my parents had." He looked up at her, and his green eyes were lined with silver. "But Maggie, love, this is so much more than I could ever have imagined. I didn't know love could feel like this. It's like I spent my whole life half in the dark until you. And married or not, I know that this, you and I, are forever. Nothing else could ever come close to this."

Tears pricked Maggie's eyes, and she swiped at her face, her heart racing.

"I thought long and hard about what kind of ring you'd like before realizing that you'd definitely want to design your own," Cal continued with a watery laugh. Fuck, he knew her so well. "And we can make that happen, but I still wanted to pick out a ring, and then I thought about how this all started…" He opened the box, revealing two platinum bands, smaller than she expected. Cal reached for her, and Maggie didn't hesitate to slide her hand into his. He brushed his thumb across her pinky. "With a pinky promise."

He plucked the smaller of the two rings from the box and turned it to show her the inside, and the tiny word engraved on the inside of the band. *Promise.* The size of the rings suddenly made sense; one for her pinky, one for his. A pinky promise to tie them together forever.

"I pinky promise to love you forever, Maggie. Whether you want to get married or not, I'm yours, heart and soul, every second of every day. I love you so much."

A single tear slipped down Cal's cheek and Maggie leaned in, catching it with her thumb and holding his face while her heart felt like it was going to explode out her chest. "Fuck, Cal." She brushed her thumb across his lips, and Cal pressed a gentle kiss to it. "Of course I'll marry you. Yes."

Cal's face split into the most beautiful smile Maggie had ever seen as he slid the cool band on to her pinky. It was perfect—the perfect proposal and the perfect ring. Proof that Cal knew her particular ways and embraced them, that he loved her brain as much as he loved her heart.

Maggie's fingers were trembling as she took the second ring from the box and slid it over Cal's finger. "I pinky promise to love you forever, for longer than forever, because nothing in the entire universe could stop me from loving you, Cal. We were made for this, for us."

"Yeah, we were."

Cal clasped her face and kissed her, claiming her lips like he'd claimed her heart all those months ago. He still made her heart flutter and electricity crackle all over her body with every touch. They broke apart, panting, cheeks pink from more than the November chill. "We're getting married. I'm going to be your husband," Cal said with a breathy laugh and a grin.

"I'm going to be your wife. Shit, I'm going to be a Michaelson." *Maggie Michaelson.* Nothing had ever sounded more like it was meant to be.

"You've been a Michaelson since the moment you agreed to come home to meet my family before we were even dating, love," Cal said, smiling down at the hand and running a finger over the platinum band. "Wait." He looked up at her, wide-eyed. "You're changing your name? I didn't think you'd want to."

"Are you kidding?" Maggie asked, laughing. "Why would I want to be a Burlington when I could be a Michaelson? Also, when I change my name, our initials will be MMM CUM. I can't think of anything more us." Maggie had never been a monogram kind of girl, but that might have to change.

"Jazz is going to have a field day with that," Cal snorted.

"Jazz is going to have a field day with all of this. If you think she's chaos at work, imagine her helping us plan a wedding. I'm guessing you didn't tell her about this?" Maggie nodded towards the now-empty ring box.

"Are you kidding? If I'd told Jazz, everyone would already know. I didn't tell anyone, actually. I wanted this to be just for us, and I didn't want you to feel any pressure to say yes."

Maggie drew in a shaky breath. She knew, logically, that people weren't split into bad and good; Nathan and

Cal. But she couldn't help compare how different they were. Nathan's proposal had been for Nathan; Cal's had been for Maggie. If she'd married Nathan, she was sure their marriage would have been all about him too. Maggie knew that her marriage with Cal would be a partnership of two people just stupidly in love, who respected the hell out of each other. It was everything she'd never allowed herself to dream of.

"Cal."

"Yeah, love?"

"I'm going to need us to go inside now. It's too cold out here to get naked."

She hadn't even finished her sentence before Cal had her in his arms, bridal style, carrying her into the lighthouse. Her head fell back, and he kissed the hollow of her throat, dragging his lips up her neck, across her jaw, the tip of her nose, ignoring her lips entirely.

He lay her down on the pullout bed and kneeled between her legs, his lips traversing her torso, her thighs, her fucking knee. And she was still wearing too many clothes. "Cal," she whined, and he looked up at her with a wicked smile.

"Feeling a little impatient, love?"

Maggie showed him just how impatient she was feeling by grasping his collar and tugging him up to her. "Yes."

"So you don't want me to take my time, showing every inch of your body exactly how much I love you?" Cal lightly gripped her chin, his thumb brushing her lip.

"I want you to claim me and fuck me like I'm going

to be your wife," she replied, and Cal's eyes turned molten, his grip on her chin tightening and all of a second before he was gone, tearing at her clothes. Jackets and sweaters and underwear were tossed aside, but Maggie's thigh high socks stayed on, like they always did.

Cal nudged her thighs apart and buried his face between her legs. He didn't start slow; Cal knew her body by heart, knew she could take it. He pressed two relentless fingers inside her while his tongue and teeth played gently with her clit. The combination, the soft and slow and deep and hard, felt like flames licking her skin. Maggie's back bowed off the bed, and she fisted the covers, her wool sock covered legs wrapping around Cal's head.

Cal ran the flat of his tongue over her clit, followed by a light graze of his teeth, before pulling back. His fingers didn't still as he said, "Do you want to come on my fingers or my cock, baby girl?"

Fire lashed at Maggie, Cal unrelenting as he fucked her with his fingers. She opened her mouth to respond, but the only sound she could manage was a whimper.

"Answer the question, love."

Maggie's head fell to the side with a sob, her eyes rolling back. She wasn't going to last long enough to answer the question.

"Don't even think about it." Cal grasped her chin, gently turning her head until she was facing him again. "You don't get to come yet, baby. Fingers or cock?"

It took every ounce of Maggie's concentration not to tighten around Cal's fingers as he continued to stroke inside her. Because as good as they felt, they both knew she wanted to come on his cock; he was just making her work for it.

"Your c… your… fuck," Maggie cried. Every inch of her was poker hot, like at any moment she might burst into flames.

Cal pressed harder against her G-spot and black teased the edges of Maggie's vision. "You want my cock, baby?"

"Y-yes."

His fingers slowed but didn't stop. "Yes, what?"

Maggie's thighs were shaking, her fingers numb where they were tangled in the covers.

"Yes, Daddy."

"Good girl." Cal bent his head and licked her pussy one last time before pulling his fingers out. He sat back on his knees and rubbed the tip of his cock over her clit, torturously close to where she wanted him—where she needed him.

"*Please,*" she begged, and Cal took mercy on her, positioning his cock and leaning in to brush his lips over hers.

"Maggie, love?" he murmured as he pressed the tiniest fraction inside her.

"Yeah?"

"I love you."

Maggie released the covers, and with a shaking hand, cupped the side of his face. "I love you. So much."

"You're going to be my wife." He placed his hand over hers, his thumb brushing the platinum band.

"You're going to be my husband." *Husband. Cal was going to be her husband. Holy shit.*

"Fuck yes I am, baby girl." He crushed his lips to hers as he pressed into her, drinking down her cries.

Cal and Maggie's bodies knew each other like two halves of something that were made to click together; they moved almost instinctively, Cal's cock hitting the most perfect spot inside of her with every thrust. The flames were no longer teasing Maggie. They engulfed her, her nails raking down Cal's back as she splintered beneath him. But Cal didn't stop, didn't even slow, and Maggie's orgasm didn't end, just spiraled and spiraled until she felt almost separate from her body.

"You feel so fucking good coming on Daddy's cock, baby girl," Cal gasped as he slammed into her. He pushed her thighs further apart, opening her wider to him and, somehow, hit somewhere deeper within her.

"*Fuck*," Maggie sobbed, writhing beneath him, fire after fire rolling through her.

"Are you going to be a good girl and take Daddy's cum?" Cal's voice was rough, his grip on her thighs tight enough that Maggie knew she would feel ghosts of his fingers long after he let go.

"Yes, yes, *please*, Daddy."

Maggie squeezed her pussy around Cal's cock and he faltered, his eyes glazing over as he fell to pieces. Maggie's name slipped from his tongue. She should be used to it by now, but Cal's accent was still fucking lethal; lethal enough to make her come again while he filled her up. She held on tight to Cal, his cum spilling out of her as he fucked her through one last orgasm, his face buried in the crook of his neck, whispering, "I love you," against her skin.

For the first time since finding out Eliza was pregnant, Cal wasn't nervous walking up to his parents' front door. Maggie's hand was twined around his, the cool platinum of her ring pressed against his skin, reminding him that she'd agreed to marry him. As if he could forget.

If she hadn't wanted to get married, he would have been completely okay with it. Who could blame her, really? She hadn't exactly had a shining example of married life growing up. The way Cal saw it, they didn't need a piece of paper, a ring, or a fancy party to show how much they loved each other. But he couldn't deny he wanted that with Maggie. His Maggie.

Gravel crunched beneath their feet as they approached the door. They reached the steps just as the door burst open, a gaggle of Michaelsons appearing before them, his parents at the helm.

"Next time you bring Maggie home, you better not introduce her as your assistant," his mom had told him when he and Maggie were leaving last time. Back then, he hadn't let himself hope that they might one day be more. But now... now, they were everything. They didn't

need sixty years, because time stood still when they were together.

Cal took a deep breath and smiled at his family. "Everyone, allow me to re-introduce you to Maggie. My fiancée."

THE END

Thank you for reading Legally Binding!

I hope you enjoyed Maggie and Cal's love story. If you did, please consider leaving a review and sharing Legally Binding wherever you like to talk about books!

This isn't the last you'll see of Maggie and Cal! Legally Binding is the first book in the Spicy in Seattle Series and book two, Jazz and Liam's book, is up next.

In the meantime, you can find a sweet and spicy Maggie and Cal extended epilogue by visiting www.sophiesnowbooks.com/bonus-scenes, or scanning this QR code:

The Spicy Stuff

If you should, for whatever reason, wish to revisit *just* the spicy moments... you'll find no judgment here! But you will find the spicy scenes here:

- Chapter Three
- Chapter Eight
- Chapter Twelve
- Chapter Thirteen
- Chapter Nineteen
- Chapter Twenty-one
- Chapter Twenty-five
- Chapter Twenty-eight
- Chapter Thirty-four
- Epilogue

Enjoy!

Acknowledgments

Putting myself out there to release The Rule of Three genuinely filled me with dread, but the entire experience of my first release, and now the release of Legally Binding, has been overwhelmingly positive, and I'm so grateful for everything.

My dearest, Kyle—thank you for every single time you held me when I had yet another meltdown about my books. I know the past few years have been a lot of ups and downs, but I'm so grateful to have you by my side for all of them. I love you.

Claire, I don't even want to think about what my life would be like if we hadn't met in 2020. Books have brought a lot of wonderful things into my life, but you, by far, are the best. Thank you for being the best, most supportive friend.

My incredible beta readers, Emily Shacklette, Cara Dion, and Lila Dawes—you helped me shape Legally Binding into the story that I wanted to tell, and I'm so grateful for all of your kindness, feedback, and friendship. Thank you.

I feel so lucky to have so many people in my corner cheering me on—Gemma, Alaina, Leigh-Ann, Terry, thank you for all your support.

My wonderful Street Team—Aimee, Shannen, Molly,

Lil, Kai, Hayley, Jenna, Jess, Rebecca, Abigail, Claire, Charley, and Sophie—thank you for taking a chance on a completely unknown author and embracing The Rule of Three. You all made the release of my debut so special.

As always, to Taylor Swift, without whom I wouldn't be writing, and this book wouldn't exist.

To whoever gave me COVID in March 2023—no one warned me that COVID could cause an increase in horniness, but, without it, I would never have written Legally Binding. So, thanks I guess.

I fell in love with romance through fanfiction, and Legally Binding's setting is my nod to my first love—Twilight fanfiction, most of which is set in or around Seattle. I will be eternally grateful to the writers who put their blood, sweat, and tears into stories and share them online. I learned far too much, at far too young an age, and I wouldn't change it for the world.

To the readers who have made my first few months as an author the most amazing experience—thank you. This has been a lifelong dream for me, and I couldn't ask for better people in my corner. I appreciate every single one of you.

And to the pathological people pleasers who see themselves in Maggie, I see you. There's nothing more powerful than learning to love yourself for *you*, and not for the things you do for others. You've got this.

Love,
Sophie

Sophie Snow lives in Scotland with her husband and cat, Pumpkin (who she loves dearly, even if he does bite.)

She writes spicy romance books with messy, queer characters and too many Taylor Swift references to count. She has been in love with love stories for as long as she can remember, and writing them as songs and novels since she was twelve.

A forest fairy in a past life, Sophie loves spending time in nature, drinking too much coffee, and trying out more hobbies than she can keep up with.

You can find more from Sophie by visiting her website at www.sophiesnowbooks.com, or scanning this QR code:

Made in the USA
Monee, IL
24 March 2024